I0637265

Santa's Special

MARK BASFORD

Published by Mark Basford, 2016

Copyright © 2016 Mark Basford

Mark Basford has asserted his right to be identified as the author of this work in accordance with the Copyright, Designs and Patents Act of 1988

All rights reserved. No part of this publication may be reproduced, stored in a retrieval system, or transmitted in any form or by any means, electronic, mechanical, photocopying, recording, or otherwise, without the prior written permission of the copyright owner and publisher of this book, nor be lent, re-sold, hired out or otherwise circulated in any form of binding or cover other than that in which it is published and without a similar condition including this condition being imposed on the subsequent purchaser. All characters in this publication are fictitious except for those in the public domain; any similarity to persons living or dead is entirely coincidental.

ISBN: 978-0-9934345-2-5

CHAPTER 1

The gas mantle glowed inside the glass cage crowning the wrought iron Victorian streetlamp, casting a soft green light on a family of four, huddled below in the freezing fog. Helen watched Edwin watching Alice, recalling how pleased he had been to put on his brand-new fleece-lined olive-green waxed jacket. She turned her gaze toward Alice, remembering her delight on receiving the space-to-grow-into, hand-me-down dark blue anorak, and wondered when her attitude to her brother's cast-offs would change. To assuage her conscience, she had bought her a new scarf; the bright hoops of yellow, green, red and purple, interspersed with broad bands of beige, now looked to her like a harlequin snake that had wrapped itself around her daughter's neck in two coils. To ward off the cold, Helen had threaded one end of the scarf down the coat front; like Edwin, she now found herself mesmerised by Alice, who was holding the free end in her woollen-gloved hand and rhythmically swinging its dangling pom-pom to-and-fro.

Anticipating the imminent arrival of the Christmas Special, Marcus peered along the platform and into the grey mist. He observed the stationmaster step out of his office and approach him, noting how his usual quick march had been replaced by slow, deliberate steps as he threaded his way through the throng of children.

Gordon, a heritage railway volunteer, had decked himself out with various accoutrements of a bygone era.

In the centre of his peaked cap glinted a bright golden badge that in the nineteenth century had signified a so-called servant of the local Manchester, Sheffield and Lincolnshire Railway. Eight brass buttons from the Great Western Railway paraded in two proud columns down the front of his thick black overcoat; though he had earlier polished them to a high shine, they had lost their sparkle due to condensation from the mist. The coat was unfastened, leaving a gap that revealed a black woollen waistcoat adorned with a silver chain. As he approached the Priestley family, he pulled the chain and withdrew a silver full-hunter Great Central Railway pocket watch; he allowed it to nestle snugly in his hand for a moment, before depressing the crown that released the steel latch, causing the front cover to spring open.

Marcus called out, 'Merry Christmas, Gordon.'

He checked the time, then closed and pocketed it. 'Merry Christmas to you all. We're running a bit late. It was touch-and-go whether we'd be able to have the final Santa's Special; the crew are struggling to see the track in front of them.'

Marcus glanced at his children. 'I'm glad it's going ahead; they've been looking forward to it for ages.'

Helen put a hand on Edwin's shoulder. 'It was also touch-and-go whether one particular young man would be allowed to have this treat.'

Edwin rolled his eyes at her. 'What's the point of having candles if you don't light them?'

Helen frowned at him. 'Don't start again; you've already lost that argument. Why can't you behave, like Alice? She's younger than you, but far more sensible.'

Edwin turned his head and raised his eyebrows at his father. 'Am I really expected to answer that question?'

Marcus gently swivelled him by one shoulder so they were facing each other. 'Don't cheek your mother! Remember, it's Christmas day tomorrow and only well-behaved children get presents.'

Edwin grinned. 'Yeah, right!' Seeing his father point surreptitiously at Alice, he added brightly, 'And Father Christmas will be leaving Lapland at seven o'clock, because it's a long way to travel by sleigh; so, I'll have to behave myself until then.'

Alice looked with concern at her brother. 'Don't risk it, Ed; you can't be sure exactly what time he'll set off.'

Marcus swelled with pride at her innocence, as he wondered if she would still be willing to believe their well-intentioned lies next year.

Gordon peered into the gloom. 'It'll be a Hunslet 'Austerity' saddle tank. That's an o-six-o, of course.'

Helen raised her head and looked him full in the face, responding with an overly-enthusiastic voice. 'Really? A saddle tank o-six-o? How marvellous!'

Gordon's eyes widened. 'Yes; it's ideal for this line, though we do sometimes have bigger visitors. We're planning to host a *Pacific*; a four-six-two.' He leaned in conspiratorially, his voice quasi-religious. '*The* most famous A3.' After reverting to his earlier stance, he continued in a normal voice. 'Subject to clearances, it'll be here next spring. Should I let you know about it?'

Helen, embarrassed he had failed to recognise her overt irony, knew she must maintain the pretence; she widened her eyes to match his, and nodded repeatedly. 'Yes please; could you send us an e-mail?'

He puffed out his chest. 'Of course. Anyway, must go, things to do.' He meandered back to his office.

Marcus frowned at Helen with mock-sternness.

'That was very naughty of you, wasn't it? Perhaps you'll be the one not getting a visit from Santa.'

Alice took hold of her mother's hand and looked up at her. 'Don't worry, Mummy; I'm sure you'll get *some* presents.' Helen smiled at her.

Marcus lifted up his daughter so they were face to face. 'And I'm sure you'll be getting *lots* of presents, my little sweetheart.' She hugged the back of his neck.

Several fathers at the opposite end of the platform began to point into the impenetrable greyness and declaim excitedly to their children, having heard the heavy breathing of a steam locomotive. The tank engine emerged from the fog, black smoke belching from the chimney and mingling with the mist, producing droplets that deposited soot on the upturned young faces gazing earnestly at the massive machine. Marcus glanced at the red buffer beam, and then up to the smoke box door with its painted Christmas pudding cover, the two centred black levers tight at half past ten.

Helen held Alice's hand as they headed down the platform in the direction of their carriage, past a dozen carol singers who were proclaiming in *a cappella* four-part harmony, *peace on earth and mercy mild*. Marcus followed close behind, his hand resting on Edwin's shoulder, ready to collar him if he should attempt to deviate. They joined the queue of families at the carriage door. Nearby, a juggler in a light blue two-piece suit with coloured court card and dice designs was keeping three green-and-yellow balls in the air for the amusement of a little girl.

Inside, they settled quickly into their four table-seats, the children by the window. Marcus spoke quietly to Helen. 'The fog and the gaslight outside made it feel like a Gothic horror scene, or maybe Jack the Ripper; but here it's more *Murder on the Orient Express*.'

She shook her head. 'Why not something nice? What about *A Christmas Carol*?' Raising her voice a notch, she nodded in turn to Alice, Edwin and Marcus as she recited, 'God Bless Us, Every One!'

Edwin narrowed his eyes at her. 'You don't really believe in God, do you? It's like Fa...'

Marcus quickly put his hand over Edwin's mouth. 'You know what we said about that particular subject.'

The train juddered and began to move. Marcus took the two Christmas present tickets out of his wallet and handed one each to the children. When Edwin began to fold his into a dart shape, Helen reached over and took it from him. 'I'll keep it for you.' He made a grab for it. 'You know what you've been told about snatching. If you don't promise to behave, you won't be getting it back, and then you can't get a present.' She saw him scowl, knowing crying was something else in which he no longer believed. 'Well?' she asked.

'Shan't,' he muttered, as he turned away and pressed his nose and mouth to the chilled window. Through the swirling fog, he looked over at the brambles bravely scrambling over the barbed wire that stretched between crumbling concrete posts, and then beyond to the rimed iron railings, each pair of vertical rods joined above the upper horizontal retaining bar in a semi-circular arc. After a few moments, he switched his focus to the spectral silvered trees beyond. Alice imitated him, her lips, nasal facet and columella pressed to the window, before she decided the glass was far too cold.

Edwin bumped his nose as the carriage swayed, so withdrew his face a little way from the window. Alice leaned over to him and whispered, 'I'm sure I'll be getting lots of presents, so you can have my ticket.' He silently palmed it from her outstretched fingers and transferred it to his jacket pocket.

When an accordion player announced herself with an ascending *glissando*, Edwin quickly stood to watch the musician over the seat backs. She began to sing *Jingle Bells*, passengers spontaneously joining in with the chorus. After a rapid rendition of *Good King Wenceslas* and *Deck the Hall,* and an instrumental *O Tannenbaum*, she closed her set with *Rudolf the Red-nosed Reindeer*. Following a fast final flourish, she moved to the next carriage, as a tall Santa Claus accompanied by an elf appeared at the other end. Santa worked his way along, speaking with each child as the elf fetched the presents.

When Santa reached the Priestleys, he delivered a rumbling 'Ho! Ho! Ho!' Then, lightly, he asked Alice, 'And what is your name, little girl?'

She looked up in wonder. 'Alice,' she whispered.

He broadened his smile, just visible through the mass of white whiskers. 'You've been a very good girl this year, haven't you, Alice?'

Without the slightest sense of immodesty, she breathed, 'Yes, I have.'

He turned to Edwin and asked, a little louder, 'And you are her brother?'

Edwin spoke up clearly. 'Yes I am; I'm Edwin.'

'And have you been good this year, Edwin?'

He chewed his lower lip. 'Sometimes.' Before his eligibility for a present could be discussed further, he thrust out the ticket with its pink sticker displaying the category "6 to 8 years". Santa squinted at it over his small rectangular spectacles. 'But this isn't your ticket.'

Edwin looked shocked that he knew, being a firm disbeliever in any sort of magic.

Helen handed to Santa the crumpled ticket with the blue sticker bearing the legend "9 to 15 years". 'This one is my son's; that one is my daughter's.'

Santa examined the ticket. 'So, Edwin, I think you must be nine years old.' Edwin felt relieved to know this Santa was not omniscient; he opened his mouth and prepared to respond.

Marcus interjected, 'In some ways he's a lot older.'

Santa passed the two tickets to his runner, a slender young teenage girl with faun-like features that fully complemented her elf costume. She scurried away, quickly returning with two diagonally striped bags: one, white and pink; the other, black and gold.

Santa handed Alice her bag; she took it in silence, believing simple thanks were too mundane to be offered to this legendary figure. He asked, 'And will you be a good girl next year, Alice?' She nodded vigorously.

When accepting the black and gold bag, Edwin gave a chirpy 'Thank you, Santa.' Marcus stared sternly at him to discourage any further conversation.

Having noticed the interaction, Santa laughingly asked Marcus, 'Do you think Edwin will be a good boy next year?'

Marcus smiled warmly. 'I'm sure he'll be trying.' He frowned. 'Very trying.' His smile returned.

After Elf and Santa had moved to the next carriage, a helper appeared in a red hat with white fur trim and fluffy pom-pom, carrying a board with round holes that held tumblers of mulled wine; as he set about delivering the drinks to the adults, he was joined by another helper in similar attire, who distributed mince pies from a tray.

Next to arrive were two painted clowns wearing matching star-spangled blue dungarees, the man an Auguste with large red nose and lips, the woman a Whiteface. Auguste asked Alice and Edwin if they had seen the red light that Rudolf had lost from his nose. The children shook their heads. He palmed an unlit bulb into Helen's sleeve, then turned it on so that it showed through, before pulling it out with a flourish. 'Here it is,' he laughed. Helen giggled. Edwin frowned, certain it was a trick. As Alice stared wide-eyed in wonder, the clown gently asked her, 'And what's your name?'

'Alice,' she whispered.

'Cor-rect!' he responded heartily. 'You have won a balloon animal!' Alice smiled sweetly, unsure why she was being rewarded simply for knowing her own name. 'Would you like a sausage dog?' She nodded.

Whiteface pushed a nozzle into a long thin pink balloon and pumped air into it, inflating all but the last four inches. She twisted the distended section rapidly to form the head, the ears, the fore-legs and the hind-legs. Finally, she grasped the residual tail a few inches from the end and squeezed air into the uninflated section, creating a pom-pom effect. As Alice gratefully accepted the so-called sausage dog, she thought it looked more like a poodle. After the clowns had moved on, she held the balloon animal carefully, unsure what to do with it.

Helen picked up Alice's bag. 'Would you like to open your present now, or will you wait 'til tomorrow?'

Edwin distracted her, thrusting a hand into his own bag and taking out a clear-sided box; on seeing it contained a digital watch, he remarked to no one in particular, 'That's good.' After yanking open one end, he slid out the cardboard-and-plastic display mount and

prised off the chronometer. Declining offers of help
with adjusting it to his wrist, he discovered for himself
that even on the tightest setting it was still a little loose.

Helen smiled at Alice. 'You can open yours as well.'

Alice carefully extracted her present and examined it
closely. 'It's beads for making necklaces and things.'

'Do you like it?'

'Yes; I'll make us all some bracelets at home.'

Edwin asked his mother, 'Did you forget my age?'

She tittered. 'Do you think that's at all likely?'

He shook his head. 'You had to have a reason.'

Marcus turned to him. 'We thought you may be a bit
too old for the six-to-eight presents, so we just rounded
you up to the next year.'

Edwin grinned. 'I'm glad you did.'

As Marcus grinned back, Helen suddenly glowered
at Edwin. 'Why did you take Alice's ticket?'

Edwin took a deep breath and prepared to mount a
defence. Alice piped up before he could begin. 'I gave
it to him, Mummy, because he looked sad.'

Marcus smiled at Alice. 'You love your big brother,
don't you, sweetheart?' She nodded repeatedly. He
turned to Edwin. 'And do you love your little sister?'

Edwin contemplated the question at length, before
murmuring, 'I suppose so.' Seeing his father frown at
him, he tried again, in a sing-song voice. 'Yes, I do love
my sister; she's very sweet and nice and good and I
should try to be more like her.' Seeing the frown
intensify at the perceived insincerity, Edwin turned
away and found Alice gazing at him with pure joy.

CHAPTER 2

When the train came to a halt, Marcus looked out of the window to see which station they had reached, only to find they were still flanked by trees. Helen widened her eyes questioningly. He shook his head. 'I don't know why we've stopped; maybe the fog's too dense.'

She shrugged, having no likelier suggestion herself. 'I hope it isn't too bad for the drive home.' Turning to Alice, she smiled and spoke softly. 'We need to be back before midnight, don't we, sweetheart?' Seeing Alice's look of concern, she added, 'Don't worry; Father Christmas knows what a good girl you've been, so he'll make sure he visits our house before the morning.'

A few minutes later, a septuagenarian in a black woollen suit hurried into the carriage; the insignia on his matching peaked cap proclaimed him a British Rail guard. He called out, 'Is there a doctor on the train?'

Edwin ceased exploring his digital watch's various functions. Leaping to his feet, he raised his newly adorned arm, and shouted, 'My Mummy's a doctor.' When the man looked at him, he pointed to his mother, who was already standing up.

As the guard hurried over, she gave a confirmatory nod, before asking him, 'What's the problem?'

He jerked his head in the direction of the window. 'The signalman's unconscious... or worse. Someone's phoned for an ambulance, but with this fog...' His voice trailed off. Helen quickly followed the guard to the external door. He pressed his fingers to the steel lip attached to the upper edge of the window, and pulled down the glass; reaching through, he located the outer brass handle and released the lock. After yanking the door open from the outside, he pushed it wide from the inside, then turned to face into the carriage before edging backward onto the top tread. Holding onto the vertical handrail, he took the two steps down before dropping to the ground. As Helen copied him, his hands hovered either side of her, ready to offer gentlemanly assistance if she should slip.

To avoid her high heels sinking into the ballast, she extended her stride to bridge the two-and-a-half feet gap from one sleeper to the next. Fearing the seams of her tight skirt would not take the strain, she discreetly eased the hem high above her knees. Once she had settled into a rhythm, she asked the guard, 'What more can you tell me about the man's condition?'

He glanced up briefly. 'All I've been told is, he's lying on the floor and doesn't appear to be breathing.'

When they reached the level crossing, he found the wooden gates too daunting. Seeing they were as tall as her, he assumed she also would be unable to scale them. He looked around for an easier route, but found only a dry stone wall of similar height on one side of the track, and a higher wire mesh fence on the other. Unsure how to proceed, he offered, 'I could maybe help *you* up, but I don't think *I* can get over.'

Smiling, she responded, 'It's alright; you stay there.' She considered her options, made her decision and turned her back on him. Though she was relieved her anorak had enough padding to cushion her stomach, she wished she had been wearing trousers. Masked by the jacket, she hitched up her skirt even further, then placed a foot on the second-lowest of the five transverse wooden beams. Holding onto the top of the gate, she stepped up to the middle beam. Leaning right over, she grasped a diagonal metal support bar at the other side, as a mesh was blocking her access to the crossbeams. Executing a traditional five-bar gate vault, she swung herself over and down, keeping one hand firmly on the metal bar to minimise her dismount velocity, while raising her free arm for balance. The guard watched appreciatively as she landed lightly.

After crossing the empty road, she saw there was a tall, narrow gate blocking her access to the steps at the foot of the high, slender signal box. As she considered how best to tackle it, he called out, 'There's a bolt on the other side; you'll need to reach around the wall.'

She located the cast iron bolt and withdrew it, then hastened up the middle of the broad stairway to the deck at the top. Through a grimy glass panel in the soot-stained, once-white wooden frame, she saw a man lying motionless on the floor, his bald head pointing toward her. She gingerly pushed the door open and stepped inside. On seeing his wide staring eyes, she was certain he was dead, but nevertheless stooped down to check for vital signs. Below his full beard she located where a pulse should have been, and experienced a momentary shock on discovering the man's neck had been broken. Bending in closer, she checked her initial findings. With a forced calmness, she stepped out of the signal box and called down to the guard, his head just visible above the gate. 'When they phoned for an ambulance, did they ask for the police as well?'

He called back, 'I don't know.'

After she had descended the steps and was crossing

the road, he asked over the barrier, 'How is he?'

She stopped by the gate and looked through the mesh just below the top rail; he stooped to listen. 'I'm sorry to have to tell you this, but he's dead.'

Knowing she would have to swing her legs away from the guard to avoid flashing her underwear, she again hitched up her skirt. First stepping onto a metal support, she hauled herself up and reached over to the middle wooden bar, before executing another perfect vault. As she lightly planted her dismount, she thought of Ginger Rogers performing the same dance steps as Fred Astaire, only backwards and with less functional footwear. After surreptitiously pulling down her skirt and smoothing it a little, she adopted her professional sympathy face and turned to him.

He looked at her and sighed. 'Poor old Stan; but it comes to us all in the end.' They hurried back to the train in silence.

She stopped at the carriage door. 'You stay there; I'll fetch my husband, Marcus Priestley. He's a policeman, a detective chief inspector; he'll know what to do.'

After again discreetly raising her skirt, she hauled herself up the steps with the aid of the handrail. Inside the carriage, she walked toward Marcus until he was in her line of sight. Curling her index finger to bring him to his feet, she mouthed, 'Come.' He quickly followed her as she retreated to the door. Glancing around to check no one was within hearing distance, she leaned in closely. 'There's a man in the signal box who's had his neck broken; I'd say it was done by a professional.'

Marcus turned his face and spoke into her ear above the sounds of people having festive fun. 'You're sure it couldn't have been an accident?'

She moved her head away and looked him in the eye. 'I'm certain. The guard says someone's phoned for an ambulance, but he doesn't know if they requested police as well. I know there's no point in asking you not to get involved, even if you are on holiday, but you can hand over and drop out when help arrives, can't you.'

Marcus went back to his seat to fetch his coat, with Helen following. As his children looked up at him, he forced a smile. 'I have some police work to do, so you need to keep Mummy company.' He looked directly at Edwin. 'And be on your best behaviour.'

Helen took Marcus's seat to block Edwin's potential escape route. Marcus stepped into Helen's place as Alice stood to receive a parting kiss on the forehead.

At the door, Marcus eschewed the prominent brass handrail and jumped down from the top step. As soon as he had landed, the guard pointed up the line. 'Your wife says the signalman has died. His name's Stan; Stanley Hicks.' Without waiting for a response, he set off trotting toward the signal box, as though there were still a need for urgency. At the gate, he stopped and turned to Marcus. 'It's a bit high for me.'

Marcus looked around and wondered if it would be easier to climb the dry stone wall. Trying not to sound too perplexed, he asked, 'How did my wife get past?'

A smile flittered faintly across the guard's frowning face. 'She just vaulted over the gate like it was nothing; she's very fit, your wife.'

Silently agreeing with both interpretations, he set out to prove his own athleticism. Placing one foot on the central wooden crossbeam, he grasped the top of the barrier and hoisted himself up. After swinging first one leg over, then the other, he supported himself using only his hands, balancing for a moment before pushing himself off. Landing awkwardly, he staggered slightly. Noticing the guard grimacing, he assumed his vault had not achieved as high a score as Helen's.

He crossed the road and swung open the unfastened narrow gate. At the bottom of the stairway he checked the lower treads for shoe prints, and found a series of moderately small boot marks ascending fairly near the left side, some of which were partially overlaid by a similar series of descending prints closer to the centre. Avoiding touching the handrail, he stayed to the left of the suspect footprints as he climbed the steps.

At the top, he looked in through a glass panel next to the door, and saw the body sprawled on the floor. He moved to the side and observed how the head was at an unnatural angle. After a cursory glance around the signal box from the outside, he stepped back to the wooden rail that skirted the deck; unsure how solid it was, he avoided putting any pressure on it as he leaned over. Seeing the guard looking up, he called out, 'Are you sure someone dialled nine-nine-nine?'

The guard took a step closer, then removed his peaked cap before tilting his head back further. 'The fireman phoned the stationmaster for him to call for an ambulance, but with this fog there's no knowing when they'll get here.' Seeing a look of uncertainty, he added, 'The fireman on the locomotive; he found the body.'

Marcus tested the strength of the rail and leaned further over. 'What's his name?'

'Mick Collett.'

'I'll need to talk to him later. What's your name, by the way?'

'Roderick Stapleton. Rod.'

'I'm DCI Marcus Priestley.'

'Yes, your wife said.'

'Right. Excuse me, I need to make some calls.' He took out his mobile phone. Discovering there was no signal, he wondered if the fog was in some way responsible. Leaning over the rail again, he called down, 'I'll use the phone in here, if that's alright.'

Rod shook his head. 'It only connects with other phones on our system; it doesn't do external calls.'

Marcus blew out his cheeks. 'How do I phone the stationmaster?'

'If you dial three-five-three you'll get either the stationmaster or the operations duty manager. All the numbers you can reach are listed next to the phone.'

Marcus entered the signal box, stepped carefully around the body and lifted the receiver from the beige telephone cradle hanging on the wall. Gordon answered almost as soon as he had finished pressing the buttons. 'It's Marcus Priestley here; I understand you've already been contacted about the signalman.'

'Yes. Mick said he thought he was dead. Is he?'

'I'm afraid so; Helen's checked him for vital signs. When you called for an ambulance, did you ask for the police as well?'

'I didn't make the call myself; I got Dave to run to the pub and use their landline. I never said to ask for the police, so I don't expect he did.'

'Right. Look, Gordon, I'll have to co-opt you. My mobile phone isn't getting a signal, so I'd like you to send someone to dial nine-nine-nine again. Do you have a pen and paper? You'll need to take notes. ... Ask for the police. Tell them Helen has confirmed the man's dead and that it's a crime scene. Remind them to let the ambulance crew know; they won't want to be dashing about in this fog. Then say I'd like SOCO ASAP. … Sorry, I mean Scenes of Crime Officers as soon as possible. Tell them I want the ops wagon, and to make sure the floodlights are all working; it'll be dark soon and we'll need some decent lighting to check out the whole area. If they have any questions for me, you can relay them, can't you. And one more thing: the police will want to speak to anyone working on the railway who may have seen something. I know it's Christmas eve, but it would be good if they could wait at the station. … Thanks, Gordon.'

Marcus thought of Alice and how anxious she would be to make it home before Father Christmas arrived. He stepped outside and called down, 'Rod, I've spoken to Gordon. Now, can we get this train going? I wouldn't want all those children getting upset, stuck out here.'

Rod pointed down the railway line to the upper horizontal semaphore arm. 'The signal's against him.'

Marcus glanced at both signals, not knowing which was relevant. 'Can't we just swing these gates open and you tell the driver it's alright to go?'

Rod looked shocked at the suggestion. 'There's things that have to be done first. Has the next signalman given you permission to pass the train on to him?'

Marcus suppressed a shrug. 'How would I know?'

'What's it showing on the box? Is it "Train on Line" or "Normal" or "Line Clear"? If it isn't "Line Clear", you'll need to ding him once to get his attention, then tap him a three-and-one. But under the circumstances, I think you ought to talk to him; there's a direct line, or you could dial one thirty on the main phone.'

Marcus stepped into the signal box. Finding three

line status indicators, he returned outside. 'There's a "Down Passenger" at the top and an "Up Passenger" in the middle, and below that is another one that has a knob on it. How can I tell which one to look at?'

Rod quickly explained, 'Our line was originally "Up" to Derby, but now it's "Up" to London like all the other lines in England; so, that's the one you want.'

Marcus checked the central indicator and stepped outside again. 'The "Up Passenger" is pointing to "Line Clear" in the green band.'

'That's good. If you're not going to change the signal, the driver will expect to see a yellow flag.'

Marcus sighed. 'Where can I get a yellow flag?'

'There's one in the signal box.'

'Where exactly?'

'It's just above the far window, next to the red flag. But don't go waving it yet; he still won't be able to go.'

Marcus spoke more sharply than he had intended. 'Well, why not? What else do we need?'

Rod replied curtly, 'Annett's key for the gates.'

Marcus barked out, 'Who's Annette and where is she? And why does she have the key?'

Rod raised his eyebrows and called out, slowly and deliberately, 'The Annett's key sits in the frame where all the levers are for changing the signals. You have to take it out of there to lock the frame before you can move the level crossing gates. And obviously, until the gates are blocking the road, the train can't go through.'

Embarrassed at having inappropriately pressed for action, Marcus softened his voice. 'I'm sorry, Rod, I should have simply asked you for instructions. Can you talk me through the procedure?'

Rod's voice changed similarly. 'Will do. Take the

big brass key out of the right hand side of the lever frame; it says something like "Lever Frame and Gate Locks" on it. Then bring it down here.'

Marcus went inside and located the key, turning it first one way and then the other before finding the position to extract it. Grasping it firmly, he exited the signal box, hurried down the steps and crossed the road.

Rod put his hand on the barrier in front of him. 'This gate is number four and the one next to it is number three.' He pointed across the road. 'That one's one and that one's two. You'll need the key to unlock each pair of gates. Start with the other pair; move gate two first.'

After detaching gate two from gate one, he swung it into the road, keeping a tight hold of the top rail. When he returned to his starting position and grabbed gate one, Rod snapped, 'Leave that; you need to do gate four next.' Marcus used the key to release gate four from gate three, and began to walk it across the road, enabling Rod to step through the gap. When it was in position, Rod stood at his elbow and explained, 'Now you can do gate three, and then gate one. You have to lock each pair with the key.'

Marcus noticed a blue flashing light approaching gate two and recognised the outline of an ambulance through the fog. He offered the key to Rod. 'Do you mind taking over? I'd better have a word with the paramedics.' Rod accepted the key and went to move gate three.

To avoid becoming isolated from the crime scene, Marcus stepped to the rail side of gate two. He waved to the driver as Rod walked gate three into position and closed the road. The paramedics conferred briefly, and then the co-driver stepped down from the ambulance;

Marcus thought he looked vaguely familiar.

The paramedic raised a hand in greeting. 'Greg Smith. Detective Inspector Marcus Priestley, isn't it? We met a while back at an RTC.'

Marcus imitated the gesture. 'I'm a DCI, now.'

'I'm now a Senior Paramedic. Are you in charge?'

'Just until the duty officers arrive; I was a passenger on the train. You're here for the signalman, I presume.'

'That's right. We've been told over the radio that life expired has been confirmed by a doctor.'

Marcus sought to dispel the doubt suggested by Smith's slight inflection on his final syllable. 'Yes, my wife; she was on the train as well. She identified the cause of death as a broken neck.'

Rod locked the final pair of gates into position and walked over to Marcus, holding out the key. 'Now the road's blocked, we need to get a move on.'

Marcus took the key, gave a departing nod to Greg, and walked with Rod toward the signal box. 'What do I need to do now?'

Rod stopped at the foot of the steps. 'You need to wave the yellow flag. When the driver passes, you have to grab the line control token. Once the train has gone, you need to move the gates back in the opposite order; that's one, three, four, two. Have you got that?'

Having discovered enabling the train to move was not a simple matter, Marcus felt concerned there may be yet more unfamiliar procedures to be performed. Recognising Rod was better qualified, he asked, 'Do you have to go back on the train for some reason? If not, I'd like you to stay here with me.'

Rod screwed up his eyes as he considered the question, and then responded firmly, 'I can stay here.'

Marcus handed back the key. 'Right, then; you just do whatever's needed.'

'In that case, I'll speak to the signalman up the track to start with, to get him to confirm that the line's clear. Then I'll change the signal. After that, I'll collect the token from the driver and put it in the machine. Am I alright to go into the signal box, now?'

'Yes, please do. I'll come with you. Squeeze up to the left edge, if you will; but don't touch the handrail.'

Inside the signal box, Rod edged past the body and inserted the key into the rack, then picked up the grey telephone and jabbed the red button twice, one second apart. After a short delay, he pressed the black button and held a brief conversation.

Marcus looked down the track at the two horizontal arms on the semaphore signal pole. Hearing a tinkling sound behind him, he turned and saw Rod pull the fourth lever and then the sixth. On turning back, he saw the upper signal was now pointing down at forty-five degrees. When the train had remained motionless for a short time, he asked, 'Is there something else we need to do? Perhaps they haven't seen the signal change?'

Though confident they would have noticed, Rod felt obliged to offer to check. 'Shall I go and tell them? If I'm not here when they come past, you'll need to stand on that platform and collect the token from the driver; they shouldn't be doing more than ten miles an hour.'

Marcus felt torn between trying to grab something from someone on a moving train, and leaving the crime scene; he reluctantly chose the latter. 'I'll go. Please don't touch anything you don't have to.'

He hurried out of the signal box, down the steps, across the road and along the side of the railway line to the train. As he was approaching the engine, the driver leaned out and looked at him. Marcus raised a hand and shouted, 'Hello.'

When he had almost reached the cab, the driver called down, 'How do.'

Marcus responded, 'The signal's changed.'

The driver rubbed his eyes and made a show of staring. 'Yep, you're right, it's definitely changed.'

'So you can go now.'

'So that's what it means, when it's pointing down; I never knew that.'

Recognising the heavy sarcasm, he remembered his earlier ignorance, so decided not to make any more assumptions. 'Is there a reason why you can't go?'

'Yep.'

'What is it?'

'We've lost steam.'

'What can be done about it?'

'Why do you want to know? Are you offering to help? You can come into the cab and shovel some coal, if you like.'

Realising the driver's attitude was probably down to not knowing who was asking, he introduced himself. 'I'm Detective Chief Inspector Priestley, by the way, based at Midshaw.' The driver's expression changed instantly. 'The signalman's dead, I'm sorry to say.'

A blackened face appeared behind the driver, a set of teeth suddenly flashing white. 'I'm the one that found him; I was pretty sure he was dead.'

'You're Mick Collett?'

'That's right.'

'What are you wearing on your feet?'

Collett looked at him incredulously. 'Boots.'

'Let me take a quick look.' Collett waved first one foot out of the cab, then the other. 'What size are they?'

Collett shook his head in disbelief. 'Eights.'

'When you walked up and down the steps to the signal box, do you remember where you trod?'

Realisation dawned on Collett's face. 'Leftish on the way up, same line coming down, so Tom could see me if I needed to attract his attention about something.'

The driver turned from the polished brass gauge he had been monitoring. 'That's me, Tom Duddington.'

'Right. The police may need to interview you both. Does the stationmaster have your contact details?'

'Yes. So, it wasn't a heart attack or anything, then?'

'No, nothing like that.'

'An accident?'

By way of an answer, Marcus clamped his mouth tight shut, his lips pulled inward.

Duddington turned back to his bank of levers and gauges. 'We're up to pressure now, so we'll be off.'

When the engine emitted a scream like a whistling kettle forgotten on the hob, Marcus stepped well away. As the train began to move, he heard a clanking sound relayed into the distance as the couplings took up the slack. Watching for his family's carriage, he was rewarded with enthusiastic waves from his children, Helen giving more restrained signals. He waved back until they were no longer visible.

Due to the curvature of the track, the train was now restricting his view of the signal box, so he stepped to the edge of the woods to improve his line of sight. From his vantage point he saw Rod, standing on the rail side upper deck, deftly grab from the driver a large yellow plastic hoop with a black leather pouch attached.

After the rear of the train had passed the level crossing, Marcus heard a clicking noise issuing from the signal post. He looked up and found the arm was again horizontal. Confident this was one occasion he could be certain there would be no train coming, he stepped over the near rail and walked on the sleepers down the centre of the track, feeling fraudulently brave.

As he approached the signal box, he saw Rod was already opening the barriers. Only the ambulance was waiting when the final gate was swung away from the road and across the track. Seeing Rod disappear back into the signal box, he realised he was again isolated from the crime scene. Placing a foot on a crossbeam, he looked forward to improving his vaulting performance. Rod saw him and hurried down the steps, key in hand, calling out, 'Hang on; I'm coming.'

Rod opened one gate just wide enough for Marcus to slip through, before closing and locking it behind him. Marcus stated without obvious equivocation, 'Thanks; you saved me from having to do another vault.'

Rod grimaced. 'I thought I'd better, seeing how you performed last time.'

As he climbed the steps two at a time, trusting Rod to follow his line, Marcus tried not to take the comment too much to heart. He made a mental note to add gate-vaulting to Helen's extensive superiority list, and reminded himself he was being immature to see her in a competitive light. A thought suddenly struck him: her one fault was that she was too perfect, and that, in turn, condemned him to be forever flawed.

At the top, he walked to the far edge of the deck and looked down the track at the disappearing train, his tongue tasting the bitter tang of soot in the air. As Rod reached the top, Marcus moved back and opened the door for him. Rod hesitated briefly before stepping inside and edging past his fallen colleague. Marcus silently followed him in.

After Rod had inserted the Annett's key into position at the end of the rack, he asked, 'Can we cover him up? It seems disrespectful just leaving him here like this.'

Marcus shook his head. 'It's important for the forensics people that the body be disturbed as little as possible. Are you finished, now?'

'Apart from the token.' Rod placed a large iron key into a domed machine reminiscent of a 1920s Bakelite radio, then opened the door and stepped out. Marcus followed him, reminding him to keep to the right.

At the foot of the steps, Marcus called over to Greg, who was standing a little way off. 'Would you mind completing the formalities?' Both paramedics walked over. Marcus invited them to follow him up. Inside, Greg asked, 'Do you know his name?'

Marcus replied, 'Stanley Hicks.'

Greg looked at his watch and noted the time on a Validation of Death form, before turning to Marcus and inflecting as though a question, 'We'll wait outside.'

Marcus stood in the empty signal box and looked around. The stove still had some warmth, but there was no sign of combustion; he assumed Hicks had been allowing the fire to die down, synchronised with the end of his working day. Being previously unfamiliar with the innards of the signal box, he was aware he could not know whether everything was in its correct place, yet he felt confident there was no evidence of a struggle. He decided to invite Rod back into the box to see if he could make any useful observations. From the deck just outside the door, he called down, 'Do you mind coming back in, Rod? I need your expertise.'

Marcus watched him trudging slowly up the steps, clearly reluctant to re-enter; he decided to give him a little encouragement. 'Thank you for all your help so far, Rod; and could I ask you to do one more thing? Just look around and tell me if there's anything you think is out of place, or missing, or shouldn't be here.'

Inside, Rod began to scan the room conscientiously, though avoided looking too near the dead body.

Marcus noticed a novel next to an open log of train-related events. 'Was this his? Please don't touch it.'

Rod peered at it. 'Yes, I'm sure it's the one he was reading; it's a crime novel about the death of an artist. He liked detective fiction; that, and anything to do with codes and code-breaking.' Rod examined the adjacent log book. 'Stan entered his last three-one properly; you can tell it's his handwriting.'

Marcus edged closer and leaned over to see where Rod was indicating. 'Thanks for pointing that out to me; we'll need to take both these books into evidence.' He stood aside as the guard continued to scan the room.

Rod finally delivered his assessment. 'Everything looks just like it should.'

Marcus responded, 'Thank you for checking.' After a brief silence, he asked, 'Have you had many dealings with the police?'

In contemplation, Rod cupped his chin in his hand and rubbed the short silver bristles of one cheek with his fingertips. 'None as I can remember, except for reporting car drivers who swerve through the barriers instead of waiting. Some people have no patience; a signalman will be killed one of these days.'

Seeing Rod's face register shock at his own words, Marcus decided now would be the time to ask about the deceased, as he would be least reserved and therefore most susceptible to disclosing confidential information. 'What can you tell me about Mr Hicks?'

Rod's words flooded out. 'For a start, he didn't like drivers blowing their horns at him; he said it was illogical of them to think the gates would be opened any quicker just because they're honking. He told me one time there was just one car waiting, a sporty-looking Toyota with a cheap sort of personalised registration number; you know, letters, numbers and a single letter. He had a theory about personalised registrations: people who go to all that expense just to tell everyone who they are, tend to see themselves as more important than other road users, which makes them bad drivers. He reckoned the more personalised they are, the more self-important the driver; he described it as a positive correlation.' Marcus nodded to indicate he understood the term. 'I think he was a bit of a commie at heart. What I mean is, he believed all men are born equal, and disliked anything that made anyone seem more important than anyone else.' Marcus noted how older folk had no qualms about saying "men" instead of "people". 'You can guess what he thought of the royal family. Not personally, mind; just as a principle.'

There was a pause. Marcus resisted the temptation to comment, believing Rod might deliver further insights if left uninterrupted.

Having checked that Marcus was still fully engaged, Rod began again. 'Well, anyway, he was hurrying to open the gates when the driver of that Toyota started to blast their horn at him, so he slowed down a bit to keep them waiting a while longer. He told me he wondered if it was being driven by a bishop, because it was purple; I guess he had a dry sense of humour. When he finally opened the gate, he saw the electric window coming down. The driver leaned out and gave him a load of abuse; but the thing he hadn't expected was what sort of a driver it would be. It wasn't a bishop; it was a small, thin, pasty-white woman in her sixties.'

Marcus recognised Rod was waiting for some sort of appreciation of the anecdote; he gave a short 'Hmm', then followed up with an audible sigh. 'It's a sad thing, Rod, but you'd be surprised how many women of all ages display signs of road rage nowadays.'

'I suppose it's all this equality thing, isn't it?'

'Maybe it is, but men are still the main offenders.'

Rod glanced at the corpse. 'Perhaps I shouldn't have told you that; it makes him sound mean, but I'm sure he was just trying to teach the driver good manners.'

'Educating people into better behaviour is good in theory, but some just don't have enough sense to get the message. It probably isn't related to this case, but we'll try and track her down if we don't get any other leads. After all, the woman clearly has self-control issues and a motive of sorts, so I'm glad you mentioned it.'

Rod stared at him. 'What do you mean, motive?'

Marcus looked him steadily in the eye. 'I know this will come as a shock to you, Rod, but my wife is certain it wasn't an accident.' Seeing the colour drain from his face, Marcus pressed on quickly. 'Now, what about people who've been swerving through the barriers: did Mr Hicks report any? They might bear a grudge.'

'I think there's been four car or van drivers he's reported to the police, but I could be wrong.'

'We can check it out ourselves. Could there be any others that weren't logged with us?'

'He believed in reporting every offender, apart from cyclists who nip through when they're not supposed to; they don't have registration numbers, so he thought it was pointless reporting them.'

'Unless they were seen by at least one police officer or two independent witnesses, he'd have needed film of them doing it. You don't have CCTV, do you?'

'No; it's been discussed, but it didn't seem worth it.'

'Do you know of anyone with CCTV around here?'

'Sorry, no.'

Marcus pursed his lips. 'I wonder, is there anything else connected to his work at the railway that might have made him enemies?'

Rod shook his head firmly. 'I really don't think so. Apart from the odd motorist, everybody loves heritage railways, and the volunteers who keep them running; at least I think they do.'

'I'm sure you're right. So, what about away from the railway: what did he do with his time?'

'He never said.'

'Was he married, or living with a partner?'

'As far as I know, he was single with no family ties; that's why it was easy for him to move up here when he stopped work. Nobody to please but himself, you see.'

'Do you know when he stopped working?'

'Not exactly, but it was less than a year ago. He said he moved up from London straight after retiring.'

'Do you know what his job was in London?'

'He was a Civil Servant.'

'Do you happen to know which branch of the Civil Service he was in, by any chance? Or what he did?'

'I think he was some sort of accountant; he said his job was very boring, which is probably why he never really spoke about it.'

'Is there anything else you know about him?'

'I know he had a fantastic memory for numbers. He could recite every preserved British railway locomotive number, and some others that have now been scrapped. And he knew their names as well, of course.'

'How many would that be?'

'There must be thousands of preserved engines, but only a fraction are "Namers". Huh, that's a word I haven't used in a long time. Just last week he was telling me there's been more than one Black Prince.' Marcus fleetingly thought of the eldest son of King Edward III, and then of Machiavelli. 'He reeled off some numbers, starting with nine double-two o-three; everybody knows that one, of course, though not everybody knows it didn't always have a name. Next, he said seven treble-o eight. That one was designed in Derby; I actually saw it pulling an express, years ago. Then, he mentioned the narrow gauge number eleven at Romney, built before the war by Krupp in Germany. And then he listed two numbers that I hadn't come across before; I'm not sure, but I think he said sixteen seventy and twenty-six thirty-one.'

'It sounds like you've a fair head for numbers yourself, Rod.'

'Maybe steam locomotive numbers, especially the ones that were around when I was a train-spotter; that was back in the days when it was fashionable, before it gained the anorak reputation.'

'I expect it was more interesting with steam engines, before diesels took over.'

'Yes, though I thought some diesels were alright; maybe *Peaks* and *Deltics*. DMUs were the worst; that's diesel multiple units. We used to call them bug-cars.'

Marcus doubted Rod knew anything else pertinent to the investigation, and assumed he would prefer not to be with the dead man, so invited him to step outside.

At the foot of the stairs in the fading light, Marcus cast around for something sociable to chat about while waiting for his colleagues to arrive. He glimpsed in the distance a flashing blue light struggling to cut through a bank of fog, and found the effect reminiscent of the fireworks exploding within low clouds that he had witnessed in the previous month with his family; he recalled how the weather had largely spoiled the organised bonfire display, and how disappointed the children had been. Looking sideways at Rod, he nodded in its direction. 'Here comes the cavalry.'

Marcus began to scan the surrounding area, looking for anything that might prove significant to the inquiry.

Realising the officer's attention was now directed elsewhere, Rod walked away a short distance, then turned and looked up at the signal box. Thinking of the sudden death of his colleague, he began reflecting on his own mortality.

CHAPTER 3

The first officers to arrive at the crime scene were Frank Cargill and Neil "Witty" Whittington. Priestley called out to them, 'Over here.'

When the two detectives were still a few metres away, Priestley addressed them with an air of formality. 'DI Cargill, DS Whittington, this is Rodney Stapleton. Rod has been helping me; you'll need to take his fingerprints because he's been in the signal box.' He realised Cargill was eying Stapleton with an air of suspicion. 'He's not a suspect; he was on the train when the signalman died. I've made a start on getting some information about the deceased, and...'

Cargill raised his hand to stop Priestley in mid-sentence. 'Sorry, boss, but you're off the case. Your wife phoned in to say she can't get through to your mobile, so could we relay a message: the train is forty minutes behind schedule and she'll assume you're making your own way home if you're not at the car when they get there. And she asked us to remind you that your children will need you at home for "special duties", whatever that means, so don't be too late.'

Priestley stifled a grin. 'I'll fill you in on what I know, and then I'll cadge a lift home.' He turned to Stapleton. 'I asked Gordon to keep key people back at the station; I'd like you to join them, but please don't divulge any information about the incident.'

He frowned. 'What if someone asks?'

'Just say, the police don't want any discussion until

we've had the chance to talk to them all; it's so that if someone misremembers something, they don't confuse other people.' Stapleton confirmed acceptance of the instruction and set off in the direction of the station.

As several more service vehicles arrived, Priestley briefed Cargill and Witty on events so far, commencing with the train's unscheduled stop at around ten past three. He referred to the final ledger entry, which had a recorded time of 15:04 and was apparently in the victim's handwriting. Lastly, he described prominent boot marks on the steps, and suggested they probably belonged to the fireman from the locomotive.

Cargill asked, 'Is the fireman a suspect, then?'

Priestley rubbed his chin. 'Only if the signalman was complicit in his own murder. He'd have had to stop the train in order to get the fireman to leave the locomotive so that he could come along and do him in.'

'So that's a no, then.'

'Yes, Frank, that's a no.'

'Well, if that's everything, boss, it must be time you were going home.' He called over to a male uniformed constable loitering by the Ops wagon. 'You're not busy are you? DCI Priestley needs taking to Sheffield.'

DC Linda Plummer, who had been waiting for an opportunity to involve herself, rushed over and spoke past Priestley to Cargill. 'I could take him home, sir; I shouldn't be too long, and he can fill me in on the way.'

Cargill frowned. 'It might take you quite a while.'

Plummer's attempted smile faltered. 'I'll be quick; I won't stop off anywhere.'

Cargill raised his eyebrows. 'I meant because of the fog. Well, one volunteer is worth two pressed men. Or women,' he added, trying to be Politically Correct.

Priestley addressed the air above Plummer's head, his voice acquiring a harsh edge from his determination to exclude any hint of softness. 'Right, let's get off.'

When they reached the open road, she glanced briefly at him. 'I have a Christmas present for you.'

He winced and hissily sucked in a lungful of air. 'You really shouldn't have, Lin. You know we need to keep things under the radar, and giving a present could set tongues wagging.'

'Don't worry, I know how to keep a secret.'

'Well, what is the present?'

'You have to guess.'

'Is it wrapped up?'

'Yes.'

'Would I be embarrassed if I unwrapped it in front of my wife?'

'Definitely!'

'Where is it? Not back at the office, I hope.'

'No, it's in the car.'

'I'd better unwrap it here, then.' She giggled. He scanned the detritus on the back seat. 'I can't see it.'

'I'm sure you can.'

He looked again. 'What's it wrapped in?'

'Coat, shirt, trousers, bra, knickers.'

'Oh! You mean you.'

'Of course I mean me.'

His nervous laughter faltered. 'It is fun together, but don't you feel it's time you found yourself someone for a serious relationship? Someone you could commit to?'

She gave a relaxed laugh. 'I'm happy with things just the way they are. So, when can you come over and unwrap your present, do you think?'

'I'll be spending all Christmas with my children; it's

a very special time for them. I guess we might have to wait until the New Year.'

She sighed heavily. 'I was really hoping you'd come sooner.'

Once away from the valley, the roads had just the occasional bank of fog. He replayed his earlier briefing, concluding as she drew up on his driveway.

Keeping the engine running, she turned to face him. 'Right, off you go. And don't worry about the rest of us, stuck out in the cold.' She shivered theatrically.

'You should wear a vest.'

'I'm not expecting any knife attacks.'

He smiled. 'A thermal one.'

She smiled back. 'Do I get a Christmas kiss?'

Tutting repeatedly, he shook his head slowly. 'Don't be naughty, DC Plummer.' He put on a serious face, stepped out of the car and walked around the front. She lowered the passenger window. He called out, 'See you in the New Year.' She reversed away.

As he turned his key in the lock, Helen opened the inner door. When he stepped inside, she asked, 'Why didn't you invite her in to say hello?' Before he could respond, she giggled like an adolescent. 'You might even have got a kiss off her under the mistletoe.'

He suppressed a smile, leaving him looking severe. 'She's on the clock, and she knows me well enough not to take any time out when it's a murder inquiry.'

'Ooh! She must think you're a hard man.'

Smiling inwardly at Helen's unintended *soupçon* of *double entendre*, he responded in kind. 'She *knows* I'm a hard man.' A small burst of adrenaline told him Helen had perhaps laid a trap, and if so, he had walked right into it. He scrutinised her face, and felt a wave of relief on finding nothing but innocence displayed there.

'Well, you can forget about the case now; you're on holiday, aren't you.' She watched him extend his arm and wiggle his hand a few times to suggest some doubt. 'Aren't you?'

'Officially, yes; but we're short-staffed, so I need to be flexible.'

She shook her head. 'You're always short-staffed. You need to deal with our problems at home before you even think about getting involved in the inquiry.'

His initial surprise quickly gave way to an uneasy feeling she had suspicions about him and Lin. 'What problems are those, love? I didn't know we had any.'

'Well, today we have two. Problem number one: Edwin says he intends to prove Father Christmas doesn't exist. I assume that means he'll try to stay awake all night on the lookout. If you wish to avoid being unmasked, you'd better be extra careful.'

'He's bound to fall asleep eventually. So, what's problemette number two?'

'Alice saw two father Christmases at the same time, and would like you to explain to her... actually, I'd like to hear your explanation as well.'

'Where did she see two of them?'

'We left one behind on the train, and she caught a glimpse of another one in the stationmaster's office.'

'Maybe one was a reserve. Alright, let's deal with Alice.'

In the kitchen, Alice was sitting quietly at the table, designing bracelets. Edwin was nearby, pressing the buttons on his new watch. Marcus sat opposite Alice, with Helen next to her. 'I understand you saw two Father Christmases at the station, today.'

'Yes, I did. One was tall and thin and the other was short and fat.'

'Right, well, you see, it's like this...'

Edwin interrupted him. 'If one was made of matter, then the other must be made of anti-matter, and if the two of them ever touch, there'll be a massive explosion that will rip the universe apart.'

Seeing Alice looking utterly shocked, he sighed at Edwin. 'That was unhelpful, wasn't it?' Edwin grinned. Marcus smiled at Alice. 'It isn't true; he's just making it up. Now, as well as the main Father Christmas who lives in Lapland, there are lots more all over the world; it's to make sure there are enough of them to deliver all the presents to all the children everywhere.'

Alice pondered on this revelation. 'So the one from Lapland doesn't deliver all the presents?'

Edwin blurted out, 'If the one from Lapland had to deliver all the presents in just one night, he'd have to go so fast the friction would make him burst into flames, along with the reindeer.' Alice blinked slowly, twice.

Marcus regretted having started the explanation in Edwin's presence, but decided to keep going. 'That's why there are so many Assistant Father Christmases, or AFCs. But don't worry about it; they're very well organised, so there'll be an AFC here sometime tonight to deliver *your* presents.' Seeing she looked reasonably convinced, Marcus made a strategic withdrawal to the living room, Helen following closely behind.

He settled at one end of a settee. She climbed into the other end, drawing up her legs between them. Holding a warm smile, she asked, 'What does AFC stand for, again? Was it Assistant something? Or did you say Association Football Club?'

He shook his head. 'You won't confuse me like that. In the army, I was trained how to keep track of my lies. But then, you know all about that.'

Thinking she had seen a dark shadow pass over his face as he recalled his army days, she refreshed her own smile to distract him. 'And, since then, I've taught you other techniques for lying convincingly. You say it's essential for police work, but I can't help thinking some officers lose the ability to tell the truth anymore.'

He hoped her words were not intended as a personal accusation. 'I don't mind lying to criminals, but not to Alice.' Puffing up his cheeks, he breathed out, slowly. 'This has to be the last year. I'll put it in my diary for September to tell her the truth about Father Christmas.'

'Unless she's already found out.'

'If she did, she might not believe us about other things. I'll tell her in January. It's interesting though, that there were two Father Christmases at the station. I'll phone Neil and check he's aware of it, just in case.'

'By which you mean you'd like to find out how the investigation's going. You'll need a much better excuse than that. I'll put some Christmas music on, and you can relax. That's an order.'

He stretched his arms out to either side, across the top of the settee. 'I've started relaxing, boss.' … 'I'm relaxing some more.' … 'I'm fully relaxed now.'

She loaded a disc into the CD player and picked up the remote control box, before returning to the settee to nestle under his arm. After pressing a button on the box, the first track began: an *a cappella* rendition of the *Ukrainian Bell Carol* in English by a choir of women. When the final sonorous note had faded away, she touched the pause button. 'Originally, it would have been performed by unmarried girls as a simple chant. The English lyric relates to Christmas, whereas the Ukrainian version is to do with the New Year and the coming of spring, about a swallow that tells of future prosperity. Its timing isn't as strange as it sounds, as their year used to begin in April, before they changed the calendar.'

'Before they changed the calendar? Did four pages get stuck together and they lost three months? Didn't anybody notice?'

'Don't be simple, Marcus; they would have had to lose nine months that way, and someone would have been bound to notice ten pages stuck together.' She waited for him to finish counting on eight fingers and a thumb as he mouthed the months. 'You must know I'm talking about the Julian and Gregorian calendars.'

He wrapped her closer into him. 'Do you think we're sometimes a bit too, um, intense? What about just listening for enjoyment?'

'When you say "we" you mean me. I know how deeply you can be affected by music, but I'm different; I like to know everything there is to know about anything I listen to.'

He kissed her forehead. 'Sorry; it wasn't meant as a criticism. I love you for what you are, and I wouldn't want you to be any other way. But I'm just a simple copper, whereas you're always totally full-on brilliant.'

'And we both know that isn't true.'

'But you are brilliant.'

She dug her elbow into his side. 'The other part.'

He reached over, took the remote control from her and set the CD playing again. It restarted with a double choir rendition of *In dulci jubilo*. With his eyes closed, he silently sang a bass part, his jaw muscles tightening as they suppressed the requisite changes to the shape of his mouth. Despite accepting his real voice was now bass-baritone, he imagined himself making a solo tenor entry with *O Patris caritas*. His muscle memory was fighting to control the movements of his diaphragm, and his mind was telling him his vocal chords were straining to make the higher notes. Thinking he should try harder to relax by allowing the music simply to wash over him, he smiled as he recognised the paradox.

She had felt the tensing of his thorax, which she interpreted as symptomatic of a different malaise. When the carol was ending, she looked up at his face and caught his smile before it could fade. With carefully chosen words, she endeavoured to preserve the moment in him. 'I sometimes envy your ability to become calm and peaceful when you hear music.'

Interpreting her words as intended to reinforce his apparent positive emotional response to the singing, he maintained the smile for her benefit: he wished to look relaxed because she wished him to feel relaxed.

He tried employing another calming technique she had taught him, imagining himself sifting through his conscious mind and discarding any negative thoughts. When he had convinced himself only positive ones now remained, he again tuned into the music. A soloist opened with *Three Kings*. He silently doubled *from Persian lands afar*, knowing he would always prefer to sing choral music than to listen passively.

CHAPTER 4

At the crime scene, DS Neil Whittington and DI Frank Cargill were prepared to work late, having made no plans to celebrate Christmas eve. They had in fact both volunteered to be on duty for the whole of the festive period. Cargill's reasoning was that he had no close relatives to visit, and no religious beliefs requiring attendance elsewhere, so preferred to keep busy in order not to suffer the dismal feeling of being left out of the joyful occasion. Witty's motivation came from his desire to retain as much time off work as possible for spending with his partner, Lily; she was currently working in Paris and not due back until late January.

The Stanley Hicks case fell under the auspices of the Derbyshire and Nottinghamshire Major Crime section of East Midlands Special Operations Unit, a regional tasking structure designed for marshalling resources across five forces. Cargill had earlier been notified he was assigned to the case as Deputy Senior Investigating Officer. After he advised Control over police radio that a doctor in the vicinity had confirmed life expired, and that paramedics had completed a death Validation form, he was informed he was now Acting SIO; he wished it were due to someone having confidence in his ability, but thought it was almost certainly down to the very high level of holiday-related absences. Any lingering doubt disappeared when he was informed he was also now the designated Crime Scene Manager, and must find a stand-in Crime Scene Photographer.

Cargill briefed Witty. 'I'm now Acting SIO and the Scene Manager; see if you can find me a clipboard and some forms, will you? Failing that, I'll have to make do with blank sheets of paper. And you need to rustle up a camera for yourself; you're the official Photographer.' Witty accepted the instructions with equanimity.

Shortly after, Control informed Cargill not to expect a police surgeon, and then relayed instructions from the pathologist, Dr Patel. 'He's unable to attend due to fog, so he's asked you to bag up the hands and have the paramedics take the body directly to the mortuary.'

When Witty returned with the requisite equipment, Cargill took a pound coin from his pocket. 'We won't be getting a medic; let's see which of us will have to cover for that job as well. I'm heads.' He tossed the coin, then pocketed it without revealing the outcome. 'When you've taken your photos, bag up the hands and tell the paramedics to pick up the body. The pathologist wants it taking to the mortuary straight away.'

Witty looked askance. 'Shouldn't we at least wait for the CSIs?'

He shrugged. 'Is there any point? The body isn't their job.'

'They might learn something from seeing it in situ.'

'Something they wouldn't get from your pictures?'

'I suppose not. I'd better get snapping, then.'

Witty donned an all-white disposable scene suit, before extracting a pair of pale blue latex gloves from a sealed bag, and working his fingers into the ends.

In lieu of stepping plates, as he climbed the stairs he laid two lines of yellow numbered markers, defining the previously forensically compromised route.

Knowing the door handle had already been used

several times subsequent to the incident, he had no qualms about grasping it. Inside the signal box, he took photographs with the police-issue digital camera, selecting various angles to record the position of the body relative to its surroundings. Next, he drew a chalk outline around the body on the wooden floor. Then, he explored the camera's video facility and made a short recording. Satisfied he had captured the entire scene, he carefully placed the camera on the bench seat by the window, before putting plastic bags over the deceased's hands and sealing them with tape.

From the top of the steps, he called down to the paramedics, and invited them to take away the corpse following the defined route. He watched as they ascended in single file with their equipment. Inside, they gently eased the deceased into a body bag and attached it to the stretcher, before carefully descending the flight of steps between the lines of plastic brackets.

Back in the signal box, he picked up the camera again and slung it around his neck. He contemplated the chalk outline and decided to take a complete set of overlapping shots, to facilitate the creation of a collage encompassing all the adjacent fixtures.

When finished with photographing, he reviewed every image on the small digital screen, and appreciated just how simple and reliable the process had become since the days of exposing, developing and printing from film. Confident of having a comprehensive set of pictures, he exited and returned to the foot of the steps.

Cargill noted down Witty's egress on the locus log. When he looked up, he saw two men running cables from the generator to the floodlights. After a short while, he judged they were almost ready to turn them on. He called out, 'Make sure you give us a ten second countdown before you blind us all, this time.'

A voice shouted back, 'Will do, Frank. Ten, nine, eight, six.' Someone laughed. 'Three, two, one.' The lights burst into life, though the usual initial impact was lessened by the diffusing effect of the swirling fog.

Witty and Cargill saw a small van arrive, white with a side stripe of blue and yellow squares, and "Crime Scene Investigation" stencilled on the side. They watched as CSI Nick Evans carefully parked the SOCO van, and then exchanged amused glances as he re-parked it just a few inches further into the edge.

Evans and Lead CSI Jenny Merton climbed into their scene suits, white with thin, pale blue lines that defined a collar and a vertical cross at the front and back. Merton put on purple latex gloves and then joined the detectives. She acknowledged Witty, and then asked Cargill, 'Where's the body, Frank?' His response was lost in a raking cough. 'You don't sound too clever; have you seen somebody about it?'

Cargill shook his head. 'It's just this bad weather.' He held his cough in check and swallowed hard. 'The paramedics have taken the deceased to the pathologist; he didn't want to turn out in this fog.'

'OK, so where *was* the body?'

'In the signal box. Neil took some photos before it was moved.'

Witty interjected, 'I drew a chalk outline on the floor, as well.'

Cargill continued, 'Helen Priestley was the first medic on the scene. She reckoned it was a broken neck, and could well have been done by an expert. If so, he may not have left any clues. He or she, I mean.'

Merton snorted at him. 'Have you been on a Gender Equality Awareness course recently?'

He grimaced. 'Does it show?'

She grinned. 'Only a lot.'

Cargill grinned back at her for a moment before pointing to the steps behind him. 'Marcus was here earlier and kept everybody as close to the left edge as possible; the markers are only there to show his route. The smallish boot marks to the left of centre probably came from the locomotive fireman who found him. Other recent footprints could be worth a closer look, though any stilettoes probably belong to Helen.'

'Well, if you'll move away and stop messing up the ground with your size thirteens, we'll begin here and work our way over.' She turned to Evans. 'OK Nick, down on your hands and knees and make like a dog.'

Witty and Cargill adjourned to the nearby Ops wagon for a drink. When Cargill had finished his tea, he poured the dregs away and stared into the empty beaker. Witty asked, 'What future do you see, Frank?'

Cargill gave a lopsided smile. 'A meeting with a tall, dark stranger. That'll be just after midnight on New Year's Day, I guess; someone first-footing. Do they still do that round your way?'

'Yes, though it's more organised than it used to be. One bloke has advertised himself with a card in a shop window; the one that has a post office in it. All very professional-looking, with a photo and contact details. So, what do you have lined up for New Year's Eve?'

'Nothing. I'll be home alone.'

'In that case, what about seeing the New Year in with me? Lily won't be back until the end of January, so I wasn't planning on going anywhere.'

'OK, maybe. It's a nice idea.' He jerked his thumb in the direction of the signal box. 'Anyway, we'd best crack on with this. House-to-house enquiries would be a good start point. There's only one property that's very close, but there's another half-a-dozen down the road that'll need checking out.'

'I know it's best to strike while the iron's hot, but I doubt anyone will really appreciate being disturbed on Christmas eve.'

'I should have kept Lin here; she's good at charming people.' He pretended to cough. 'Perhaps I should do it myself; someone might offer me a medicinal whisky.'

Witty glanced around. 'There's a couple of uniforms looking for something to do. Shall I give them a shout?'

'Yes, let's get it kicked off.'

WPC Holly Grenfell, single and fast approaching forty, had joined the service at thirty-five; she had been a social worker who had dedicated all her time to her vocation until she ultimately felt burnt out. WPC Paige Anderson, twenty-one, though plain, was very popular with her single male colleagues due to her accessibility. After a briefing, they began house-to-house enquiries, starting with the cottage opposite the signal box.

The doorbell was answered by a woman in her thirties, tall and thin, with a Modigliani drawn face. She was dressed in skin-tight blue jeans, and wearing a thick sweater that displayed a snow scene with reindeer. 'Oh, hello. I thought it might have been some relations. Come in and tell me what's going on.' She turned away and headed for the living room, relying on them to close the outer door.

Mrs Emily Thompson introduced herself and invited them to sit. The officers gave their names and showed their IDs. Grenfell asked, 'Did you notice any unusual activity in this vicinity between three and three fifteen.'

Mrs Thompson responded without hesitation. 'Not that I recall.' Suddenly, a small boy popped up from behind the sofa. She pretended to be startled. 'I've told you before about that, Alan; making people jump.'

He ignored the reprimand and spoke in a monotone to no one in particular. 'I saw Father Christmas.'

His mother waved him away. 'Go and play upstairs.' When he had left the room, she asked, 'Can you tell me what happened?'

Grenfell replied, 'I'm sure you appreciate we can't divulge any details, Mrs Thompson, but I can tell you that someone died in the signal box. Did you notice anyone earlier, say from two o'clock onwards?'

She shook her head. 'Sorry, I've only seen my boy this afternoon. I've been baking for hours, though I probably shouldn't have been; I always do too much. I've just finished masses of sausage rolls; would you like to try some while they're warm? Or maybe some quiche?' They declined politely and took their leave.

Before the row of terraced houses was a large plot of untended ground with a mud path that led to the woods. Grenfell pointed to it and asked rhetorically, 'I wonder where that leads?'

At the first house, Grenfell knocked and waited. An elderly woman opened the door and invited them into her parlour. Her ancient husband explained they had closed the curtains at three o'clock to block out the bad weather and make the place cosier. When Grenfell informed them that someone had died, they appeared anxious, so she assured them there was no evidence to suggest a dangerous felon remained at large in the area.

As the officers approached the next house, a young couple stepped out, dressed up to the nines. When asked if they had seen anything unusual that afternoon, she turned to him and giggled. He adopted a serious expression and responded to Grenfell. 'We've been busy together all afternoon and haven't even looked out of the window, so I'm sorry but we can't help you.'

Grenfell asked, 'Busy, as in… ?'

The woman giggled again. 'Yes, in the bedroom.'

He shushed his companion. Grenfell stepped aside so they could pass. 'Well, thank you for your time.'

When the next bell failed to attract the attention of the occupants visible through the window, Grenfell knocked loudly on the door's central panel and flicked the letterbox a few times. A youngish man rushed to open it and apologised for not hearing the bell, explaining it was because he had been playing with his three children, the oldest just six. He invited them into the hallway and to close the door behind them to keep the place warm. His wife joined them there, where she expressed concern their children would become upset if they were to hear someone had died on Christmas Eve, as though the date made the event far worse. Neither of them could recall having looked outside all afternoon.

At the next house, Grenfell refrained from knocking, as she had observed a shadowy figure through the frosted glass moving quickly toward the door. Mrs Karen Eckersley, a dumpy woman in her forties, beckoned them to follow her into the kitchen. On the rectangular table, seven circular dishes of different nibbles plotted a parabolic arc, a half-empty glass of red wine at its focus. Away to one side stood an empty bottle of Bordeaux. *Good Kind Wenceslas*, emanating from a portable CD player, sounded apologetically subdued as he requested *flesh* and *wine*.

Grenfell began, 'You'll have been wondering what's going on outside.'

Mrs Eckersley stared anxiously at her. 'Yes.'

'A gentleman died at the signal box up the road, sometime between three o'clock and a quarter past. We're making enquiries in the area. Did you see any unusual or suspicious activity in the vicinity of the signal box around that time? Or earlier?'

An almost inaudible reply of 'No,' was accompanied by an incongruous nod of the head. Grenfell tried again. 'Are you saying you saw nothing unusual?'

Mrs Eckersley responded 'Yes,' and nodded again.

Grenfell tried once more. 'Did you see anything at all between three o'clock and a quarter past?'

Mrs Eckersley pointed at the window. 'I was in the kitchen until I heard all the palaver outside. You can see it looks the other way.'

Grenfell asked, 'Is there anyone else at home? Anyone who might have seen something?'

Mrs Eckersley stammered, 'Mmm my husband is in the other room, but *he* won't have seen anything.'

Grenfell empathically felt the tension rising in her. 'I'm sure you're right, but we'll just check with him.'

They were led in silence to the living room. After several seconds, Mrs Eckersley coughed lightly. 'Bill? These policewomen would like to talk to you.'

Mr Eckersley kept his can of lager in his hand, as he reluctantly took his eyes off the television for just a moment to glance at the WPCs. 'What do you want?'

Grenfell waited for him to look around again, but his eyes remained focused on the screen. She walked in front of the television and stared at him. 'Something's happened near here and I need your full attention. Would you mind turning off the sound.'

With his free hand he picked up the TV remote control box and pressed the mute button, then glared at her with unconcealed annoyance.

She returned his stare, refusing to be cowed. 'Just before a quarter past three this afternoon, a body was found in the signal box. Could you tell me what you were doing between three o'clock and a quarter past.'

He snarled, 'What are you accusing me of? I've been sat here since two; she'll back me up.'

'I'm not accusing you of anything, sir, but I would like you to think back and tell me if you saw something around that time that may help with our investigation.'

He sneered at her. 'I've been watching telly since two and I haven't seen nowt.'

Grenfell continued to obscure the screen for a few seconds longer. 'Then I'll leave you to your television.' As she moved away, she adopted an acid smile. 'And a very Merry Christmas to you, sir.'

He responded slightly less icily, having missed the irony. 'Well, thank you.' Before the three women had filed out of the room, he had turned the sound on again.

Back in the kitchen, Grenfell checked his alibi. She asked with apparent incredulity, 'Surely he hasn't been sat in that chair all this time?'

Mrs Eckersley gave an almost imperceptible sigh. 'Yes, he has. He never moves, except to go for a pee. I keep out of his way as much as I can.'

Anderson, uncomfortable with the silence that now hung in the room, swung her head back and forth in two exaggerated arcs, as she scanned the array of nibbles.

'Christmas must be a bit quiet for you, then?'

Mrs Eckersley looked first at Anderson and then at Grenfell. 'Very quiet. I could do with a bit of company. Will you have a drink with me?'

Grenfell replied, 'It would be nice, only we're on duty, so we're not allowed.' Seeing her intense look of disappointment, she added, 'But thanks for the offer.'

As they walked to the next house, Grenfell snapped, 'Why do women put up with someone like that?'

Anderson shook her head. 'Beats me.'

Grenfell migrated the emphasis to the first word. 'Beats me! I wouldn't be at all surprised. If ever I'm called out to a domestic at that address, I'll know exactly what to expect.'

As they approached the fifth and final terraced house, Anderson commented, 'No lights on.'

Grenfell responded, 'We'll try anyway.' She rapped loudly at the door until confident no one was at home. As they began to walk away, they heard a creak behind them. An old man standing in the doorway called out, 'Hello. Come on in. Let me get this door closed.'

After introductions, Samuel Youens led them to his front room and invited them to sit on the settee. When he had settled into the armchair by the gas fire, Grenfell looked him steadily in the eye, checking for signs of anxiety as she spoke. 'There's been an incident at the signal box. A man was found dead this afternoon at a little before quarter past three. We're asking anyone who lives locally if they saw anything suspicious around that time.'

Youens closed his eyes for a few seconds. 'I must have dozed off around half two, and I didn't wake up again until just a little while ago when I saw some blue flashing lights reflecting off the ceiling.'

Grenfell acknowledged his testimony with a deep nod. 'Then I won't trouble you further, sir.'

He began to stand, but changed his mind and settled back into the armchair, a smile creasing his wrinkled cheeks. 'Will you have a sherry and a mince pie?'

Grenfell failed to respond immediately, so Anderson trotted out the official line. 'We're on duty, sir, so we're not allowed.'

Grenfell stood and took a step toward the door. 'Don't trouble yourself, sir; we'll see ourselves out.'

Once Anderson had closed the external door behind them, Grenfell admitted, 'I was thinking we might just have a sip of sherry with him. God, I hate the idea of getting old and being forgotten about.'

As Grenfell trudged slowly away, Anderson spoke brightly in an attempt to lighten her colleague's mood. 'We don't know if he's really been forgotten about; he could have people who're coming for Christmas.'

Grenfell stopped and turned to her. 'You could be right, Paige. It would be nice to think so, but I didn't see much evidence of contact with other people. I only counted eight Christmas cards. I really wish there was something we could do for folk like that.'

They walked in silence the short distance to the final property, a newly built stone-faced detached house with double garage and large garden. Grenfell looked at the two bell buttons and pressed the one that was shining the brighter. In place of standard chimes, they heard the first two bars of *God rest you merry, gentlemen.* Anderson grinned at her. 'They're obviously into the Christmas spirit.'

A tall, silver-haired, late-middle-aged man opened

the door to them. After inspecting their IDs, he introduced himself as 'Dr Freddie Forbes,' and seemed disappointed when they failed to react to the name. Grenfell explained the reason for their visit. He ushered them into the dining room so they could question all the guests. As they entered, the conversation stopped as suddenly as if an electric switch had been flicked. All eyes turned to the newcomers, and then to Forbes, as though awaiting his direction or an explanation.

Grenfell glanced initially at the central table that was scattered with platters of finger food, and then around at the score of well-dressed middle-aged people holding glasses of wine and balancing paper plates precariously. When she began to speak, she felt unnecessarily loud for the attentive guests. 'I'm sorry to have to interrupt the festivities, but there's been an incident at the railway signal box. The body of a man was discovered there just before a quarter past three, and we'd like to interview anyone who may have seen anything out of the ordinary in the vicinity, leading up to that time.'

After a pause, there followed a chorus of denial of any knowledge. Then, a high male voice asked, 'What exactly do you mean by "out of the ordinary"? I don't know what normally happens there, so I can't know what constitutes "out of the ordinary".'

Grenfell invited the man to come away from the others and into the hallway. 'Did you see something?'

He ran his fingers through his thick, blond hair. 'My wife and I walked here so we could both have a drink. We went through the level crossing up the road and I noticed the light was on in the signal box. I'm sure someone was standing inside, but I didn't really look properly so I couldn't give you any sort of description.'

Grenfell took out her notebook. 'Could I have your details, please.' She noted down the address, landline and mobile phone numbers of Oliver Brownlow and his wife Nancy. 'If you remember something later, please get in touch. Here's my card. Will you be home over Christmas if we need to contact you?'

'We're not planning to go far, but you can always get me on my mobile.'

'Good. One other thing: can you tell me exactly what time you were passing the signal box?'

'I'd say it was about three o'clock.'

'Thank you, Mr Brownlow. And could you point out to me the lady you were walking with.'

Brownlow considered saying, 'That's no lady, that's my wife,' but thought better of it. He stepped into the dining room and indicated a cluster of three women and two men. 'She's the one in the dark red top.'

'That's all for now, then. Thank you again.'

Brownlow headed for his wife. Anderson followed closely on his heels, and addressed her before he could speak. 'Mrs Brownlow, would you mind stepping into the hallway. My colleague has some questions for you.'

Grenfell began, 'You are Nancy Brownlow?'

She enunciated her response. 'I am indeed.'

'I understand you walked here with your husband. Could you tell me exactly what time you arrived?'

'Yes, of course. We know the route very well, so I set us off in good time to be fashionably late. I checked my watch as my husband rang both doorbells at once; he seemed determined to produce a cacophony. The time was a little after five past three; just coming up to six minutes past, in fact.'

'And it's just a minute or two from the level

crossing. You did walk straight here, I assume?'

Mrs Brownlow smiled. 'We didn't dilly dally on the way, if that's what you mean.' Seeing Anderson's puzzled frown, she explained, 'It's from an old music hall song. Everyone here belongs to the same amateur singing group. Dr Forbes is our conductor. We do songs from musicals, old time stuff, anything that takes our fancy, really.'

Anderson interjected brightly, 'How lovely. Who comes to hear you?'

'All sorts. We've sung in church halls, old people's homes, hospitals, the local hospice. It's good to bring a bit of cheer into people's lives, you know.'

Grenfell thrust her notebook forward. 'That's nice; now, let's get back to the incident. First of all, could I check your watch.' Mrs Brownlow held up her slender arm and displayed a gold wristwatch, ten diamonds twinkling all the hours except three and twelve, the former showing "24" under a bubble of glass, the latter a five-pointed crown. After observing the second-finger march a few steps, Grenfell compared it with her own, digital watch, and commented, 'It keeps good time.'

Mrs Brownlow gave a tiny laugh. 'Actually, it doesn't. I set it accurately before coming here, but it loses quite a lot. I only wear it on social occasions.'

Grenfell peered at it again. 'It does look very good. Now, can you tell me anything you noticed, at or near the signal box, while you were walking past it.'

'Well, the light was on, and there was a man inside. He was standing up and leaning over something, with his back to the row of levers.'

'You could see the levers, could you?'

'I could see the tops of them, and I've seen enough

old films to know what to expect inside a signal box.'

'Did you notice anything unusual about him?'

'As we passed by, he turned his head and looked directly at me. At the time, I thought nothing of it, but now I think perhaps there was a cold glint in his eyes.'

Grenfell tried unsuccessfully not to reveal her flood of despair on hearing the melodramatic interpretation. 'Can you give me a description of the man?'

Mrs Brownlow, realising her *faux pas*, now strove to be accurate and succinct. 'Bald, with a full set.' She checked for signs of comprehension, but found only uncertainty. 'I mean, a large beard and a moustache. I don't have any idea of the man's height, as I couldn't see the floor. I think he was wearing a green parka. At least, the hood was trimmed with fur.'

Grenfell displayed the immense relief she felt at her witness's recovery. 'That's brilliant, Mrs Brownlow. We'll take a formal statement later.'

'So, did I see the murderer, do you think?'

Grenfell quickly adopted a neutral expression. 'I said nothing about murder.'

Mrs Brownlow responded immediately, 'You didn't have to; you wouldn't be here if the death had been due to natural causes.'

Grenfell nodded a tacit confirmation. 'Well, thank you for your help. Your husband gave us your contact details; I'll just check them with you, if I may.'

Mrs Brownlow confirmed the information before returning to the dining room. The officers circulated and took the details of the other people present, asking everyone individually what they had seen. At the end, Grenfell closed her notebook and commented quietly to her colleague, 'Apart from Mr and Mrs Brownlow, everyone arrived too early to have seen anything.'

They took their leave and went to report their findings to Cargill and Witty. When Grenfell described the man Mrs Brownlow had observed in the signal box, Cargill noisily sucked spittle through the narrow gaps between his lower front teeth. 'Sounds like she saw the victim making his three-o-four log entry. That gives us about a five minute window for the murder, between five and ten past three. It certainly sounds like a professional hit, quick and efficient. Well done, girls. I mean ladies. I mean women. I mean... oh, what the hell. You can knock off now. Merry Christmas.' The officers exchanged the compliments of the season.

Grenfell turned to Anderson as they walked toward their car. 'Shall we have a drink before we go?'

'Yes, a cup of tea would be nice.' Anderson changed direction for the Ops wagon.

Grenfell took hold of her elbow and steered her away. 'I have a better idea.'

'What is it?'

'I fancy bringing some Christmas cheer to a couple of people. It's a bit off-the-wall. Do you trust me?'

'Go on then. I'm game for anything.'

They returned to the last house and Forbes again came to the door. Grenfell smiled warmly at him. 'Sorry to disturb you, Dr Forbes, but I'd like to speak to Mrs Brownlow for a moment.'

Forbes stepped back and invited them in, then brought her to them in the hallway. Grenfell explained to Mrs Brownlow, 'The man you saw was probably the victim, not the perpetrator. I thought you'd like to know that, so you don't go having nightmares.'

Mrs Brownlow smiled. 'That's very kind of you.'

Grenfell acknowledged her thanks with a nod. 'It's the season for kindness, isn't it? Earlier, you mentioned how your singing group performs for people who are old or ill. That's a really wonderful thing you do. You must be proud of yourselves.'

Mrs Brownlow looked ever so slightly guilty. 'Well, we do it for our own pleasure, too.'

Forbes appeared more smug as he interjected, 'We do like to bring joy into other people's lives.'

Grenfell saw her opportunity. 'What a kind-hearted man you are, Dr Forbes. So, when I say there are people who are alone this Christmas eve, I think you're the very type of person who would immediately want to invite them into their home. I am right, aren't I?'

Forbes realised he had been played, but was unwilling to admit as much in front of Mrs Brownlow. 'To be honest, I'm not sure how comfortable homeless people would feel, mixing with my group. Who exactly are you thinking of?'

Grenfell increased her smile. 'Not homeless people, Dr Forbes. I'm thinking of Mr Youens, your next-door neighbour; and Mrs Eckersley up the road. I could go and ask them for you, if you like.'

Relieved that the invitees would not be down-and-outs, he happily switched to being the genial host. 'They would be most welcome.'

Grenfell returned to the Eckersley house. 'Hello again. Do you know Dr Forbes down the road?'

She stared. 'Not very well. Has he done something?'

Grenfell smiled. 'Not that I know of. May I come in?' She followed Mrs Eckersley into the kitchen. 'He's having a party with twenty or so guests, and was saying there's plenty of room for more. So, to cut a long story short, he asked me to invite you to join them.'

She shook her head. 'Oh, I couldn't do that; Bill might want something.'

'Well, why don't you tell your husband you're accompanying a policewoman who has some questions, and you'll not be back for a while?'

'Do you have some questions?'

'I always have some questions; just not for you. Except, why don't you bring one of those bottles of wine and come and enjoy yourself?'

'What if he finds out where I was?'

'What if he does? Will he be violent?'

Mrs Eckersley opened her mouth for a moment, but no words could escape.

Grenfell was confident she could read the signs. 'If he ever assaults you, report it to the police and press charges. It's the only way.'

Mrs Eckersley trod lightly into the living room. 'There's a policewoman here again. She wants me to go with her. She has some questions.'

He glanced up at her. 'Well, get off then.'

She returned to the kitchen, picked up a bottle of Bordeaux, grabbed her coat that was hanging on a hook by the door, and headed out with Grenfell. 'It was very nice of Dr Forbes to invite me.'

Grenfell smiled at her. 'Yes, I thought so, too.'

'Did you know he's a musician? He used to teach violin at a college. Now he just does private lessons.'

'That's interesting.' She considered for a moment whether his pupils might represent a possible line of inquiry, but put the idea aside, at least for now.

As they neared the Forbes house, Mr Youens emerged, hanging on Anderson's arm. He called over to

Mrs Eckersley, 'Are you invited as well then, Karen?'

She stepped closer to him. 'Yes, Sam.'

He relinquished his hold of Anderson and locked arms with Mrs Eckersley. 'You and me can have a good old chin-wag.'

Anderson and Grenfell delivered the invitees to Forbes, who gave them a fulsome welcome. As the officers began to head away, he called after them, 'And won't you two ladies join us for a drink?'

Grenfell turned right around before responding, 'That's very kind of you, Dr Forbes. We're finished for the evening, so I suppose we could just have a small one.' She gestured to Anderson to enter first, then held back as she proceeded to the dining room. 'I hope you really didn't mind, Dr Forbes; but I just don't like seeing people left on their own, especially at Christmas. Anyway, it's a tradition; you could think of yourself as Good King Wenceslas.'

He frowned. 'You played me very well.'

She smiled. 'Do I need to apologise?'

He smiled. 'Do you really believe in traditions?'

She frowned. 'Yes, I do. Honestly.'

He pointed up. 'Good. We're under the mistletoe.'

She shook her head. 'I'm in uniform.'

He laughed. 'For me, that adds a certain frisson.'

She laughed. After a quick check behind her, she held up her face for a chaste kiss, and found herself reciprocating when he demanded far more than she had initially offered.

CHAPTER 5

Cargill observed the CSIs undertaking their external inspection of the signal box. As they prepared to enter, he called out, 'Found anything yet, Jenny?'

She pulled aside her face mask and bawled back, 'Very keen, aren't you, Frank? Can't you wait?'

He swept a hand in the direction of the stairs. 'Any footprints?'

She carefully descended halfway. 'Are you waiting for us to find a muddy shoeprint that has "killer" written all over it? The steps are covered in marks, so there's no way of knowing.' She waited for him to register his disappointment. 'Though, one of the most recent visitors wore size twelve, broad-fitting boots.'

He rubbed his chin. 'So we could be looking for a very large man, well over six feet tall.' He paused. 'Or woman.'

Merton laughed loudly, then stopped abruptly as she realised onlookers might misinterpret her levity. She joined him and Witty at the foot of the steps. 'No doubt you're also considering whether it was just someone with exceptionally large feet for their height. And then there's the possibility it was someone wearing over-sized shoes.' She was not at all sure he would be thinking along these lines, but she rather liked him and had no wish to see him miss a trick.

Held overlong by her steady gaze, he guessed she was waiting to be invited to explain further. 'Can you test for someone being too small for their boots?'

She had recently attended a seminar under the Continuing Professional Development programme, where a graduate in forensic podiatry had delivered a lecture followed by a Q&A session. With hindsight, she thought she must have shown too much interest with her many Qs, as he had insisted on giving her more As throughout lunch than she could ever have wished for. Nevertheless, she had learned a substantial amount from him, beyond how unwise it was to disclose her mobile phone number to a serial divorcee. 'There are techniques for interpreting the relative depth of various parts of a shoe impression, but they need a softer surface. It's also possible to establish someone's gait from consecutive impressions, only it doesn't work on stairs; the need to step up or down generally overrides any walking pattern or style.' She hesitated, realising she was heading into the mire. 'I know an expert on the subject, if you think it's worth checking out.'

He assumed he was doing as she wished. 'Yes, that would be great, Jenny.'

She unzipped the top of her scene suit and fished out her phone, then selected his name from the directory; it was programmed in, so she could screen out his calls. 'Would you like to talk to him yourself?'

'If he's answering; it is Christmas eve.'

She felt certain he would pick up her call. 'You give him a try; his name's Roger Rosenkranz.' As it began to connect, she handed him the phone.

The man at the other end spoke immediately. 'I'm glad you've changed your mind.'

Cargill was taken aback by the opening gambit, but recovered quickly. 'Is that Roger Rosenkranz?'

'Yes. Who are you and what are you doing with

Jenny Merton's phone?'

'I'm Detective Inspector Frank Cargill; Jenny's here with me at a crime scene. She says you're an expert on footprints.'

'Do you mean plantars?'

Cargill detected the emphatically territorial tone of a determined expert. 'I'm not sure what you mean.'

'Perhaps it would be best if I talked directly to Jenny, then.'

Cargill whispered, 'He wants to talk to you.'

She reluctantly accepted the phone and walked sufficiently far away that her side of the conversation would not be overheard. Cargill watched, trying to interpret her body language. When she stepped back, he asked, 'Is he a boyfriend, then?'

She flushed. 'Certainly not!' Feeling the pressure of the ensuing silence, she added quietly, 'I haven't had a boyfriend for ages.' As he pondered at length, she gave up hope of ever eliciting a response. With a dismissive, 'He'd nothing to add,' she headed back up the steps.

Wondering if he had perhaps missed an opportunity, Cargill forced his mind back to the case, and called over to a uniformed constable loitering nearby. 'Come and make yourself useful. You can go with Neil to the train station. There'll be some people there, waiting to be interviewed.' He turned to Witty. 'They're all yours. I have to stay, to control access to the crime scene.'

Witty peeled off his oversuit and left with the PC. They crossed the railway track and walked along the compressed earth footpath between the railings and the grass-bordered woodland. He looked back at the signal box, sighed, shook his head, and asked rhetorically, 'Who'd want to kill a retired Civil Service accountant.'

The PC assumed he should respond. 'That's what he was then? An accountant? I haven't the foggiest.'

Witty shrugged. 'Me neither. It doesn't seem very likely he would have made a mortal enemy in the Civil Service, and it's difficult to imagine it's anything to do with his volunteer work on the railway. Maybe there's something in his personal life. Top of the list is sex or money. Sexual motives are less common by his age, unless there's a paedophile connection. He still had his wallet on him, so if it was about money, it wasn't for petty cash. We need to keep an open mind until we've got some intel. He could be pure as the driven snow, and it's just some nutter that's chosen him at random.'

'Aren't random killings as rare as rocking-horse shit? I thought we only have domestics around here.'

'You're right, but this one could be an exception. Anyway, let's see if someone can shed some light.'

The PC fished out a torch. 'I could shed some light. Shall I lead the way?' Witty waved him past and followed in his footsteps.

When they approached the gently shelving ramp at the edge of the station platform, Witty noticed someone silhouetted near the far end. He overtook the constable and kept them in view, a misty halo of light from a gas lamp now directly above them. As he drew nearer, he recognised it was a man dressed in the railway uniform of a bygone era, standing sentinel outside the waiting-room door. He asked, 'Are you the stationmaster?'

The man responded crisply, 'Yes; Gordon Wheeler.'

Witty introduced himself and the PC. When they proffered their IDs, Wheeler took them quickly as though collecting used tickets. He peered closely at each warrant card in the gaslight, then held them up to a string of decorative coloured bulbs for a second view. Finally, he stepped into the waiting-room and inspected their credentials under fluorescent lighting. Satisfied, he returned their cards and invited them inside.

Witty looked around the room in surprise. Dozens of people were sitting or standing, all with their eyes focused on him. He turned and asked, 'Is everyone here connected with the railway, Mr Wheeler?'

The stationmaster surveyed the assembled throng. 'Yes. I asked everyone to stay who was either working on the trains or at this station; I didn't ask the engineers to come over from the sheds, or anyone from the other stations. I've listed all their names and jobs from the duty roster; would you like to go through it?'

Witty nodded. 'Yes; that's an excellent idea.'

Keeping the original for himself, he handed Witty the photocopy and began to read each duty aloud. His accompanying identification of the individuals became increasingly sporadic as he progressed through the list. 'Steam engine driver and fireman. Diesel engine driver and crewman. Two guards. Father Christmas, carriages A and B. Father Christmas, carriages C to E. Two more Father Christmases for the relief shift. Four elves. Eight mulled wine and mince pie servers. One accordion player. One juggler. Two clowns. One chef. One sous chef. Four waitresses. That makes thirty-two. Next, four who are based here at the station. Operations Duty Manager. Shop manager and assistant. Ticket seller, not that we were selling any today; we were sold out weeks ago. Then, people who work nearby. Four volunteers with general duties. Four fire and first aiders. And four telecoms guys. That makes sixteen.'

'Seventeen including yourself. Is there anyone else

here you haven't mentioned?'

'Two signalmen joined us after I'd made the list. They're standing over there at the back, Ian and Colin.'

Realising it would take hours to question all fifty-one witnesses separately, Witty considered his options. Experience told him the longer anyone is kept waiting, the keener they become to complete their testimony, and this can be reflected in a tendency to skimp on detail. He thought this effect would be particularly pronounced at Christmas. Aware how few officers were currently available to conduct interviews, he knew he could not reduce the problem sufficiently by drafting in more people. He therefore decided to use a quicker method for garnering evidence: asking everyone to write their own initial statements, and only following up later with formal interviews where necessary. His main concern was that, by failing to employ the correct procedure for recording and witnessing statements, they would be inadmissible in court.

Though fully aware the matter should be referred upward, he felt reluctant to seek permission from Cargill, knowing he was a stickler for the rules. He recognised he would not now be hesitating if the more pragmatic Priestley were in charge. For a moment, he considered bypassing Cargill and referring the question direct to Priestley, but realised the damage that could inflict on their working relationships. Recalling the mantra that it is often easier to ask forgiveness than to request permission, he decided to press ahead without seeking prior approval. He asked Wheeler, 'Is there some A4 paper I could use? One sheet per person.'

Wheeler replied, 'There's some next door.' He despatched an elf to fetch a pack from the office.

While waiting for the paper, Witty reconsidered his strategy, anxious not to be the subject of disciplinary procedures. He borrowed the PC's radio and made a back-to-back call to Cargill on Channel 2, to outline his plan. When he was given permission to proceed, he felt a twinge of guilt at having lacked confidence in him.

By the time he had finished speaking with Cargill, the elf had returned with a ream of A4 paper. He asked her to distribute one sheet apiece. The other three elves took some of the sheets from her and shared the duty. He smiled inwardly as he watched the elves being so elf-like in their helpfulness.

The original elf collected up the remaining four hundred and fifty sheets and returned them to Wheeler, who placed them on a table nearby. Witty picked up the top sheet and offered it to him with a smile. 'Don't forget yourself.' Wheeler accepted it with a nod.

Witty took a deep breath and addressed the assembly in a faltering voice, feeling somewhat overwhelmed by the size of his audience. 'May I have your attention, ladies and gentlemen.' The babble continued unabated.

Wheeler pitched in at a volume just below a shout. 'Everyone, listen up! The officer wishes to speak to you all.' A hush quickly descended. He turned to Witty and spoke slightly less loudly. 'You can go ahead now.'

As he responded with a murmured 'Thank you,' he felt a tad embarrassed. Scanning the crowd, he raised his voice to Wheeler's last level. 'You may already have heard about what happened to Mr Stanley Hicks. The police investigation so far has revealed he died at some time between three o'clock and three fifteen this afternoon, in the signal box on High Church Lane. We need to know where everyone was, around that time.

I'm going to ask you all some questions, and I'd like you to write down your answers on the sheet of paper provided. Does everyone have something to write with?' There was a babble of voices. 'Could you all get hold of a pen or pencil.' Realising he had departed even further from standard procedure, he added, 'Ideally a pen.' Among the hubbub of overlapping conversations, he heard the strident voice of a woman in dungarees, warning others not to use pencils as the police could easily tamper with their testimonies.

When everyone appeared to be fully equipped, Witty spoke again, this time in a more confident-sounding voice. 'First of all, would you print your name, address, home telephone number and mobile at the top of your sheet.' There followed a lengthy delay, as people manoeuvred into positions where they had a hard surface to rest on. 'Now, if you're planning to be away from home at any time during the next seven days, write down where you'll be, including address and telephone number.' Witty noticed some were quickly ready to proceed; as time dragged on, he told himself the others must be composing their memoirs.

When the final scribe had looked up, Witty asked, 'Are we all ready to carry on?' Nods and murmurs indicated they were. 'Now, write down, "At three o'clock I was…", and then put down where you were.' He watched them complete the short task. 'Now write, "At three fifteen I was…", and then put down where you were at that time.' He waited until everyone had finished. 'Now write, "Between three o'clock and three fifteen I was…", and then put down what you were doing, and who you were with; it's very important to say who was there. If you were on your own at any time between three o'clock and three fifteen, write down, "I was on my own from…", whatever time it was, "to…", whatever time that was.'

During the lengthy interlude that followed, he scanned the faces of those present in the forlorn hope of identifying someone with a guilty look. When everyone appeared to have finished, he made a concluding request. 'Finally, please sign your name straight after the last thing you wrote, and put today's date next to it.'

A few people held up their papers to indicate they had completed the task. The rest quickly followed suit. Witty turned to Wheeler and asked quietly, 'Would you mind collecting the sheets yourself and checking that every name at the top matches the person?'

Wheeler responded, a little louder than Witty would have wished for, 'I'll check there are no imposters.' He walked around the room and collected up the sheets. When he finally handed them to Witty, he asked, 'Is that everything you need from us?'

Witty felt sure he would think of something else, but knew any moment of inspiration could be a long time coming. He therefore decided to release all but Wheeler. 'Would you mind staying behind for a few minutes? But everyone else can go. I'll just thank them first.' He raised his voice again. 'Thank you everyone for your co-operation, and I'm sorry we're meeting under these unhappy circumstances. Despite your sad loss, I hope you will all still have a Merry Christmas.'

Over the subdued festive responses, Wheeler added loudly, 'I'll arrange for an e-mail to be sent to you all, once I have any news.' As people prepared to leave, he turned to Witty. 'Let's talk in my room.'

Witty followed him into the stationmaster's office,

the PC close behind. There were just two chairs, either side of a desk. Wheeler took his usual seat and invited Witty to sit opposite. The PC stood to one side and leaned against the wall. Witty began, 'Mr Hicks' death must have come as a big shock to everyone. Do you happen to have any idea what might be behind it?'

Wheeler put his elbows on his desk and repeatedly punched his knuckled hands together. 'No idea at all. It makes no sense to me that anyone would want to murder him. You did say it was murder?'

'Murder, manslaughter, whatever the court decides. But at the end of the day, for me it comes down to the same thing: someone killed Stanley Hicks, and it's my job to find out who. And why, as well, if I'm ever to make sense of it. Is there anything you can think of that might have given someone a motive of any kind?'

Wheeler rested his hands flat on the desk, pressing them down hard as though it might otherwise fly away. 'I can't imagine anyone having a motive. He was just an ordinary chap who'd recently retired from a boring job in the Civil Service. It makes no sense at all.'

Witty nodded. 'It rarely does. Well, I'll not detain you any longer. I'm heading back to the crime scene, to report to my boss.'

'Marcus Priestley?'

'He's my boss's boss, but he's not on duty. My immediate boss is Detective Inspector Frank Cargill. I'll leave you his contact details, along with mine.'

Witty picked up his pile of papers and put them into a plastic shopping bag that Wheeler had provided. After solemn goodbyes and an undertaking to keep him informed of any significant developments, he headed out with the PC. At the end of the platform, the constable switched on his torch and led the way back.

When Cargill saw them approaching, he dispensed with the usual pleasantries. 'What have you got, Neil? Anything useful?'

'Only fifty-one statements!'

Cargill gave a few silent claps. 'And what have you learned from them?'

'I haven't actually read any of them; not yet. I'll need to collate the information and check for any discrepancies on where people said they were. It'll be a long job; I could do it tonight if you think it's necessary, but I don't see any of them doing a runner.'

Cargill understood what was being asked of him. 'You're in tomorrow morning, aren't you? That'll be soon enough. You may as well get off; there's not much you can do here, now. I'm waiting for Jenny to finish; she might find something interesting for me to look at.'

'Should I leave you the car?'

'Yes, that would be good. You can get a lift back, can't you. And before you clock off, will you phone Marcus, just to let him know everything's in hand; my mobile isn't working here.'

'Of course. Cheers, Frank.' He left with a wave.

Cargill had time for two more teas before the SOCOs had finished. When they emerged from the signal box, he walked over to the foot of the steps and spoke to Merton, as Evans went to disrobe by the CSI van. 'Find anything useful, Jenny?'

'Lots of fingerprints everywhere. Some body fluids, but no blood. I've taken pictures of the size twelve boot prints on the steps; there's some wear on the soles that should enable us to make a match. Apart from that, there's no evidence of a struggle; it's as though the victim simply waited to be done in.'

'OK. I look forward to reading your report, when you have the time to complete it.'

She combined a smile with a frown. 'Are you alright, Frank? Whatever happened to wanting it first thing in the morning at the latest?'

'Well, it's Christmas eve, isn't it. I'm sure you've better things to be doing for the next few days.'

'I'll be looking after the kids, even though they think they don't need it; they're becoming more independent. Before long, they'll be leaving home, so I need to make the most of them while they're still here.'

'And what about yourself? Anything nice planned?'

'I'm happy just to be with my kids; when you become a mother, you give up all thoughts of your own needs.' She held his gaze, challenging him to suggest she was lying.

He hoped her assertion constituted enough of an opening. 'Well, perhaps you should allow a little bit of time for yourself. I was thinking, once we've sealed the crime scene, I could maybe take you for a drink?'

Responding too quickly, she felt she had revealed a desperate edge to her forty-six-year-old single-mother status. 'That would be nice, Frank.' He became tongue-tied, having only thought through a response to the anticipated rejection. Recognising his difficulty, she helped him out. 'If you don't have anywhere specific in mind, I'm sure I could think of somewhere. Have you got a car, here?'

His 'Yes,' almost stuck in his throat. To cover up his embarrassment, he repeated his response in a stronger, deeper voice. 'Yes.' He felt that made it worse.

'Well, Nick can take the van back; he does all the

driving anyway. I'm too reckless for him; I sometimes let the needle almost touch thirty miles an hour.'

Not realising he had been holding his breath, he laughed too loudly as he released the pent-up air. Quickly, he stopped himself and frowned. 'It'll be busy, wherever we go.'

She smiled. 'I'm sure we'll squeeze in, somewhere.'

Back at the office, Witty phoned Priestley. The call was answered almost immediately by Edwin. 'Hello. Who are you?'

Witty recognised the boy's voice. 'Hello, Edwin. It's Neil Whittington here. Is your Daddy there?'

'No; he's downstairs.'

Witty waited, until it became clear Edwin had not gone to fetch him. 'Is he busy? Can he come to the phone?'

'I'll ask him.'

Marcus retrieved the telephone from where Edwin had left it, on a shelf by the top of the stairs. 'Hello, Neil. What's happening? Am I needed? I'm staying sober, just in case.'

'I was simply phoning to let you know everything's in hand.'

'So I won't be called in, then.'

Witty detected a hint of disappointment in his voice. 'Nothing much will happen until I've time-lined my fifty-one statements and looked for any contradictions.'

'You have been busy, haven't you.'

'I did it a quick way, I got the witnesses to do their own notes. Just like I did when that sports master was found dead in a school changing-room. He would have become Tony's brother-in-law.'

'Speaking of Tony, you could ask him to assist you.

Identifying logical inconsistencies is right up his street.'

Witty gave a short laugh, unsure whether Marcus had made a pun on *Up Your Street*, the name of the new software package Tony had been helping to develop. 'I'll definitely be in touch with him sometime soon.'

'I spoke to him just yesterday. He's off secondment and will be back in the New Year. I'm not sure what I'll do with him, though; he's more cut out for behind-the-scenes analysis than foot-slogging detective work. He seemed almost embarrassed to have been promoted to sergeant for doing what was his job before he joined up. They've been trialling the computer system in parts of Derby for over a month now, and everyone's really impressed with it. They're talking about a target of a twelve per cent decrease in property crime and a twenty-six per cent decrease in burglary.'

'It's all a bit too futuristic for me. It doesn't seem right, this idea of letting a computer tell us which streets the patrols should be focusing on.'

'Don't let him hear you say that; he's still excited about what it can do. He told me it took him a week to come down from the clouds, after he'd seen the super-smart stochastic system they use in Los Angeles.'

'I don't even know what that means, Marcus; but you've reminded me of a story I heard about a plane that developed engine trouble.' Witty waited, hoping to be invited to explain.

Marcus had heard it before, but had no wish to quash Witty's enthusiasm for telling amusing tales. 'What plane was that, Neil?'

'It was a four-engined bird. When one of the engines stopped working, the captain announced, "One of the engines has failed. This is nothing to worry about, but due to the loss of power, we will be arriving an hour late." After a second one stopped, he announced, "A second engine has failed. This is nothing to worry about, but due to the loss of power, we will be arriving four hours late." Then another one stopped, and he announced, "A third engine has failed. This is nothing to worry about, but due to the loss of power, we will be arriving nine hours late, and if the last one goes, we'll be up here all day."'

Marcus laughed dutifully. 'Very good, Neil.'

'They were obviously not Rolls-Royce engines. Did I tell you about the Rolls-Royce driver who was on his way back from playing golf and gave a tramp a lift?'

Marcus empathised with Neil, understanding how lonely he must feel with Lily away, but decided he had given enough support for now. He responded with an emphatically dismissive, 'Yes, Neil; about five times.'

'Right. I'll not keep you any longer then, boss. Have a good break, and I'll see you in the New Year.'

'Merry Christmas, Neil. And give my love to Lily.'

'Will do. I'll be Skyping her, later.'

As Marcus terminated the call, a creak from the third stair told him Helen was letting him know she was coming up. He poked his head around the banister and called down to her, 'They have it all in hand.'

She reached the top of the stairs and took the slim black handset from him. 'Oh, you poor boy; no one wants you... except me. It'll be nice to have you here right through Christmas; that's something to celebrate. Shall we have a drink? Wine, maybe?'

'You're letting me off the leash?'

'Within reason.'

'I'll have a small glass with you, then.'

She led the way down the stairs and deposited the phone onto its charging base in the living room, then fetched two large glasses and a chilled bottle of Prosecco Spumante. He opened it with a satisfying pop. She commented, 'There's nothing wrong with alcohol in moderation. It can even do you some good. It's like many things, only a problem when taken to excess.'

'Like honey,' he responded innocently.

She wrinkled her nose. 'Why honey?'

He felt smug; for once, he was the one with the knowledge. 'It's in the King James Bible; Proverbs. "It is not good to eat much honey." It was years before I found out what that really meant.'

'Ah, that; you don't need to explain.'

'Well, it's something *we* don't have too much of.'

'I thought we were having plenty.'

'It's different for men and women, despite what some feminists have written on the subject. A woman complains to her psychiatrist that she gets it three times a week. A man complains to his psychiatrist that he gets it *only* three times a week.'

After giving her naughtiest schoolgirl giggle, she suddenly adopted a serious expression. 'But what if she *is* his psychiatrist? I suppose she might just tell him to be grateful for what he *is* getting.'

Accepting she would always strive to go one better, he laughed brightly at her clever twist, relieved that its implicit assumption was that she was his sole mate.

CHAPTER 6

Cargill crept into the office ten minutes late and saw Witty already beavering away at his computer. He took a circuitous route and slipped into a conference room at the far side; Witty pretended not to notice him sneaking past. Half-a-minute later he strode out, treading heavily to attract Witty's attention. 'Merry Christmas, Neil.'

Witty stood and proffered his hand. 'And the season's felicitations to you too, Frank.'

'So, you're hard at it, then. I wonder if the general public really appreciate us for having to come in on Christmas Day.'

'Probably not, but it could be worse: we could work for Royal Mail.'

'What makes you say that?'

'An old guy was in earlier, reckoned the postman must have nicked a fiver from the money Father Christmas sent him.'

'Go on, I'll buy it.'

'On Christmas eve, he'd written to Santa Claus asking for fifty quid so he could go and visit his sister on the train. This morning a card arrived with just forty-five quid in it. I phoned the sorting office and they said they'd found his letter and knew it was too late for delivery to Lapland, so they'd had a whip-round and the collection came up just five quid short.'

Cargill's laughter was interrupted by his cough. It was several seconds later before he could speak. 'Very funny, Neil. I'll have to think of one myself.' He fixed a broad grin, and then allowed it to fade slowly. 'Right, what do we know?'

Witty considered listing a few irrelevant facts, such as the height of mount Everest, or the length of the world's longest river, but decided he had inflicted enough humour. 'It's like yesterday, we're covering all the jobs until they start allocating resources. So, as well as a detective, I'm an analyst, an indexer and a typist.'

'That leaves tea-maker for me, then.'

'Yes, whenever you're ready. I've set up a case file on the system and logged the documents. I read through the interim SOCO report; it's a bit sparse. The size twelves have been checked on FIT, but no match; Cinderella analysis suggests handmade boots. The only other identifiable footprints have been explained away. There are lots of fingerprints in the signal box, but no matches on IDENT1. There's some trace evidence that'll take longer to check out: urine and spittle, but no blood. There's also a few hair and fibre samples, but I'm not optimistic they'll give us anything.'

'You never know what she'll turn up, she always does a thorough job. Jenny, I mean.' He felt ridiculous to be blushing at his age. 'Let's hope we get something off the body, then. Who's doing the autopsy?'

'Dr Patel, but he isn't due in 'til noon.'

'OK. Well, seeing as there's nobody but us to do the spadework, I'd best get stuck in. What's top of the list?'

'If you don't mind, you could try ferreting around and seeing what you can find out about our Mr Hicks. I kicked off a few searches first thing, but drew a blank.'

'I'll get right on it, unless you'd rather I help with cross-checking alibis?'

'No thanks, I usually find it's easiest done on my

own. It'll keep me busy for hours, though.'

'OK, I'll leave you to it. I'll work in one of the conference rooms, so I don't distract you if I need to make phone calls.'

Cargill headed for the most distant room. He took a moment to compose himself, then telephoned Jenny Merton. She answered with a typically breezy, 'Hello.' His mouth dried up in an instant. 'Hel-lo,' she repeated.

'It's me, Frank.' He felt physically strangulated, his larynx refusing to deliver any more words.

'Hello, Frank. Are you at work?'

He stammered, 'Y-yes. Thanks for the report.'

'You didn't phone me for that, did you? Or are you going to complain it's too skimpy and tell me I've got to re-do it?' She gave a light laugh, just in case he was taking her seriously.

He swallowed hard. 'You're right, I didn't phone for that. I just wanted to say how much I enjoyed being with you last night, and to check if I'm still invited to come over to your house later. I completely understand if you've changed your mind, what with your children being there; you could have had second thoughts about me meeting them. Maybe you were just being polite, so I'm not holding you to it. Perhaps you were even feeling a bit sorry for me, and it didn't mean anything to you; I am a bit of a sorry mess at times, I know that. And if you were simply wanting a bit of company yourself, that's alright as well; I completely understand about women having needs.'

She waited until certain his well of words had dried. 'So, you think I might have been a bitch with an itch, and you were the nearest dog?'

'No, no, I didn't mean that. All I'm saying is, don't

feel under any obligation to see me again if you don't want to. Away from work, I mean.'

She thought she understood where he was really coming from, but tested the ice first. 'What if I were to say I'd like to spend more time with you? How would you respond to that?'

'I'd say, that's fine with me.'

'Only fine?'

'More than fine.' She waited. And waited. 'I'd say it was grand.'

'Well, that's good, because I was thinking it would be grand to spend more time with you.'

His tightening chest and pounding heart reminded him of his teenage schooldays whenever any sixth-form girl happened to walk within a yard of him. He took a deep breath and blurted out, 'That's settled, then. I'll see you later.' Hearing him terminate the call so abruptly, she smiled at the telephone and gave it a slight shake of the head.

Unsure what searches Witty had already performed, but afraid he would disclose his current preoccupation if he spoke with him, he decided to start from scratch. The standard queries on Stanley Hicks revealed he was a homeowner and a registered voter, with no history of criminality. He tried to think around the subject in the various ways Priestley had patiently explained to him on numerous occasions, but found his thoughts kept returning to his rediscovery of sexual intercourse after a decade of reliance on the furtive habits of his youth.

During the morning, feeling guilty at undertaking so little work himself, he made regular sorties into the office to check on Witty's progress and to offer to make him drinks. At midday, he asked him if he would like another mug of tea.

Witty stood up. 'I'll do this mash; I need to stretch my legs, anyway.' He took away their heavily tannin-stained mugs, Cargill's "Keep Smiling", and his own "*Illegitimi non carborundum*", both gifts from Priestley.

Shortly after Witty had left the office, his telephone rang; Cargill answered it. 'DS Whittington's phone.'

'Hi, its Paal Patel, here. Is that Frank?'

'Yes. Neil's just gone to make a drink.'

'It's really you I wanted to speak to, anyway. I tried your number earlier but you weren't answering.'

'No, I've been in conference. Are you letting me know when you're doing the post-mortem?'

'Yes. Or do I mean no? You're going to find this really weird, Frank, but the body was taken away this morning; it'll be in London by now. I wasn't due on shift 'til midday, so I've only just found out.'

'Has Neil put you up to this?'

'I'm not making it up; honestly. The documentation looks to be in order, but I still phoned to find out what was going on; I was a bit worried someone didn't trust me to do my job properly. Anyway, they said it's simply because jurisdiction for the investigation has been transferred to the Met. Did you not know?'

'There must be some wires crossed, somewhere. I can't see why our own Major Crime wouldn't keep the case; after all, the bloke was killed in Derbyshire.'

'Well, it's out of my hands now. Literally. Would you mind keeping me in the loop on this one?'

'I'll let you know when I find something out. Thanks for telling me about it, Paal.'

Witty arrived with the teas and caught the tail-end of the conversation. 'Why are you talking to a pal of yours on my phone? Is yours not working?'

'I took a call from Paal Patel, about the autopsy.'

'Sorry I wasn't here; I could have wished him all the best. Him and his pretty wife, Priti. Pretty Priti.'

'Neil, you need to wipe the rabid foam from your mouth and listen to me. You won't believe this, but the body's gone to London.'

'Did it catch the train, or was it driving down.'

'It's been taken.'

'Aliens?'

'The Met. They've claimed jurisdiction, so you'd best put your work on hold. I'm going to find out who's in, upstairs, and get to the bottom of this.'

'Get to the bottom of the corpse? This is starting to sound too suspect, but we don't yet have one suspect.'

'Neil, Neil, you're not making any sense.'

'And you think you are?' He laughed.

'I'll find out what's going on, but it's no laughing matter.'

Cargill hurried out of the office. Believing some elaborate joke was behind the tale of the disappearing corpse and the Met takeover, Witty returned to his work on collating information from the statements. As time dragged on, he began to wonder why Cargill had dashed off, just before they were due to have lunch.

When Cargill finally reappeared, Witty gained the impression he was deep in thought. He called across the office, 'You've been a while, Frank; did you get lost?'

Cargill initially blanked him, then engaged him with an unflinching stare. Finally, he responded. 'Come on; let's get some snap.'

As they headed for the canteen, Witty caught his arm. 'You're looking a bit worried, Frank; don't tell me you're pregnant? Like that male baboon I told you about?'

Cargill shook his head. 'It's nearly as weird as that. Stanley Hicks used to live in London, so the Met are claiming it's their case as it must have something to do with when he was there. Everyone I talked to passed me up the chain, until I ended up having to phone the Chief Constable at home. He told me we're simply to hand everything over; statements, photos, the lot. We're to pack it up and have it ready for collection later today. Someone's already on their way here to pick it up.'

'That certainly is weird. I thought you were joking, earlier. Should we tell Marcus? He won't like it.'

They had reached the canteen's heavy swing doors, their rubber seals failing to hold back the waves of hot food smells. Cargill pushed hard at the left side, and half-whispered, 'We'll talk about it later.'

In the canteen, the serving lady welcomed them brightly. 'Christmas Dinner alright for you both? This sitting's nearly finished, but there's plenty left.'

Cargill shook his head. 'I'm not really in the mood for a Christmas Dinner; I'm not that hungry.'

She looked downcast. 'But it's a treat. Anyway, it's all we have on the menu apart from the vegetarian option, and I'm sure you wouldn't want that.'

As Cargill hesitated, Witty intervened. 'You could give him one with small portions, couldn't you?'

Her response was immediate and automatic. 'I can't go making exceptions.' She sighed. 'We go all out to do our best, and this is the thanks we get.'

Cargill forced a smile. 'Sorry, love; it'll be grand.'

They picked up their trays, the dinner plates equally heavily laden with large portions of turkey and stuffing, pigs-in-blankets, roast and boiled potatoes, parsnips, carrots and half-a-dozen sprouts. She instructed them to collect their Christmas puddings after they had finished their main course, so they would not be going cold.

The furniture had been rearranged into long rows, forcing diners to sit sociably at the same tables; most had left empty seats to either side of them. Cargill and Witty sat at the very end of a table, facing each other. A heavily-built constable, four seats down, stood with his empty plate on a tray and walked in their direction. As he passed by, he announced loudly, 'This is my third Christmas dinner. I had the first one before I started last night, and then another for breakfast, and now this one. It's a great day for working a double shift!'

Witty responded, 'Certainly is! The others don't know what they're missing, spending Christmas at home with their families.'

The constable took the reply at face value. 'Too right. I'll be volunteering every year from now on.'

When he had passed out of earshot, Witty quietly enquired about the Hicks case. Cargill shook his head. 'Not here; somebody might hear. I'll tell you all about it somewhere private after we've finished.'

Having waited longer than normal for his meal, Witty had felt he was starving, so ate every last morsel. Cargill, too preoccupied to have been hungry, cleared his plate in an unselfconscious reflection of his humble upbringing, a legacy from his mother who had drilled it into him that to waste food was a sin.

When Cargill stood with his tray and headed for the conveyor belt, Witty reluctantly did likewise, having been looking forward to his one-and-only Christmas pudding of the year.

Cargill led the way to the largest conference room and held the door open. Witty entered the so-called boardroom and sat at the stern of the boat-shaped beech table. Cargill pushed the door until it clicked shut, then sat conspiratorially close to him. 'I said to the Chief Constable, "With respect, sir, the case should be ours because the murder happened on our patch." He said, "Frank,"; I didn't even know he knew my first name. "Frank," he said, "you need to walk away from this one. If I'm not allowed to question it, you certainly aren't." When I asked him if he could tell me something about the reason behind it, he said, "I could, but then I'd have to kill you." And, as God is my witness, I heard him laugh as he put the phone down. I think he must have been on the juice.'

After cogitating for a while, Witty spoke in hushed tones. 'It all smells very fishy to me. Are you certain we shouldn't be telling Marcus?'

'I'm not certain, no. I'd like to tell him, but it might spoil his Christmas. We'll hold off, at least for now.'

In the office, Witty labelled two evidence boxes and began to pack away the case documents. His telephone rang. On hearing Paal Patel, he prepared to exchange some banter involving his wife's first name. Before he could begin, Patel spoke hurriedly. 'Neil, I honestly don't know what to do. I checked up on the autopsy through the official route, and was basically told to bugger off. So I used the old pals network…'

'You've got your own network?'

'This is not a time for frivolity, Neil. I asked a contact, who shall remain nameless, and was told the autopsy had been completed in double-quick time and the finding was "Accidental Death". But yesterday I was led to believe this was an open-and-shut homicide.'

'Thanks for letting me know, but if I were you I wouldn't go telling anyone else. There must be a conspiracy that goes right to the very top; we've been told to lay off by the Chief Constable. I can see me having to contact Anti-Corruption.'

Overhearing certain key words, Cargill's interest was piqued; he walked over to Witty's desk as he was putting down the telephone, and asked him to explain the conversation he had had. Witty briefed him on the salient points. Cargill picked up Witty's telephone and prepared to dial. 'I'm calling the Chief Constable again. I'm sure he'd like to know what's happening, and I can't believe he'd be part of a cover-up. But if he is, I'm going to have to give him a piece of my mind.'

'And of course he'll take notice of you, Frank; what with you being on first name terms, now.'

'Only him to me, Neil; and after this, maybe not even that.'

Cargill stood to attention as his call was answered. 'This is DI Frank Cargill, sir; sorry to disturb you again. I've found out from one of my sources that the autopsy on Stanley Hicks will be concluding his death was accidental, but we all know it wasn't. Does this change anything about how we proceed, sir?'

Witty listened to Cargill's *staccato* contributions to the conversation. 'Yes sir. ... Yes sir. ... Absolutely, sir. ... Definitely, sir. ... Of course, sir. ... At once, sir. ... I'm sure you're right, sir. ... Thank you, sir.'

As Cargill replaced the handset, Witty looked up. 'That was "sir", then. Well, you certainly gave him a damn good listening to.'

Cargill pursed his lips. 'He said it isn't in the

national interest to pursue it any further. That usually means the CPS thinks it's a waste of money because there's no prospect of securing a conviction. I forgot to ask if he's going to put Marcus in the picture.'

'Do you need to phone him back again, to check?'

'No, I don't think he'd appreciate it.' He breathed deeply, triggering a cough. 'I'm going to leave it five minutes to give him time to phone Marcus if he wants to, and then I'm going to call him myself.'

Witty resumed boxing up the papers, inserting coloured dividers to layer them by category. Cargill perched on the edge of Witty's desk and stared morosely out of the window, frequently glancing at his watch and a wall clock and comparing their times. After resisting for almost three minutes, he stood and telephoned Priestley. Witty stopped work and listened. 'Hello, Marcus; there's something I need to tell you. … Oh, sorry. And a Merry Christmas to you too. … Could I just say first of all, don't shoot the messenger! … Really? That's barbaric. In that case, I'm glad I'm at the other end of a phone line. … Right; here goes. The Met have claimed jurisdiction over the Stanley Hicks case. … I know that, but it isn't my fault. I spoke to the Chief Constable and he told me, in no uncertain terms, just to let it go. … Well, we've been told to box everything up, for collection by someone from the Met. … The body was whisked away this morning, and I've learned through a back-channel that the autopsy report will state "Accidental Death". I can't really see a coroner questioning a pathologist's report, so that'll no doubt become the official verdict. … Yes, I know she did. … Maybe you should just not tell her? … Of course, sir; it was wrong of me to suggest it. … Right; I look forward to getting your call; I'm on Neil's number. Erm, and Merry Christmas again.'

Cargill replaced the handset. 'I thought this was going to be a grand day, but all I'm getting is grief.'

'I didn't think you saw Christmas as that special.'

'This one is. I had a drink with Jenny Merton after work, yesterday; and then she came back to my place.' He added hurriedly, 'For a chat.'

'Just a chat?' Witty was surprised to see Cargill's colour rising. 'You randy git!'

'It wasn't like that! Anyway, she invited me over to her place later today for a meal. With her children.'

'That's a bad sign, Frank; she's looking to get her claws into you.'

'Maybe you're right, and maybe I wouldn't mind.'

'Should I set the rumour-mill going?'

'Don't spoil things, Neil; I'm serious about this. If she thinks I've been gossiping about her in the office, that could really put her off.'

'Understood. So, what about Marcus?'

'He's not happy; not happy at all.'

'I can see how it would annoy him to have a case taken off us; people will think we're incompetent.'

'That wasn't what he was concerned about. It was having to tell his wife that a Home Office pathologist had disagreed with her about the cause of death.'

Cargill sat himself at an adjacent desk and waited for Priestley to call. He looked over the untidy mess of unfinished drinks and empty food wrappers, and guessed at the underlying reason: the litter was there to discourage claim jumpers. A firm of consultants had proposed the introduction of "hot-desking", and the Top Brass had accepted the recommendation provided it did not apply to them personally. The same attitude had cascaded down until only the most junior officers would be impacted, but no one had considered their official job descriptions, which made no mention of responsibility for making the tea, fetching sandwiches, et cetera. Consequently, to keep them onside, desk numbers reduced only slightly, and officers were largely permitted to claim one for themselves. He assumed the most recent occupant of his current desk was employing a protectionist policy against anyone from other shifts; either that, or they simply had very untidy habits. Having exhausted his interest in the desk's detritus, he stared at the ceiling, watching a spider in a corner, and wondering how long he would have to wait for Priestley to call.

Witty completed boxing up the papers before quietly sitting and mulling over the situation. His thoughts were interrupted by the sudden ringing of his telephone. He snatched it up. 'DS Neil Whittington. ... Merry Christmas, Marcus. ... No, I wasn't; honest. ... He's right here. I'm putting you on speaker, now.'

Priestley rattled through his instructions. 'I want to see copies of everything, so before you part with any documents, photocopy them on a basic machine that can't do reprints. Don't scan them, because that would leave an electronic footprint. And don't forget the photos. I can't come in, today; that would be against regulations, after I've been drinking. I know there's other regs about taking copies of docs for me to look over at home, but I'm trusting you to say nothing, alright? So, can you both come over here after work?'

Witty responded, 'I'm OK, but Frank's got a date. And it's with a real woman, not his inflatable one.'

'Very funny, Neil. Are you free, Frank?'

'Yes, sure.'

'Good. One last thing: cancel any media briefing, if you haven't already. If I decide to leak anything to the press, I don't want anyone to have queered my pitch. Right then, I'll see you both later. And don't either of you say "Merry Christmas", because it bloody isn't.'

Witty unpacked the case documents and copied them. When he had repacked and resealed the originals into the boxes, he sat back with an air of satisfaction, announcing loudly, 'That's that, then.'

Cargill stepped over and rested a hand on the nearer box. 'I'll take one to reception.'

Witty moved a pile of photocopies closer to Cargill. 'Why don't you put these in your car boot, instead? That way, if one of us is caught, it won't be me.'

Cargill gave a hollow laugh. 'Thank you for that comforting thought, Neil!' He fetched two plastic bags from his desk and put the copies into them.

When all the documents had been removed, Witty settled back at his desk. Suddenly, he thought: the photographs! He had earlier uploaded all his crime scene pictures onto the central computer system, and left the originals on the camera's memory card as a belt-and-braces backup. Concerned that downloading them to a memory stick would leave a system footprint traceable back to him by the usage monitoring software, he decided it would be better to take a copy direct from the original memory card. In the storeroom, he tracked down the camera and looked for his pictures. On discovering all the JPGs had been wiped from the card, he put the camera back into its bag and brought it to his desk, in the hope that he could somehow restore them.

A check of the central computer system revealed the absence of the photographs he thought he had earlier uploaded. Wondering if he had somehow deleted them in error, he checked his computer's waste basket, only to find someone had emptied it while he was at lunch. He concluded the conspiracy must include someone with the security privileges or technical skills necessary to override his password protection.

On finding a manual in the camera bag, he searched each page for mention of a file restoration facility. Disappointed, he trawled through the menu options on the camera itself. Again unsuccessful, he became convinced the JPGs were now irretrievably lost to him. Believing he should nevertheless follow standard police procedure and check everything, he conscientiously examined the contents of each sub-directory. Among the tiny control files employed by the camera's software, he discovered one substantially larger file, with the unfamiliar suffix MTS. He opened it and felt a wave of relief as it played back the video he had taken in the signal box. Rather than risk the monitoring software catching him copying the file, he removed the memory card from the camera and slipped it into a plain brown envelope. Though a new memory card could be requisitioned, it would have to be signed for, and he had no wish to leave a forensic trail of his subterfuge; he therefore returned the empty camera to the storeroom, hoping no one would take it away before he could reinsert the original memory card.

Back in the office, he walked over to Cargill and explained to him about the video and the missing photographs. When he offered him the memory card in the envelope, Cargill quipped, 'You keep it; they're doing random searches today.'

Witty returned to his cleared desk. Realising he would need to employ some tactic to throw any casual visitor off the scent, he delved into a filing cabinet of current cases and found one that had stalled due to a lack of forensics. Having spread a selection of the documents in front of him, he explained his subterfuge to Cargill, who collected an inactive file for himself and papered another desk nearby.

When it was approaching time to finish for the day, Cargill went into an empty room and telephoned Merton. 'Hello, Jenny. I'm just phoning to say I have to visit someone with Neil straight after work and I don't know how long we'll be. I'll get away as soon as I can.'

With growing unease, she waited for further explanation. Eventually, she broke the silence. 'Are you standing me up, Frank?'

His words tumbled out. 'No, no, of course I want to see you, but this is something I really have to do.'

Hearing the desperation in his voice, she accepted there must be a valid reason. 'Do you want to tell me what it's all about?'

He laughed nervously. 'I'd like to, but if I did I'd have to kill you! That's what the Chief Constable said to me earlier.'

'Name-dropper! OK, I'll see you when I see you.'

Witty led Cargill in convoy. The light was fading fast by the time they reached the Priestley residence. Witty turned into the driveway and drew his car tight up against a low boundary wall. Being unfamiliar with the property, Cargill parked on the road.

CHAPTER 7

On Christmas morn, Helen and Marcus woke as usual when the clock-radio crackled and burst into life at a minute to seven. He muttered into the darkness, 'I expected Edwin to have been up for ages by now.'

She reached over and turned on the lamp that stood on a short chest by the bed, then extracted a red veil from the top drawer and placed it over the shade. Pressing her body against him, she whispered into his ear, 'Shall I give you *my* Christmas present?'

He smiled in knowing anticipation. 'Mmm, please.' His fingers blindly roamed and groped for the buttons on the nearby radio. He finally found the third in the row, depressed it, and the wireless fell silent.

Half an hour later, she slipped out of bed and slowly peeled off her short, sweaty, diaphanous nightdress. His sonorous breathing remained constant, telling her he had missed that particular part of her performance. In her bathroom, she turned on the small striplight above the mirror, then came back for a moment to turn off her bedside light so that it would not disturb his slumber.

She returned from her shower wrapped in two peach towels and found him breathing heavily in a deep sleep. After dressing, she woke him gently, tugging his cheek as she spoke softly. 'Come on, love; let's get this show on the road.' He turned away. She nibbled his ear. He wriggled down the bed. She grasped the top of the duvet with both hands and folded it over. Defeated, he sighed, climbed out and shuffled off to the bathroom.

Helen, hoping to see her children sleeping, switched on the ceiling lights at the far end of her bedroom so as to illuminate the area outside in a more subdued manner than the bright landing lights, which tended to wake them if their doors were open; finding both were closed, she tiptoed first to Alice's room. Hearing no sound from within, she eased open the portal and stepped into the inner sanctum, then closed it softly behind her, and listened to the regular ebb and flow of her daughter's gentle breathing. The only relief from the unremitting blackness was a thin sliver of silver illumination from the limned crescent moon, glimmering through a chink in the thick, brown curtains. She wondered if Alice had pulled the drapes apart in the night to search the skies for Father Christmas.

When her eyes had adjusted to the dim light, she gazed lovingly at Alice, before thinking of herself at her daughter's age and imagining how her own mother might have gazed on her as a child. While growing up in Belfast, there had been an undercurrent of gang violence spilling over from the Troubles, but this had never really touched their lives directly. Though nominally Protestant by her father, she had always felt independent of the segregated communities when with her mother, whose oriental features, almond-shaped green eyes and long, straight black hair, afforded her an exotic distinction from the two warring factions.

Helen's mother, Pearl, was the greatest treasure her merchant seaman father ever discovered on his lengthy journeys, though he continued to search every foreign port. After just a few years, he had sailed away for the last time, leaving Pearl to bring up their daughter alone.

Belfast's Shankill Road bombing of 23 October

1993 persuaded Pearl she should take Helen to live somewhere safer. Having secured employment as a radiographer at the Hallamshire Hospital in Sheffield, they departed by ferry for England on Helen's tenth birthday, 10 January 1994.

In Sheffield, Pearl began to instil in her daughter a love of learning, inculcating in her an understanding of a broad range of scientific subjects. Helen memorised her twenty-times table, became familiar with Linnaean taxonomy, and explored the atomic structure of elements and the ways in which ions can interact to form complex molecules. By her teens, she had begun to study the interconnectedness of the human body's organs, muscles and bones. She knew academically her mother had sculpted her precisely, and hoped her own attempts to mould Alice would be just as successful.

After retreating from Alice's room, Helen stepped noiselessly along the landing and quietly eased open Edwin's bedroom door. She left it ajar when she saw his curtains were firmly closed, so that a few reflected beams from her bedroom lights would shine on him. Hearing his quiet, measured breathing, punctuated with the occasional deeper intake of air, she contrasted this with the previous year when he had been noisily roaming the house from the early hours. Seeing he was lying across rather than down the bed, she edged closer with tiny steps to avoid any collisions, and discovered he was fully clothed. She guessed he had dressed as soon as he had been put to bed the previous evening, and had kept a long vigil to prove there was no Father Christmas, before finally succumbing to tiredness.

Standing close to the bulging white pillowcase on the floor at the foot of the bed, she bent down and checked its contents; it was still crammed with wrapped presents. Hanging at the end of the bed was a football sock stretched with yet more gifts; she recalled topping it off with an anachronistic apple and orange, an echo from her own childhood when her only presents were the simple ones found in her repeatedly reused white-fur-edged red Christmas stocking. As she stealthily exited her son's room, she wondered how he would explain away the undetected deliveries.

With the children's doors closed again, she switched on the landing lights. Elfin-like, she floated down the stairs, stepping over the creaky tread. In the kitchen, she prepared a breakfast of fruit and cereal, and turned on the filter coffee machine. The water had just completed its gurgling passage from funnel to flask, when she heard a noise from the third stair that heralded Marcus's imminent arrival. She picked up the jug as he opened the door and peered inside. 'Coffee?', she asked.

'Let's get them up, first.' He turned and headed back the way he had come.

She put down the jug and hurried to catch up with him. At the top of the stairs, she fretted, 'I do like to see them opening their presents, but it's always a bit nerve-racking, finding out if we chose the right things.'

A frown lightly creased his brow. 'I'm still not sure about you experimenting on them.'

She took a deep breath. 'It may provide me with an insight into the extent to which behavioural stereotypes are visited on children, rather than being innate, and whether introducing them at an early age to other-gendered toys will subsequently ameliorate the rigid boundaries society seeks to impose.'

He laughed. 'I haven't a clue what that means.'

She shrugged. 'Well, Edwin might decide the doll and the little pink oven are his favourite presents.'

He immediately dismissed the idea. 'I don't think they can compete with the train set; I had one when I was young and I really enjoyed playing with it.'

He led the way to Alice's bedroom and pushed the door open carefully in case she was behind it.

As light flooded in from the landing, Alice's eyes sprang wide open. She sat up in bed and looked at her father. 'Has he been?'

He pointed to the foot of the bed. 'It certainly looks like it; there's a sack full of presents down here.'

She threw back the duvet, jumped down, and ran a few steps, so she could see for herself.

Helen asked her, 'Are you going to come down and have breakfast before you open them?'

Normally compliant, for once Alice resisted. 'I'll just open some of them first.'

Having heard his parents talking, Edwin emerged from his bedroom and barged past them to reach Alice. 'I've loads of presents in my room; I'm going to open them all now.'

Helen asked him, 'What about breakfast?'

He responded firmly, 'That can wait.'

Marcus understood resistance was futile. 'Let me take them all downstairs for you both, and then you can open them in front of the tree. There's one more present each, under it; you can save those for after breakfast.'

In the living room, Helen and Marcus observed how Edwin took only seconds to tear away each layer of wrapping paper they had so lovingly cut and folded and taped together, and contrasted this with Alice who was more circumspect. When she had opened her final present from the pillowslip, she asked her father, 'Will we be getting an AFC next year?'

Marcus racked his brains for the present she might be wanting. 'What's one of those, sweetheart?'

'An Associate Father Christmas.'

He swallowed hard. 'I expect so.'

'Can't we have the real Father Christmas?'

'He is *very* busy. Do you not like having an AFC?'

'No, not really.'

'Why is that, my little darling?'

'Because he gets the presents wrong. Edwin has been given two of my presents, and I've got two of his.'

Edwin looked first at his father, then at his mother, as he grinned from ear to ear. He picked up the doll and the oven and walked on his knees over to his sister, where he swapped them for the garage and the robot.

Seeing Helen appear nonplussed, Marcus pretended to try not to look smug. She quickly recovered and corralled everyone into the kitchen for breakfast.

After bolting his food, Edwin jumped off his chair and rushed away. Marcus sluiced down the last of his coffee and hared after him. In the living room, Edwin dragged out the large box-shaped present from under the Christmas tree in the corner. As he tore off the outer wrapping, he announced, 'It's a train set.'

Marcus used a thumbnail to split the tape that was holding the lid in place, before rattling off his research. 'It's a double-o scale model of the first locomotive to do a hundred miles an hour. The real one is seventy-six times longer. It was built almost a hundred years ago, not far from here in Doncaster. Ours shows it how it was in 1963, with a single chimney and a banjo-shaped steam collector dome, after it had been upgraded from an A1 to an A3 and converted to left-hand drive. It's in LNER colours; that's Doncaster Green, which most people call Apple Green. The real one is now painted in British Railways Green, which is darker. It hasn't always been green, though; during the Second World War it was painted black, like all locomotives were. And it's been other numbers as well, over the years.'

Edwin extracted the engine from its moulded plastic bay and read out the nameplate. '*Flying Scotsman.*'

Marcus gushed more information. 'It was pulling a train that was derailed in 1926 by striking miners; seven of them were sent to prison for years over it.' Edwin inspected the engine minutely. 'We might even see the real one someday if we're lucky; there's a rumour it'll be near here in the spring.'

Edwin finally looked up at his father. 'Will we see it doing a hundred miles an hour?'

Marcus shook his head. 'No; it isn't allowed to do more than seventy-five, nowadays.' He added, largely for his own amusement, 'Elf and safety.'

Edwin looked disappointed. 'How fast can we make ours go?'

Marcus remained enthusiastic. 'I don't know, but if it was doing two miles an hour, that would be like the real one doing a hundred and fifty-two miles an hour, which would be a new world record.'

'Can we try and break the world record, then?'

'We need to build the track first. There's enough pieces to have one loop at one end and two loops at the other. We can choose which loop it travels on by changing the points; I'll show you what I mean.'

As they laid the track, Helen watched Alice putting on her doctor's outfit, knowing in reality it was a nurse's uniform plus a stethoscope; she hoped this would prove in the fullness of time to have been a more successful experiment than the robot and garage.

Marcus showed Edwin how to use the tiny green oilcan to provide lubricant for the locomotive's pistons. Next, he fetched a small beaker of warm water from the kitchen and a plastic bottle of baby oil from upstairs, and then dribbled a few drops of the oil into the beaker. As he poured the immiscible liquids down the funnel and into the boiler, he explained, 'When this heats up, the water will turn into steam, just like the proper one; and the baby oil will make it smell like the real thing.'

After plugging in the transformer, he demonstrated how to vary the train's forward motion by turning its dial clockwise to differing degrees; then, he turned it anticlockwise a little way and made the train reverse slowly. When Edwin was invited to drive, he grasped the dial and turned it immediately to maximum, causing the train to derail on a bend. Marcus took back the control box and set the train on the rails again, then manually derailed two bogies on a passenger carriage and made the rerailer deflect them back onto the track.

A sudden explosive noise attracted Helen's attention. She asked Marcus, 'Is it supposed to do that?'

He held up a black metal box and showed her its extensible arm. 'It's a fog warning device; it works like this.' With eager, boyish enthusiasm, he repeatedly tensioned the trigger and made the device bang for her.

She gave an exaggerated sigh. 'Marcus, if you can't play quietly, I'm going in the kitchen.' He feigned abashedness.

Much later, when Edwin finally brought the train to a halt at the station, Marcus suggested they might like to make a signal on a pole to control when the train could move again, and perhaps even build a miniature signal box. Edwin responded, 'You can do that if you like, but I want to try out my robot.'

Marcus reluctantly unplugged the transformer, then decoupled the locomotive and took it into the kitchen. Helen watched him cross the room to the sink and pour away the contents of the boiler before putting the inverted engine onto the draining board. As he stood silently staring through the window at the garden, she thought he seemed wistful, and guessed he was thinking of his own childhood. She asked, tenderly, 'Have you enjoyed yourself, playing with your train set?'

He pretended to stand on his dignity. 'It's a model railway and I've simply been helping Edwin appreciate how it operates.'

She giggled, 'Yes, I heard you being helpful.'

He retained his earlier tone. 'I'm always helpful.' His voice softened. 'Would you like me to give you a hand with anything?' He felt certain she would decline.

'Yes, you can do the carrots and the parsnips. When you've peeled them, I'll explain how to cut them to get the dimensions just right.'

He listened to an analysis of the cooking techniques necessary to achieve a perfect meal, asking occasional questions to prove he was paying attention. She described an aptitude test once set for a cook by a founder of the Rolls-Royce marque: the potatoes must be segregated by size before being boiled for different lengths of time so that they each receive the same degree of cooking. Suspecting a small flaw in her meal preparations, he asked, 'Why haven't you sorted our spuds into sets?'

She gave a superior smile. 'I went through the whole bag and chose praeties that are all about the same size; when I quarter them, each piece will need the same boiling and roasting time.' He told himself he should have known better than to question her thoroughness.

At midday precisely, she pointed to the wall clock. 'We can have a drink, now; there's Prosecco in the fridge.' Knowing the house rule of no alcohol before noon, it occurred to him she had spoken at exactly twelve o'clock to avoid him self-consciously having to delay for fear of appearing too eager.

He caught the initial fizz in two glasses, then filled them close to the top and passed one to her. She lifted it up high and offered a toast: 'Here's to a wonderful Christmas together.' Having taken too large a gulp, she found the bubbles had effervesced behind her nose, forcing her to stifle a sneeze.

Quickly raising his glass in salute, he accidentally splashed a libation on the floor as he responded, 'To a wonderful Christmas.' She squeezed out a damp cloth and wiped up the wine he had spilled.

They reminisced about earlier Christmases together, the first when she was nearly seven weeks pregnant and abstaining from alcohol. He kept their glasses topped up as she monitored the vegetables that were boiling prior to roasting. Just when he thought they had settled into a comfortable silence, she began a brief lecture on historical, cultural and geographical factors that had influenced the celebration of Christmas around the world. She concluded, 'There may be a benign hidden agenda such as a drive toward religious inclusivity, that this year has led a certain high street store to promote the Jewish menorah as a symbol of a Christian festival.'

He refilled her glass once again and drained the bottle into his own. 'Or maybe someone simply thought that style of candelabra looks good?'

She gave a wry smile. 'Perhaps you'd like me to dumb down for the day. Here's a question for you: why are train sets like mothers' breasts?'

He was pleased the alcohol had loosened her almost invariably controlled tongue. 'I don't know; why are train sets like mothers' breasts?'

'They're meant for the children, but it's the father who ends up playing with them all the time.' She giggled at her boldness in the kitchen, her less inhibited conversation normally being restricted to the bedroom.

He laughed loudly, his voice thickening as he asked, 'Shall we have another?'

They were reaching the end of the second bottle when the telephone rang. He picked up the handset and answered brightly. She watched intently as his jolly demeanour drained away. 'Hello? ... Let me guess: Merry Christmas. ... So, what's the problem? ... That idea may have started in a play by Sophocles called *Antigone*. Then there was something in Plutarch's *Parallel Lives*: Tigranes didn't like some news, so he cut the messenger's head off. ... Alright, I've wasted enough of your time; just spit it out. ... We shouldn't let them! ... Let it go? What does that mean? ... Nicking our evidence! ... But Helen examined him and found his neck had been broken. ... She really won't like it when she finds out; I hope she doesn't blow her top. ... I have to tell her; we don't keep secrets from each other. ... Don't worry, Frank; you weren't to know she's standing right next to me and listening to everything I say. I'll talk to her about it and call you straight back. … Pah!' He slammed down the phone.

She cocked an eyebrow and waited for him to speak.

He took a moment to collect his thoughts. 'You know that body you examined in the railway signal box? The Met have taken over the investigation, and it's obvious they're just going to close it down; they've rigged the autopsy to declare it an "Accidental Death".'

Her face flushed as she clattered her empty glass onto the table. 'What are you going to do about it?'

'The Chief Constable has authorised the transfer, so there's nothing much I can do, really.'

'That may be the official line, but what about unofficially?'

'I can't see how I can do anything.'

Her voice leapt in pitch and intensity. 'Sometimes it doesn't work to do things the official way, does it?'

'What do you mean?'

'Remember that twenty-first birthday party someone had on Dobcroft that kept the whole area awake until gone half-past two in the morning with their pop-concert speakers blasting bass noises that we couldn't block out and that made the whole house vibrate, and the neighbours with the autistic boy had to drive him around for hours but finally gave in and took him to the hospital to be sedated because he screamed all the time when the noise wouldn't STOP?'

He raised his voice several notches to match hers. 'You're not still going on about that, are you? It was ages ago.'

Her voice ratcheted up even further. 'It was only last year, October the seventeenth. You made me stick with the official route for reporting it, which is why three-and-a-half hours later nothing had been done about the torture we were all suffering. I told you what you should do, but you wouldn't do it.'

'I couldn't do anything officially; it was outside my jurisdiction. And if I'd called in a favour from South Yorkshire, that might have led to me being charged with Misconduct in Public Office. And anyway, I couldn't have known the bloody council wouldn't get their finger out and do something about it.'

Her voice was sharper and louder than he had ever heard it before. 'So you left me to keep phoning the police; me, the wife of a senior officer. And they just fobbed me off each time because they'd already had so many calls they didn't see any point in logging mine as well. And later, when I twice complained in writing to our Lib Dem councillor, he didn't even deign to reply. Well, I shall not be ignored this time! Either you do something about it, or I shall! I'll find out who the coroner is and tell them the truth, and if that doesn't get me anywhere, I'll give the story to the press, and if they won't take it, I'll leak it over the internet!'

Though he found words he hoped might appease her, his voice remained stubbornly stretched near breaking point as he delivered them. 'You want me to jeopardise my career? Well, fine! I'll call the Chief Constable right now and tell him that if he's a party to this cover-up, I'll personally come and slap the handcuffs on him.'

She realised the argument had escalated into new territory and was wishing she could have stayed calm. Her voice became subdued, though the emotion was still vibrating within it. 'You shouldn't speak to anyone until we've had a proper think about what to do.'

He felt relieved to know the worst was over. Though his voice became more mellow, his sharpened hearing warned him it still sounded strained. 'We shall do something about it; we're both too principled to allow ourselves to be drawn into a cover-up. I promise you, I'll do everything in my power to make sure the dead man gets justice.'

Believing she was unwilling to respond for fear of betraying her heightened emotional state, he decided to continue speaking, to allow her to settle herself. 'And, if I might just put forward a few words in my defence on the noise front, earlier this year I did speak to that lad who was racing his incredibly loud liquid-fuel model car up and down the road. I'd guess it was knocking out well over a hundred decibels.'

As the pause lengthened, she felt she must contribute to the conversation. 'Yes, I remember; May the twenty-first. Jet engines can do a hundred and forty decibels, and it must have been approaching that level.'

He nodded, relieved to find she was simply agreeing with him rather than correcting or improving on his estimate. 'What I found interesting was the lad's reaction; he complained he wasn't being treated with respect. That was so ironic, seeing as he was the one who was showing disrespect to everyone in the entire neighbourhood. In the criminal world this focus on perceived disrespect has developed into a big issue. There's the obvious problem of people walking around with vicious dogs as a way of asserting their status within a gang culture, but the worst case I ever came across was a father who was killed by someone who felt he was being dissed. A couple had been driving home in the early hours, and their children were asleep in the back of the car. There wasn't room at the kerb for him to park outside his house, so he just stopped in the road while he carried them inside, still asleep. When some gang members found their way blocked by someone who evidently believed their children took precedence, one of them shot him.'

Having regained her composure, she added her own perspective. 'The phenomenon of parents believing their children should take priority over all other people has been the subject of various studies; the concept can also be extended to other family members in proportion to the degree to which they share genes. Parents don't always comprehend that just because their children are the most important thing in the world to them, they're no more special than any other child to everyone else. It's the same underlying misconception in both the shooting and that incident with the model car.'

He rushed to agree with her. 'Yes, I see that. When the lad's father came to our house to complain at me for complaining at his son, he even offered up the excuse that it had only just come back from being repaired and he'd been waiting to play with it, as though that had some relevance. You know, if his son was acting with his permission, I'd say he was more responsible for the noise than his son was, so he should have come over to apologise rather than complain. But not everyone has the sensitivity to recognise when they're in the wrong. I always recall what Pagnol said: *"Comme on est faible, quand on est dans son tort!"*, "How weak one is, when one is in the wrong!" But if someone doesn't recognise they're in the wrong, they don't behave appropriately; they don't apologise when they should.'

Her eyes began to water as she felt a tinge of shame for having allowed her emotions to overcome her usual self-restraint. Thinking that perhaps the accusation was also intended for her, she reached out and took hold of his hand. 'I'm sorry I flew off the handle.'

He grasped the olive branch, lifting her four fingers and kissing them individually. 'I'm sorry for how I reacted, too. And you were right about everything.'

In the calm after the storm, she looked around for some mundane task to bring them back to normalcy. She picked up the teaspoon she had used earlier for measuring cornflour. Rather than putting it into the dishwasher, she ran hot water through the mixer tap to wash it, fully aware she was being unusually inefficient. After drying it with a linen dishcloth, she suddenly felt an urge to check on the roast. Hastily opening the oven door using just the thin cloth, she felt the heat penetrate the linen. As she grabbed an oven mitt to close the door again, the glass front slipped from her grasp and crashed shut. She looked apologetically at Marcus. 'Sorry. It'll be coming out soon; you'd better tell them to wash their paws.'

Marcus opened the kitchen door that led into the hallway, only to find his way blocked by his children standing together holding hands. As they stared at him with wide, accusing eyes, he felt a stabbing pain in his chest that went beyond anything merely physical. He tried to smile, but found his face muscles had contorted and were refusing to adopt the relaxed arrangement he so desperately craved.

Edwin spoke with a gravitas that belied his age. 'We want to stay together.'

Marcus was dumbfounded. Helen rushed to stand next to him, and bent low to speak closely to Edwin. 'What do you mean, sweetheart?'

'When we're sent to a children's home, or given to

foster parents, or adopted, we want to stay together.'

Helen's cloudburst of blinding tears chased down her cheeks in scalding rivulets.

Marcus recovered his voice. 'We're never going to part with either of you, my little loves.'

Hearing Alice sob, Edwin began to cry in sympathy. Between gulps of air, he forced out an accusation. 'You were arguing.'

Helen recovered herself sufficiently to respond. 'We were having a heated debate, but that isn't really the same as arguing. And everything's alright now, so you can go and wash your mitts and come straight back.'

As they went upstairs, Marcus grabbed the phone. 'I'm going to do something about it.'

He dialled Witty's number. 'Hello Neil. ... Are you being ironic? ... Can you get hold of Frank? I need to talk to both of you.' Helen listened intently as Marcus arranged for copies of all documents to be made before the Met could take away the originals, and for them to be delivered to him at home later in the day.

As he put down the phone, a ting announced their goose was cooked. Helen slipped her hands into a pair of heat-resistant gloves and opened the oven door, then pulled the basting tray forward. Using a carving knife and fork, she tipped the bird onto its end to drain away the fat; it gushed out, sizzling and spitting angrily. Marcus watched and waited for the moment when the flow of hot, clear liquid would reduce to a trickle. Right on cue, he picked up the aluminium studded carving tray and held it close by, so she could lift the bird with the utensils and transfer it over.

Alice and Edwin returned to the kitchen together, glancing at each other for mutual support. Helen, observing small indications of their continuing distress, sought to defuse the tension by becoming wildly enthusiastic about their plans for later. Edwin sensed it was all an act. When Marcus admitted he may have to work with colleagues in the evening, Edwin relaxed a little, feeling things were returning to normal. Alice continued to eye her parents with suspicion.

After presenting the goose to the children, Helen despatched them to the dining room and began to transfer the vegetables into warmed tureens. As Marcus carved a breast, he asked, 'What shall we have with it? We were going to have that nice red.'

She waited until he looked up at her. 'You see what happens when people drink too much? I'm sure we'd both have handled the issue better if we'd been sober.'

He agreed emphatically. 'It's been a long time since we've shared a couple of bottles of fizz; we're simply not used to it, so of course we were bound to overreact.'

She reflected for a moment. 'But don't be under any misapprehension; I stand by everything I said. If you don't deal with the problem, I shall.' Her face softened and her voice lightened. 'As to my overreaction, it was actually an excellent example of the lack of self-control that results from imbibing alcohol to excess; perhaps I was merely wishing to demonstrate this as a learning point for you.'

From her concluding smile, he knew she had merely acted out her defence with as much belief in her words as an average criminal lawyer. He blew her a kiss. She watched it glide through the air for a few seconds before puckering her lips to accept it.

While he transferred the slices of meat to a serving plate, she took a two-litre clear glass pitcher from a cupboard, and a tray of ice cubes from the fridge. Untypically, she allowed two of the cubes to escape into the sink as she emptied the tray into the jug. He knew how irritated she would be for having made a slip, so resisted drawing attention to them. She ran cold water through the mixer tap for a few seconds to clear out the hot water that had passed through earlier, all the time checking the temperature of the stream with a little finger. He watched as she filled the jug with tap water. Accepting her implied decision without objection, he fetched the bottle of red wine from the dining room and returned it to the pantry.

As though concluding a very recent discussion, she referred back to the scientific justification she had given him years earlier for allowing red wine to *chambré* but not to breathe: 'And that's another good reason for not opening red wine in advance.'

CHAPTER 8

Marcus stood in the living room, watching through the net curtains as Neil manoeuvred his car into position by the low front wall. When the vehicle lights were turned off, he drew the heavy brown velvet drapes and went to unlock the front door. The movement-activated external globe light switched itself on and illuminated Neil and Frank, walking in step, each carrying a plastic shopping bag. Marcus opened the outer door and invited them in. Frank stepped into the porch, put down his bag and untied his shoe laces, then pulled off his black brogues and left them by the inner door. Neil followed suit, though aware it was not a house rule.

Marcus led them into the streamer-festooned dining room. Realising the smell of food still permeated, he asked, 'Would either of you like something to eat, before we start?'

Frank answered for them. 'We're not hungry; we had a big Christmas Dinner in the canteen.'

'What about a drink?' They both declined. 'Well, let's see what you've brought, then.'

They removed the documents from their bags and placed them on the dining table. Neil stacked them into four piles, then pointed to his leftmost. 'These are statements from people working on the railway and claiming to have been on the train at the time of death.' He indicated the next pile. 'These are from the railway volunteers who claim to have been elsewhere at T-O-D. I've cross-checked both sets of alibis for three o'clock and three fifteen. I would have started on the timeline in between, but I couldn't go looking at their statements in the office this afternoon, so I'll have to do it at home. To corroborate them fully, we'd need to take statements from people who are not railway volunteers.'

Marcus inverted the third pile and picked up the document that was now on top. After scanning through, he placed it face up on the table to start a new stack. Repeating the process with the other documents, he rebuilt the original pile. As he put down the final sheet, he commented, 'Most of the neighbours claim to have seen nothing at all.'

Neil responded, 'There's only the one couple who saw anything, and that wasn't much.'

Marcus took the SOCO interim report from the top of the fourth pile and skimmed through it, searching for any conclusions. 'Well, it looks like we'll be having to rely on good old-fashioned police work.' He flicked through the fourth pile, giving closer scrutiny to reports from officers who had attended the scene. When he had restacked the documents in their original order, he looked first at Frank and then at Neil. 'Thank you both for collecting everything together, but I think we'd have to agree there's not a lot to go on. Tony Beresford has just completed his secondment in Derby and isn't due to start back with us until the New Year; I'll phone him tomorrow to see if he's willing to do some unpaid work before then, to construct the timeline covering T-O-D.'

Neil bristled. 'I can do the timeline.'

Though having previously decided what he wished to say to them both, Marcus waited a moment to create the impression he was now giving some thought to the proposal. 'I'm not doubting you for a moment, Neil, but

I need to make sure I don't drag you into something that could damage your career prospects; that applies to you too, Frank. You both need to be seen to be handling other cases, and not be visibly putting any time into this investigation. As Tony isn't due in yet, no one's going to suspect him of working on it.'

Neil, who had recently been Tony's Best Man, still felt a need to protect his once naïve protégé. 'When Frank and I were talking about this case earlier, we agreed we're both willing to stick our necks out; but Tony wouldn't know what he's walking into. Besides, he and Susan may be busy with their new relations.'

Recognising Neil's concern, Marcus sought to ease the tension. 'Are you talking about them discovering sex?' Seeing Neil remain stubbornly unamused by his risqué misinterpretation, Marcus became serious again. 'I'll make sure there's no pressure on him to volunteer.'

Neil appeared appeased as he responded, 'If he does anything on the computer system, it'll show up on the audit trail, so he should only work off the documents we brought with us.'

Though Marcus was fully aware of the monitoring system, he nevertheless responded, 'Thank you for reminding me. From now on, we all need to avoid running any queries that are obviously linked to this case, or accessing information we can't justify for other reasons. Expanding on that theme, we should avoid putting anything in writing, electronic or paper, and not go disclosing information over the phone; we need to stick to face-to-face communications. If we must refer to this investigation, call it Operation Semaphore, but better not to mention it within earshot of anyone outside our team. And one more thing: if anything new turns up in the office case file that you think might prove useful, it would be good if you could make an untraceable copy. But don't take any unnecessary risks.'

Neil pulled a plain brown envelope from an inside pocket and held it open. 'Speaking of taking risks, this is the memory card from the camera I used in the signal box; I need to get it back before anyone notices it's gone missing. Someone has been deleting all my crime scene photos; not just off the camera, but the entire system, except they missed a short video I made. The SOCOs didn't arrive until after the body had been moved, so it's now all we have of the victim in situ.'

Marcus extracted the black plastic card, avoiding touching the row of gold contacts. 'How do I access it?'

Neil smacked the heel of his hand to his forehead. 'Sorry, I should have brought the camera to connect to the computer. Unless you have an adaptor?'

Marcus pursed his lips. 'We don't have one, but we do have a camera of our own that might do the trick.' He took the card away. Minutes later, he returned with a compact camera and a laptop. After putting down the computer, he held up the camera. 'This one can read the card.' He plugged one end of a cable into the camera's dual-purpose logic and charging port, and the other into the laptop's highest baud-rated USB port, then opened the memory card as an external hard drive and proceeded to copy the MTS file. When it had completed successfully, he thought out loud, 'I'll take two copies, just to be on the safe side.'

He walked to the walnut-veneered Victorian bureau in a corner of the room by the French windows, then closed the curtains in front of them in an unnecessary act of security-consciousness. A key projected from the top of the bureau's sloping drop-leaf writing-flap; he turned it and pulled open the front, revealing a tier of pigeonholes and a small drawer. As he lowered the leaf to the horizontal, a pair of disguised wooden arms emerged from the fascia to support it at the edges. From the drawer, he extracted a two-gigabyte memory stick, its cleverly engineered folding structure harking back to the days when smart design of such items was deemed important. After opening it out, he inserted it into one of the laptop's unused USB ports.

While waiting for a new device driver to install, he explained his plan for disguising the video. 'I'll rename the file on the memory stick so no one can recognise it.' He backed it up as "familysummer.hols", then clicked the hidden icons chevron on the Status bar and chose the option for safe removal of hardware. As the laptop logically detached first one device, then the other, he in turn extracted the stick and disconnected the camera.

Returning to the bureau with the memory stick, he reached into a recess and slid aside a veneered panel that revealed a secret compartment. After depositing the stick inside, he slid the panel back into place so it once again merged with the surrounding wood. As he closed the bureau's writing-flap, he decided to leave the key in the lock to suggest there was nothing of value inside.

Back at the laptop, he explained, 'I'm going to attach a copy to an e-mail.' After a couple of minutes, he finished the task and looked up.

Neil asked, 'Who did you send the e-mail to?'

Marcus put on a smug face. 'No one at all; who's to say it wouldn't be picked up under some surveillance operation.' He waited while they registered curiosity. 'I attached it to a draft, so it wasn't sent to anyone.'

Frank declared, 'Clever!'

Neil added, 'As always!'

Marcus ran the video from the laptop's hard drive. Frank had not previously seen it, and Neil had only been able to watch it on the police camera's small screen, so they pressed up against him on either side for an unobscured view. As it ended, Marcus remarked, 'I'd say there's clear evidence of a snapped neck, but I need to ask Helen to take a look.'

He fetched her from the living room and introduced Frank; she responded formally as they shook hands. Having met Neil on many previous occasions, she acknowledged him more casually. No one thought it appropriate to offer season's greetings.

Helen watched the video and took a moment before delivering her considered opinion. 'The angle of the head certainly suggests a broken neck that goes beyond a simple severing of the spinal cord; but the beard is covering up the actual break point, so someone could argue it's a *trompe l'œil.*'

Marcus leaned closer to her. 'Are you saying it isn't clear beyond reasonable doubt? That someone could interpret it as simply fooling the eye?'

She held his gaze. 'I'm saying it's in the grey area between being enough to convince a rational individual, and proving sufficient to satisfy a group of a dozen people thrown together at random. Plenty of books mention the wisdom of crowds, but not so many refer to the collective stupidity of juries. The problem usually lies with lawyers who are determined to confuse people by throwing doubt on anything and everything.'

Marcus felt disheartened. 'So we've no proof.'

Her eyes stretched wide, transforming her gaze into

a mesmeric stare. 'Don't forget I examined him myself. I'd like to think people would take my word as gospel; but even if it's me against the world, I've no intention of backing down over this. Anyway, the video would support me to some extent.'

He blinked firmly, hoping she would do likewise to release her magnetic hold over him. 'As well as the copy on the hard drive, I've put one on a memory stick and another on a draft e-mail. So, I'm going to delete the original from the camera card, if that's alright?'

She held up a hand, Ulster Banner style. 'Wait a minute.' Without another word, she left the room and rushed upstairs. Soon after, she returned with a blank CD. 'Burn a copy onto this as well.'

Marcus did as she bade. When the process had completed, he turned on the camera and deleted the video. As he extracted the empty card, Neil took out his envelope and held it open for Marcus to drop it in.

Helen went upstairs with the CD, and hid it in her underwear drawer wrapped in a pair of plain blue knickers. Back downstairs, she looked in on Alice and Edwin in the living room, and found them kneeling by the railway line. Around the track, she saw various small plastic animals, with more in the cattle wagon. She watched as Edwin stopped the truck next to a horse, for Alice to walk it up a cardboard ramp made from a cereal packet top. Her initial reaction was delight on seeing them playing together so nicely, until she considered how it may be a legacy of the earlier argument she and Marcus had had. As she stole guiltily away, she heard Alice say, 'You need to stop at this field, Ed, so the cows can get off.'

The dining room fell silent as she entered. She tried

to sound unconcerned. 'Were you talking about me?'

Marcus knew he had delayed too long to deny it. 'We were just discussing who needs to be involved in Operation Semaphore; that's what we're calling it. I've already told these guys I'm expecting to have to tread on a few toes to get anywhere, and I might find my career's all washed up if I fall foul of the wrong people, so I don't want them risking their careers as well.'

Neil interjected, 'But we've both said we're fully committed to staying involved in the investigation.'

Marcus acknowledged his contribution with a nod, before continuing to address Helen. 'Only, at the office, they have to be seen to be working on other things. That's why I need someone such as Tony Beresford, who's on holiday. I'll be giving him a call tomorrow, to see if he's up for it.' He turned to the others. 'If he is, I'll need just one more recruit: a DC who can question people without making waves.'

Neil asked, 'Do you have anyone in mind?'

'No,' he lied. 'But it needs to be someone who can be trusted to keep the investigation under the radar. Perhaps someone who's been working over Christmas and has time off until the New Year, so they can be away from work without anyone missing them.' He found himself willing Neil to nominate Linda Plummer. After a couple of seconds, he continued, 'This might be a better job for a woman; someone flexible who can deal with all types.' After more silence, he tried again. 'Perhaps someone who attended the crime scene and already knows something about the case.'

Frank spoke up. 'What about Linda Plummer?'

Marcus felt a hot flush; he had hoped someone would make the correct suggestion for him, but now he feared he had spelled it out too obviously. With Helen watching and interpreting, he decided to cast doubt on the proposal. 'That isn't a bad suggestion, Frank; but do you not think she might be too open and honest to be capable of covering her tracks?'

Neil interjected to support Frank. 'I agree with you about her not being the naturally deceitful type, but she's very adaptable, so I think she could cope with a bit of cloak-and-dagger stuff if it was for the right reasons. She gets my vote.' Realising he had overstated his authority, he added, 'Not that this is a democracy.'

Marcus smiled, relieved he was apparently having to be persuaded to do what he wished to do all along. 'But this is off the books, so perhaps we should all get a vote. I take it you're in favour, Frank?'

He nodded, 'Sure; she's very capable.'

Before Marcus could continue, Helen piped up. 'Don't I get a vote? You haven't mentioned me as part of the team, but I'll be doing whatever I can to help.'

His smile faltered. 'Err, yes, of course, Helen. Do share your thoughts with us.'

She made eye contact equally with all three men as she delivered her omniscient opinion. 'Just because this is a clandestine operation, it doesn't mean the command structure should be undermined; if anything, I believe it should be applied even more rigorously. As a matter of principle, I would say it should be the boss who makes the decision in this type of situation, so that later there can be no hiding behind an excuse of pressure from the persuasive forces of democracy.'

Marcus waited until sure she had nothing to add. 'Well, if it's the boss who makes the decision, tell me who I should invite, Helen.'

Neil laughed at once. Frank quickly joined in. She turned to Marcus, realising he had outmanoeuvred her. For a fleeting moment, she wondered why he should have wished to avoid being seen to make the decision himself. 'I don't know many of your colleagues, but Lin is certainly the best candidate of those I do.'

Marcus now felt secure in making it unanimous. 'I agree; I think she's the best choice. I'll ask her, but I'll make it clear she can say no without a stain on her character, otherwise she might think she's letting the side down. I'd better go and see her in person, and if I get any negative vibes I'll drop the subject entirely.'

Neil asked, 'Are you going to visit Tony, as well?'

Having previously stated he would only telephone him, Marcus backtracked seamlessly. 'Certainly; what's sauce for the goose is sauce for the gander.' He added amiably, 'We had goose for our Christmas Dinner.'

Recalling his invitation from Jenny, Frank's hands came together unconsciously in supplication. 'Speaking of which, boss, if we're done here, I have…'

Neil interrupted. '…a hot date!'

Marcus turned to Frank. 'Anyone I know?'

Frank replied before Neil could intercede again. 'It isn't a date; I'm simply going around to a colleague's house for a bite to eat.' Seeing Marcus's questioning stare, he blurted out, 'Jenny Merton's, in fact.'

Helen spoke authoritatively for her husband. 'In that case, Frank, you'd better get off straight away.'

Marcus led him out of the room and toward the porch. As he was putting on his shoes, Marcus asked, 'Is it a hot date, Frank? You can tell me!'

He mouthed with the tiniest whisper, 'Scorching!', then flapped his hand vigorously in front of his face to dissipate the implied heat.

After Frank had hurried away, Marcus returned to the dining room, where he found Neil explaining how Lily would be working in Paris until the end of January.

Helen empathised. 'You must be really missing her, especially with it being Christmas.'

Neil responded, 'Yes, I do miss her; but we'll be Skyping once I get back, unless she's already gone out.'

Helen turned to Marcus and spoke commandingly. 'You'd better not keep him any longer, otherwise he might miss her; I mean, she might not be in.'

Marcus echoed her sentiments and ushered him out, Helen trailing behind. After putting on his shoes at the door, he brightly wished them both a Merry Christmas, before heading back to his cold, empty flat.

CHAPTER 9

Boxing Day began as early as every other day in the Priestley home. By seven fifteen Helen was out of the shower and drying herself. Marcus had pressed the snooze button on the radio in the hope of grabbing a few more minutes of sleep, something that had evaded him for much of the night as he cogitated on the Hicks case and played out various scenarios in his mind. While dozing, he had the impression Helen was gliding by. Debating whether to wake, he found the decision had made itself. Reluctantly, he dragged his tired body out of the warm bed. In the bathroom, he forced his eyelids to extend from mere slits, so that he could see to have a wet shave. The hot shower eventually rendered him fully conscious. He stayed under the deluge longer than was his custom, as he marshalled his thoughts.

When he trudged into the kitchen, he saw Helen had just finished pouring him a coffee. She swept a gracious hand toward the window as though an act of largition, and delivered her usual opening phrase for the first snowfall of the winter. 'It's a white world.'

He delicately turned her to face the garden, and put his arms around her midriff to hug her from behind. 'It makes everything seem so clean. And look at the way the trees have silver edges; it's just so beautiful.' Confident they would be happier today than yesterday, he bent and kissed her neck. She squirmed as he found an erogenous zone. He nibbled his way up to her ear lobe. She leaned forward a little way and squeezed her buttocks to his groin. He rubbed against her, slowly, gently, tenderly, rhythmically. The door opened quietly behind them. They froze.

'Does this mean you love each other again, today?'

They separated unhurriedly to avoid any suggestion of embarrassment. Helen responded, 'We always love each other, sweetheart. Yesterday we found out about something that made us very cross with some people, but we were never really cross with each other.'

Edwin scrutinised her face for insincerity. Satisfied, he declared, 'I could make a snowman with Alice.'

She interpreted his joint enterprise proposal as another beneficent legacy of yesterday's argument. 'We could all build one together, when it's light.'

He dashed out of the kitchen and galloped up the stairs, returning shortly after with Alice, who had dressed sensibly for playing outdoors in the cold.

The children unceremoniously despatched breakfast, before hurrying to the living room where the train track was still laid on the floor. Marcus followed them and plugged in the transformer. 'Shall I help with the train?'

Edwin responded, 'It's OK, we know how to do it.'

Marcus returned to the kitchen. Helen mischievously misinterpreted his visible disappointment and gave him a sympathetic smile. 'Don't fret, love; you can always play with the train set when they've gone to bed!'

He grimaced. 'I sometimes think you don't give me the respect I'm due as your lord and master.'

She laughed. 'As if!'

He glazed his smile with a frown. 'Anyway, if we're planning on building a snowman, we'd better not leave it too late; I want to see Tony this morning, if he's in.'

She directed his gaze to the wall clock with her eyes.

'You'd better not call him too soon; not everyone gets up this early on their days off. For all you know, he may be planning not to get up at all.'

Marcus felt an all-pervading warm glow. 'Or get up repeatedly! Remember when we were newly-weds?'

'That's not something I'll ever forget.'

'We couldn't get enough of each other. You were amazing! You were fantastic!'

'The older you get, the better it was.'

'Come on, Helen; we had a great time. And we will again, once they've flown the nest.'

'In your dreams! Work it out; you'll be fifty before Alice has her twenty-first.'

'Then you'd better make the most of me while I'm still young.' She raised an eyebrow, prompting him to add '...enough.' He turned her away from him and put his arms around her, his hands on her belly. 'Remind me where we were up to, earlier.' She wiggled her fundament against his groin. As he began to rock hard between her buttocks, the kitchen door burst open and Edwin charged in. Though somewhat irritated to have been interrupted again, he was relieved his son was back to normal. Alice hurried in after him, her words tumbling out. 'Are we going to make a snowman, yet?'

Helen shrugged Marcus away from her. 'When it's a bit lighter.' The children rushed out. She assembled various accoutrements for later: a strip of cloth for a scarf, a battered hat, two glass marbles, a pair of old sunglasses, ten pieces of penne pasta and a carrot.

Initially, all four were fully committed to Helen's snowman construction project, until Marcus rebelled by throwing a snowball at Edwin. The two chased each other around the garden, launching white missiles that would drop out of the sky onto the unwary Edwin or his well-positioned father. Helen, remaining focused on the primary objective, showed Alice how to roll snow into a compact ball to achieve a sturdy foundation.

As the building phase neared completion, the boys joined in again and added finishing touches using twigs and stones. Helen fetched her camera to record the team's ephemeral achievement for posterity. Her first disposition placed Marcus behind the snowman, with the children to either side of it. She rearranged the tableau, putting Marcus between the children, with Alice next to the snowman. The parents changed places for more pictures, before Marcus took a set of children-only snaps. When every combination and angle had been covered, he turned off the camera, making the telescopic lens retract. Edwin stepped over to him, holding out his hand. 'Can I do a picture of you and Mum together?'

Marcus was taken unawares by a wave of profound sadness that washed over him. Was it that Edwin was suddenly growing up, as evidenced by his asking to use the camera? Or was it that he had said "Mum" instead of "Mummy"? Or did he still fear his parents would separate, and he wanted proof that they had once been together? Or was it just the very idea of a photograph at home without the children in it? He mulled this over, rendering him too slow to respond. Helen answered for him. 'Take your gloves off, first.' Edwin complied promptly, squashing them into a wet woollen ball that he quickly stuffed into his jacket pocket.

Marcus held open the carrying-loop for Edwin to put his hand through. Without relinquishing his hold of the camera, he explained, 'To take a photograph you have to press this button, but first you have to look here to make sure we're in the picture. If we're too small, you can zoom in by turning this bit clockwise; and if we're too big, you can zoom out by turning it the other way.'

Helen added, 'Or you could just move closer to us, or further away. Try not to cut our heads or feet off, won't you, sweetheart?'

Marcus put an arm around Helen's shoulder; she put hers around his waist. Edwin concentrated on locating them in the centre of the digital viewing frame, then walked forward a few steps until confident they were correctly positioned. As he pressed the button, he heard the unanticipated click of an electronic shutter.

Helen showed him how to display the picture on the camera's small screen. They took turns in examining it, and everyone agreed it was a great photograph. Alice responded quietly to her mother's invitation to take one herself. 'No, mummy; mine wouldn't be as good.'

When they returned indoors for hot chocolate and a thin sliver of Christmas cake, Marcus picked up the telephone and selected 'Beresford Ho'. Susan identified the incoming caller's number. 'Hello, Marcus?'

He responded, 'Merry Christmas, Susan.'

She replied abruptly, 'Are you wanting Tony? You do know he's on holiday until the New Year.'

He smiled at her directness. 'There's something I'd like to discuss with him. Is he free?'

'I'll fetch him.'

After a short pause, Tony came to the telephone. 'Hello, Marcus; are you wanting me to go into work?'

'No, quite the opposite. I'd like a quiet *tête-à-tête*.'

'A one-to-one meeting? What's it about?'

'There's something I'd like your help with, but it's

not for general consumption. You could be doing Susan a favour if you keep her in the dark. Like rhubarb.'

'In the, erm, manure? That's a joke, isn't it. Isn't it?'

'Not entirely. It really could be best if she doesn't know what you're working on.'

'Really? Shall I come over straight away?'

'No, I'll come to you for eleven, if that's alright.'

'Surely. I'll roll out the welcome wagon.'

'Where did you get that expression?'

'The States.'

'The States! I can see I'll have to re-educate you in how to speak the Queen's English! See you at eleven.'

When he had terminated the call, Helen asked, 'What time do you intend to see Lin?'

He looked up at the ceiling as though he were only now considering the question. 'She's on duty 'til four, and I wouldn't want her to be taking the call if anyone can overhear, so I'll try her around five.'

'Right then. Is there anything I can contribute? It feels like this investigation is more for my benefit than for anyone else; it's too late for the guy himself.'

'Don't think of it that way; you simply reminded me I have a duty to uphold the law. Perhaps you'll be able to do something later; but for now it's just police work.'

Marcus joined the children in the living room and knelt by the railway track. They listened intently as he explained about shunting and how to detach carriages. When he offered to demonstrate switching the engine and tender from one end of the train to the other, Edwin reluctantly relinquished his grip of the velocity control knob. After completing the manoeuvre, Marcus invited Alice to take over as the train driver, and was pleasantly surprised to find Edwin made no objection.

Helen remained in the kitchen, preparing food and turning the pages of a recipe book. When Marcus was due to leave, she went to the living room and cautiously opened the door, mindful of anyone behind it. Seeing the three of them clustered around the track, she thought how engrossed they all appeared. As Marcus finally looked up at her, she tapped the non-existent watch on her wrist. 'It's time you were going.'

He endowed his response with childlike inflections. 'Oh, Mummy, can't I play a bit longer?'

She giggled, before responding severely, 'You can play later, but right now you have some work to do.'

Though Edwin had recently begun objecting to overt displays of affection from either parent, he laughed as unrestrainedly as Alice at their father's silliness as he gave them slurping kisses on their cheeks.

When Marcus went to collect his coat and car keys, Helen opened the inner door and unlocked the outer. They shared a lingering kiss in the hallway.

Marcus found the roads to Dronfield largely clear of snow, the gritting boundary disputes between Sheffield and Derbyshire having been resolved long ago. With little traffic to command his attention, he took in the picture-postcard scenery along the way. Below the white peaks glistening in the wintry sun, dry-stone walls divided the hills into fields; he thought they looked like layered liquorice allsorts, displaying black-and-white lines where they had provided shelter on one side as snow had drifted in from the other. The lower-lying land, light brown with flecks of white, reminded him of a huge Yuletide log powdered with icing sugar.

He drew up directly outside the house and lifted the rucksack off the front passenger seat, then climbed out of the car and onto the cleared pavement. As he walked up the gritted path, he saw the front door open a little way and Susan peer around the edge. When he reached the stone step, she opened it wide. Aiming for some originality, he boomed, 'Merry Boxing Day, Susan.'

The tone of her response suggested a correction. 'Merry Christmas, Marcus.' Her usual shy, polite smile never quite materialised. 'Tony's in the kitchen.' She ushered him down the hallway. He opened the door and stepped inside; she remained outside, and closed it behind him firmly enough to rattle the jamb.

Tony looked up apologetically. 'She asked me why you were coming over, so I told her you'd told me not to tell her; she wasn't at all pleased about that.'

Marcus sat at right-angles to Tony around the round table. 'I thought it wasn't only the wind that felt icy.'

Tony shuffled uncomfortably. 'It isn't you; it's just that she doesn't like us keeping secrets from each other. She even called you a distinguished guest, and said I'd have to clear the snow from the path and pavement and put some grit down; only, then she realised the grit would be walked into the house, so she said you'd have to come into the kitchen.'

Marcus put on a confused expression. 'You had to clear the snow because I'm supposed to be a special guest, but then I'm sent to the kitchen. So, are we both in the doghouse?' Tony took a deep breath and prepared to restate the situation. Marcus smiled and held up a hand to stop him. 'There's no need to explain. But I thought you and Susan were made for each other. Is married life not quite what you expected?'

'We're very happily married... she tells me!' He grinned; Marcus reciprocated. 'She's very much into the idea of equal partners; we share household chores, except she's the one who decides who does what! And she's maybe a bit house-proud at times; it was a big step for us, getting a massive mortgage, and I think she's worried about if we did the right thing.'

'Well, doing the right thing is what I'm here about. I'll fill you in on an off-the-record investigation, and then you'll need to decide whether or not you'd like Susan to know. Not only that, you'll have to decide whether you wish to be involved yourself.'

'Really? Perhaps you'd better give me the facts.'

'Of course, though some of them are in dispute. First of all, a man was murdered. Fact. Helen examined the body and found the victim had had his neck broken. Fact. The Met have taken the case off us. Fact. They arranged an autopsy in London. Fact. It concluded the death was accidental, which is not a fact, so I'm treating it as a fact that there's a cover-up going on.'

Tony looked genuinely shocked. 'A conspiracy?'

Marcus echoed, 'A conspiracy! Helen has agreed with me I should investigate what really happened, and she understands I might upset some very senior people, which could put the kibosh on my career. But that doesn't mean you should be putting your career at risk. Before you decide whether to get involved, you need to consider what might happen to you. What if you were dismissed: who'd pay the mortgage. You can decide to drop out right away, or Susan could decide, either.'

Tony stared at the varnished wooden-planked floor as he weighed the information. Finally, he raised his head and looked intently at Marcus. 'If it were just up to me, I'd say count me in straight away. But it's like you say: who'll pay the mortgage. I can only come on board if Susan gives me her seal of approval.'

'I understand entirely. So now the question is, do you wish to ask Susan or not? Once she's aware of the facts, she can't then unlearn that information, and she may not wish to know. What do you think?'

'I think she'd wish to know. Actually, I think she'll not let it drop until she does know, so there's no point in my second-guessing her. Shall I ask her to join us?'

'Yes; let's get it out in the open.'

Susan walked into the kitchen and chose the chair facing Marcus, casting a jaundiced eye over him. As he explained the background to Operation Semaphore, and the attendant communication restrictions, he felt her animosity toward him dissipating. At the end, he asked, 'What do you think, Susan? Should Tony risk getting involved? I can understand perfectly if you say "no".'

She held his gaze unflinchingly. 'As a solicitor, I would be bound to disclose any knowledge I may gain of a criminal conspiracy. Also, it would be immoral of me to join with those who would seek to deny the victim justice by their action or inaction. I therefore give my unequivocal support for the investigation.'

Having so often complained that lawyers were all ethics and no morals, Marcus felt abashed to find one who would calmly, if not a little pompously, jeopardise her husband's career and risk repossession of her house. He turned to Tony. 'If you'd like to discuss it together without my being here, I can make myself scarce.'

Tony shook his head. 'Just as you trust Helen's judgement, I trust Susan's. I'm in.'

Marcus squirmed inwardly as he recalled his guilty secret and considered his own untrustworthiness.

Susan sat up straight. 'Give us the details and we'll

make a start; we'll be going to Chesterfield later to see my mother, but we've a couple of hours.'

Marcus lifted his rucksack a little way, then put it back down. 'Are you personally intending to help? Are you sure you shouldn't just leave this to Tony? I appreciate you giving him the green light, but should you really risk being drawn into this yourself?'

She walked around to Marcus, grabbed the rucksack, hoisted it up and plonked it on the table. 'Let's not waste time debating this; just show us what you've got.'

He took out the plastic bags that held the documents, and then stacked the contents onto the table in four piles, just as Neil had done the previous evening. After giving a broad overview of the case, he described the contents of each stack. In addition, he explained that Neil had cross-checked the statements from the railway volunteers as at 15:00 and 15:15, and asked Tony to complete the process by time-lining the gap in between. Finally, he extracted a memory stick from a pocket. Tony asked, 'What's on the thumb drive?' Seeing the look of apparent puzzlement, he tried again. 'The flash drive? The micro-drive? The USB drive?'

Marcus frowned. 'The memory stick contains a short video Neil made. It appears to show the deceased had his neck physically dislocated, but Helen says it isn't definitive because the victim's beard blocks the critical juncture. Anyway, let's back it up to your computer.'

Tony fetched his laptop and placed it on the kitchen table. When it had booted up, he inserted the device and examined its contents. 'Are you sure this is the right one? I can only see a family summer holiday file on it.'

Marcus declared smugly, 'I renamed it to cover my tracks. You should give your copy a new name as well;

that way, anyone would think it wasn't the same file.'

Tony responded, 'Some of the metadata will be the same, so it could still be matched up.'

As Tony copied the file, Marcus looked over his shoulder; seeing him rename it "NTSFA2358X.doc", he asked the significance. Tony pointed to the characters on the screen as he read out, *staccato*, 'Not The Same File As Two Three Five Eight X. The numbers are part of the Fibonacci sequence; someone might waste ages looking for a hidden meaning. And the suffix is to pretend it's an old-standard word document, so anyone looking for pictures won't be interested, unless they check the file's properties: at sixty megabytes it's way too big. But aren't you being a bit paranoid, boss? Do you really think someone's going to be tracking down every copy? Perhaps I should back it up to the Cloud?'

Marcus rubbed his chin. 'What if someone hacks the Cloud? Maybe it's better to keep it local.'

Tony smiled at Susan. 'Definite signs of paranoia.'

Susan pretended to be serious. 'You really shouldn't be talking about your boss like that.' A faint smile played on her lips. 'At least, not while he's listening.'

Marcus laughed. 'Alright, I'll leave it up to you to decide how to back it up. I already have some copies…' His tone became didactic. '… the exact number of which I am keeping secret for security reasons; that way, you would be unable to disclose the information under interrogation.'

Tony and Susan began to laugh, until Susan stopped, leading Tony to do likewise. She asked, 'Joking apart, do you really think this is a vital piece of evidence that needs special protection? If so, I could deposit a copy at the firm; we have a safe at our Sheffield offices.'

Marcus smiled warmly at her, aware she was a tightly wound spring who needed encouragement to uncoil. 'Perhaps it's best if I don't know about any copies you take, so I can't spill the beans if I'm grilled.'

Tony looked intently at him. 'Surely, you wouldn't crack under interrogation, would you, Marcus? I thought you'd been trained how to resist, in the army.'

His brow furrowed. 'Techniques are very different from the old days, when people like Kim Philby were only subject to polite questioning; he got away with it by simply keeping his nerve and denying everything. I'm not meaning torture, though; that just makes people say anything to stop the pain. There are now so many methods, I expect everyone talks in the end, and the only doubt is over the truth of what they say. Simply keeping shtum tends to incur the wrath of your jailers, so a better tactic is to give the impression of talking freely, while not disclosing anything significant.'

Tony responded, 'Have you ever tried doing that? You'd have to keep your wits about you.'

Marcus shook his head. 'No, but I've seen plenty of people attempt it; only, they all tripped themselves up in the end. Anyway, let's watch the video.' They played it through twice, and agreed the deceased's neck appeared to be broken, but accepted Helen's opinion it may be insufficient to convince a court of law.

To begin time-lining, Tony proposed they subdivide the statements into groups of people who were together at 15:00. Susan picked up the first pile and set to work. Tony began sorting through the second pile. Seeing how focused they were, Marcus took his leave without waiting to be offered a drink.

CHAPTER 10

Edwin groaned. 'Not goose, again.'

Helen tutted. 'Most children would be delighted to have goose at Christmas; you should be grateful.'

He gurned. 'But we had goose yesterday.'

She sighed. 'And I was planning we'd have goose again tomorrow. If we don't, your father might have to have it in sandwiches all week.' Realising she had no knowledge of his plans, she turned to Marcus. 'Will you be wanting sandwiches?'

He shrugged his shoulders. 'I haven't a clue. It all depends on what the investigation turns up.'

She picked up her knife and fork. 'Well, if you're to avoid being seen in the office, you can hardly use the canteen; and other places might be closed.'

Alice leaned closer to her brother, and whispered, 'Would you like my sausage, Ed? I could have some of your meat if you don't want it.'

Helen pointed at her, then swung her index finger toward Edwin in concert with a disapproving glance. 'Eat what's in front of you.'

Marcus grinned at them. 'It's what you have to do as you get older.'

After the main course, Helen fetched a layered red, orange and yellow jelly trifle from the refrigerator. She looked apologetically at Marcus as she passed him his serving. 'You have to eat what's put in front of you as you get older. I know you'd prefer a traditional sherry trifle on Boxing Day, but think of it as another pleasure waiting for you when they've fledged.' Marcus checked that Edwin had missed the hidden meaning, before exchanging smiles with Helen. She added, 'There's port and Stilton for us, after.'

At five o'clock precisely, Marcus went looking for Helen. He found her in the kitchen, sitting at the table with the goose in front of her. Casually, he asked, 'Is there anything I can help you with?'

She glanced around before returning his gaze. 'Not really; everything's done apart from stripping the carcass. But don't you need to phone Lin?'

He knitted his eyebrows together for a moment, as though the thought had escaped him. 'I suppose now is as good a time as any.' He walked nonchalantly to the telephone and scrolled through the directory, choosing Lin's landline in preference to her personal or work mobile numbers. 'Hi, Lin. Merry Christmas.'

She responded crisply, with an air of formality. 'Hello, sir. How's the surveillance operation going?'

He understood she was asking whether Helen might be listening in on an extension. 'It's been stood down.'

Her voice softened. 'So, are you coming over?'

'Yes, I'd like to see you about an investigation.'

'I'm looking forward to being investigated!'

'It's hush-hush.'

'I'll try not to scream too much.'

'There's something we have to keep under wraps.'

'Under the duvet?'

'I need to explain something to you, face-to-face.'

'Fine, if that's how you want it.'

'Could I come over straight away?'

'Yes; you're sounding desperate.'

'I've a lot to say to you.'

'I can't wait!'

'It may take quite some time.'

'That'll make a nice change.'

'I'll be asking if you're prepared to do something that you may not be entirely comfortable with.'

'Don't start going all weird on me, Marcus; you know I'm satisfied with simple pleasures.'

'I'd better not say any more over the phone. See you soon.' He terminated the call and reviewed his side of the conversation. Confident that nothing incriminating had slipped out, he placed the handset in its charger and turned to face Helen.

She stopped pulling morsels of meat from the carcass and looked up at him. 'How long do you think you'll be with her?'

He set his face rigid, in case the *double entendre* was a trap. 'It's difficult to say, really. I have to give her all the facts, so that she can make an informed decision.'

'Are you going to get off straight away?'

He remained stone-faced in case this was a second attempt to trip him up. 'The sooner I go, the sooner I can come home.'

As he drove the short distance to Lin's flat, he began to wonder if he was lucky, or stupid, or both. He recalled his reasons for declining her first seductive offer: one, happily married with children; two, her senior officer; three, an age difference of thirteen-and-a-half years. But he had succumbed under the influence of the powerful emotions they had felt when she had been the subject of a murder attempt, heightened by his feeling of having negligently put her in harm's way.

They had now been regularly enjoying sex together for almost a year and a half, and she was still as keen as ever. Though they always protested their relationship was entirely physical, he wondered to what extent they were guilty of self-deception. He found her uninhibited expressions of sensual pleasure reminiscent of Helen in their first years of marriage, though he felt disloyal for comparing the two. Knowing he remained very much in love with Helen, and doting as he did on his children, he asked himself why he would imperil his happy family life. He admitted to being dissolute, but hoped his good fortune would continue into the future.

His musings ceased as he approached her block of flats. He fished out her spare zapper that opened the gates to the underground garage where she rented a parking space; to avoid the possible ramifications of anyone reporting his car for being in their bay, he always used her reserved space, leaving her to borrow someone else's or to park outside. The full-height metal gates screeched open; he wondered if he should bring an oil can with him on his next visit, to inhibit them from announcing his future furtive comings and goings.

As usual, he took the stairs instead of the lift, so he would be less likely to meet other residents. Though he believed they had taken every reasonable precaution to keep their affair secret, he knew the young woman in the adjacent flat was aware Lin had a lover, from Lin's ecstatic screams having penetrated the thick walls.

His gentle knock at the door was unnecessary as she was about to open it, having seen his car arrive and knowing how long he took from garage to flat. She closed the door behind him while he hung up his coat.

As she put her arms around him and grabbed his buttocks, he pulled his head away and looked down at her. When she stared up at him questioningly, he began,

'You wouldn't take me seriously on the phone, but I really do need to talk to you about an investigation.'

She released her hold of him and stepped back, before grabbing his hand. 'You can tell me all about it in bed.' He allowed himself to be led away.

After a brief yet pleasurable experience for both of them, he waited for what he judged to be the minimum respectful duration before he could mention work. He turned onto his side to face her. 'You need to know what's happening with Operation Semaphore.'

She propped herself up on one elbow and pulled the duvet to cover her shoulders. 'I haven't heard of it.'

'That's because it's off the record; it's my name for the murdered signalman investigation. Officially, the case has been taken off us by the Met, but they're doing a snow-job on it. They've kicked off by getting a tame pathologist to declare it an accidental death. Helen knows that's a lie, and she won't let it rest, so I'm going to have to keep pushing until I've proved it's murder. Or I get suspended for insubordination.'

'And you want me to be on the team?'

'I do, but you need to understand what you'd be letting yourself in for; it could wreck your career, so it really would be alright to say no. If you say yes, and there's ever a Professional Standards inquiry, you could always claim you thought it was a pukka investigation, and that way it would just come back to me.'

'I'm not sure they'd believe me, but even if they didn't, I expect they'd simply assume I was doing as instructed by you, because of our relative ranks; so it would still come back to you. And if we were put under surveillance and they found out about our relationship, they'd assume I was acting under duress. That means you're the only one whose career is on the line. I don't think I'm risking anything, so I've no reason to say no.'

'I think you're underestimating the contagion effect, but I promise I'd do everything I could to keep you clear of any fallout. So, what storyline should we take?'

'I'd like to stick as close to the truth as possible: believing there to be a cover-up, we felt it was our duty to press ahead with the investigation.'

'They'd ask why we didn't pass on our concerns to Anti-Corruption. I could honestly say I wouldn't trust AC not to be part of the conspiracy.'

'It sounds like you have some history with them.'

'Let me put it this way: past experience suggests they can be as human as the next man.'

'And some of them are more human than others?'

'You've hit the nail on the head, Lin.'

'Alright, tell me how this sounds for my statement to Standards: I felt professionally and personally obligated to pursue the inquiry in accordance with my Oath of Attestation, knowing I would be failing in my duty to protect the public if the perpetrator remained at large to commit further murders.'

'That's very good. I'll make sure my own statement doesn't sound too similar to yours, and I'll throw in my concerns about AC as well.'

'This has turned into a highly effective meeting; perhaps we should always get into bed together when we need to discuss a case?'

He pretended to take her suggestion seriously. 'That would certainly be efficient, briefing and de-briefing at the same time.' She laughed, and brought her head closer to him, her blonde hair cascading over her face; he pushed it behind her ears as he struggled to resist a powerful urge to kiss her on the lips, believing it would go against their understanding that the relationship should remain strictly sexual. Trying not to become aroused again, he dredged up some dusty facts from history. 'Did you know, in mediaeval times, kings used to have meetings with their courtiers in the royal bedchamber; so we're actually following an ancient tradition by discussing a plan of campaign in bed.'

She responded firmly, 'It's agreed, then: all future meetings are to take place in bed, by royal decree.'

He smiled for a moment, before becoming serious. 'Actually, it could be the most secure place. I told the other members of the team to make all communications face-to-face, rather than discussing the case over the phone. They also know not to leave any electronic footprints, and to put nothing down in writing.'

'Do I get to know who else is on the team, or is that confidential?'

'Disclosure is on a need-to-know basis.' He paused for effect. 'And you need to know. I've asked Tony to look at some statements and produce a timeline. Frank and Neil are under orders not to be seen to be working on the case, though they've already provided copies of all the documents on the system, and they'll be looking out for anything new. Helen's straining at the leash, but I'm keeping her out of it; she isn't qualified for police-work. Susan knows exactly what Tony's up to, though I don't think she should be quite so closely involved; she may find a conflict between solicitor-client privilege and rules on disclosure. And that's everyone. I don't intend to ask anyone else unless it's essential; the fewer who know what we're doing, the less chance there is of something leaking out.'

'So, what do you see us doing?'

'Let's meet up tomorrow morning at nine and review everything properly. I'd better have a quick shower and go back before I'm declared AWOL.'

'Don't forget to use your own shower gel; we can't have you going home smelling different. I decanted it into a washing-up bottle and hid it under the kitchen sink. It's quite thick; you'll have to pull the top off.'

He climbed out of bed. 'I wonder how good we really are at covering our tracks? Let's hope we're never put to the test.'

After drying himself, he dressed and prepared to leave. She tilted her face to him to receive the usual perfunctory parting kiss. He found himself weakening under the steady gaze of her deep blue eyes, but forced himself to remain within their conventional bounds. When he had completed the formality, she pulled him back to her and gave him a more luscious one; he reciprocated without restraint, unable to resist. Driving back, he felt the parting kiss was suffused with greater significance than the carnal act that had preceded it.

On arriving home, he stepped out of the car and opened the garage; in the deep mid-winter he preferred parking under cover overnight, to save him having to clear ice or frost from the windscreen in the morning. He had once suggested they have an electric door fitted, but Helen had dismissed the idea as a boy's toy.

Hearing the rattle of the garage door closing, Helen went to let him in. He had already unlocked the outer door to the porch by the time she had opened the inner. She stepped back as he locked it again. Without a word, he walked up to her in the hallway and took hold of her, kissing her with an intensity for which she was entirely unprepared, having just breathed out. She pulled her mouth away, fighting for air, then allowed him to begin again. When he finally released his embrace, she asked, 'What was all that about?'

He kissed her once more, gently on the lips. 'I just wanted to get my money's worth out of the mistletoe.'

She laughed. 'Typical Yorkshireman!' Initially, she was pleased to have been greeted so passionately, but then began to wonder if there might be an underlying cause for concern. Recognising she needed further data to process before she could reach any firm conclusions, she focused on the most recent potential factors. 'You'd better tell me everything that happened over at Lin's. Has she bought into the investigation?'

'Yes, she's a willing volunteer. Our meeting is set for nine a.m. prompt to go through the evidence. Then, I'll put together a strategic plan and task list, and allocate resources. It'll all have to stay in my head, though; nothing's to be put in writing.'

'Should I come, too? I'm sure Amanda would be happy to look after the children for a couple of hours.'

He delayed his response as though weighing the suggestion. 'For now, I really don't think there's very much you could contribute; it's just a matter of getting her up to speed. After that, I expect the two of us will be on the road, re-interviewing witnesses.' He smiled inwardly. 'We might be at it all week.'

'In that case, I'd better make you some sandwiches in the morning; it's a Bank Holiday, so most places will be closed. It'll be goose and cranberry; do you think Lin would like some?'

'I'm sure she would.'

To avoid having to answer questions about his visit,

he joined in with the children around the train track; as it had been his suggestion for Edwin's main Christmas present, he was relieved it had been such a success.

That night, recalling how ardently Marcus had kissed her under the mistletoe, Helen picked up where he had left off. He hid his initial reaction, that he was too tired. When he had given her everything she craved, he wondered if his age was beginning to catch up with him. Drifting off to sleep, he considered how much he and Helen had just enjoyed tenderly making love, and contrasted this with the sheer physicality of his encounters with Lin. As he lay in the warm glow of Helen's body, he decided he should stop risking losing her, despite the huge pleasure he invariably felt when having sex with the younger woman. At that moment, he believed his only uncertainty was when and how he should finish the affair.

CHAPTER 11

Marcus was soundly asleep when the radio turned on and opened with the 7:00 a.m. pips. Helen listened to the news headlines before slipping out of bed. Marcus pressed the snooze button and drifted back to sleep. When the radio burst into life for a second time, he pressed the snooze button again and nodded off. Within a dream, someone in a darkened room encouraged him to get up. It dawned on him that Helen was speaking. He offered a guttural sound to indicate he was awake.

She turned on her bathroom light to avoid dazzling him with any sudden brightness. 'It's time you were up, love; you have a nine o'clock meeting.' She watched him rub his eyes and blink them open several times. A shiver bounced between her shoulder blades as she leaned over and whispered the name of the clandestine investigation. 'Operation Semaphore.'

He shaved and showered. When he stepped out of the cubicle and grabbed a warm towel off the radiator, he caught sight of himself in the large round mirror on the opposite wall. Seeing an ostensibly untroubled face staring back at him, he looked away, ashamed of his lying eyes. He told himself he must stop having sex with Lin; after all, Helen was always a delight, and Lin ought to have someone nearer her own age. And then there were all the other factors to consider, top of which was the risk of hurting Helen.

When he came down for breakfast, the children were still in bed, having stayed up late to watch a lengthy animation on television as a holiday treat. He watched Helen as she gathered his fruit and cereal before settling quietly at the table to drink her coffee. She interpreted his silence. 'Thinking about the case?'

'Yes,' he responded quickly, though his thoughts had been focused on how she would be the only woman he would ever make love to, for the rest of their lives together. Despite his certainty he would always love her, he found the prospect daunting; instinctively, he felt it signalled the end of his primeval manhood at the age of just thirty-five, only half way through his three score years and ten.

She poured him a coffee and left him to his brown study. Alice crept into the room, for once arriving before Edwin. She looked first at her father and then at her mother. 'Aren't you talking?'

Helen saw the concern written in her usually placid features. 'We're both having a good long think. People do that, sometimes, when everything is fine and they just want to plan their day.'

Hearing the emphasis on "fine", Marcus added his support. 'Yes, sweetheart; when people really love each other, they can be happy just to sit quietly together and think about things.'

Alice brightened. 'What are you thinking about?'

He responded with a sigh, 'Oh, just work.'

As Helen was pouring Alice's cereal into a bowl, they heard Edwin thundering down the stairs. He burst in, holding a torch. 'The train's really great in the dark; it looks like it's going even faster.'

Marcus assumed Helen's stare must be an invitation to reprimand Edwin for turning on the power to the train track when no one else was present, as they had long ago given up discouraging him from roaming the house at night. Fearing that imposing yet another stricture would cast him as a spoilsport in his son's eyes, he decided to misinterpret Helen's intention, and declared, calmly, 'I'm glad you didn't say it *actually* goes faster, because that would make no sense.'

Edwin tried out his current favourite word. 'It would be illogical.'

Helen asked Marcus, leadingly, 'Is it dangerous for Edwin to play with the train on his own? What about the electricity transformer?'

He backed down, though doubting there was any real danger. 'You have to be very careful with electricity; it's best if you don't play on your own. And don't do anything silly, like poking a screwdriver into a socket.' He turned to Alice. 'You can keep an eye on your brother, can't you, sweetheart?' She giggled.

Edwin felt affronted. 'I know not to do things like that, now. I'm not stupid; I'm not illogical.'

Helen extended a hand to attract Edwin's attention. 'That isn't quite the right way to use that word, my little love; I'll give you a talk about logic, later.'

Marcus grinned at him. 'And she'll test you on it, too; so pay attention to what she says.'

Helen gave smiles all around to show she had taken the jibe in good part.

Edwin bolted his food and headed straight for the railway track. Alice dogged his footsteps, intent on keeping him safe. Marcus followed them and closed the curtains. Edwin demonstrated shining his torch at the moving train. After finally bringing it to a halt at "Adlestrop", the name Marcus had inscribed in black marker pen on the cereal box station wall, he redirected his beam to the light switches. Marcus turned them on, opened the curtains, and asked, 'Are you sure it doesn't go faster in the dark? It certainly looks like it does.'

Edwin snorted. 'That would… make no sense.'

Marcus returned to the kitchen and waited for a reprimand. Helen duly obliged. 'You need to be stricter with him when it comes to playing with electricity. I'd tell him myself, but he takes more notice of you.'

'I'm sure that's not true, love; he hangs on your every word, just like I do.'

She watched the grin spread over his face. 'You and he are so alike: so subversive.' Seeing his over-acted shamefaced expression, she released a laugh. 'Anyway, you need to be getting ready, soon. I've made lots of sandwiches for you and Lin, and a flask of black coffee. She takes milk, doesn't she. It's best to keep it separate. I could put some in a screw-top water bottle.'

'It's only Derbyshire we're going to, not the back of beyond; there'll be plenty of places to get drinks. But I'll take the coffee, now you've made it.' He fetched his rucksack, which she filled with the provisions.

At ten to nine, he gave workaday goodbyes and set off to see Lin. As he drove, he made a firm decision: he must begin by finishing their affair. He decided the best way was to heap approbation on her and disapproval on himself. He would take the blame for having allowed their relationship to continue long after he had realised he was taking advantage of her. Yes, of course she enjoyed the physicality, but sex without full emotional engagement did not constitute love, and that was something which she fully deserved but he could never give her. He discovered one single crumb of comfort, that he had never said he would leave Helen for her.

The gates screeched open, triggering another train of thought. If he had set off this morning intending to continue visiting her, would he not have brought the oilcan? So, the affair was over, all bar the shouting; and how much of that would there be? Would she be very upset? How would they cope with working together in the aftermath? Would he try to avoid her? Would he bar her from working closely with him on future cases? If he did, she would become unhappy, even depressed, and feel the need to confide in someone. Knowledge of their affair would spread like wildfire, and when it reached the upper echelons, his career would go tits-up; he regretted thinking that expression. He regretted... just what exactly did he regret? For himself, it had been sheer unadulterated pleasure; he regretted thinking that inappropriate word, with its implicit threat to his marriage. And what about from Lin's point of view? She had said she just wanted to come along for the ride. Well, he had ridden her long and hard, but their revels now were ended. The phrase made him smile, and gave him hope their affair might simply melt away, like small chocolates in the mouth. He wondered if he should have perhaps brought a box of expensive chocolates. Or maybe flowers to spell out the word "Linda". Lilac for first love; he was hers. Iris for inspiration; she was his. Narcissus for his crushing ego and her crushed echo. Daisy for innocence; hers, taken by him. Amaryllis, dramatic; no, he could do without the drama. Anemone, fragile; he hoped not. Aster, contentment; his, taken by her. He recalled lines from Housman's poem on the land of lost content, learned by rote at prep school but only now fully felt: "The happy highways where I went and cannot come again."

Through the spyhole, she saw him approach but stop short of the door. She opened it and beckoned him in. When he prepared to speak, she silenced him with a finger to her lips. He stepped inside. As she closed the door behind him, he began, 'I've been thinking…'

She cut him short. 'Not a word; don't you remember what we said?' He saw she was wearing the blue silk dressing-gown he had given her last October for her twenty-second birthday, when they had had a weekend away at a B&B in the Lake District that catered for walkers. They had barely noticed the incessant rain.

As she led him silently to her bedroom, he decided he must tell her at once. 'Lin, wait a minute.'

She looked puzzled. 'Not in the bedroom? What, you want to have me in the kitchen?'

'No, not in the kitchen.' He felt his resolve waver. 'I'm not pansexual.'

'Oh, you are clever!' she over-enunciated. 'Anyway, we can't talk here.'

She headed for her bedroom again. He followed, accepting what inevitably lay ahead. As she reached the pure white cotton sheets, she slipped off her only item of clothing. He breathed in her beauty, asking himself how he could ever have thought of giving her up.

Afterwards, he lay on his back, staring at the ceiling, and wondering when something would come along to spoil everything.

She commented in a matter-of-fact voice, 'If I didn't know better, I'd think you'd forgotten we'd agreed to have all future meetings in bed.'

He turned and smiled. 'I'll have to take an inflatable one to my office.'

She laughed only briefly. 'Let's get on, then. What

developments have there been?'

'None, yet; I'm waiting for Tony to report back to me, or maybe Neil or Frank to find something out.'

'In that case, let's stay in bed until something comes up. Or shall we just have a cuddle and a sleep?' He closed his eyes. She turned her back to him. He put an arm around her and pressed up to her.

Woken by his personal mobile phone alerting him to an incoming call, he jumped out of bed and hurried to retrieve the device from his coat pocket. Seeing the number was withheld, he answered flatly, 'Yes?'

Tony responded, 'Is that you, Marcus? I'm using Susan's phone. I haven't just woken you up, have I?'

He checked the time display; it was approaching midday. 'I've been up since seven. Have you something to tell me?'

'Yes, but shouldn't we meet face-to-face? It's about you-know-what. Shall I come over?'

'No, I'll come to you.'

'Right; see you in twenty?'

'No, I'll be a bit longer.' Hearing the speed and stress in his own voice, he began again, more slowly. 'I have one or two things to deal with first. Shall we make it one o'clock?'

'Sure. Should I do some food?'

'No, we'll be fine.'

'We?'

'I'll be coming with... one other.'

'OK. See you then.'

When he had terminated the call, Lin slipped out of bed, put on her silk dressing-gown and headed for the bathroom. She stopped by the door to ask, 'Anything?'

'We're going to Tony's for one o'clock.'

'That gives us time to go back to bed for a bit.'

'Lin, you're going to wear me out; I'm an old man.'

'Nonsense! Thirty-five is the new eighteen.'

'Even so, let's just get showered and have a chat.'

As he was enjoying the sight of her through the misty shower door, he struggled to resist the powerful urge to join her. She saw him watching, and pressed her body against the glass, leaning forward and tilting her head back to make firmer contact; he was sure it was an image he would never forget. When the show was over and she stepped out, he edged past her. She twisted a towel around her hair and wrapped herself in a bath sheet. 'I'll make us something to eat.'

A sense of guilt suddenly coursed through his veins as he responded, 'Helen made us some sandwiches.'

Lin also felt uncomfortable, but avoided showing it. 'That was good of her.'

After dressing, he took his rucksack to the kitchen and extracted four sandwich bags. 'These are goose with cranberry. Edwin turned his nose up at the goose yesterday, so Helen didn't want to give him any more. That's probably why she's done enough for an army.'

Lin picked up a polythene bag and twisted off its tie, then took out a sandwich and bit into it. 'This tastes very nice. Perhaps she expects you to be out for tea, as well. So, we can come back here later, can't we?'

'I'd better not push my luck. I expect she'll demand a project status report when I get back, so it'll come down to how much progress we make this afternoon, which in turn will depend on what Tony has found out.'

In Dronfield, Tony was watching as Marcus and Lin arrived precisely on time. After exchanging pleasantries at the door, he remarked to Marcus, 'I see you dressed for work; makes me feel quite scruffy in my jeans.'

Marcus responded, 'Well, you are on holiday; at least, officially.'

Tony led the way into the kitchen, where Susan was standing waiting. 'Hello Marcus; Lin. We conducted a joint investigation; I shall present our findings.' With a flick of her hands, she invited them to take their places on the empty chairs either side of her around the table.

Marcus heard the formality in her voice and adopted a similar tone. 'The floor is all yours.'

Tony missed the seriousness. 'And the walls; and the ceiling.' Marcus walked around Susan, flashing a grin at Tony as he was passing behind her.

Lin looked around, before delivering a conventional response with plausible sincerity. 'This is a nice room.'

Susan brightened visibly. 'Thank you; we've just finished decorating it. The lighting is new as well; we chose it together.'

Tony held his tongue in check, recalling how he had meekly accepted instruction on what he should like.

Marcus waited for Lin, before settling onto his own unsculpted wooden seat. Susan began to descend, Tony following suit. Marcus noticed she hovered a few inches above her chair until Tony was fully down, thereby appointing herself head of the round table.

Susan began, 'I checked Tony's cross-correlation of the statements given by the people working on the railway, and confirmed his tentative conclusion; barring a conspiracy involving at least three individuals, none were unaccounted for at the time of death.'

Into her pregnant pause, Tony began, 'But…'

Susan raised a finger to silence him. 'BUT, this is based on the assumption that none of them confused any one Father Christmas with any other; people tend to see only their clothing, beard and whiskers. There were in fact four Santas, two on the train and two in rooms adjacent to the ticket office. It *is* feasible that only one Santa was at the station, being seen first in one room and then the other. This would leave the second Santa unaccounted for. So, what if one of the Santas slipped away unseen?' Smugly, she pressed herself against the chair's unyielding splat, before sitting forward again on rediscovering how uncomfortable it was.

Tony waited until certain she had finished. 'An alternative scenario is that the second Santa lent their outfit to someone else. The other railway staff are all accounted for, which would mean it would have had to have been passed to an outsider.'

Marcus saw Tony taking his turn to look smug; he peered at Susan out of the corner of his eye, and concluded she was annoyed he had sprung this on the court without prior disclosure to her as leading counsel. He addressed his response to Tony, nodding repeatedly for emphasis. 'That was a good piece of analysis. We need to eliminate those two Santas from our list of suspects, either as the perpetrator or as an involved party. Lin and I will go and interview them.'

Tony plucked the top two sheets from a pile at his right hand. 'I thought that's what you'd say. Here are their statements; Billy Padley and Jan Kowalski.'

Lin asked in surprise, 'Jan? A woman?'

Susan blasted a response directly at her. 'Why not? Why shouldn't a woman be Father Christmas?'

Lin, taken aback, jerked her head away. Tony, aiming to defuse the tension, called out, 'Chick Fight!'

Susan turned on him. 'I. Am. Your. Wife. You do

not refer to me as a chick!'

Marcus intervened. 'I think we may find "Jan" is actually male. I was at school with a polish boy called "Yan", spelled "J-A-N". The clue is in the surname.'

Tony picked up his iPhone and began touching the screen. The others watched him in silence. 'Kowalski comes from Kowal, meaning Blacksmith. Could be a powerful kind of bloke, with a name like that.'

Marcus responded, 'We'll find out soon enough.'

Tony asked, 'Are you intending to re-interview the people who live near the signal box? I have to say, I don't think you'll get much joy there.' He handed over a few sheets of paper. 'But these might be worth a visit. Mrs Emily Thompson's house is directly opposite, and there were two visitors to Dr Freddie Forbes who lives down the lane: Mrs Nancy Brownlow and her husband, Oliver.'

Marcus noticed the conventional ordering had been reversed, and wondered if this was due to Susan's influence. As he accepted the recommended contacts, he asked Tony, 'Are the others definitely non-starters?'

Susan responded for him. 'We both agree they're very unlikely to have anything to offer. There's two old people with their curtains closed, an old man who was asleep, a couple with young children, and a woman who wouldn't say boo to a goose.'

Tony waited before adding, 'There was also a young couple who were busy all afternoon having sex.'

Susan looked daggers at him. 'Allegedly!'

Seeing her blushing a deep red, Tony smiled at her before continuing. 'You may also want to interview the timid woman, Karen Eckersley; she was keeping out of her husband's way, so neither of them has an alibi.'

Marcus responded, 'I'll take her address. And the couple who were busy having sex... allegedly!'

Susan averted her eyes when Marcus turned to offer her a smile. Tony rustled the papers noisily, then added the requested sheets to the selected set. Marcus glanced through the documents, passing each reviewed page over to Lin, who read them more thoroughly.

After Lin had completed the final paper, Marcus asked her, 'Where do you think we should begin?'

Though certain he had intended the invitation as an opportunity to display her prowess as a detective, she wished he had not asked in Susan's presence. Feeling self-conscious, she responded quickly, 'We should start with the two Santas, and then review progress.'

Marcus nodded in agreement. 'That makes sense.' He turned to Tony. 'Right; we'll be on our way, then.' Switching his gaze to Susan, he smiled with sincerity. 'Thank you for your input; it's greatly appreciated.'

Susan nodded without smiling. 'You're welcome.'

Tony asked, 'What should we do with the rest? I've scanned everything, so I could shred them if you like.'

Marcus grinned at him. 'Looks to me like you're the one with signs of paranoia! Just bag 'em up and put 'em away; you never know, they might be needed later.'

Marcus led the way to the door. Lin stopped to speak to Tony. 'How does it feel to be a sergeant, Sergeant?'

Tony looked sheepish. 'I haven't got used to it, yet.'

Susan interjected. 'He fully deserved his promotion.'

Lin turned to her. 'I don't doubt that for a moment. Well, we'll be off. And thank you for the hospitality.'

Marcus smiled inwardly at Lin's subtle cattiness, a side of her he had never seen before.

CHAPTER 12

In the car outside DS Beresford's house, DCI Priestley was taking a second look at the brief statement given by Billy Padley, while DC Plummer reminded herself of Jan Kowalski's far lengthier testimony. He waited for her to finish, then exchanged papers. After skimming Padley's notes, she glanced out of the window for a moment. He completed reading Kowalski's missive and handed it back to her, asking, 'Which do you think would work better: telephoning in advance, or arriving unannounced? And who should we see first?'

She thought for a moment. 'Well, I'd say, give no advance warning if they're genuine suspects, and see Kowalski first because we can be confident he'll be in. Neil asked everyone to write down where they'll be, and he certainly did that; he should be walking home from a local Polish club right now.'

Marcus leaned over and glanced at Kowalski's notes. 'And he'll have been there since noon, so he's probably three sheets to the wind.'

She waggled her head. 'Unless he's a teetotaller.'

He shrugged. 'I'm not aware of any application for a liquor license from that address, so it might be an alcohol-free club; but if the Polish friends I've known in the past are anything to go by, I'd be amazed if it really is. Anyway, shall we phone, or just go?'

'Let's just go.'

'And that's your considered opinion, is it?'

She stared ahead. 'It is, when Susan's watching us.'

Without looking around at the house, he turned on the engine and engaged first gear, commenting, 'We don't need the satnav, yet; I know the way to Rowsley.'

He set a strictly professional conversational tone for the journey. She followed his lead, accepting they should practise their duplicitousness. Only when they were passing through the Chatsworth estate did he offer a lighter topic than police work. 'Have you seen this place when the sun catches the gold window frames?'

'Not as I recall. It can't be real gold, can it?'

'I believe it's gold leaf. If it were solid gold, people wouldn't need to break in to rob the place; they'd just steal the frames.' She gave him a suitably brief smile, which he acknowledged with an even briefer one.

As they waited at the traffic lights before the hump-back bridge, she complied with his request to enter the destination on the satnav. When the lights had changed and they were on a stretch of road with no turnings, she related an instruction. 'Continue straight ahead.'

He glanced at her and jibed, 'Does it think I might drive through the hedge?'

She pointed forward. 'Keep your eyes on the road.'

He grinned. 'Cheeky!'

As they approached the A6, she looked through his side of the windscreen. 'Turn right. Then there's a left, next to an old lamp on a stone pillar on a little traffic island; it's before you get to the Peacock on the right. You might be able to park up by the church hall.'

He laughed. 'You didn't get that from the satnav.'

She smiled. 'I sometimes come out this way with my friend.' She caught his quizzical look. 'Female.' Seeing him raise his eyebrows further, she added, 'Platonic!'

He saw the sign for Stanton in the Peak, and found a

space to park on School Lane. She stepped out of the car and glanced around. When he climbed out, she pointed toward a row of stone cottages. 'It must be one of those.'

They crossed the road and headed along a narrow path, careful not to hurry on the compacted snow. She grasped his arm. 'You wouldn't want me to slip, would you, sir?'

He looked down at her walking boots, and compared them with his lighter shoes. 'I think maybe I should be the one who's hanging onto you.'

She gave his arm a squeeze. 'I'm relying on you to hang onto me for years and years.'

He grimaced. 'Get your mind back on the job, DC Plummer.'

They checked they were at the correct cottage by scanning those at either side, the property itself having no visible number among the patches of snow that clung to the wall. He knocked at the door and was greeted by a paunchy, bald man of small-to-medium height with an age he estimated at around seventy hard years. 'Mr Jan Kowalski?' he asked, pronouncing the first name with an initial Y.

'Jan Kowalski,' he responded, with Y and V sounds replacing the J and W. 'You must be the police.'

'Must we? You *are* correct, but how did you know?'

'You're here together, but you're far too old for her to be a couple, and she's too young and pretty to be going around with you knocking on doors on a cold Bank Holiday to be anything else.' He smiled at her. 'Come in, my dear; make yourself at home.'

Plummer found Kowalski's observations amusing, but hid this from Priestley, believing he may have been offended by them. She followed him into the flat and sat where indicated on the two-seater settee. Priestley brought up the rear and closed the door. He declined Kowalski's invitation to sit next to Plummer, preferring a Windsor chair by the window, of mellow yellow yew with an ornately hand-carved splat.

Kowalski picked up a long poker and made a few sparks fly from the log atop the incandescent coal fire. Satisfied with the effect, he settled into a high-backed red leather armchair and stretched out his legs, warming his feet in their ankle-length woolly blue slippers.

Priestley waited for Kowalski to look over in his direction, before holding up his warrant card; Plummer immediately copied his action. Kowalski waved them away, before addressing Priestley. 'You must be here about Stan Hicks. It's a shame, what happened to him.'

Priestley responded, 'What do you think did happen to him, Mr Kowalski?'

'Well, he was killed, wasn't he; and only just retired. I don't know anything else about it, but I do know we should all raise a glass to him. Polish vodka alright?'

Priestley shook his head. 'Not when I'm driving.'

Plummer added quickly, 'Or on duty. We both are.'

Kowalski nodded acceptance. 'I'll not have one either, then; I've already had quite a few at the club. Well, I call it a club, but it isn't really.'

Priestley asked, 'So what is it, really? A shebeen? I mean, an illegal drinking establishment?'

Kowalski laughed loudly and held his arms forward, wrists together, as though waiting to be handcuffed. 'You got me!' After a few moments, he explained, 'It's just a friend's house and we all take it in turns to bring stuff, so no money changes hands.'

Priestley nodded. 'Anyway, that's not why we're here. I have a copy of your statement, detailing where you were on Christmas eve between three and three fifteen, and I'd just like to check something with you. Were you actually wearing your Father Christmas outfit throughout that quarter of an hour?'

Kowalski frowned pensively, his gnarled fingers steepling. 'Let me see... Yes, I was; it was too much of a faff to take it off. Except the hat and the whiskers. I took them off at some point, but I can't say exactly when. They were too warm for me.'

'Before you removed the hat and whiskers, would people know it was you and not Billy Padley?'

'Well, that's a tricky one; the outfits are the same.'

'So they wouldn't be able to tell you apart, just by looking at you?'

'I expect some people could tell, and they'd know for certain if I had the hat off; he still has hair.'

'Right. Did you talk to anyone in the office before you took off the hat and whiskers?'

'Probably, but you can't expect me to remember something like that, can you?'

'No, not unless there was something in particular that stuck in your mind.'

'Well, I can't recall anything. Anyway, why are you interested in what I was doing? You're looking for the murderer, and I haven't bumped anyone off for years.'

Priestley gave him a warm smile. 'Well, I can't condone your past behaviour, but I'm glad to hear you've mended your ways.' He waited until Kowalski had returned the smile. 'Thank you for your help, sir.'

In the car, Priestley looked at Plummer. 'What did you make of him? Is he reliable?'

She glanced again at his original statement. 'I would say so. The notes he made about where he'll be over the next few days were certainly thorough, so there's no suggestion his mind's going.'

'No, he isn't gaga, but could he be lying to us about something?'

'It is possible, but I think he's just a nice old man.'

'Yes, well, you would say that, wouldn't you, because he said that you're pretty…'

She interrupted, '… and that you're too old for me! Well, don't worry about it; I know there's still plenty of life in the old dog, yet.'

Priestley was unable to keep a smile from spreading across his face as he remembered how she had looked against the shower glass, and how the term "pretty" was such an understatement. He shook himself mentally, and asked, 'Shall we carry on, then? Billy Padley, next. I wonder if that's his real name.'

'You think he might be living under an alias?'

'I only meant "Billy" is a diminutive of "William".'

Less than ten minutes later they were drawing up outside a large, old house on the outskirts of Bakewell. Priestley commented, 'This is rather grand.'

The door was opened by a tall woman in jogging bottoms and designer sweatshirt, whose bottle-red hair did little to detract from her fine features, clear skin and athletic physique. Plummer hoped that twenty years hence she would be in as good a shape.

Priestley showed his warrant card and introduced them both, before asking, 'Is Mr Billy Padley at home?'

She stepped back. 'Come in. I'm his wife, Jan.'

As Priestley was led through the narrow hallway, he felt her brush up against him several times, apparently oblivious to Plummer who was directly behind them. Unable to avoid her determined contacts, he speeded up and tried to deflect her with mundane conversation. 'Is "Jan" short for something?'

She giggled. 'January.' They hurried through to a solid stone extension in the style of the original house. Inside, a small, gaunt man with long, dyed black hair lay relaxing in swimming shorts on a lounger by a pool.

Priestley began, 'Mr Billy Padley?'

The man sat up. 'That depends.'

Priestley frowned at him theatrically. 'What does it depend on, sir?'

'Personal or business; as in, the music business. You don't recognise me, do you?'

'Sorry, sir; I haven't a clue.' He took out his warrant card. 'I'm Detective Chief Inspector Priestley, with Detective Constable Plummer.'

'A detective without a clue? That's a new one. Well, what can I do for you, Detective?'

'First of all, could you just clarify about your name?'

'My real name is William Padley, but I'm famously known as Granite, frontman with the Hard Rocks. Look on the wall over there: two platinum discs.'

'I'm sorry, sir, I don't recall ever hearing of your band; but then, hard rock was never really my thing.'

Jan nudged Priestley. 'And don't you recognise me, either? I was Miss January for a special millennium edition calendar that sold millions. I could sign a copy for you, if you like?'

Padley stood up and put on a towelling dressing gown. 'Yes, take one; otherwise she won't be happy. She likes everyone to see what great tits she had when she was young.' Jan glared at him. He accepted the prompt. 'Still has.'

She turned to Priestley. 'Am I wanted for anything?'

He knew not to encourage her with a witty response. 'It's really only your husband I need to speak to.'

'I'll leave you to it, then.' She cat-walked away.

Priestley cleared his throat noisily. 'I'm here on a very serious matter, Mr Padley.'

'This must be about Stan. I'll give you whatever help I can, but I was nowhere near the signal box so I doubt I've much to tell you.'

'I see you state you were sitting in an office at the station between three and three fifteen. Is that correct?'

'It is, as well as I can remember.'

'And were you wearing your Father Christmas outfit throughout that time?'

'No, I'd already taken it off. I went for a smoke a while before then, and I could hardly be seen strolling about looking like Santa Claus.'

'Where and when were you smoking, do you recall?'

'I had a wander away from the station; between half two and three, I'd guess. I went down the path toward the next signal box up the line, by the trees.'

'You say the next signal box?'

'Yes, not Stan's box on High Church Lane.'

'And did you see anyone while you were walking?'

'I remember there was a young woman with a dog. Quite pretty.'

'The dog? What breed was it?'

'No, the woman. I hardly looked at the dog. Was that one of those trick questions the police are supposed to be famous for?'

He retained his serious expression. 'It can often be easier to track down a witness if we have a description of their dog. Did you see anyone else?'

'Just a couple with a small boy. Look, what's this all about? I know Stan was killed after I'd got back, so why do you want to know who I saw earlier?'

'It's just possible the perpetrator was making their way to the signal box along that footpath.'

'Well, the young woman was more of a girl, really; maybe seventeen. And the couple were having a laugh with their kid. So, I don't think they're your suspects.'

'And there was no one else?'

'Not as I recall.'

'So, when you came back after your walk, you sat in the office for a while?'

'Yes, just having a chat.'

'Where did you put your Santa outfit, by the way?'

'I hung it up in a cupboard. That would have been around ten past two, just after I'd finished my stint. It was still there when I took it out again after I'd made my statement to the sergeant.'

'Could anyone have taken it away and returned it between those times?'

'If they had, they'd have been spotted for sure; there's always someone around in the office.'

'Right. I think that's everything, at least for now. Is there anything you'd like to tell us, that might have a bearing on the case?'

'Nothing comes to mind. I only ever met Stan once; I just help out occasionally, you see.'

'Did you form any sort of impression of him?'

'I'd say he was different. Yes, different. Unworldly, in a way. He hadn't heard of me, either; but it went deeper than that. I'm not even sure he knew what rock music was. It was as though he lived in a different place to the rest of us. Sorry, these are just my idle thoughts; I can't really justify them. But the thing I remember most was, he said he didn't believe it was right for someone to earn millions from "pop music", when other people work hard their entire lives for a pittance. I suppose he had a point, but how else would someone from my background make this sort of money, legally?'

Priestley glanced around the room in response to Padley's sweep of an arm. 'Yes, I can see you've done very well for yourself. Do you think it's changed who you are?'

'That's a bit deep, isn't it? Is that the way police question people nowadays? I hope I'm still who I was. The only thing is, I have too much time on my hands, which is why I like volunteering at various places. It's great fun playing Santa Claus with all the kiddies. We never had any of our own, you see; so it's especially nice for me to spend time with other people's.'

Priestley waited until sure he had nothing more to add. 'Well, thank you very much, Mr Padley; you've been most helpful. Perhaps I could telephone you if I have any further questions?'

'Yes, feel free, any time. Or call in. You could bring your sidekick and we could all have a swimming party.'

'That's very kind of you, but there are rules against fraternising during an investigation.'

'After you've caught the culprit, then. I mean it.'

'Well, that's very generous of you. Shall we see ourselves out?'

'Jan will want to show you the way; hold on.' He cupped his hands together and shouted in a high, reedy voice. 'Jan? Our visitors are leaving.'

A few moments later, Jan appeared at the doorway

holding a brown envelope. 'This way, Detective Chief Inspector.' As she led them out, she extracted a calendar from the envelope and held it up. 'Do you remember me now?'

Priestley stopped to look. 'Oh, of course; how could I ever forget.'

She slipped the calendar back into the envelope. At the outer door, she prepared to hand it over to him. Plummer stepped forward and grabbed it, commenting, 'I'll take care of it.'

He smiled at the disaffected hostess. 'Thank you ever so much, Jan; I'll always treasure it.'

Plummer hurried to the car and waited impatiently for Priestley to catch up. Inside, Priestley turned to her. 'Let me have another look, then.'

'Don't be so disgusting! It's demeaning to women, having to show off their bodies like that.'

'Surely it's their choice if they wish to flaunt their assets. Anyway, there might be some obscure detail in the photograph that could aid the investigation; I should examine it closely.'

'That's not going to happen.'

'Yes, but…'

'No buts; I said no and I mean no.'

He shrugged. 'No matter, I don't need to look at it again; it's already indelibly etched on my mind.

'Well, you're not going to look at the others.'

'Fine. It doesn't interest me, anyway; once you've seen two, you've seen 'em all.'

'You don't really mean that.'

'You're right, I don't. I was eighteen when it came out, and I spent a lot of time looking at it, as you do at that age. Some of the others are even more impressive. I think Miss July is my favourite out of the whole lot.'

Plummer extracted the calendar. Holding it to one side so that Priestley was unable to see it, she turned to July. 'Is she really your favourite?'

'Yes, I'd say so.'

'But she couldn't possibly ride a motorbike with her breasts on the petrol tank like that. You probably didn't even notice the tank.'

'I didn't even notice the motorbike!'

'Ugh! You're disgusting. Well, I'm not letting you have it.'

'But it's evidence.'

'Yes, it's evidence of your inappropriate attitude to women. Perhaps you should take up Mr Padley's offer of a swimming party, so you can see what Miss January looks like now in a bikini.'

'The invitation was to both of us together.'

'Perhaps he wants to see me in a bikini, then.'

'Actually, Lin, he never mentioned swimwear; my guess is, he was hoping to see very much more of you.' Seeing her blushing a deep crimson, he rubbed his hands together and held them close to her cheek, as though he were warming them at a brazier.

She blazed at him, 'Just get going, will you?'

CHAPTER 13

Priestley started the car and headed off. 'We'll see the Brownlows, next.' Plummer sat quietly, contemplating what it would be like to know that everyone could see pictures of them in the nude, and found herself fixated on the distress young people can suffer when they discover their private sexting has gone viral. Priestley finally broke the silence. 'Penny for them?'

She turned and looked at him. 'What?'

'A penny for your thoughts?'

'Oh, I was just wondering if the law does enough to protect young people from having embarrassing photos put out on social media. Or elsewhere on the web.'

'I think the law does too much.'

'Seriously? You can't mean that.'

'Actually, I do mean it. What brought it home to me was hearing two women healthcare professionals on the BBC debating the subject, oblivious to their underlying assumption that sexting was commonplace and should be accepted as a fact-of-life. They failed to recognise that, by normalising such behaviour, they themselves were guilty of propagating the problem, and at the same time were lulling young people into a false sense of security. The real fact-of-life is that revenge porn will always be put out by ex-partners of any age.'

'Don't all the adult prosecutions act as a deterrent?'

'Do you remember the homosexual pop star who had an injunction brought in the High Court, to stop details of his husband's behaviour being published? The media were permitted to report that someone had obtained an injunction, but not who it related to. If anyone was sufficiently intrigued to find out about it, all they had to do was to plug in a simple query over the internet. To my mind, it brings our legal system into disrepute, when we have judges saying what can and can't be published in Britain, when they obviously know they're powerless to stop what happens outside our borders, real and virtual.'

'Yes, but that's not the same thing as putting out revenge porn, is it?'

'Think about it, Lin. If someone wants to distribute explicit photos over the internet, do you really think Britain can stand alone in blocking them? Anyone can get away with it fairly easily, so long as they mask their identity as the originator.'

'You think our judges are like King Canute, then; trying to hold back the waves?'

'Yes, so far as the common misinterpretation of his behaviour is concerned, though I think he simply had bad press; but that's rather wandering off the point. What I'm saying is, it would be better to de-normalise sexting by putting out the clear message that, if you ever let anyone have an intimate picture of yourself, you should assume at some point in your life it will be visible to everyone who cares to take a look.'

'I'm unclear where you're coming from on this. Do you think it shouldn't even be a criminal offence to publish revenge porn?'

'We have more than enough laws that are virtually impossible to enforce, without adding another one to the statute books. And it comes from the Nanny State concept that people need protection from their own stupid behaviour, when we should be focusing on educating them to understand what is, and what is not, appropriate. Rather than allocating massive resources to protecting people from themselves, our job should be to stop bad behaviour that's totally outside their control. Take noise, for example: someone can blast out enough sound from their home or car in one form or another to disturb thousands of neighbours. In effect it constitutes mass assault, but it isn't taken as seriously as other forms of assault. To my mind, every noise-generating device is a potential weapon of mass disruption.'

Her obligatory laugh was less than the generally accepted minimum. 'Oh, that's very clever.'

'Helen says I'm too clever by half, sometimes; but she's hardly one to talk.'

'Well, anyway, back to the porn question; if it's the law, we have to enforce it.'

'Yes, for now, but if you look back at nineteenth century legislation, you'll find the previous porn laws lasted little more than three decades before they were repealed.'

'I didn't even know there were any porn laws in the nineteenth century.'

'Oh, hang on a minute; I must be confusing myself. Now I come to think of it, they were the Corn Laws.'

Surprised by the unexpected punchline, her laughter was sincere. 'That sounds familiar, from my school days. I can't remember much about it, though; apart from something to do with a potato famine in Ireland.'

'You mean, you don't remember it was Sir Robert Peel who had the Corn Laws re-peeled, despite the opposition of his own party?'

She sighed. 'It must have slipped my mind.'

'The same Sir Robert "Bobby" Peel who founded the Metropolitan Police Service? The very organisation that has now claimed jurisdiction over our own homicide investigation? And the reason for the term, Keep Your Eyes Peeled? You were a Peeler, yourself; and I'm not referring to 'taters, precious.'

'I don't know where you're going with this, Marcus; but I can't help thinking you're trying to lead me away from the problem I was talking about, of people posting pictures on the internet, that the subjects only intended for private consumption. What can be done about that?'

'One possible solution would be to ban the wearing of clothes in public, so that nakedness becomes entirely commonplace.'

'Now I know you're not being serious.'

'Hmm, perhaps that isn't such a good idea; at least, not in this weather. I can feel myself shrivelling up just at the thought of it.'

'Too much information! But don't you think people lose something by showing off their naked bodies to everyone? Don't we lose some of the mystery? The joy of discovery?'

'You're absolutely right, Lin; it's the "tease" part in striptease that makes all the difference. That's why that calendar isn't of any real interest to me; you can see straight away what they have to offer.'

'So I'll just get rid of it, then.'

They were now drawing up outside the Brownlow's detached cottage. He stopped the vehicle and pulled on the handbrake, before responding, 'We ought to apply rigid rules of evidence, which means you shouldn't be handling it at all. I'll take it off you and hide it away somewhere at home.' By the time she had exited, he had opened the car boot and was holding out his hand. 'Just give me the envelope and I'll chuck it in here.'

She clutched it resolutely behind her back. 'You make some very convincing arguments, but I'm not stupid; you just want to look at the mucky pictures.'

'It's evidence.'

'It's no such thing.'

'Well, it's art, then.'

Before she could respond, she was distracted by the sound of music emanating from the cottage. "My old man said follow the van..." He grabbed the envelope, threw it into the boot and slammed the lid.

She frowned at him and wagged her finger. 'This isn't over, Marcus. Why would you want photographs when you can see the real thing?'

He grinned. 'Alright, Lin; to be continued. But now, we need to focus on the Brownlows.' He hurried along the de-iced tarmacked path and then waited for her. When she caught up, he rang the bell.

A woman in a Laura Ashley dress opened the door. 'Yes? Can I help you?'

Priestley showed his warrant card. 'I'm Detective Chief Inspector Priestley. This is Detective Constable Plummer. Are you Mrs Nancy Brownlow?'

'I am. Is this about the dead railwayman?'

'It is indeed. May we come in?'

'Of course. Go through to the far room on the left.'

When Priestley approached the end of the hallway, the door opened and a man stepped out in green cavalry twill trousers and a Fair Isle jumper. Nancy called over to him, 'It's the police about that railwayman.'

He backed away toward the music room. 'I'm Oliver Brownlow. Come through.'

Priestley and Plummer followed him and accepted his invitation to sit. They settled into opposite ends of the three-seater chintz-covered settee, while he and Nancy dropped into matching chairs from the same suite. Priestley began, 'We're making further inquiries into the death of the railwayman on High Church Lane. I have here some notes based on interviews with you on Christmas eve, which I'd like to revisit.'

Oliver responded unnecessarily, 'Go right ahead.'

Priestley turned to Nancy. 'I understand you saw some activity in the signal box at approximately four minutes past three, and you arrived at the house of Dr Freddie Forbes some two minutes later. Based on your description, it would seem you saw Mr Hicks alive and well, so what I'm wanting to know is whether you saw any other activity in the vicinity prior to entering Dr Forbes' house.'

Nancy stared unseeingly at the wall, as she cast about in her memory. Eventually, she responded, 'Once we were at the house, and Oliver had rung both bells, I was really only focused on the door, waiting for Freddie to open it and invite us in. I never looked around.'

Priestley nodded before turning to her husband. 'And does that apply to you as well, Mr Brownlow?'

He pushed his fingers through his hair. 'Yes, I suppose it does.' After a moment, he added, 'Though I did notice a black Range Rover going slowly, nearby.'

Priestley registered his interest with widened eyes. 'What can you tell me about that vehicle, sir?'

'Not very much, really. I couldn't see who was in it, because the windows were blacked out.'

'Would that be, blacked out at the sides? Could you see through the front or the back?'

'I think all the windows were the same; a really dark, smoky colour. Or maybe they were made of one-way glass, like you have in your interrogation rooms.'

Priestley was too pleased with the information not to offer a grateful smile, though he knew closed-circuit television had rendered such glass obsolete at his own station. 'Is there anything else at all you can remember about the vehicle, sir?'

'Sorry, no. Except it was new. The numbers were sixty-six. I don't recall the letters.'

Priestley maintained eye-contact, encouraging him to keep trying. When he finally looked away, Priestley sought him out again until he glanced back. 'If I could ask you to think about that number plate whenever you have an idle moment, it's possible you'll remember the letters. I know it isn't something that can be forced, but you might suddenly recall some or all of them, if they ever registered with you in the first place. I'll give you my contact details, and if you remember anything, anything at all, just give me a call.' He walked over, proffering a card. Oliver stood to receive it. Nancy and Lin rose in unison. 'We'll leave you to your rehearsal.'

Nancy responded, 'Oh, you heard us, then.'

Priestley smiled. 'Just briefly. Who's the pianist?'

She returned his smile. 'That would be me. Do you ever sing yourself, Chief Inspector?'

'I used to be in a choral society, but had to drop out because I couldn't be relied on for concerts; I'm often called away for work at short notice, you see.'

'In that case, you should consider joining our little group. What voice are you? Baritone, I would have thought, tending toward bass.'

'You're spot on, though I have occasionally been

known to stretch to tenor; only, it really is a stretch.'

'And how's your sight-reading? Let me audition you now. I'm sure I have some suitable pieces in my box.'

Priestley grinned. 'Perhaps I'll be in touch once the investigation is finished, but until then I'm obliged to limit my interaction with witnesses.'

'Well, you know where to find us.'

After amiable goodbyes, Priestley and Plummer returned to the car. She asked, 'What is it about you, that people always want to see you again?'

He put on a serious face. 'I suppose it's my charm, charisma, aura, personality, general attractiveness and devilish good looks.' He laughed. 'Only joking!'

She leaned forward to look at him more directly. 'Except it's all true, isn't it? And you forgot to mention intelligence and handsomeness.'

He shook his head. 'Beauty is in the eye of the beholder. I may be those things to you, Lin; but to other people, I'm just someone starting on the downhill path to decrepitude. Anyway, we really must press on; that Range Rover could be the lead we've been looking for. Let's try the people at the house opposite the signal box and see if we can jog someone's memory.'

They drove the short distance to the Thompson cottage. Seeing unbroken double yellow lines in the vicinity of the signal box, they squeezed into a small parking area off the road at the front of the property.

Priestley rang the bell. The door was opened by a stocky, muscular man with a dark five o'clock shadow. Following introductions, Priestley explained the reason for their visit. Danny Thompson inspected his warrant card, and invited them to follow him into the living room to meet his wife, Emily. They found her flicking through a magazine that lay open on her lap. After the two officers were seated together on the sofa, Danny began, 'I'll be no help to you; I was working on Christmas eve, fixing a problem at an electricity sub-station. Should I leave you to talk to Em on her own?'

Priestley replied, 'I'd like you to stay; I just have a few questions.' Danny settled into an armchair.

Emily dropped the magazine onto a table by her side, and sat up straight. 'Do you have any news about what happened?'

Priestley responded, 'It's early days, yet; but there is something I'd like to ask you about. Have you ever, at any time, seen a black Range Rover in this area? It may have had darkened windows made of smoked glass.' She shook her head. 'And you, Mr Thompson?'

He scratched his neck. 'Not as I remember.'

Priestley turned back to Emily. 'On Christmas eve, do you recall seeing anyone in the vicinity of the signal box between three o'clock and three fifteen?'

'Sorry, no. As I explained to the other officers, I was busy baking and looking after our boy, Alan.'

'Is it possible Alan saw anything?'

Emily and Danny exchanged glances. She replied, 'There's no point in asking him; he's autistic, you see.'

Danny responded abruptly to her. 'He's perfectly capable of doing lots of things, including looking out at what's happening. Just because he's got this label, you seem to think he can't do anything.'

She replied sharply to him, 'You don't see as much of him as I do, all day long through the holidays.'

Priestley knew there could be insights to be gleaned from listening to arguments, but felt this one would be unproductive. He asked Danny, 'What sort of autistic behaviour does your son display, Mr Thompson?'

Danny frowned as he considered the question for a few moments. 'He enjoys repetitive activities, and he counts just about anything. He looks for patterns, and he likes to do certain things in ways that only he can understand. Like when he's walking, if he accidentally treads on the join between two paving stones, he has to tread on more joins in some order involving his left and right feet, until he's completed the set; sometimes, that means he suddenly has to take a big jump to get over a join because it isn't in the sequence, which takes a bit of getting used to when you're simply walking along with him. And I can't hold his hand to keep him in check, because he doesn't like being touched.'

Priestley put his hand to his chin and pulled it, as though extruding a beard. 'Is it Asperger syndrome, by any chance?'

'Yes, that's what we've been told. Are you some sort of expert on this?'

'My wife's an expert; I suppose I've picked up some knowledge from talking to her. Would now be a good time to ask him if he saw anything?'

'I can fetch him, if you think it's alright for you to question him.'

'If you believe it's necessary, I could ask my wife to conduct the interview; she's a qualified psychiatrist. But perhaps we could just test the water, so to speak?'

'Alright, I'll get him.'

Danny returned with Alan four steps behind, and proceeded to introduce everyone to him in painstaking detail. He encouraged him to sit on his favourite high stool, incongruously positioned between two matching soft chairs. As Danny settled into the adjacent vacant seat, he nodded to Priestley as a sign he could begin.

Priestley looked over in the boy's direction, until it became clear he would refuse to meet his gaze. 'Alan, I want to ask you about something that happened on Christmas eve. First of all, could you tell me if you saw a big black car near the signal box at about three o'clock in the afternoon?'

The boy remained focused on the patterned carpet as he responded in a virtual monotone, 'What sort of car?'

'It's a type called a Range Rover.'

'A black Range Rover.'

'Yes, with dark windows. Did you see it?'

'Yes.'

'Where did you see it?'

'Across the road.'

'Would you recognise it if you saw it again?'

'Yes.'

'How would you recognise it.'

'By it's alphanumeric.'

'It's what, Alan?'

'What people call its number plate, but it isn't, because it doesn't just have numbers; it has letters as well. Computer programs use fields that can hold numbers and letters, and they're called alphanumeric.'

'Right. I see. So, what was its alphanumeric?' As Alan reeled off the seven characters, Priestley was relieved to hear "sixty-six" included within the index. He noticed Plummer was writing it down on a scrap of paper, rather than putting it in her police notebook.

Priestley asked Alan, who was maintaining his focus on the floor, 'Do you know anything about who was in the Range Rover?'

He glanced up for just a moment. 'Yes; lots.'

'Tell me everything you know, then.'

'He lives in Lapland. He has nine reindeer. He has only thirty-one hours every Christmas to deliver all the presents around the world.'

Priestley recognised the description but was puzzled by the time limit. 'Why thirty-one hours?'

'Because of the time zones.'

He made a mental note to check the answer later. 'Do you think Father Christmas was in the car?'

'I know Father Christmas was in the car, because I saw him get out of it. He was dressed in red and white with black boots, but he wasn't carrying a sack.'

'What did you do when you saw him?'

'I went to get my autograph book.'

'Did you get his autograph?'

'No.'

'Did you cross the road to his car?' He remained silent.

Emily spoke up. 'You know you're not supposed to cross the road, but it's alright if you did this time.'

Priestley signalled his appreciation to her, then asked again. 'Did you cross the road to the car?'

'Yes.'

'And what did you do then.'

'I wrote down the car's alphanumeric.'

'And then?'

'I opened the car door and picked up his iPhone and wrote down his phone number.'

He heard Emily's sharp intake of breath, and was relieved when she decided not to interrupt. 'Why did you do that, Alan?'

'So I can call him next Christmas before he sets off, to make sure he's bringing me what I want.'

'That makes sense. What did you do after that?'

'I wrote down some more data about his iPhone.'

'What data was that?'

'The Apple ID, the Carrier, the Serial Number, the IMEI and the ICCID.'

'Why did you write down all those things?'

'So that Stan could help me find out where Father Christmas goes when it isn't Christmas.'

'You mean Stan the railway signalman?'

'Yes.'

'Do you know him very well?'

'He was my friend.'

Priestley noted the past tense. Seeing how shocked Emily appeared, he repeatedly pressed the air under the splayed fingers of both hands to ask her to remain calm. 'Why do you think of him as a friend?' Receiving no response, he rephrased the question. 'What did he do that made him your friend?'

'He told me all about codes and numbers and how to write things down so nobody knows what they mean.'

'Did the two of you do anything together?'

'We did some encryption and decryption.'

Priestley raised an eyebrow on hearing the technical terms. 'Anything else?'

'He showed me how to use his iPhone; he was an expert on iPhones.'

'Anything else?'

'No.'

Priestley glanced at Emily and saw she now seemed slightly less worried.

'When you were at the car, why did you not stay until Father Christmas came back.'

'Mum called for me.' For a moment, Alan's gaze

swung in Priestley's direction, his eyelids flickering. 'Was Stan murdered?'

Priestley checked with Danny and received a nod of permission. 'It's possible, Alan; that's why we're here asking questions, to try to find out what happened.'

After a brief silence, Priestley asked, 'Alan, may I borrow your autograph book to see what you wrote?'

Danny stood up. 'We'll fetch it together, Al.'

Alan followed his father upstairs, four paces behind.

Emily explained, 'It's his prize possession. He keeps it in the gap next to a drawer, only I'm not supposed to know where it is. Sometimes it gets stuck, so I have to be careful when I'm putting his socks away.'

Alan followed Danny back into the living room and placed the book on his father's chair arm, before perching on his stool again. Danny picked up the book, opened it to the relevant page and handed it to Priestley, who looked at the first two entries; there were seven letters and numbers for the car, plus twelve numbers for the phone. After waiting for Danny to sit down, he asked, 'Alan, can you remember the phone number?'

The monotone response was immediate. 'Yes.'

'Tell me what it is.' He checked the reply against the book. 'Can you remember the other things you wrote.'

Again, there was no hesitation. 'Yes.'

Priestley looked through one of the entries, a twelve-character series of numbers and capital letters, trying unsuccessfully to recognise some significance. Then he glanced along a fifteen digit number that had been divided by three spaces into two, six, six and one, again without gaining any insight. Finally, he reviewed an unbroken series of nineteen digits, but discovered nothing meaningful. Based on Alan's earlier correct recollections, he saw no reason to doubt that the boy had committed them all to memory. Rather than risking upsetting him by taking the book away, he quickly photographed the page using his phone, before standing and returning it to Danny's chair arm.

Danny rose next, and then the two women. Alan stayed seated as he reached out and picked up the book. Priestley tried unsuccessfully to catch his eye. He tried again by bending low, and was rewarded with a brief glance. In a deeper voice, replete with gravitas, he explained, 'Alan, it's very important that you don't try to make contact with Father Christmas until I say you can. Will you promise me not to use his telephone number or any of the other data until I say it's alright?'

Danny prompted him. 'Mr Priestley needs you to promise, and you know you mustn't break promises.'

Alan responded, 'I promise.'

Priestley stood and addressed Alan's parents. 'I'm sure you recognise the potential significance of what has just happened here. Please make sure none of this conversation goes beyond these four walls.'

Danny thrust out a hand for Priestley to shake, and stated proudly, 'I knew Alan would be a star someday.'

Priestley turned to Emily. As he shook her hand, he held her gaze and smiled warmly. 'He really is a very special boy.' Seeing her eyes begin to water, he hastened to leave before they gushed into a cascade.

CHAPTER 14

As Priestley drove Plummer back to her flat, he offered an ungrammatical assessment of the investigation. 'It's starting to look like Father Christmas done it.'

She took a deep breath and blew the air out slowly. 'But who was wearing the costume?'

He glanced at her. 'What do you mean, costume? What if it was the real Father Christmas?'

She tittered. 'You do know there's no such thing?'

He gasped loudly. 'I'm shocked, Miss Plummer; you've just destroyed all my illusions.'

She chuckled. 'Someday, when you're all grown up, I'll tell you the truth about Father Christmas.'

They settled into a period of silence as they reflected on the facts of the case and the latest information. Finally, Priestley spoke gravely. 'I'm going to give the suspect Father Christmas the code name *Fish*.'

She nodded emphatically in mock-approval. 'Now the investigation is *really* moving forward.'

He turned for a moment to frown at her. 'It's a very good name. We are now on a fishing expedition. If he resists arrest, we'll batter him. And if he's extradited to Kentucky in the US, he'll fry like a chicken.'

She smiled briefly. 'Very funny, but shouldn't we be having a proper case review? I need to know where we're going from here.'

He glanced at her again, his face serious. '*We* are not going anywhere. *You* are going back to your flat. This is the point where you drop out.' Knowing she was staring at him, he kept facing forward to avoid eye contact.

Finally, she complained, 'It's not fair. Why am I being taken off the case?'

He turned and gave her a brief smile. 'I told you before, I'd do everything I could to protect you, and the best way I can do that is to terminate your involvement here and now.'

She tugged irritably at the seat belt, annoyed at it for restricting her squirming. 'Well, at least tell me where *you're* going with the case; I assume you've thought it through, and the joking earlier was just to soften me up, before you let me down gently.'

He nodded. 'That's very astute of you, Lin. Alright, I'll give you a run-through of how I see things panning out from here; but let's wait until we're back at your flat and I can focus my thoughts.'

As they entered the car park, he reflected on how the screeching gates seemed to have become a symbolic reminder of his infidelity. He asked himself, 'To oil or not to oil, that is the question.'

Inside, she pulled off her outdoor clothes and headed for the bedroom door. He called out, 'Hang on, Lin; I know there's a "discussions only in bed" rule, but I really wouldn't be able to concentrate, next to you.'

She heard the sincerity in his voice and changed direction. 'OK, but just this once.'

As she drew her legs up under her on the settee, he sat in a chair and half-closed his eyes to collect his thoughts. 'I appear to have two main routes for finding Fish: through the car index; or via his iPhone. If only I knew his password, I could log into the iCloud and trace where the phone is, providing it's turned on and has the "track" facility activated.'

She responded quickly, 'Don't we have experts for getting around password security?'

He shook his head. 'We have people who can bypass some security mechanisms, but to the best of my knowledge no UK police force has the ability to get into an iCloud account without knowing the password, even if they have the phone number. Maybe there are some hackers who could do it; I don't know.'

'So we can't find its location directly.'

'Not without the password. As to the phone itself, there may be information on it that could lead me directly to Fish. There's evidence to suggest the FBI knows how to search through the data if they have the physical phone. That raises two possible issues with trying that route: one, I don't know if they can do it remotely; and two, I'd be amazed if they'd let someone like me in on the secret. Again, if only I knew a hacker, perhaps they could help me trawl Fish's data.'

She smiled briefly to indicate she had seen the pun. 'I could work on tracking down a hacker. Or couldn't we just get Apple to help?'

'Do you remember in December twenty fifteen there was a terrorist attack in San Bernardino, California?'

'Only vaguely.'

'Well, two terrorists, a husband and wife, shot and killed fourteen innocent civilians, and seriously injured another twenty-two. They also tried to murder yet more with pipe bombs, which, fortunately, failed to explode. People over here might think Americans would be inured to the suffering of the victims and their families, what with all the mass shootings we hear about, but it was clear there was a deep sense of shock. I don't know if that was more because of the attempted bombing as well as the shootings, or down to the fact that one of the perpetrators had been born in the good old US of A. Anyway, in the aftermath, the FBI wanted to find out what was on an iPhone one of them used.'

'Ah, so that's the connection with our investigation.'

'Sort of. I'd be happy just to be able to track down our phone, whereas the FBI needed to know everything there was on theirs. They started out by asking the NSA to help, but they couldn't break the encryption. So they asked Apple, like you suggested I could do. Depending on who you believe, Apple either refused point blank, or gave them some ideas on how they might go about doing it for themselves. One mechanism Apple declined to countenance was creating a version of the operating system that was breakable; they argued their customers relied on the tight security for their own protection, and wouldn't want it undermined, so it would be bad for business. Anyway, it was heading for the courts, when the FBI suddenly withdrew their request. Most people assumed that meant they'd solved the problem. I seem to recall Apple then planned to take the FBI to court to force them to explain how they'd done it.'

'That's so ironic.'

'The boot was certainly on the other foot. I do remember talking to Tony about it at the time. He was speculating they might have somehow taken a bit-copy and recreated the entire device as a virtual machine, to avoid triggering the feature that wipes the data after ten failed attempts. Since then, he told me they may have exploited a weakness in Apple's software that made it vulnerable to bypassing the ten-try limitation, and that the FBI had employed some professional hackers to break the password security.'

'Alright, so I'll enquire about hackers.'

'Not so fast, Lin; there's the question of what would follow on from that. Let's say I could trick iCloud into allowing me access to the location finder; if he had GPS turned on, I'd then know where he is, but it could take a lot of travelling to get close to him. He could be in another part of the country, or even another country entirely. So I'd need to employ local resources if I'm to find him in real time, which would mean making other people aware of the investigation.'

'And I thought we'd had a major breakthrough with all that phone data the boy collected.'

'Well, some of it may still prove useful. Take the phone number itself, for example. If I had a suspect in close proximity and called the number, I'd know he was our man if he answered it. But I can't use that method to work through a long list of suspects. If Fish received too many wrong numbers or nuisance calls, he may realise the phone had been compromised, and ditch it.'

'At least it's a strategy we could adopt when we're fairly certain we know who Fish is.'

'True; but by then I'd expect the inquiry would have had to have been made official, in which case I could be employing other strategies, such as examining previous phone usage to give a picture of his recent movements. Network providers make a record of which mobile phone towers were active when a call's being made, though I'm told it doesn't necessarily work for iPhone texts. To find out where he is now, it ought to be possible to work with them to ping the phone remotely without it registering on the device, and to see which cell towers become active. If three towers can get a simultaneous distance and direction fix, they could use trilateration to triangulate the phone's location.'

'To define a triangular boundary for the search area.'

'Actually, it's the towers that make a triangle; the search area itself would be formed by three pairs of concentric arcs, where they intersect. The shape of the area would be dependent on the specific arcs, as you'll no doubt recall from your geometry lessons.'

'Damn! I should have paid more attention in class! And I was so sure I'd never need to know any geometry once I'd left school. Or algebra, for that matter.'

He sighed. 'You do disappoint me, Miss Plummer. Anyway, by repeated use of the method, I could whittle down the potential population pool for finding Fish.'

'So, is that the way we're going?'

'Probably not. A simpler route is to make a DVLA enquiry using the car index, either by phone or via the PNC. But queries are logged on the auditing system, making them visible to anyone who's monitoring the vehicle. There are several alternatives for obtaining the information covertly, such as utilising an online system trapdoor, or obtaining batch extracts or backup files to examine offline. Perhaps the most feasible option for me is to speak to a contact I made at that data security course I went on; an IT manager at the computer centre. I think I could probably persuade them to authorise a troubleshoot.'

'What's a troubleshoot?'

'It's when someone bypasses the user interfaces and goes directly to the raw data. Normally, it's used when a system has suffered corruption that can't be fixed using standard access routines, so a troubleshooter has to change any faulty bits manually. The regular audit reporting works off normal user activity, which is why all troubleshoots are supposed to be logged in writing, to complete the picture. Only, thinking about it, I don't believe it would be fair to ask my contact, because it could cost them their job if someone higher up found out and didn't accept the troubleshoot was justified.'

'You carefully avoided indicating the gender of your IT contact; so, who is she?'

Priestley grinned. 'No names, no pack drill.'

'Don't tell me, then. But couldn't we trace Fish by checking places that hire out Father Christmas outfits?'

'In theory, yes; if it was hired locally, we could hook him that way. I'm confident that Fish wasn't wearing any of the outfits used on the railway, so I'd have to check out every supplier on an expanding radius basis. I could strike lucky with an early hit, but if not, I'd be facing a mammoth task. Even so, it's a strategy that avoids having to break cover.'

'So, is that what we're going to start with?'

'You keep saying "we" and I keep saying "I". Don't you remember I said you're off the case?'

'You need all the help you can get.'

'Except I don't, because, talking it through with you, I've decided how to play it: I'm going to make an official enquiry on the vehicle. I don't know if the cover-up relates to the victim, or the perpetrator, or both. If the victim only, my index query shouldn't raise a red flag; but if the perpetrator, the warning bells will be ringing straight away. Either way, I'll have to wait and see what happens.'

'That sounds like watching a kettle and waiting for it to boil; it always takes forever. And yes, I know that's illogical, but it's still a well-known fact.'

He grimaced. 'Actually, it's called a factoid.'

He made the call from his work mobile, and was unsurprised to find the information had been blocked. 'The index has restricted access status.'

She smiled. 'I know what we could do while we're waiting for something to happen.'

He spat out, 'Yes; have the rest of the sandwiches.'

She made the coffees. After twenty minutes of chat that swung between speculation and small talk, he checked his watch. 'Well, it doesn't appear to have triggered an immediate reaction.' He picked up his rucksack and prepared to leave. 'I'm going back to give my status report to Helen.'

Her disappointment registered clearly on her face. 'Are you sure you don't want to stay a bit longer?'

He pecked her on each cheek, the innocent way he had seen French girls greet each other in the morning on their way to school. 'Now I want you to forget all about Fish and Operation Semaphore.'

She blocked his way to the door. 'You should let me make my own decisions; I want to stay involved. The least you can do is to keep me informed of progress. What about a review over here every morning at nine?'

He smiled. 'I can imagine the tangible benefits, but let me see how things move forward.'

When he arrived home, he picked up his rucksack and collected the envelope from the car boot. Inside, he explained to Helen, 'I've some evidence to review, and then I'll put you in the picture.' She took the rucksack from him and went into the kitchen. After checking on his children in the living room, he took the envelope to the dining room, extracted the calendar, and began to give each entry a thorough examination; he argued his behaviour was justified as he had missed out on this rite of passage when it had first been published.

As he turned over the leaf to where Miss October was revealed, Helen opened the door. She was behind him too quickly for him to cover her up. When she said nothing, he quickly flicked over to Misses November and December, before returning to Miss January.

She asked, icily, 'Have you finished examining your evidence, then? What's your excuse?'

He pointed to the head of the featured model. 'I met this woman today. It was a reasonably straightforward interview; I don't think she had anything to hide.'

'Well, she certainly doesn't look like the type to hide anything.' She quickly picked up the envelope, took the calendar off him and placed it inside. 'So, where does she fit into the investigation?'

'Well, she calls herself Jan, which she said was short for January, but maybe it's Janet or Jane or Jannifer.' Receiving no appreciation, he continued, 'Her husband was one of the two Father Christmases who were at the station; he used to be a rock star, apparently. Anyway, he's in the clear, as is the other one.'

'And the two on the train, obviously.'

'Obviously. After I'd said my fond farewells to Jan, I went and interviewed a couple who had walked past the signal box just before the incident, and the man recalled seeing a black Range Rover with dark tinted windows. So I tried the people who live opposite the signal box, and that's where I hit pure gold. Their boy saw a man, dressed as Father Christmas, step out of the Range Rover. He didn't see where he went, but he noticed he was wearing boots. You know the SOCOs found some boot marks on the steps, so my working assumption is, that's our man.'

'You said you interviewed various people, but you haven't mentioned Lin at all; wasn't she with you?'

'She was; I'm airbrushing her from my testimony. I did all the interviewing, to try to keep her out of things as much as possible in case there's an inquiry. In fact, once we'd had the breakthrough, I told her she's off the investigation, only she's insisting on staying involved.' He laughed. 'She's such an innocent! I couldn't help having a bit of fun with her about the calendar. When Jan was giving it to me, she snatched it away so that I couldn't look at it; she's quite a prude, at times. So I pretended I'd seen the whole thing before, when it first came out, and she fell for it completely.'

'You really shouldn't make fun of her like that; she's such a nice girl. So, where are you going to store that particular piece of so-called evidence?'

'The best place of all, in plain sight. I was thinking I'd hang it up in my bathroom.'

'Think again, Marcus; I can be as prudish as the next woman.' He quickly dismissed the thought that Helen wondered if Lin was indeed the next woman.

'Well, the garage, then; the children never go in there. And it does have a motor vehicle theme to it.'

'How about I hide it somewhere you can't find it?'

He jutted out his lower lip. 'You don't let me have any fun anymore.'

She stared at him. 'I don't know how you have the cheek to say that. Anyway, the investigation: you have to track down a Father Christmas who was driving a black Range Rover with tinted windows. It sounds like it could be a long job.'

He grinned. 'But that's where you're wrong. The boy has Asperger's, and under my expert interviewing he eventually revealed the car registration. Not only that, he also gave me the suspect's iPhone number and some other information about it.'

'You are so lucky, aren't you, Marcus Priestley!'

'Maybe I am, but it's an important part of being a DCI. You know what Napoleon used to say: I know he's a good general, but is he lucky?'

'He never did.'

'Are you sure? It's often quoted.'

'Yes, I am sure; he would have spoken in French.'

'*Touché*. Anyway, one important development in the case is that I've come up with a code name for the suspect. I'm calling him Fish.'

She frowned. 'Why "Fish"?'

'It makes sense. One man's fish is another man's *poisson*, and this case could *poisson* my career.'

'Your mind does seem to wander about a bit, doesn't it just? So, the vehicle registration number: when are you going to start the ball rolling?'

'If it were done when 'tis done, then 'twere well it were done.' She looked at him quizzically. 'So, just go and wash your hands again. And again. And again.'

She expressed her understanding with an 'Ah!'

'It came back blocked, which makes me wonder if someone is protecting the perpetrator, or maybe they're the subject of another inquiry. Anyway, I've certainly put the cat among the pigeons.'

'That doesn't exactly generate a pleasant image.'

'Especially if we're the pigeons.'

'How long ago did you make the call?'

'About an hour.'

'I'll do us something to eat straight away in case it kicks off this evening and you're called out.'

'Good idea, but not too much for me; I finished off those goose sandwiches at Lin's.'

The children were in bed long before the telephone rang just after nine o'clock. Helen took the call. 'Hello. … Yes, it is; how very nice to hear from you.' Marcus used hand signals to ask who was calling. She shooed him away. 'No, he isn't here right now, but if you've called to wish him a Merry Christmas, I'll be sure to pass it on. Or would it be a Happy New Year? We're between the two of course, so it could be either. Both would be nicest. I know he'll be delighted to hear you called. … Oh, there was something else? … I see. … Should I expect him to be away for long? Just so I can make plans for the children. … Right. … I'll let him know, and do pass on my best wishes to Maddy.'

Marcus watched to ensure she had disconnected the call, before he burst out, 'What were you up to?'

She gave him a two-handed sign to quieten down. 'The Chief Constable wishes to see you in the morning at eight thirty for a meeting that he anticipates, or at least hopes, will be brief.'

'So why didn't you just pass me the phone?'

'I thought if I came over as a chatterbox, he might reciprocate and let something slip that he wouldn't have divulged to you; but he didn't really give much away.'

'Well, I reckon the game's afoot. I'd better have an early night to make sure I'm alert in the morning.'

'I'll give you a good breakfast; condemned man, and all that. And something to help you sleep tonight.'

He tried his best to look enthusiastic, but was finding acceptance of so many offers from Helen and Lin had started to take its toll.

CHAPTER 15

Priestley noticed the unusual absence of any other staff in the vicinity, as he knocked on the unexpectedly open door of Chief Constable Charles Coker's office. He was surprised to see Coker quickly stand and walk toward him with a hand held forward for shaking.

Coker called out to him, 'Marcus, it's good to see you. Season's greetings. Come in and have a seat.'

Priestley thought Coker's smile looked more worried than welcoming. He stepped smartly into the office and responded with a simple 'Good morning, sir.'

After a normal handshake, Coker walked around him and closed the door. 'You're supposed to be on holiday, aren't you? We should be informal today, then; call me Charles. Let's have ourselves a cosy little chat.'

'That would be nice, Charles; about anything in particular?'

'Oh, this and that. As you know, I had the pleasure of speaking to your charming wife yesterday; she's such a bubbly young woman, intelligent and attractive. She has it all, hasn't she? And so do you, what with your career, and Helen and your two lovely children. I trust they're all in the pink?'

In the pink? 'Absolutely ripping, sir.' *Perhaps I just overdid it.* 'And you have the, erm, interesting Maddy, Charles; so you have it all, too, if I may say so.'

'Maddy? Yes, Maddy by name, Maddy by nature. She's as mad as a box of frogs, you know.'

Is he trying to be "modern", now? 'I've always

considered her to be fascinatingly original.'

'Well, that's a very pleasant way of thinking of her. Whereas Helen is always so, erm, reliable. Very logical sort of woman, I've always found.'

Having only met her twice! 'Yes, I think I can say Helen is definitely logical.'

'So, what would Helen think if she thought you were risking everything you have by going on some wild goose chase? Logically, she'd say it makes no sense. Do you see what I mean, Marcus?'

'Yes, Charles; she'd say it would be illogical to go on a wild goose chase.'

'Well, I'm glad we've got that sorted. So, I suggest you go back home and enjoy the day with your lovely family, and don't give work another thought.'

'I'll be off, then; once I'm clear on what it is we've just sorted.'

'This tomfoolery; you know.'

'I wasn't aware of a jewellery heist.'

'No, no, not that type of tomfoolery. Do I have to spell it out?'

'I'm afraid you do, Charles. I'm obviously slow on the uptake this morning; I think it must be all that holiday spirit I've been enjoying.'

'Well, you know the chap from London who died. Why shouldn't the Met take him back home? Hmm?'

'When you put it like that, it makes complete sense that he should have his funeral back there.'

'Yes, I knew you'd see it the right way. So that's why the case it out of our hands.'

'With respect, Charles, that only explains why his body should have been taken back eventually; it doesn't really appear to justify the case going south as well.'

'I know exactly what you mean; it's our case and we can do a good job of investigating it. No, an excellent job; you always do an excellent job, Marcus. That's why I can see you progressing to the very top… so long as you don't let some little case mess it up for you along the way. Just like you don't want to mess up everything else you have; your wife, your family… Only, as you operate higher and higher, up the chain of command, you have to become increasingly pragmatic, as you'll no doubt discover for yourself in due course. And that's what the Hicks case needs, a big healthy spoonful of pragmatism.'

'Well, I certainly believe in pragmatism.'

'Good. Marvellous. So you'll not be making any further enquiries into it.'

'There's just one little problem with that, if I might explain. I'm aware the autopsy claimed the death was accidental, but I know it wasn't. I can't permit the Met to cover it up; I have to answer to a higher authority.'

'Oh, god, no, Marcus; you haven't caught religion, have you?'

'Sorry, I didn't mean that higher authority; I meant Helen. She examined the body at the scene and was certain it wasn't an accident, so now she's insisting I pursue the case to prove her right. It's as you say, I'm lucky to have her; and logically, in a pragmatic way, that means I really have to do as she wishes so as not to risk losing her.' *Try worming your way around that argument!*

Coker hesitated before responding, 'Alright, Marcus, I'll contact my own higher authority and run this by them. Go to your office and wait; and don't do anything until I say you can. Is that clear?'

Priestley thought he had glimpsed a heavy weariness in Coker's eyes. 'Yes, Charles; perfectly clear.'

His voice hardened. 'Try that again, DCI Priestley.'

'Yes, sir; perfectly clear.'

Priestley had only a few minutes to wait before his telephone rang. 'I've been speaking to a Mr Brown who would like to talk to you; he has something important to say. I'm putting you through now.'

The voice on the telephone sounded to Priestley like a tenor straining to reach a high note. 'Good morning DCI Priestley; this is Mr Brown speaking on behalf of the intelligence services.'

'Good morning, Mr Brown; what can I do for you?'

'You can drop your investigation into the death of Stanley Hicks; that's what you can do for me.'

'Much as I'd like to accommodate anyone from the intelligence services, I don't know you from Adam, so how do I know you are who you say you are?'

'I've just been put through to you by your own Chief Constable; what more do you need?'

'I may be only a simple copper, Mr Brown, but I always check everything thoroughly. That's what we plodders do, you see.' He heard an exasperated sigh.

'Right, Mr Priestley; get yourself down to London for a meeting straight away.'

'Would that be at Babylon-on-Thames, by any chance? Or maybe Thames House?'

'Neither. Get to Bruton Street for one o'clock; if you get lost, you can always ask a policeman. And then call this number.' He read it out condescendingly slowly. 'Have you got that, or do I need to repeat it?'

'I have it, Mr Brown. I'll just check with the Chief Constable that he approves of our having a meeting. If he's happy with it, I'll see you this afternoon. May I ask if there will be anyone else present?'

'You can ask all you like.' The line went dead.

Priestley went to Coker's office and found the door closed; he knocked and was kept waiting for the regulation six seconds. When Coker called out, 'Yes?' Priestley opened the door and stepped inside. Coker held up a hand to stop him. 'Close the door, first.'

Priestley complied, before walking to Coker's desk. 'Your Mr Brown has asked me to go to London for a one o'clock meeting.'

Coker nodded. 'You'd better be going, then; you wouldn't want to be late. I'm not sure how reliable the trains will be today; have yourself driven down, give yourself time to think about what I've said.'

When Coker dismissed him by staring at the papers on his desk and raising his pen, Priestley noticed the top sheet was simply an old circular no longer needing his attention; he found himself feeling sorry for his boss, recognising he was feeling pressure from on high.

Priestley eased himself into the back of the liveried BMW, before looking over at traffic pursuit officer Vardy behind the wheel. 'Hi Craig. I'd have driven myself, but I need to get my thoughts together.'

'Big meeting is it, then?'

'I really couldn't say.'

'Shall I put the blue light on?'

'I'm sure we'll be in plenty of time.'

'Are you certain? This Beamer's ever so quick, but I can't really go above seventy, without.'

Priestley heard the disappointment in Vardy's voice. 'Sorry, Craig; maybe next time.'

Priestley looked out of the window, feeling lost to be

carrying none of the usual paraphernalia. As there was no official investigation, there were no files needing to be carried in a briefcase. Neither was there a laptop, as there was nothing to be retrieved from it. He had just his work and personal mobile phones to hug in his pockets for reassurance.

After the one comfort break and a bite to eat, they were approaching Bruton Street in good time, with Priestley now in the front passenger seat. Vardy asked, 'What's the exact address?'

Priestley took out his work phone. 'I have to ring to find out.' He dialled the number. The call was answered immediately by the same strangulated tenor as had spoken earlier.

'Where are you?'

'Ten minutes from Bruton Street.' Vardy raised one finger to indicate they were only a minute away.

'Plug in this postcode and number.'

When they were approaching the final turn, Priestley pointed to the near side of the road. 'Drop me off here, will you, Craig? I'd like to do this last part on foot. I'll call you when I'm ready to go back, always assuming they let me leave.'

Priestley walked around the corner and along the opposite side of the road to the glass-fronted building advertising "Business Lounge Meeting Rooms". After passing it by, he stopped to look at its reflection in the window of an art gallery, quickly finding the perfect angle for observing anyone coming or going. For nine minutes, he shuffled along the window to face other paintings, all the time retaining his view of the target building. By the time it was almost one o'clock, the only activity had been six people entering in pairs: two men in black suits; two women in overcoats, one of green tweed, the other navy blue; and a heavily built man in a grey greatcoat, accompanied by a towering woman in a tan trench coat. He crossed the road and passed through the revolving door. Before he had reached the reception desk, a man touched his arm. 'Marcus, I'm so glad you finally decided to join us.'

As they shook hands, Marcus asked, 'And you are?'

'Mr Blue; I'll also be attending the meeting that Mr Brown has arranged, but I thought I'd like to have a pre-meeting meeting with you to check the lie of the land. Let's take the stairs.' He led the way past the lifts and pushed open a swing-door.

When Priestley began to take the steps at his usual pace, Blue spoke quietly to him. 'Marcus, let's go very, very slowly, if you don't mind. Have you identified the killer, yet?'

Priestley stopped entirely. 'I'm hoping to be the one who is given information, not the one who is asked to divulge details of any investigation, real or imagined.'

Blue nodded in appreciation. 'Good answer, Marcus. The meeting will consist of myself, two cousins from across the pond, and Mr Brown. If you take my advice, you won't tell them anything; but at the same time, try not to antagonise them by suggesting you're holding something back. Now, we'd better carry on, otherwise Mr Brown might suspect I've waylaid you for my own sinister purposes, and that would never do.'

Blue led the way to a small room packed with two settees and four matching chairs. They approached the three people standing together in a huddle. 'Gentlemen, lady, this is Marcus. Marcus, meet Pamela, Brett, and Mr Brown with whom you spoke earlier today.'

Pamela was the first to respond. 'Hello, Marcus; I'm so pleased to meet you.' The statuesque woman held her arm so far out, he wondered whether she expected him to kiss her hand. He took it gently to shake it, only to have his fingers crushed in her vice-like grip.

After overtly contemplating his released hand, he smiled at her. 'The pleasure is all mine, Pamela.'

Brett was the next in line. 'Howdy.'

Priestley thought his brief greeting sounded too clichéd to be real. He immediately formed an opinion. *A wholesome American with a little too much flesh in his cheeks and jowls, as though mom had always allowed him an extra scoop of ice cream on his home-made apple pie.* 'It's good to meet you, Brett.'

Brown held out a begrudging hand. 'Marcus.'

'And do you have a first name yourself, Mr Brown?'

He eventually offered, 'Call me David.'

Blue added, 'And call me Ben.'

Pamela and Brett settled onto one settee, Marcus on the other, facing them. David and Ben chose chairs where Marcus could hardly see them. From behind his left ear, David began, 'Now, Marcus, you've obviously been very industrious, for which of course you should be congratulated; but we'll be taking over from here, once you've given us a comprehensive briefing on what you have discovered so far.'

Priestley stood and moved to a chair from which he could see everyone. As he resettled himself, he gave a satisfied sigh. 'Ah, that's better; let's start again. David, you obviously have some knowledge relating to the death of a Mr Stanley Hicks; it's your legal duty to disclose that information, otherwise I may have to arrest you for withholding evidence.'

Brown jumped to his feet. 'Look, you cretin, there are matters of national security involved here. Now, just tell us what you know.'

Priestley stood and stretched himself to his full height, which was a good nine inches more than Brown. 'My understanding of the British legal system leads me to believe the police are obligated to hold the entire nation to account, with the possible exception of the Queen; members of the intelligence community do not have the right to ride roughshod over people's hard-won freedoms and democratic rights.'

Blue spoke quietly from his chair. 'Perhaps we could explain the situation to Marcus, so that he can form his own opinion of the way we should proceed.'

Brett stood and walked to an internal telephone. 'I reckon we need a powwow; let's order some food and chew the fat.'

Pamela spoke authoritatively, 'I agree.' She looked over to David. 'Don't worry, I'll be picking up the tab, as per usual. You British and your budgets!'

Brett dialled a two-digit number. 'Bring us a bottle of... hold on a minute.' He turned to the various occupants. 'Bourbon alright for everyone? Apart from water for Pammie.'

Priestley sensed a tactical opportunity. 'That sounds great, Brett; if we're *all* drinking.'

Pamela read his move and turned to Brett. 'Me too; what the hell.' She exchanged a sly smile with Marcus.

Brett again addressed the telephone. 'A bottle of bourbon and some finger-lickin' food for five.'

The victuals were delivered in minutes, as though someone had been waiting in readiness. While the others each collected a few assorted sandwiches, Brett poured and distributed five large glasses of bourbon, before adding a pile of chicken drumsticks to his personal mountain of beef sandwiches.

To set a precedent, Marcus ostentatiously raised his glass to Pamela and drained half the contents; she winked at him before doing likewise, then stared in turn at David and Ben until they drank half of their own. Marcus felt he had won a small battle, and perhaps gained an ally. Brett emptied his glass, then picked up the bottle to refill it, before topping up everyone else's.

After finishing his final sandwich, Ben put down his glass and cleared his throat to attract attention. 'Before I say anything about the purpose of our meeting, I need your signature on this.' He passed him a form relating to the Official Secrets Act. Priestley saw that his details had already been entered in block capitals; he gave it no more than a glance, before signing it.

David spoke through clenched teeth. 'There's no time limit on it; are you aware you already signed a copy, and that it's still legally binding?'

Marcus pretended to look surprised. 'I do recall, yes. I thought maybe it's like tetanus shots; you have to get a ten-year booster.'

Ben laughed. 'I'm starting to warm to you, Marcus; you're a bit of a rebel, aren't you. Well, I'll kick off with some background. Stanley Hicks was employed at GCHQ as a cryptographer. I can see no valid reason for giving you all the details of his work, so let it suffice to say that our American friends were grateful to him for helping them overcome a technological barrier that was restricting their investigation into the activity of two terminated terrorists.'

Brett punched the air ahead of him. 'Stan worked out

how we can bite into an apple.' He laughed loudly in appreciation of his own witticism.

Ben continued, 'He advised on various projects over many years, so you can appreciate how concerned we all were to learn he had been assassinated. Being a loyal servant of the Crown, he had deserved to live out his old age in peace and tranquillity.'

After a long silence, Marcus accepted they were waiting for his contribution. 'What I don't understand is, assuming you'd like to track down the assassin and bring him to justice, why have you taken steps to cover up the killing?'

David responded immediately. 'This investigation is best conducted by people in London who have all the right knowledge and contacts; it isn't something that can be left to a regional police force from up north.'

Marcus nodded repeatedly. 'I can imagine how some people from down south might think that.' He added as an aside to Pamela, 'Despite our superior clear-up rate for major crime.' He winked at her, before turning back to David. 'By rigging the autopsy to mislead an inquest into concluding the death was accidental, you would be blocking the police from acting, as there would be no underlying criminal offence. So, how do you see the assassination being investigated?'

David shook his head. 'We have our ways. What I'd like from you, in the spirit of co-operation, is all the information you have obtained so far, that might help us to track him down.'

Marcus knew they already had the car registration, so decided to use it to appear helpful. 'We had an untraceable, anonymous tip about a car that was parked in the vicinity, so we made a system inquiry.'

David responded, 'And it raised a red flag with us, because we'd been monitoring activity on that vehicle.'

Marcus asked him, 'So, who does it belong to?'

Brett growled, 'Some damn Russkie.'

Priestley turned to him. 'But it couldn't have been someone with diplomatic immunity, could it. I mean, the registration wasn't the standard type for the Russian embassy: three numbers, D for Diplomat or X for other staff, and another three numbers.'

Ben commented, 'Some like personalised numbers as well. But you're right; it wasn't an embassy official.'

Marcus continued, 'Accepting that we all want the killer brought to justice, I still don't get why there's this cover-up; I mean, what's to be gained by it?'

The room fell silent. Eventually, David spoke up. 'My predecessor instigated it.'

Ben responded, 'That's rather misleading, David. Mr Green only sought to control the flow of information. And he was not your predecessor, inasmuch as you have not inherited his position.'

David snapped back, 'Not yet.'

Marcus addressed them all in turn. 'As there's no good reason to continue any cover-up, I propose that, whichever of you has the authority, should rescind the earlier actions, arrange a second autopsy which would reach the correct conclusion, and ensure the coroner is permitted to do his job without being fed lies. Then, the police would do their job and identify the perpetrator. If the killer is beyond British jurisdiction, that would be the time when people such as yourselves could take on responsibility for pursuing the case to an appropriate conclusion. Do we all agree?'

Pamela answered swiftly. 'Agreed.'

Brett weighed in without hesitation. 'Agreed.'

Ben reflected for a moment. 'Yes, agreed.'

David shook his head. 'No, I can't agree to that. It would make the service look bad, people knowing we'd failed to take care of one of our own after he'd retired to rural England.'

Marcus responded, 'It isn't that rural, you know.'

David quickly rose to his feet. 'Thank you all for your input to the meeting, but I'm going to have to call a halt right there.' He went to the door and opened it. 'Marcus, this is where you say goodbye.'

As Marcus stood and prepared to leave, Pamela jumped up and held out her hand. Remembering the earlier crush, he prepared himself better, but had to alter his grip when he realised she was surreptitiously slipping him something small. He was taken aback when she pressed her cheek against his, and whispered in his ear, 'Don't be a stranger.'

Brett walked over and punched him on the shoulder. 'Adios, amigo.'

Ben went to the door. 'I'll see you out, Marcus.'

After a perfunctory goodbye to David, without a handshake, Marcus followed Ben out of the room and took the opportunity to deposit the unknown contents of his right hand into his trouser pocket. Ben stopped and turned for a moment. 'Put this one in a different pocket, so you don't get them mixed up.'

Marcus looked at the tiny, flat package. 'What is it?'

'A SIM card. Get yourself a disposable phone, put it in and give me a call on the number I've listed. Then we can have a proper talk. Pamela will be expecting the same, but it's best if you speak to me first.'

After Ben had escorted him out and returned inside,

Marcus strolled aimlessly around Mayfair for a while, before window-shopping for women's lingerie on New Bond Street. As he imagined first Helen, then Lin, wearing the various skimpy items, he found he was unable to decide which would look the better in them, so gave up and chose nothing for either.

Eventually, he decided to call Ben, so headed away from the area and found a shop where he could buy an inexpensive smartphone. It came in a bulky box, with a booklet of instructions and other papers, along with a charger and various wires. He extracted the mobile and decanted the remaining contents into the store's bag, which he thrust deep into his overcoat pocket, the charger's prongs facing upward to protect the lining.

Feeling slightly grubby for having allowed himself to be drawn into their murky world of intrigue and subterfuge, he remembered he was himself already inhabiting such a world.

CHAPTER 16

Marcus sat on a bench by a small island of grass, just sufficiently distanced from the constant hum of London traffic to be confident of hearing clearly. He swapped out the SIM card in the new smartphone and found the replacement had five pounds loaded onto it. When he called the specified number, Ben answered, 'Yes?'

Marcus began, 'You asked me to phone you.'

Ben responded, 'I'll call you back in five minutes.'

Marcus looked at his watch and calculated when he might receive a call-back. Six minutes later, as he was staring out a pigeon, the phone buzzed like an angry bee. He accepted the call and answered, 'Yes?'

'Come for another meeting, now; I'm sending you the address.' The call terminated.

As Marcus walked to the nearest tube station, he called Vardy from his work phone. 'Hi, Craig. It looks like I might be here for quite a while; I don't want to waste your time, so do you want to get off?'

'I'm filling my time productively, boss; if it's alright with you, I'll stay.'

Priestley knew better than to ask for details of what constituted productive time. 'Well, if you're sure; but I'll be at least another hour, and probably a lot more.'

He took the tube to what he knew professionally was a Red Light District. When he emerged into the pale afternoon light, an attractive young woman approached him, brazenly under-dressed. 'Would you like to come with me?' His mouth fell open but no words emerged.

To clarify the situation, she half-whispered, 'Mister M dot P dot.'

He found himself flushing, despite the cold. 'Ah, you're the welcoming committee.'

She pointed up the road. 'We're going to that hotel over there. You'd better link arms with me.' As they walked together, tightly bound, he thought her perfume smelled far too expensive to be right for someone of her supposed profession operating in this vicinity.

She ignored the man at the reception desk as she picked up the key he had placed there when she had entered the shabby lobby. Marcus walked with her to the lift, arms still linked. Once inside, she shrugged him off. 'Ben is waiting for you.'

As the lift rattled to the second floor, he asked, 'Do you, erm... Are you, erm... Do you come here often?'

The lift opened and she walked quickly to the furthest room in her impossibly high heels. Without knocking, she walked in and held the door open. Marcus entered and saw Ben standing close enough to the edge of the window to look down without being visible to the outside world. 'Come in Ruth, Marcus.'

She sat herself on the bed and addressed Ben. 'Your guest thinks I might be on the game.'

Ben smiled. 'Well, you are very convincing.'

Marcus turned to her. 'Actually, there was one thing that gave you away.'

She frowned at him. 'Really? Or are you just being mean because I fooled you?'

He smiled at her. 'Ruth, if that's your name, if you're supposed to be working this end of the market, you really shouldn't be wearing that lovely perfume.'

She put her hand to her face, as though to smell

herself better. 'Damn!' She turned to Ben, who was now sitting in one of the two chairs. 'Your man's good at sniffing women; I have to give him that.'

Marcus sat in the remaining chair. 'So, what's it all about? A bit of plain speaking wouldn't go amiss.'

Ben interlaced his fingers at chin height. 'My section chief is a Mr Green, who is currently suspended for failing to provide Mr Hicks with adequate protection. Mr Brown is as keen as mustard to take over from him, whereas I would be by far the better man. Now, I can understand why Green may have wanted the liquidation hushed up, but the only reason I can see for Brown continuing with the charade is that he has been tipped the wink he'll be rewarded if he can keep the section looking clean. I, on the other hand, may well benefit if Brown fails. Consequently, I would like to see the case investigated thoroughly, and the killer to be identified.'

'So that Brown looks bad and you get promoted.'

'In a nutshell, yes. Now, is that a sufficiently cynical explanation, for you to accept its veracity.'

'I'd say you've taken cynicism to a whole new level. But our objectives coincide, so we're on the same team. Can you now give me information on the assassin?'

'Some, but perhaps less than you were hoping for. The vehicle has often been seen entering the Russian embassy at Kensington Palace Gardens, but there have been several different drivers, and none of those seem to fit the bill. Checking records for the twenty-fourth of December, none of the staff covered by diplomatic immunity appear to have been unaccounted for, so it would seem the assassin works for the Russians but isn't officially on their books. Now, what I need is someone who can go blundering about and kick the hornet's nest, while we watch and see who reacts. At the same time, that person has to be someone who is not directly associated with the intelligence services, to afford us plausible deniability.'

'And of course, I'm expendable.'

'Well done! This cynicism thing isn't so difficult after all, is it?'

Marcus sighed. 'With so much honesty from you, I'm starting to think you must be lying through your teeth. Cynically speaking.'

'Excellent! Now you're really getting the hang of it. So, are you the man I think you are?'

'If you mean am I a blundering copper who'll take all the flak while you sit back and watch the show? Absolutely. Bring it on.'

'And now I know *you're* lying. I've checked you out and I know you possess a razor-sharp mind. But how do you wish to proceed? I'm afraid the autopsy finding is somewhat problematic; any opportunity for a second post-mortem has now gone, along with the corpse.'

Marcus shuddered at the thought of Helen's threat of contacting the coroner, which would expose her to any number of dangers from both the Russians and the British. 'I need some time to think.'

'I would expect no less of you. Contact me again when you know what you want to do and how I can help. Now, I need to go; you will please stay here with Ruth for half an hour to maintain her cover.' He picked up his coat. 'When you leave, you should use the rear service entrance, as though wishing for anonymity.'

Ruth went and sat in the vacated chair. 'I know your first name is Marcus, but I don't know your surname. We could play a guessing game, if you like? See if I can guess your surname, which begins with a P, and you have to try not to let me know if I get it right.'

He decided to try a mind game of his own. 'I've a better idea. I saw from your reaction to my comment about scent that you're aiming to be the consummate professional, and that you'd do anything to improve your performance. You were trying to act like you're a prostitute, but my guess is, you've never actually sold your body for money; so, if you want to learn how to be more convincing... Call it "on the job training". I've a tenner in my wallet and a couple of quid in my pocket, to make it authentic. Hmm? What do you say?' He watched her wrestle with how to respond.

Finally, her laughter burst out. 'I wasn't sure about the idea of recruiting you, but I can see you have hidden depths. Only, do tread carefully; this isn't a game.'

He smiled. 'And you need to be careful as well, Ruth; there's something else that isn't authentic about this rôle you're playing.'

Deep concern registered on her face. 'What is it?'

He pointed to the bed. 'When we leave here, this needs to look like it's had two highly active occupants; otherwise, the maid will know it wasn't really used.'

She laughed again. 'And you're willing to do your part to ensure authenticity?'

He shrugged. 'If a job's worth doing, it's worth doing well. I'm fully prepared to put my back into it.'

She shook her head. 'It isn't something I've been trained for.'

He smiled. 'Well, we need to do something to pass the time. Perhaps we should play "I Spy"?'

She giggled. 'I spy, with my little eye, something beginning with WMD.'

An hour later, Ruth's phone rang. She put a finger to her lips and mouthed 'Shush', before answering, 'Yes?'

Ben responded, 'When you're finished with our new friend, would you mind coming back to the office?'

She gulped. 'I'll be right there.'

When she had terminated the call, Marcus asked, 'Not Ben, was it? Wanting you for a debriefing?'

She flushed. 'I'd better freshen up before I go. Could you stay a quarter of an hour on your own when I'm done, and then leave by the back way?'

He smiled. 'Sure. All the towels need to look used, and I've time for a shower, even if you haven't.'

'Oh, right; you're better at this than I am.' A few minutes later, she emerged from the bathroom. 'You will look me up, won't you?' She dashed out without waiting for a response, taking the room key with her.

After his shower, he swapped Ben's SIM card for Pamela's, noting it had fifty pounds loaded. 'Hi there; you asked me to call.'

'Yes; I'd like a one-to-one with you.'

'Ah, thereby confirming my initial suspicion you're a honeypot.'

She shrieked with laughter down the phone. 'I'm not trying to trap you; I just want you to know all the facts.'

'You want to lay everything bare for me.' He thought her shrieking this time was less spontaneous.

After her laughter had subsided, she asked, 'Will you come and see me at the embassy?'

'It would be a pleasure. Right away?'

'Yes. Ask for Pamela Fairfax.'

Knowing he would have no easy way to re-enter the room without a key, he double-checked that he was leaving no tell-tale signs of his visit.

Before catching the tube to Marble Arch, he used his work phone to call Craig. 'I'm probably going to be another hour at the very least.'

The response was immediate. 'Fantastic! Don't hurry on my behalf, boss.'

'You still being productive?'

'Absolutely!'

After changing at Notting Hill Gate, he took the Central Line and emerged at Oxford Street, then turned onto Park Lane. As an open-topped sightseeing bus passed him with just a few hardy souls bearing the cold on the upper deck, he thought he also would be taken for a tourist as he looked around at the sights.

He plugged "W1A 2LQ" into the location finder on his old, personal smartphone, and headed for the US Embassy. Circling in, he looked up at the gilded Bald Eagle with the Stars and Stripes waving behind.

When he approached the security checkpoint, he wondered how they would react to his having three mobile phones, but found no one batted an eyelid as they took them off him. The name "Pamela Fairfax" did nothing to curtail his thorough examination, though he noticed she suddenly appeared and was now waiting for him to be allowed through.

He thrust out his hand to shake, but she brushed it aside and held his shoulders as she kissed his cheek while pressing against him. 'Marcus, it's great to see you again. Call me Pammie; everyone does, bar stiff-assed Brits, and I'm sure you're not one of those.'

'I do come over a little stiff, sometimes.'

'Really! Well, anyway, I'm glad you came.'

'How could I resist an invitation from a honeypot who's keen to lay everything bare for me.'

She almost suppressed her giggle. 'I'm not really in that line of work, you know; not personally.'

'That's a pity; I was fully prepared to try to resist being seduced by you… and to fail.'

She smiled. 'You're very different to the people I normally work with; nowadays, they're all so afraid of saying something Politically Incorrect, they don't risk being familiar with me. I have associates who daren't even smile in my direction, just in case I don't like it.'

'Well, I'll keep smiling to make up for them.'

'Great. Now, to business; come with me.'

The room had no windows, but the air-conditioning kept it both warm and fresh. Marcus counted twelve chairs around the table. 'Will anyone be joining us?'

She smiled and pointed to a corner of the room. 'Don't you go imagining I need a chaperone; we're under constant surveillance. So, how was your meeting with Ben? Not as enjoyable as your follow-up meeting with the sweet young Ruth, I imagine.'

He felt his jaw stiffen. 'I thought you were going to give me the inside story on Stanley Hicks.'

'Don't worry; I'm not out to blackmail you. First of all, I think it would make sense for me to know what you've already been told.'

'Right. Ben didn't know much, except the assassin's car had been seen at the Russian embassy.'

'That's about all we know, too.'

'And my follow-up meeting with Ruth was entirely concerned with tricks of the trade and how to behave professionally when under cover.'

'Sure thing, Marcus; I'm not one for dishing the dirt. So, what else can you tell me about your investigation?'

He gave her a dissembling smile as he considered

whether to reveal more information. 'Was Brett hinting that you know how to hack iPhones?'

She frowned. 'He is sometimes a bit loose with his chat, but only in the right company. In fact, there are some models that are easier to hack than others.' She looked thoughtful. 'I can see it in your eyes there's something else you want to tell me.'

He doubted his eyes had been quite so revealing, rather believing his question had offered a strong hint. 'If I were to give you a mobile phone number, could you use it to track someone?'

'Yes; but so could you.'

'The difficulty is, with no official case, authorisation to use cell-site technology is somewhat problematical.'

'I'm sure I could find a way to authorise it, if no one worries about jurisdiction. But you asked about hacking an iPhone; come on, spill the beans.'

'I have some details of the hit-man's iPhone.'

'Let me have them and I'll see what we can do.'

He gave her a handwritten list of data items and their values, and then stared her in the eye. 'Now, Pammie, tell me why you want me to find the Russian; what do you really want?'

She locked onto his gaze. 'I've seen the unofficial report; Hicks was killed instantly. That's unusual in this type of case; normally, someone is wanting to know what someone else knows, so first they incentivise them to answer their questions, which can take some time. I want to know what the Russian's motive was.'

'Why would that matter to you?'

'It isn't personal; I never even met the vic. If the killer already knew what Hicks knew, then there must be a leak somewhere, and that's what I need to find out.

If it isn't plugged, it could put future operations at risk. But asking your guys about a leak is like asking an illusionist how he makes the tigers disappear.'

'What if he was assassinated simply because he'd previously been working against Russian interests?'

'None of us do payback without a good reason; once he was out of the game, it would just be a waste of time and effort to terminate him. That is, unless they wanted to stop him from talking in the future. But they didn't ask him any questions, which brings me back to my belief that there's a mole somewhere. I know Green is suspended, but I don't believe it was for leaking intel.'

Marcus nodded his acceptance of her explanation. 'Thanks for the straight-talking, Pammie. If there is a mole, and your reasoning suggests there is, then the British need to know, too. So, that ties it up. The next step for me is how I track down the assassin.'

'I'll give you what help I can, short of making it official; you Brits get very upset if you think we're working your side of the street. But if I have to, I'll deny all knowledge of you; that's the way it has to be. Sorry, Marcus.'

'That's alright, Pammie; I understand.'

'So, you're good to go?'

'Certainly; for the good of the nation. Queen and country, and all that.'

'What about yourself? What will you be getting out of it? You'll be taking all the risks, but getting none of the rewards.' He smiled and shrugged. She winked. 'Hey, I just thought of a reward I could give you.' He guessed what it might be. 'Let's hook up when this is all over.'

CHAPTER 17

When Priestley had had his mobile phones returned, he walked away from the embassy and called Vardy. 'Hi, Craig; I'm finished for the day. Could you pick me up in ten minutes from where you dropped me earlier?'

'Yes, boss; that's perfect timing for me.'

Priestley watched as the car drew up alongside him. He looked into the back and saw a mountain of bags bearing famous department store names. As he slipped into the front seat, he asked, 'Is this what you call being productive?'

Vardy grinned. 'It was too good an opportunity to miss; they're all having sales. Didn't you find the time to pick up a present or two, yourself? Won't your missus be expecting something?'

He instinctively felt for his new phone. 'I've been too busy; just one meeting after another.'

'Do you want me to take you somewhere now, then? They're all open 'til late.'

He sighed wearily. 'No, thanks; I could just do with getting home.'

'OK; so, shall I put the light on?'

'Not yet; I'll think about it.'

When they stopped at a service station on the M1, Vardy looked at his pile of presents. 'I'll stay with the car while you get yourself something, if that's OK?'

Priestley glanced into the back to show he had understood. 'I'll not be too long.'

After guiltily bolting a burger and chips, knowing

Helen would disapprove of his choice, he returned to the car. 'You go and get yourself something, now; I've a few private calls to make, so no need to hurry.'

His first call was to Helen. 'Hi, love; I'm on the M1, at a service station.' Believing the best policy was to admit to a sin from a distance, he continued, 'I've just had a healthy snack.'

'Was it a cheeseburger?'

'And chips.'

'You know it isn't good for you.'

'There are worse things.'

'I suppose. How long will you be?'

'At least a couple of hours.'

'They'll be in bed before you're back.' Knowing not to speak openly of Fish or Operation Semaphore, she asked obliquely, 'Any sign of our slippery customer?'

'Not yet, but I've had some offers of help.'

'So, a good day, would you say?'

'Yes, I'd say so.'

'Well, drive carefully.'

'I'm not doing the driving; our top speed merchant is at the wheel.'

'Then tell Craig to drive carefully.'

'He's always careful. See you later.'

He took out his new smartphone and called Pamela, but realised they had not discussed communication protocols. His call went to voicemail. 'Hi, Honey. Just checking on progress. Bye.' He immediately realised it had been unnecessary to say "Honey" to hint that he was the caller, as she would already have his number, having provided the SIM card.

As he took Ben's SIM card from his pocket, he considered whether he really wished to contact him.

Having little expectation of anything useful emanating from that source, and the probability that he would be subject to questioning about his own progress, he put the card away again.

Craig returned to the car. 'Shall we light the blue touch paper?'

Reflecting on how much of the day had been spent bending the rules, he decided one more infringement was hardly going to matter. 'Alright, but just don't overdo it.'

When they arrived back at the station, Vardy checked the time and looked pleased with himself. 'We only touched a hundred twice.'

Priestley knew the rejoinder. 'Yes, once when we set off, and once when we stopped.'

Vardy laughed, enjoying the camaraderie.

When Priestley checked in at his office, he found a handwritten note from Coker, instructing him to make contact without delay. He picked up the telephone and was surprised to hear Coker himself answer it. 'DCI Priestley here, sir; you asked me to get in touch.'

'My office, three minutes.'

'Three minutes? Just a short meeting then, sir?'

'The three minutes is for you to get here.'

The line went dead. Priestley headed immediately for Coker's office, checking the time as he hurried along. With seconds to spare, he rapped at the door. This time, there was no delay before he heard the response.

'Come in.'

'You wanted to see me, sir.'

'What have you been up to, today?'

'Well, it began with a meeting with Mr Brown.'

'Which went badly.'

'I wouldn't say so, sir; it seemed quite productive.'

'Not according to Brown. He wants you suspended; at least by the ankles, if I can't do it by the neck. And he's demanding you be demoted to a level where you can't interfere with their important work.'

'Then I would say it was even more productive than I'd realised. There's some internal politicking going on down there; let me make a call, if you don't mind, sir? I'd like to canvass another opinion of how it went.'

He sighed heavily. 'Alright; but make it quick. Do it here, where I can hear what you're saying.'

'Sorry, sir; the number's back in my office. But I'll let you know when I've made the call.'

'Well, come straight back.'

He transferred Ben's SIM card to the new mobile. His call was answered almost immediately. 'I've been trying to contact you for hours.'

'Sorry, I had to switch it off. I could do with your help. The other member of the colour party has spoken to my boss and given me a lot of bad press. If I don't get some immediate support, I could be suspended. Will you give the chief a call? Tell him it's just down to internal politics, and I'm the bee's knees.'

'Yes, if you promise to call me back straight after; I want to talk to you.'

'Will do.' Priestley terminated the call and again headed for Coker's office. He found the door open and realised he had probably failed to close it previously.

Coker was already on the phone. 'It's damned tricky for me to know whom to believe. All I can do is wait until someone else pushes me one way or the other.'

As Coker put down the telephone, Priestley asked,

'Was that Mr Blue, sir?'

Coker was wringing his hands as he stood up. He walked to the window in silence and looked out. When he finally turned, Priestley saw the worry etched across his face. 'He said you're a paragon of virtue and should be promoted. It's all too much; I have a force to run. If you've backed the wrong horse, you're going to lose your shirt. Are you sure you want to press ahead with this investigation?'

'Well, sir, seeing as it isn't an official inquiry, may I suggest you simply let me progress things on my own, without involving you?'

Coker's face lit up. 'Yes, yes; that would be ideal. Don't tell me anything until it's all over.'

'And if I've, as you put it, backed the wrong horse, then there'll be a time of reckoning. But until then, let's say I'm working as a liaison officer with dotted line reporting to people outside your area of responsibility, and who are therefore none of your concern. Of course, I remain with a direct line to you for everything else, such as staffing, requisitioning, expenses, et cetera.'

'That suits me fine. So, do you think you're riding the favourite, Marcus?'

'One has to give a filly her head to find out how fast she is.' He realised the analogy had taken a wrong turn.

'Filly? Well don't do anything I wouldn't do.'

'Actually, sir, I may well find myself doing things you wouldn't.'

'Then don't tell me about it.'

'Don't tell you about what, sir?'

'I've already forgotten.' He turned and again looked out of the window.

Back at his office, Priestley phoned Blue. 'Thanks

for the kind word; he's now thoroughly confused, so I'm basically on my own from hereon in.'

'Well, I'll give what support I can, but you know you're out on a limb. Now, I wanted to speak to you about that vehicle; it left the embassy this evening with two male occupants. We've been using your ANPR system to track it.'

'We? So, is it official?'

'We, as in Ruth and me; I'm not risking bringing anyone else in on this.' Priestley thought he sounded unconvincingly casual as he continued. 'By the way, exactly what happened between you and her? She now seems very keen to help you in any way possible.'

'We simply engaged in some mutually educational dialogue. Do you know where the car is now?'

'It's back at the embassy.'

'I thought you might have more to tell me than that; no matter. I only bought the one new phone, so I'm having to switch SIM cards in and out. I'll try and get hold of another, but for now I'm putting Pamela's in; I ought to hear what she has to report.'

'Well, if I need you urgently, I'll have to call your work number, in which case, take care what you say.'

'Understood. Talk to you later.'

He headed home, taking his three phones with him. When Helen heard him at the door, she hurried to let him in, and saw how weary he seemed. 'Looks like you've had a tiring day.'

'Yes, but interesting.' In the living room, he laid out his three phones.

'Wasn't two enough for you?'

'Actually, three isn't enough. Do we still have that old flip-top? I need one for a fourth SIM card.'

She found the charger and plugged the old phone into the mains. 'You do know the battery runs down really quickly?'

'Don't worry; it won't get much use. I'll just go and check on them.' He went upstairs to look in on the children.

Helen heard his new phone buzzing. Rather than risk him missing the call, she answered it. 'Hello?'

'Hi, is Marco Polo there?'

She sensed this was neither a wrong number nor a hoax call. 'Who shall I say is calling?'

'Just say, Honey.'

She creaked the third stair, then took the remainder two at a time.

Marcus heard her and exited Edwin's bedroom. 'What is it? Who's calling?'

'American, name of Honey, asking for Marco Polo.'

He took the phone from her and walked downstairs. 'Hello, Honey.'

'Hi, sweetie. I thought you'd like to know we're all geared up for tracking that phone. Is there anything else I can do for you? At a distance!'

Though he recognised she was probably playing him for her own benefit, he smiled as he accepted she did it very nicely. 'It's good to know you're with me, even if you are far away.'

'We'll meet again; be sure of it.'

'I'll look forward to that. Goodnight, Honey.'

Helen had followed close behind as he returned to the living room. She now looked at him questioningly. He placed the phone on a table. 'She's someone I met today; works at the US embassy.'

'You sounded very friendly with her.'

'I guess we just hit it off together.' She waited silently. 'I'll give you a rundown of my day.' Ruthless editing left his synopsis suitably sanitised.

As he prepared for an early night, he considered giving Lin a call, but sensed he was suffering from a surfeit of attractive females.

Helen asked, 'Aren't you going to give any of your team a call? They're putting their careers on the line over this case. Shouldn't you be giving them some support? Some encouragement?'

He picked up his landline. 'You're right, I should. I'm just a bit weary.'

She took the phone from him. 'Let me do it for you. What order do you think? By seniority? That would be Frank, Neil, Tony, Lin.'

He took the phone back. 'Even if the actual content of the conversations isn't significant, the clustering of the calls can be interpreted as suggesting group activity. It's necessary to maintain a standard call pattern.'

'You'd better phone Lin, then; you often have some reason to speak to her in the evening.'

He frowned as he nodded. 'I suppose she does tend to need more support; I'll give her a quick call.'

'I'll leave you to it; I'll lay the table for breakfast.'

He knew the phone that was plugged into a socket in the kitchen did not possess the security features of the new set of phones, and so could be used to listen in on conversations without the original dialler being aware. When Lin answered, he rattled out, 'I can't talk at the moment; are you free for a meeting tomorrow at nine?'

She answered starchily, 'Yes, sir; see you then.'

CHAPTER 18

Marcus tossed and turned all night, as his dreams belied the outer confidence he exuded when faced with threats from the unknown. The seven o'clock radio alarm came as a relief to him, giving him a reason to wake.

Helen spoke over the news headlines. 'You've been very restless; we should examine the reasons behind it.'

He stretched over and tapped the snooze button. 'There's nothing to worry about; it was probably all the excitement of yesterday's meetings, especially going inside the US embassy to see Pamela.'

'You never mentioned a Pamela.'

He quickly recalled the previous evening's edited summary of events, in which he had referred to her as Honey, and had made no mention whatsoever of Ruth. 'I told you all about Honey; that's Pamela's codename.'

'Don't they use their proper names?'

'Well, probably; but I use the name Honey when I talk to her on the phone, in case anyone's listening in.'

'Why "Honey"?'

He found he was too slow to make up an alternative explanation. 'It's from "honeypot", what we know as a *femme fatale*. I could say *Mata Hari*; she is rather tall.'

'So she's a professional seductress? Remember what you said to me: "It is not good to have much honey." Or in your case, ever to have Honey.'

'That was "eat", not "have". But she isn't in that line of work; not in the least. Which is why the codename fits her, because it's so inappropriate.'

'That's doublespeak, Marcus. Hmm, I wonder what it would be like to be a *femme fatale*; perhaps I should give it a try, before I'm past it.'

'You'll never be "past it" for me, Helen.'

'You say the nicest things. Let me see if I can work my charms on you, then.'

He quickly reacted to the touch of her hands as she began to caress his body. Just as they were approaching their climax, the radio burst into life again. Knowing it could put him off his stroke, she turned him onto his back, stretched over for the volume control wheel and turned it down to zero, before completing the seduction.

Later, relieved to hear him sleeping soundly, she remained motionless for fear of waking him, until the growing feeling of needing to start her day made her free her trapped arm and reach out for her mobile phone to check the time; it showed two minutes to eight.

He remained asleep as she edged out of bed, but woke when she opened the bathroom door which let in a little light. Seeing him open his eyes, she returned to the radio and eased the volume up a little, before quietly heading for her shower. As the pips began, he lay on his side and increased the radio volume back to its usual level. When the news headlines had finished, he climbed out of bed and headed through her bathroom toward his own. On seeing her wrapped in a bath sheet, he stopped abruptly. 'Excuse me, Miss, but don't I know you from somewhere?'

She slowly uncovered herself, allowing her towel to slip through her fingers. 'Do you recognise me now?'

'Ah, yes; it's all coming back to me.'

She laughed as she picked up the bath sheet from the floor and deposited it onto a free-standing wooden rail.

He remained watching as she took several steps into the bedroom, and was pleased to see her turn and look back, so she knew she still held his interest. With false modesty, she put an arm across her upper body, and her free hand lower down. 'How did I do as a *femme fatale*? How do I compare with your American Honey?'

He smiled as he shook his head. 'I told you, she isn't one.' He changed to nodding. 'But you're a natural.'

Pleased that the magic was still there between them, she felt a buzz of happiness as she made breakfast while he took his shower.

At eight fifty, as he opened the garage door and squeezed past the ladders, he noticed the long-spouted green oilcan, and resolutely left it on the shelf.

At Lin's flat, she opened the door to him, and he saw she was wearing unsexy jogging bottoms with a heavy jumper over some sort of shirt, her feet lost in thick woolly slippers. She noticed his cursory glance. 'I can get out of these in a flash, but it's a bit cold in here this morning, so the sooner we're in bed, the better.'

Suffering from a raised guilt level, he deployed a diversionary tactic. 'I need to be ready for action at a moment's notice.' He took out his four mobile phones and placed them side by side on a table, then settled into an armchair nearby, as she climbed onto the settee and drew her knees up in front of her. 'I'll explain what happened in London yesterday.' Though he omitted the parts that involved Ruth, he gave a detailed explanation of events, before concluding, 'If the old mobile phone rings, that should be Ben; and if the new smartphone buzzes, I expect it to be Pamela.'

She stood and walked to the array of phones. 'But we can't do anything until we get a call.'

'You mean, *I* can't do anything until *I* get a call.'

She picked up the new smartphone and put it down again like a hot potato. 'Are you really intending to do nothing until you get a call? It'll be like watching paint dry. And how sure can you be you'll actually get a call this morning, or even later today? It's all dependent on factors beyond your control, when someone drives their car or uses their phone. I suggest we do something to amuse ourselves while we're waiting.'

He collected up the four phones and put them into various pockets. 'I'd better not waste your day; I'll go back home and wait there.'

She blew out her cheeks. 'I'm disappointed, and not just because you're too preoccupied to come to bed; it has to make sense for me to stay on the case. Who's going to watch your back? It's stupidly dangerous to try to operate on your own.'

He winced. 'I'm not called stupid very often.'

She glared. 'I didn't say you're stupid; I said your intended way of working is stupid. And you know it is.'

He looked down, aware she was correct, and felt his resolve weaken. 'You're right, of course, but there's too many risks for you to get involved. Perhaps, if I track the guy down, you could stay in the car and call for backup if it all goes pear-shaped.'

She sensed her opportunity. 'And maybe I could stick to you like glue, so that it doesn't go pear-shaped.'

He nodded. 'But you have to do just what I tell you, and if I say something's too dangerous and you're to keep out of it, you must back off. Alright?'

She smiled. 'Sure thing, boss; don't I always do whatever you say? Maybe there's something I can do for you now? Come on; let's seal the contract.'

He shook his head. 'I'm going back; depending on where the search takes us, I might not see the children for a while. I'll call as soon as I hear something. Oh, and make sure you've a bag packed; we could be driving around for days, trying to pick up the trail.' Without waiting for her to approach to receive a farewell kiss, he opened the door and headed out, congratulating himself on having taken a first faltering step toward breaking their personal bonds while at the same time cementing their professional relationship.

Helen was surprised to see him return so soon. 'Is everything alright? Your debriefings normally take much longer with her.'

He opened his mouth for a moment, then paused, as he prepared to respond obliquely. 'I need to brief you; let's go in the kitchen.' He checked to make sure the children were occupied in the living room, but found it empty. 'Where are they?'

'Across the road.'

'Let's go in here, then.' She sat on a settee. He chose a chair that enabled him to face her almost directly. 'Lin understands the risks involved in police work, and especially in tracking down a killer; she's made me see sense. I need a partner, and she's the obvious candidate. It's often easier to blend into the background, when it's a man and a woman together. So I've agreed to contact her, the moment I hear anything. But I've made it absolutely clear, if I say a situation is too dangerous for her, she's to back off and keep herself safe.'

'But what if it's too dangerous for you? Or doesn't that count for anything?'

'I'll make sure I stay safe, as well.'

'In that case, what about letting me be your partner?

We'd certainly come over as an authentic couple.'

'No, Helen; you're not trained in police work.'

'I'm a fast learner; you ought to think about it.'

'I have thought, and I know I'll be safer with Lin watching my back.'

'I suppose I know you're right, but don't write me off entirely; I could be useful in some situations.'

'Sure; I'll bear it in mind.'

'What do you intend to do while you're waiting?'

'Nothing much I can do, really. I thought I'd spend some time with Edwin, make him know he's just as loved as Alice; he's seemed a bit off, since you and I had our little debate.'

'They've become a lot closer to each other, though. Like now, playing across the road; if Edwin was going, Alice had to go, too.'

'I know what I'll do, I'll make him a signal on a pole for his model railway.'

'He hasn't played with it quite so much after the first couple of days. Neither have you, for that matter.'

'Come on, Helen; you understand perfectly.'

'Recapturing one's own childhood through one's children. Well, it works for you. I adore the way you're able to become childlike. It isn't something I can do, myself; I can never really let go of being an adult.'

Sympathising with her genuine sense of loss, he changed the direction of the conversation by laughing coarsely. 'Yes, but what an adult! I remember this morning like it was…'

'This morning?' They laughed together.

When the children returned from the neighbour's house for lunch, Marcus handed Edwin the signal pole. He scrutinised it. 'You said straight across means the train has to stop, but what about when it can go?'

'With this one, you put the arm higher when the train can go. There are some that put it lower to say it can go, but that isn't as good, because if something breaks and the arm falls down, the engine driver might think it's safe when it's really just broken.'

After lunch, the children and Marcus gathered on the floor around the railway, while Helen sat on a settee with a textbook in her hands. Marcus put a small bronze tortoise on one end of the signal base to stabilise it, but found it still wobbled on the carpet. He called over to Helen, 'Any suggestions for something small and heavy to hold down the other side of the base?'

She glanced over. 'I know just the thing.'

When she fetched a brass one pound weight from the ornamental kitchen scales, Marcus declined to take it from her. He looked at Edwin. 'Should we let Mummy play with us? She could operate the signal.'

Alice answered for him enthusiastically. 'Yes, yes, Mummy can do the signal.'

Helen knelt on the floor next to Marcus and took hold of the string that held the semaphore arm in place. She asked Edwin, 'Are you ready to set off?'

He responded, 'Yes; let's go.'

Helen pulled the string downward until the arm was pointing somewhere between one and two o'clock. Edwin moved the train slowly at first, before making it pick up speed. After the engine had passed the pole, she released the string so that the signal dropped back to three o'clock.

When Helen had operated the signal for the sixth time, she asked Marcus to take over. He turned to Alice. 'Could you do the signal as well as moving the animals, sweetheart? I just need to talk to Mummy in the kitchen about something.'

Alice responded, 'I can do it easily.' She shuffled around to be closer to the string.

Helen smiled at her. 'Of course you can, my little love; we women are good at multi-tasking, aren't we.' Alice giggled at having been called a woman.

In the kitchen, Marcus looked silently at Helen. For once, she found she was unable to hold his gaze. Finally, she looked up. 'Thanks, love. But in the end, I get so bored if I'm not learning something. I mean, beyond how to operate a model railway signal.'

He laughed. 'Ah, so you admit it's a model railway.' When she tried to return his laughter, he was concerned to see her eyes begin to water. 'What on earth's the matter, love? You'd better tell me all about it.'

She shook her head. 'It's nothing. No really, there's nothing wrong, beyond my being unable to play with the children the way you do.'

He dredged up a misquote from his church-going younger days. 'When I was a child, I played as a child; but when I became a man, I put away childish things. So, clearly I haven't yet made it to manhood. Don't be sorry that you're more mature than me; I'm sure I'll grow up, someday.'

Finding a tear was trickling down her cheek, she left it untouched as an eloquent expression of her depth of feeling. 'Don't grow up, Marcus; not ever. I love you just the way you are.'

CHAPTER 19

Marcus found his sleep was again repeatedly troubled, but this time the theme was an undefined inner sadness. He knew instinctively it involved Helen and her single tear, and yet the lack of coherent meaning behind each episode left him unable to determine whether there was anything real behind them. He lay cogitating for over an hour, before the radio turned itself on at seven o'clock. Believing Helen had been asleep, he stayed still, so she could return gently to full consciousness.

She turned on her side to face him in the darkness. 'I was awake, as well. What's troubling you, love?'

He thought for a moment. 'Nothing, really, except I thought maybe something was troubling you.'

She pondered. 'If I'm troubled about anything, it's whether you're troubled about something.'

He gave a tiny laugh. 'But I'm only troubled that you may be troubled that I may be troubled that you may be troubled that I may be troubled...'

She laughed as well as she could with a dry mouth. 'In that case, everything's fine. I'm getting up.'

After breakfast together, she fed and watered the children, who then galloped off to Edwin's bedroom.

He laid out his four mobile phones and a landline handset side by side on a small table in the living room. She looked up from her textbook. 'Wotcha doin'?'

He placed his fingers to his temples and closed his eyes. 'I'm using my willpower to make them ring.' He opened them again. 'Which do you think will be first?'

She smiled in amusement. 'Which do *you* think?'

He pointed to each in turn. 'My American friend is favourite with odds of eleven to ten. British security is eleven to four. Personal mobile, five to one. Work, nine to one. And the landline, twelve to one. How much would you like to wager? Minimum bet ten pounds.'

She attempted a West Country accent. 'I ain't got no money, zur; could I earn my stake with my favours?'

He replied in a similar style. 'That would take a lot of your favours, miss; I said minimum bet ten pounds.'

She giggled, then gave him a severe stare as she responded in her usual voice. 'I can see I'll have to withdraw privileges for a while; then we'll find out what the going rate really is, when you're desperate.' He laughed heartily to cover up his secret.

All five telephones remained stubbornly silent until, at twenty minutes to nine, the new smartphone buzzed. He snatched it up and answered, 'Yes?'

'He's just used his iPhone.' He recognised Pamela's voice. 'Manchester airport. I'm sending you the last GPS and time. Grab your Go Bag.' The line went dead.

He informed Helen of the situation, as he entered latitude 53.3626, longitude -2.2717 into Google Maps GPS Coordinates. Fighting against a tide of advertising that he had accidentally triggered on the small screen, he muttered a few mild obscenities under his breath. After a second frustrating phalanx of ads, he read out the address. 'Ramp Road S, Manchester M90 3AG.' When the coordinates mysteriously altered after he had zoomed in and out, he asked Helen to fetch his laptop. She turned it on upstairs, then haltingly entered the logon details as she came down again. After placing it on the table, she brought up Google Maps. He put the phone aside and entered the postcode.

She pressed up close and looked at the screen. 'Just try the "Earth" option.' The map changed to a satellite image. 'Does that look more familiar?'

He thought for a moment. 'Terminal One drop-off?'

'Yes, so he isn't parking up.'

He called Ben's number; Ruth answered, 'Yes?'

Despite his raised stress level, for a moment a smile flickered across his lips. 'Hello, it's MP.'

'Hello MP, what can I do for you?'

'Ben there?'

'He isn't far away. Something you want?'

'Tell him our American friend has tracked the man's phone to Manchester Airport Terminal 1 drop-off point; I'll send you the precise GPS and time. Get security to check vehicle movements and scan for any passengers who first appeared on CCTV straight after, and then trace where they all went. If there's a match with the car we know about, focus on that, and find an excuse to stop it and look who's inside. I'm going to drive to the airport right now, in case I need to catch a plane, but let me know ASAP if it's the car I need to tail.' He added as an afterthought, 'I hope I see you again, sometime soon.' He heard her sharp intake of breath.

'Me too. Talk to you when I have something.'

Marcus phoned Lin from his personal mobile. 'It's kicking off! You did pack a bag, didn't you. And bring your passport; we might be getting a flight somewhere.'

'Wow! How soon to pick-up?'

'Fifteen.'

'I'll be stood outside.' He terminated the call.

While he was saying goodbye to his children, Helen used her initiative and drove his car out of the garage, leaving it parked on the road pointing up the hill.

He crammed two electrical plug adaptors into the travel bag, before stuffing his passport and three of the phones into his jacket pockets. When she stepped back into the house, he accepted his car keys from her and quickly kissed her on the lips. 'Don't worry; everything will be fine.'

She grabbed him by the lapels and kissed him fiercely. 'Be safe, love.'

Outside, he dropped his overcoat and travel bag into the car boot. As he climbed into the front seat, he was pleased to find Helen had reset it to his driving position, knowing she would have had to change it to hers.

Approaching Lin's flat, he saw her standing by the roadside with a furry green parka around her shoulders. When he pulled up, she threw her coat and bag into the back, and jumped into the front. The seat belt's motion detector refused to allow it to reel out. As she fought with it, she commanded, 'Don't wait for me; just get going.' After she had finally persuaded the belt to release, she asked, 'Where *are* we going, anyway?'

He replied, 'Manchester Airport.'

'I wouldn't risk the Snake Pass at this time of year.'

'I wasn't going to. Look after these phones, will you. Remember, the smartphone's the US contact; the other, the British. And don't use names if anyone calls.'

As time ticked by without anyone making contact, he slowed to an almost legal cruising speed. On the M67, he was glancing over at a lane-directing sign for the Hyde and Dukinfield exit, when the old phone rang. Lin answered, 'Yes?'

Ruth asked, 'Where's MP?'

'Driving,' she answered curtly. 'Talk to *me*.'

'It was the Range Rover. We had it stopped for some made-up minor traffic offence; there was only a small Russian chap in it. We think your bird has flown.'

Lin told him the caller was female, and then relayed the message.

He responded, 'Ask if she's traced any passengers.'

Ruth answered via Lin, 'We're still working on it.'

He glanced at the satnav. 'Tell her we're within half an hour of the airport, and ask if she can arrange a reception committee.'

As they approached the first point where the road split into different routes for the various terminals, the old phone rang again. Lin relayed the message. 'Go to the Terminal 1 Drop-off Point. There'll be a police car just beyond the exit, with two officers waiting. Give them your car keys. One of them will take you to a Border Force officer.'

They took the slip road and drove up the steep ramp; he smiled inwardly as he saw her instinctively duck when they passed under a two metre height restriction barrier. Having ignored the five miles per hour speed limit sign at the entrance to the multi-storey building, he found the car bounced hard over the first speed hump, so braked sharply before the second. After the third, he saw a policeman in a high-visibility yellow jacket moving traffic cones; the officer waved him into the final bay he had reserved for them.

Priestley parked the car and took his bag and coat out of the boot, while Plummer retrieved hers from the back seat. He locked the vehicle and handed the keys to the policeman. 'Good morning; I see we're expected.'

The man looked intently at him, as though searching for some indication of his special status. 'Yes, sir; I've been instructed to take you to meet a Border Force officer, and then I'm to remove your car.'

He smiled. 'Well, don't forget where you put it.'

The officer looked concerned. 'I won't, sir.'

The plain-clothed Border Force officer met them by the metal barrier next to the Check In sign. 'Come with me please, sir; I've some footage to show you.'

Priestley noted how he had dispensed entirely with introductions, and not even acknowledged Plummer's existence. He led them to a cramped office, windowless and with a faint smell of petrol, where he invited them to sit at a computer screen.

Before he played the security footage, he asked, 'Do you know what alias he might be travelling under?'

Priestley guessed he had not been fully briefed. 'No. I'm not even sure what he looks like, but I can discount most people based on their size; I'm expecting a large, muscular man.'

'That isn't a lot to go on, sir.'

'He probably has size twelve feet.'

'That doesn't exactly narrow the field for us.'

'You do know he's probably Russian, don't you?'

'Yes, I was told as much, though there's no knowing what flag he'll be sailing under.'

'Ah, so you're ex-navy.'

'Well spotted, sir; let's hope you're as successful at spotting your fugitive.'

By the end of the viewing, Priestley and Plummer had identified more than thirty men as potentially being their target. They remained cloistered alone when the officer left to initiate investigations.

Priestley watched as noon ticked by. 'I think we're supposed to stay put, but I'd quite like a bite to eat.'

Plummer looked at the numbers on a card by the phone. 'Perhaps we should order room service?'

He asked with mock-sincerity, 'Is "Room Service" listed? I'll have some sandwiches, then; and a coffee.'

'Black, no sugar, coming up.' She dialled an internal number. 'Hi, we're guests... Yes, that's us. Could we have some sandwiches and two coffees, one with milk, one without, no sugar in either... Much appreciated.'

He emphasised his surprise. 'Who did you phone?'

She replied nonchalantly, 'Head of security. Spoke to his liaison assistant; I think that means secretary.'

He smiled. 'Sometimes, I wonder about you...'

Five minutes later, a severe-looking woman arrived with two large coffees and four packs of sandwiches, two twos and two threes, made with a mixture of brown and white bread. 'Will this be alright for you, sir?'

'That's absolutely perfect; thank you ever so much.'

She smiled awkwardly. 'Thank *you* sir.' As she left, she sneaked an envious sideways glance at Plummer.

Priestley lined up the boxes of sandwiches. 'You can have first choice; prawns, I assume. And your second choice, egg and watercress, no doubt.'

'And you'll have the chicken and the cheese, and not just because they're in packs of three to my two.'

'I'm a growing boy; I need the extra sustenance.'

'Well, don't grow too much; I wouldn't want you to be crushing me by the time you're forty.'

He fell silent, reflecting on how she appeared to have assumed their affair would continue for years.

Having missed breakfast, she wolfed down all four of her sandwiches, and then took one of his.

When the smartphone buzzed, he grabbed it from the desk in front of them, and answered, 'Yes?'

'Hi; his phone just lit up in Stockholm.'

'Really? Are you certain that's where it is?'

'Yes, for sure. It wasn't on long; I expect it had been in Airplane mode, and then he just made a single call. Are you still up for the chase?'

'Of course.'

'And what about your young companion?'

'How do you know I have one?' He heard her laugh. 'Yes, she is; I need her to watch my back.'

'I don't doubt it; not for a moment. But I think I'm better qualified; do you want me to come, instead?'

Though he knew Pamela may well be correct, he had no intention of crushing Lin's hopes. 'Thanks for the offer, Honey, but I'd better stick with Plan A.'

'OK, sweetie, but if you change your mind, I'm ready to come and join you.' She ended the call.

Lin asked sharply, 'Who are you calling "Honey"? And what's Plan A?'

'You're Plan A, and "Honey" is Pamela's codename. She was offering to take your place.'

'But you definitely said no, didn't you?'

'Yes, of course I did, even though she probably has a whole range of special skills you don't possess.'

She punched him in the arm, just hard enough to let him know what she thought of him comparing them.

He phoned Ben, who immediately answered 'Yes?'

'I'm off to Stockholm.'

'Hmm, in that case you'll have to liaise with the Swedes; I'll arrange a contact for you. Anything else?'

'Yes, make sure we can get on the next flight.'

'We?'

'I have a partner; a colleague.'

'I'll have a word.'

'And what about some cash? Swedish Kroner.'

'It might take a little time to organise; and you'll need to sign a receipt.'

'You're not serious?'

'Sadly, I am. Unlike the police, all our expenditure is now scrutinised by the Public Accounts Committee, which is why we have to log everything.'

'Well, if I use my credit card in Sweden, it's going to be obvious where I am.'

'I understand that; I'll do my best.'

Seven minutes later, Ben called back. 'I've reserved two seats under your name with a Norwegian airline, and I've paid for them. It departs thirteen forty-five.'

'Marvellous. We'd better be going, then.'

'Good luck, and I'll try to get you that cash.'

Priestley ended the call and phoned Pamela. 'Hi, Honey. We're leaving at a quarter to two. Are you able to provide me with some Swedish Kroner for expenses? I don't want to be visible over there with my credit card, and our British friend doesn't seem confident he can come up with the readies in time.'

'Sure; no problem. Let me know how things are going every day, won't you. What time will you call?'

'Evening, maybe?'

'Needs to be an exact time. It's tradecraft 101, but I forget you're untrained. Let's make it eighteen o-five, local time where you are; best to avoid exact hours. If you fail to make a call, I'll assume there's a problem, so don't forget. OK?'

'Eighteen o-five, Battle of Trafalgar. Will do.'

'We're not finished yet; you need a Distress word. If you say "gorgeous", I'll know you're in trouble. And if I say "lover", I'm telling you that you're in imminent danger. We'll try it now, to fix it in your mind.'

'Alright, gorgeous.'

'Great, lover-boy. And remember, five after six.'

As he ended the call, Lin scowled at him. 'Explain!'

'It's called a Distress word,' he replied confidently, to disguise his unfamiliarity with the term. 'If I'm in trouble, I need to use the word "gorgeous" to let her know. And if she believes I'm in imminent danger, she'll use the word "lover" to warn me. You need to remember them, in case you have to make a call.'

'Don't I get my own Distress word?'

'You shouldn't need one; we've agreed you're not to put yourself in harm's way.'

As they picked up their bags and coats, the Border Force officer returned. 'Are you off, now?'

'Yes, to Stockholm on the thirteen forty-five. Our man probably arrived there not long after midday.'

'He'll have been on the SAS flight.'

Plummer spoke to him for the first time. 'SAS?'

He recognised her confusion. 'Not our Special Air Service; I'm talking about a Scandinavian airline.'

'Of course.' Though her response sounded confident enough, her rising colour gave her away.

He turned back. 'I'll show you the passengers.'

'I wouldn't want us to miss our flight.'

'It'll take no time at all.' He viewed the passenger manifest, then played the footage at high speed on the computer, freezing the image three times. 'One English, one Irish, one Swede. But no Russian.'

'That's only to be expected,' Priestley responded knowingly, trying to bolster their credibility.

The officer pressed a button on a machine nearby, and it began to whirr. He removed the three full-colour photographs he had just printed. 'These might come in handy; I'll get their details to you before your flight. Shall I'll advise the situation to your London office?'

'Yes please, that'd be brilliant; thanks very much.'

He escorted them to the check-in desk and waited for their passport details to be recorded and tickets issued. Then, he directed them to Security, where a new line opened for them, and closed immediately afterwards.

As they waited in the departure lounge, Lin looked around. 'I've only ever been to France, and that was on the ferry. It's ever so easy, catching a plane, isn't it?'

Priestley smiled at her. 'It is when they think you're someone important. If they knew who we really are, we'd still be queuing somewhere.'

When the automated announcement system invited passengers to go to Boarding, they stood up and headed for the queue that had immediately formed, but were intercepted by a young woman who asked them to accompany her. She led them onto the empty plane and showed them to their seats, then handed over a sealed brown envelope. Having no sharp implement to hand, he used an index finger to open it; the top tore jaggedly. As he took out the printed sheets, Lin leaned in close to him so they could read them together. At the end, she asked, 'Which one do you think is our man?'

He put the sheets back into the envelope, along with the three photographs from his inside pocket. 'It's possible he isn't any of them. If only this were official, it would be simple enough to do a background check on the English guy; and with a bit of international co-operation, I'm sure we could get the gen on the other two as well. I gain the impression our British spook has been doing his best to keep things under the radar, but he's obviously had to let some people know something. He's arranging a Swedish contact at the other end; I'll ask them if they can do some research for us.'

The plane was full to capacity. Priestley recalled hearing two disgruntled Englishmen near the check-in desk complaining bitterly at having been "bumped off"; he guessed he and Lin had just taken their seats.

As the plane taxied, he saw Lin looking anxiously out of the window. 'There's nothing to worry about.'

She leaned over, to explain without being overheard. 'I feel pathetic; never flown, at my age.'

He spoke quietly into her ear. 'You're not pathetic. If you didn't have somewhere particular you wanted to go, why would you want to catch a plane?'

'I'm glad you're not making fun of me. Maybe after this, we can go lots of places together?'

He gave a bittersweet smile. 'I think you sometimes forget I'm not exactly available.'

She sat back when the engines roared and the plane jerked forward before accelerating to take-off velocity. At the moment it left the ground, she took his hand and held it tightly. As the angle of ascent reduced close to level flight, he squeezed her fingers for a moment and then released them. 'That wasn't so bad, was it?'

She smiled. 'It was good; exciting, even.'

He settled back into his upright seat. 'Let me know if you see something interesting; otherwise, I'm going to try and get some shut-eye.'

For the next two hours she alternated between watching the cabin crew and staring out of the window.

CHAPTER 20

Priestley disembarked with Plummer at Stockholm's Arlanda airport and joined a queue at passport control. As he waited his turn to be vetted, he felt almost slighted to have been offered no preferential treatment.

In the arrivals area, they looked around for someone wishing to make contact. He noticed a pale young man in a grey suit, holding up a sign with "MP" written on it in thick black ink. As they approached him, he placed the sign to the back of his clipboard, which he turned around to reveal a pen attached with string. Priestley addressed him quietly. 'Hello, am I your MP?'

The man responded, 'Yes indeed. I believe you're expecting this.'

Priestley saw that the man was tightly grasping in his other hand a brown envelope bearing a red wax seal. 'If that's what I think it is, then yes.'

'Just sign here, please.'

Priestley glanced down at the form, a receipt for five thousand Swedish kroner. 'And when do I get the rest?'

The man registered surprise. 'This is all I've been instructed to deliver to you.'

Priestley took the pen, signed his name "Don Duck", and returned it with a 'Thank you.'

The man read the signature. 'Thank you, Mr Duck. Just contact the embassy if you need further assistance.'

After the man had hurried away, Priestley opened the envelope and found it did indeed contain five thousand kroner. He handed half to Lin. 'I suppose the problem is, no one knows how long we'll need to stay.'

She put her share away. 'I think there's a woman over there, trying to catch your eye.'

He turned his head slowly, his eyes always focusing further around to his right, so that he could see her before facing her. The young woman waved brightly.

As they approached her, she waved again. 'Hi.' From the single word, he guessed she was an American. 'I've a present for you, but don't open it here.' He held the chocolate box for a moment and considered whether it was safe to accept a gift from a stranger. She guessed what he was thinking. 'It's what you asked for, to cover expenses. And I'm to remind you not to forget to call.'

He smiled. 'Do give her my sincere thanks. So, will I be liaising with you while I'm here?'

She smiled back, proudly displaying her dazzling white teeth. 'I'll be around if you need me.'

'Who should I ask for?'

'Virginia Long. I was told you're new to this; I'm to keep an eye on you.'

'You're to be my guardian angel?'

She turned to Plummer and flashed her teeth and pink gums. 'Except, that's your job, isn't it?'

Plummer was startled to be suddenly brought into the conversation. 'He's given me strict orders to keep myself safe, so I'm not supposed to do any guarding, angelic or otherwise.'

'You're keeping house. OK; that's good to know.'

Feeling as though she had just been dismissed as an irrelevance, Plummer responded, 'But we're a team, so I'll be staying as close as I can.'

Long heard her defensiveness. 'We all need a partner we can rely on; I'm sure you're great together.'

Priestley, in his effort to add support, stretched the truth beyond breaking point. 'The two of us have often operated as partners; she's always my first choice.'

Long smiled again at him. 'She's got your back; I get it. OK, you need to stick with me; it wouldn't look good, giving you a present and then leaving you alone. I'll walk with you to the front of the car park. Your next contact will probably want to meet you out back, where the security cameras aren't working.' She set off.

Priestley asked, 'What next contact?'

She answered without turning. 'Elena from Säpo; she's been watching you from the moment you met the Brit from the embassy.' Receiving no response, she explained, 'Säpo, the Swedish Security Service. You really should have been briefed for this mission.'

He also felt defensive. 'We only found out which country we'd be heading for, an hour before the flight.'

Long barely concealed her concern. 'I think you need to get some orientation, and pretty damn quick. OK, I'll step into the car park with you, and you can head for the far side. Maybe go slow enough for her to catch up if she wants to without having to run, huh?'

'Will do. And thanks for the chocolates.'

Concern at their lack of preparation took the shine off her departing smile. 'Get in touch, pronto, if you hit a problem. Good to have met you both.' She rushed away, leaving them at the top of the stairwell.

He looked at Lin. 'Let's just stay on this level until someone accosts us.'

As they approached the far side, a voice came from behind them. 'My car's this way.'

He turned to see a slender young woman with dark hair, pointing back the way they had come. After glancing around and seeing no one else, he asked, 'Are you talking to us?'

'Yes, Mr Priestley and partner, I am talking to you.'

After so much subterfuge, he felt shocked to hear his name spoken openly. 'And you are?'

'Elena Andersson, Säpo. You're coming with me.'

'Where to, may I ask?'

'Headquarters. You must come for a meeting.'

He knew from her tone she would not allow him to decline. 'May I just say how thoughtful it was of Säpo to provide transport; it's always nice to feel welcome.'

She glared at him. 'Are you taking the piss?'

He responded with innocent charm. 'And what an excellent command of idiomatic English you have.'

She succumbed and smiled. 'English boyfriend.'

Hers was the eleventh Volvo. She insisted they sit in the back, their luggage in the boot. When Priestley tried to open a conversation with her, she responded, 'Would you like me to play some music?'

He took her meaning, and settled back for the ride. As five past six approached, he prepared to call Pamela. 'Sorry to disturb the quiet, only I need to make a quick phone call.' Heads turned slightly but no one spoke.

He dialled and Pamela responded immediately. 'Hi, sweetie. How are you enjoying the view?'

'Hi, Honey. Sorry you're busy; I'll call you later.' He returned to looking out of the window.

After half an hour of mute driving, Elena spoke again. 'We're on Bolstomtavägen; I'm going left down Gunnar Asplunds allé to park up. My boss is waiting to meet you at Säpo headquarters. Are you packing?'

He guessed her meaning, but feigned ignorance. 'Yes, I packed my own bag; they often ask at check-in.'

She grunted in annoyance. 'What I mean is, do you have a weapon. Did that tart Virginia slip you one?'

'The only thing that nice young lady gave me was a box of chocolates; I thought it was very sweet of her.'

'Nice? She's a total trollop and always has been.'

'Hmm, Virginia: Virgin for short but not for Long. Thanks for the information; one never knows when it might come in handy.' Lin elbowed him hard in the ribs. 'I mean, thanks for the warning.'

Elena saw the interaction and fought not to smile, being under strict orders to give them a hard time. She parked the car and instructed them to leave their luggage. As they entered the low-rise building, the guests were subject to a basic security check before being allowed to follow her up the stairs. On the top floor, she led them to the end of a corridor and knocked at a door. There was an immediate response; Marcus guessed it was Swedish for "Enter", as Elena quickly stepped inside and beckoned them to follow.

The guests approached a barrel-chested man with a bushy blond beard, standing behind a desk. '*Hej*. I'm Max Ahlberg.' He reached over and shook hands with them, Marcus first.

Priestley responded simply, 'Lin; Marcus.'

When Lin had settled into the furthest of three visitor chairs, Marcus placed the chocolates on the edge of the desk in front of him and sat next to her. Elena stepped forward and picked up the box, weighing it in her hand. Max looked at her questioningly. She put it down again. 'Your friend Ms Long gave it to him.' Marcus thought he detected a tinge of reproach in her tone.

Max motioned Elena to sit. 'She's very generous.' He turned to Marcus. 'Tell me, Mr Priestley, what is the purpose of your visit?'

Marcus put on a puzzled frown. 'We only came here because Ms Andersson asked us to.'

Max looked even more puzzled than Marcus. 'Elena, why did you invite them to come to Sweden?'

She shook her head. 'I didn't invite them to come to Sweden; he's just dicking with us.'

Marcus swivelled to look at her. 'Where did you learn your American slang, Ms Andersson? A similar source to your idiomatic English?'

She snapped, 'No; TV.'

Max tried again. 'I didn't mean why did you come to this building; I meant why did you come to Sweden.'

Marcus nodded. 'Ah, I understand.'

When the ensuing silence extended beyond several seconds, Max sighed. 'So, now that you understand the question, will you please answer it?'

Marcus felt he had baited them long enough. 'I'm investigating a murder that took place in England. The trail has led me to Stockholm. Were you not briefed?'

Max ignored the question. 'I must remind you that you have no authority to operate in my country; you have no power here to arrest your suspect. So, what would you do if you found your fugitive?'

'I would talk to him, to find out his motive.'

'Forgive me for my simplicity, but I do not believe it would be normal for an English policeman to travel to another country simply to have a chat with a suspected murderer. What else would you do?'

'I would contact your police and have them arrest him, and then arrange for his extradition.'

'And do you expect me to believe this?'

'Yes, because it's the truth. Why would you not?'

'Because of your associates, and your army record.'

Marcus found himself caught off guard. 'How do you know about my army record?'

'Do you remember Mazar-e-Sharif in Afghanistan? In two thousand six you worked with several Swedish army officers in the International Security Assistance Force, a part of NATO. And then you moved to Camp Bastion, where you showed your capacity for killing.'

Sensing Lin was staring at him, he turned and spoke softly to her. 'It was war. The rules of engagement were clear enough for me to know where my duty lay.'

Max continued, acerbically, 'And no enemy fighter would ever suggest a different version to yours, would they, Mr Priestley? Because they were all dead.'

Marcus thumped his fist down hard on the desk, narrowly missing the chocolates. 'Just what the hell do you think I'm planning to do here?'

Max responded calmly. 'My counterpart in London says you are here only to interview someone, but I fear you may decide to execute him, as that is so much more certain than relying on the courts for justice, is it not?'

Marcus made no response, taking the question as rhetorical.

'If he is one of the dozen or so spies operating out of the Russian embassy as an official employee, he would be able to claim diplomatic immunity, and we would have to honour that. The most we could do would be to expel him from the country for breaches of the Vienna Convention, but then we would no doubt suffer a retaliatory expulsion from Moscow, just as happened last year. So, that is something we wish to avoid.'

Marcus remained determinedly still.

'The situation is different, but not very much better,

if he is a NOC.' He saw Priestley's uncertain glance. 'A Non-official Cover Operative. Many of them pose as businesspeople, but it becomes obvious who they really are if we arrest them. The propaganda that pours out of Russia is aimed at weakening our resolve by claiming our evidence is flawed, and this may often trigger other actions that undermine the state machinery. Just as it is in your country, we have plenty of naïve, well-meaning do-gooders who believe the blatant lies, and are willing to sign petitions or to take part in protest marches, in order to try to have a guilty person released. In the end, sometimes we can do no more than deport the NOC, and then their place is taken by another one.'

Marcus tried for his most sympathetic look.

'Now, consider how much worse things would be if your spy is unlawfully executed. If he is an embassy official, we would have to deny any involvement and express our deepest sympathy, and hope it all dies down. But if he is a NOC, it can actually cause more of a problem for us; the average citizen may think the loss of a *bona fide* spy masquerading as a diplomat is simply par for the course, but the death of an innocent civilian makes them worry that it could happen to them. Add the idea of state collusion into the toxic mix, and we have a recipe that could topple a government.'

Marcus nodded slowly.

'The Russian embassy here in Stockholm has the official motto, "Russia is closer than you think." This is not a suggestion that our two nations may see things from a similar perspective, or that we have much in common. No! It is a direct threat, a reminder that it would only be a short step for them to invade.'

Marcus suspected Max was a little paranoid.

'Our biggest intelligence threat comes from Russian spies; they are at the top of our agenda. Since the expulsion last year, there has been a substantial increase in aggressive tactics against us. I have no intention of allowing you to make the situation worse by executing one of their operatives.'

Marcus shook his head from side to side, slowly and repeatedly. 'You've really got me all wrong, Max. The Russian assassinated someone, and there are people who simply want to know why; that's my reason for wanting to talk to him. If he doesn't have diplomatic immunity, I'll also try to get him extradited. But I've no intention of killing him.'

'So, do I have your word that, if you find your man, you will not kill him? Not under any circumstances?'

'Yes, short of him pointing a gun at my head and preparing to pull the trigger.'

Max's sigh was almost theatrically loud. 'Do you expect any help with your search, or do you intend to work alone?' He quickly swung his gaze to Lin. 'I do apologise; you are of course here to assist him in that capacity.' He looked to Marcus for a reply.

'I believe you're already aware I'm receiving some help from the US, as well as my own country.'

Max declined to confirm or deny. 'Why would the Americans send you here to work for them? It makes no sense to me; they have so many people of their own.'

'It's for plausible deniability.'

He turned to Elena. 'Plausible deniability?'

She responded in English. 'He means the Americans don't want to be seen taking action against a Russian agent outside of the US; so, by using a renegade Brit, they can deny any involvement if it all goes tits up.'

Marcus turned to her and smiled. 'You really do possess an excellent selection of idioms.'

She refused to meet his gaze, responding instead to Max. 'Perhaps we should play along; let Marcus do the tracking, while we stay in the background. After all, we do believe in justice, don't we? So, if there's a Russian murderer here, we'd want him to answer for his crime.'

Marcus thought it interesting that Max continued to use English for his discussion with Elena. 'Yes, I'm all for justice, but not if it results in a diplomatic incident that could damage Swedish-Russian relations for years. You do remember how Putin reacted when the British found out who had murdered Litvinenko?'

Elena responded dismissively, 'Yes, of course.'

Max addressed Marcus with increased gravitas. 'Do I have your word you will not execute the Russian?'

Marcus felt confident he had now won the debate. 'Certainly, Max; I'm only here to bring him to account within the rule of law. Which is what you would want.'

'*Exact*. First, then, you will need to identify him. How do you intend to do that?'

'I have an American friend who can track his phone when he turns it on.'

'And do you know where he might be?'

'My guess is, he's at the Russian embassy.'

'Very likely. Again, how would you identify him?'

'I have a shortlist of three suspects, though I can't guarantee he's actually any of them. If I can eliminate two of them…'

'I trust you do not mean *eliminate* as in *terminate*?'

'I just mean establish if any of them couldn't have done it. In fact, I have photographs of them and some details I picked up in England; could you research them for me? As this operation is being kept quiet, formal requests aren't an option. One of them is Swedish; you could check him out quite easily, I think.'

Elena responded for Max. 'Give me their details.'

'They're in my bag, in your car.' He turned back to Max. 'If I were down to just one suspect from those three, and I were standing where I could see and hear him, I could call his number and see if he answers it.'

'But you cannot call him from close by if he is at the embassy; even if you were invited to visit, you would have your phone taken away as you entered. No, what is needed is a call from outside, at the moment that the suspect is in plain sight.'

'Fine. So, how do I go about getting invited?'

'I have it from a reliable source that the Ambassador only ever gives personal invitations to attractive young women.'

Elena asked, pointedly, 'What reliable source is that, Max? It wouldn't be Virginia Long, would it?'

He smiled at her. 'I really don't know what you have against that brave, patriotic young woman; she would do anything for her country.' He addressed Marcus. 'My plan would need an attractive young woman he has never met before.' He looked at Lin.

Marcus stretched his arm forward and furiously waved his hand, as though desperately rubbing out something obscene written on a school blackboard. 'No! Lin isn't going to be whoring with a Russian; or anyone else for that matter. Absolutely not. Forget it.'

Max shook his head. 'No, that is not what I was thinking.' He turned back to Lin. 'My plan is for you to be heavily pregnant and looking for the father of your child; I am sure he would not press you for sex in that condition. The story would be that the father told you he worked at the Russian embassy as a translator. If the Ambassador thought you were the sort of girl who would eventually show him your grateful appreciation for his help, I am certain he would be very willing to appear to be assisting you in your search.'

Lin responded, 'I know you're not suggesting I get pregnant and do this in nine months' time, so just how believable can I be made to look?'

Marcus interjected. 'Hold on a minute, Lin; this isn't my idea of keeping you out of harm's way.'

She smiled at him. 'You worry about me too much; it'll be a piece of cake.' She turned to Max. 'So, let's get it organised right away. What about tomorrow?'

'Tomorrow is New Year's Eve; I am certain that the Ambassador will be too busy preparing for his party, before the embassy closes for the Russian holidays. We should aim for the middle of January.'

Marcus read Lin's disappointment. 'I think it would be safest for Lin if she could go to the embassy when there are lots of other people present. Do the Russians open their party to outsiders? If so, could we be put on the invitations list?'

Elena reacted enthusiastically before Max could speak. 'That's a brilliant idea, Marcus. Max is Virginia Long's Plus One, so you could go in his place; and Lin could go as someone else's Plus One. We just need to find someone on the guest list to take her. That can't be too difficult, if we ask nicely.'

Max scowled at Elena. 'Just wait a minute!'

She responded without hesitation. 'Always assuming you don't mind giving up your own invitation, Max. Is there some reason why you can't?'

Though his face was largely hidden by the beard, his body language reflected he had accepted defeat. 'No, of course there isn't. So, Marcus can go with Virginia. In which case, is there any need for Lin to go?'

Lin dived into the conversation. 'Yes, it's essential for me to be there; what if we don't trace our man at the first attempt? I would be the right person to get to know the Ambassador and to visit him in the future so that we can try again.'

Marcus frowned. 'I'm sorry, Lin, but I can only agree to you going with other people there. If you were on your own, who knows what might happen to you.'

She frowned back. 'Then we'll have to hope it works first time, in which case it makes sense for both of us to be there, to double our chances. That means I definitely need to go.' She turned, already smiling. 'And we'll stick with your brilliant plan, Max, about making me look pregnant. So, all that's needed is for you to find someone to take me.'

Max found himself impressed with the way she had steered the debate to the conclusion she had wished for, giving him cause for optimism that she could make the plan work. He nevertheless responded by emphasising the weaknesses. 'If you are to make your legend credible, you will have to expand on it, starting with what you have been doing in Sweden since you arrived. There are certain restrictions on pregnant women travelling on commercial flights, so you must have been in this country for several weeks, I think. SAS don't allow travel within two weeks of the due date, and a special medical certificate is required for the two weeks before that, so let us say that you have been here for a month. If so, you must have been busy doing something and seeing various places during that time. How can you cram a whole month into less than a day?'

Elena responded to Max. 'Just leave it with me; I'll drive her around and show her the main sights.'

He nodded agreement. 'But also, we need to make sure no one identifies her and blows her cover.'

Elena stood up. 'Trust me, I can deal with all that. Lin can wear wigs and changes of clothes, and they can stay hidden at our usual hotel. You're OK to authorise enough cash so they can pay for everything without using a bank card, aren't you, Max?'

'*Absolut*.' Pressing both hands down on the desk, he raised himself up. 'In case I do not see you again, allow me now to wish you the very best of good fortune.' He shook hands, first with Lin, then with Marcus.

Seeing Marcus reaching to pick up the chocolate box, Lin stepped forward and snatched it away. She giggled, 'I've only been pregnant a few minutes, and already I'm having my first craving.' Both Swedes laughed warmly. Marcus could do no more than force an unconvincing smile, concerned he was allowing Lin to be put in harm's way.

CHAPTER 21

Elena led Marcus and Lin along the corridor to her office, which was substantially smaller than Max's corner room and shared only half his view. She directed them to her two visitor chairs before settling behind her desk. 'Excuse me, I just need to make a phone call.'

While Elena was talking in Swedish, Marcus spoke quietly to Lin. 'Are you really sure about all this? You can always change your mind.'

Lin looked him in the eye. 'One of my reasons for joining the police force was for the excitement, but the reality is, it can be dull and boring for much of the time. This is the most thrilling thing I've ever done. It may not be on the same level as you in your army days, but I can feel the adrenaline pumping right now. So don't try and stop me, Marcus, because I really want to do this.'

Elena put down the telephone and looked up at them. 'I'll book your hotel rooms now.'

Lin forced herself not to glance at Marcus as she responded, 'I'd feel safer if I wasn't on my own.'

Elena nodded. 'I know how worried you must be.' She picked up the telephone and conducted two further conversations in Swedish. When she had finished, she again addressed Lin. 'Everything is arranged.'

Fearing Elena may have lost sight of the need for psychological preparation by focusing on practical arrangements, Marcus voiced his concern. 'We have a plan for Lin, but it needs a lot of work if she isn't to be exposed for who she is. What can you do to help?'

Elena responded confidently, 'I shall handle her, personally. Tomorrow, the two of us will visit various places of interest as tourists, so that she'll have the right background information.'

Marcus shook his head. 'There's much more to it than that; Lin needs to have the right persona, as well.' He turned to his colleague. 'Your observed behaviour needs to match your characterisation. You've probably read loads of popular fiction where someone behaves out of character to engineer some dramatic twist in the plot, but in real life those errors would stand out a mile. On the one hand, you've found yourself pregnant but you know next to nothing about the father, suggesting you're intellectually or behaviourally challenged; and on the other, if you were to hold a conversation with someone as your normal self, it would immediately become apparent you're neither of those things.'

'Are you suggesting I should avoid speaking?'

'I suspect that would fail to match any character we could invent that would fit the available scenarios. It seems to me the pregnancy issue will have to drive the direction we take. Either you *are* intelligent and some special circumstance led to the pregnancy, or you're an airhead. If we go with intelligent but plead special case, one option would be date rape, except that would hardly fit with you first coming looking for him eight months later. Drunkenness is another popular excuse, but again, if you were intelligent you wouldn't wait eight months to investigate. The pregnancy would be more believable if we went down the airhead route, but is it feasible for you to behave convincingly like a dizzy blonde?'

'Don't you remember me acting a part once before? At that art gallery? Not exactly a dizzy blonde, but something similar. Do you really doubt I could do it?'

'I think you *probably* could, but I don't feel one hundred per cent confident. After all, this isn't a game; if you were to get it wrong, you wouldn't just be able to go back to the beginning and start again.'

'Well, what about the alternatives?'

'No doubt we could concoct some sort of story about an intelligent young woman who gets herself pregnant by someone she hardly knows, but my instincts tell me it would inevitably sound contrived.'

'In that case, hasn't the decision just made itself? I need to act like an airhead.'

'It would need to be more than just an act to be convincing; you would have to create a persona that you could maintain while ever you were in character.'

'Do you really think it would be that difficult for me to change into some dizzy blonde?'

He looked to the ceiling for inspiration. 'In theory, it's easier for a more intelligent person to appear less so, than for a less intelligent person...'

Elena interrupted. 'Is that true? How do you know? Whatever happened to the plain and simple policeman you were trying to suggest *you* are? It seems to me you've just disproved your own theory, by displaying a considerable knowledge of psychology.'

He replied, 'The difference is, I was only playing a part before, to see how you and Max reacted; but now I know we're all on the same side, I can just be myself.'

Lin felt a strong urge to support him. 'If Marcus says I should play the dumb blonde, then that's what I'll do.'

Elena responded, 'I'm pleased that we're having this conversation, as I've arranged for someone to help you create your new characters; she's a make-up specialist.

You'll need a disguise for our day out, so no one can identify you later; and another one, for the party at the Russian embassy.'

Marcus added, 'Your biggest challenge will be to disguise your true nature when in your second persona. At least being made to look heavily pregnant will serve as a constant reminder of who you're meant to be.'

Elena caught his eye. 'You're ever so good at this, aren't you, Marcus? I think I'd need to peel away some more of your layers to find out who you really are.'

He smiled. 'Thank you for the compliment, Elena; but there's much less to me than meets the eye.'

Lin thought they had looked at each other for long enough, so addressed Marcus to distract him. 'When should I start practising playing the dumb blonde?'

He replied, 'Don't you worry your pretty little head about that sort of thing; I'll let you know when.'

She snapped, 'That's rather condescending!'

He grinned. 'Actually, that was your first test, and I'm sorry to say you failed it. Would you like to give it another try?'

She smiled sweetly. 'No; I'll just let you work things out for me and tell me what to do.'

Elena finally interrupted the long silence that hung in the air between them. 'Now I know neither of you are what it says on file. Just don't bollocks everything up for me, will you, when you put your real plan into action.' Lin gave her a warm smile in lieu of a denial. Marcus tried for hurt innocence.

There was a knock at the door. Elena called out 'Enter,' in English, for the benefit of her guests.

A well-preserved, perfectly made-up middle-aged woman strode into the room, carrying two matching brown leather suitcases. Elena introduced her to them, though not *vice versa*. 'This is Agnetha, our expert on disguises.' The two Brits listened uncomprehendingly as the other two held an animated debate in Swedish.

Agnetha finally spoke to Lin in faltering English. 'So you have red hair tomorrow, until evening when your hair is blonde with a blonde wig.'

Lin frowned. 'Why would I need a blonde wig?'

Elena replied for her. 'It will be an extension to your own hair that will be obvious to everyone, and so it will give people the impression you wish to look good, but also that you are quite careless. This would fit well with your character of having become carelessly pregnant.'

Marcus added, 'And the extra-long hair will serve as a further constant reminder of who you're playing. I mean, who you are; you need to immerse yourself in the rôle, rather than consciously act the part.'

Agnetha opened a suitcase and extracted a pair of wet-look black trousers and a black T-shirt. 'This is plain and simple, Typical Swedish Tourist.'

Elena made a quiet aside to Lin. 'More like Typical Swedish Catwalk; I'll have to get something to match.'

Next, Agnetha carefully withdrew a gold dress, and held it up. 'This is if you have meeting for discussion.'

Elena asked, 'Is it expensive? It looks it.'

Agnetha explained, 'It's cheap copy of an expensive dress, which I think is right.' She put it back, and lifted out a sparkling blue dress. 'And this is to party.'

Lin looked uncomfortably at the skimpy bodice. 'I didn't bring a suitable bra to wear with that.'

Agnetha laughed. 'You don't wear a bra with this!'

Marcus thought Lin looked more worried about wearing the dress than masquerading at the party. He changed the subject for her. 'What happened to the idea of making Lin look nine months' pregnant?'

Agnetha extracted a large rubber mound with thin straps and prominent belly button. 'This fits around the body. The straps will be hidden by the suspender belt.'

Lin gulped. 'I've never worn a suspender belt; what am I supposed to do with it?'

Agnetha smiled at her. 'I'll show you later. Try on the blue dress over the pregnant bump.'

Lin stood and began to unfasten her trousers. Marcus jumped to his feet. 'Whoa! Hang on! You've forgotten I'm here. I'll go and look out the window.'

When Lin was down to her underwear, Agnetha fastened the pregnancy bump around her, and then held up the blue dress. Lin reluctantly removed her bra. Agnetha looked closely at her bust. 'My breasts were much bigger when I was pregnant.'

Elena also took a close look. 'I think they're plenty big enough to be convincing; and firm, too.'

With a show of bravado to hide her embarrassment, Lin called out, 'Marcus, do you want to come over here and settle this dispute?'

He yelled back, without turning, 'I'm not looking. You'll just have to work with whatever you've got.'

Agnetha pulled the dress down over Lin's head, and then made small adjustments until satisfied it was fitted perfectly. Lin called out, 'You can come and see, now; I'm decent... more or less.'

Marcus walked over and saw Lin wearing the most revealing dress he had ever seen outside of the world of show business. He took a deep breath. 'That's, erm, that certainly is, um, those straps... Is it on back to front?'

Lin bowed her head and checked herself. 'I really

don't think I can wear this in public.'

Elena looked her up and down. 'If your character is to be a tart, then I think it looks just right.'

Lin shook her head. 'I'll try the other one.'

Marcus returned to the window. Agnetha carefully peeled off the blue dress. Lin put her bra back on before slipping into the gold dress with Agnetha's help, then called out, 'Marcus, come and look at this one.'

He walked over and checked her out, front and back. 'You certainly look good in it, for someone who's nine months gone. I can't help wondering if you look too good; you don't look tired enough.'

Elena turned to Agnetha. 'Can you do something to make her look tired?'

Agnetha laughed. 'Yes, keep her up all night.'

Marcus returned again to the window as Lin changed into the wet-look trousers and T-shirt. Once more, she called him back. 'I'll be wearing this tomorrow; what do you think?'

'I'm not sure it's my idea of inconspicuous; people will be looking at you and asking, "Who's that model?" Maybe you should wear sunglasses so people assume you want to be recognised, and will look the other way when they realise they don't know who you are.'

She frowned. 'I think there was a compliment hidden in there somewhere, in which case, thank you kind sir.'

Agnetha delved into her other bag. 'We haven't done your wigs, yet.' She extracted a mass of blonde curls. 'You hair is very fine. This one isn't really up to your standard, but that's OK, as people will notice.' She attached the tresses and spread them across Lin's back.

Lin brought the hair forward and let it cascade down her front. 'If I wore the blue dress, this could hide my...

embarrassment.'

Agnetha shook her head. 'It would not look good.'

Lin smiled. 'Sorry, I was only joking.'

Agnetha smiled back. 'Now for the red wig.' She fitted it in place, then returned to the first suitcase and extracted a large pair of black sunglasses, commenting to Marcus, 'I agree with you; this is the right look.' When Lin had put them on, Agnetha held up a mirror for her. 'This is who people will see, tomorrow.'

Lin examined her new image. 'If I didn't know it was me, I'd think it was some film star.'

Marcus punctiliously returned to the window before Lin removed the trousers and put on a pair of knee-length nylon stockings. After she had tried several pairs of shoes, Agnetha declared the gold ballerina pumps were a good fit and would be suitable for either dress. Lin accepted the recommendation.

Agnetha demonstrated the intricacies of suspenders and stockings, and selected various items of underwear for Lin's approval. As she collated all the agreed pieces into one suitcase, she insisted on leaving the blue dress, in case Lin changed her mind.

While Lin was putting her own clothes back on, Elena spoke with Agnetha in Swedish as she packed away the unwanted items into the other case. When dressed, Lin thanked Agnetha for her help.

As Agnetha departed with the suitcase of spares, she called out a 'Goodbye,' that was loud enough to include Marcus.

He called back, 'Goodbye; and thanks.'

Once the door had closed, Elena's smile gave way to an expression of deep concern as she turned to Lin. 'She had no suitable boots to go with the black trousers, and we don't really have time to go shopping for some.'

Lin's initial disquiet gave way to amused relief as she learned the nature of the crisis. 'I could just wear my own boots.'

'No; they wouldn't look right. Would you be willing to try some of mine? Most have very high heels.'

'Sure.'

Elena showed her relief. 'Marvellous! I have lots to choose from. And some jewellery?'

'I hadn't even thought about jewellery. Yes, I'd be happy to borrow yours, if you don't mind.'

'Good. Excuse me while I make some calls.'

Lin joined Marcus by the window and looked out at the trees. She commented quietly, 'You must be fed up of this view by now.'

He whispered, 'Not really; I was only looking *at* the window when you were getting changed, not *through* it. I saw the entire show.'

Despite their intimate relationship, she found herself blushing as she whispered back, 'You're wicked!'

Elena completed her conversations and called over to them, 'Now we must collect some cash for you.'

Marcus carried the light suitcase down the stairs. Lin took care of the box of chocolates. Elena led them to a small office on the first floor, where a tie-less man in a dark suit held out a form to her. She signed it and took delivery of a wad of Kroner notes.

As they were leaving, Elena picked up a rubber band from a desk-tidy and placed it around the money, then put the bundle into the inside pocket of her jacket. In response to Marcus's questioning look, she explained, 'It'll be easier if I pay the bills; not everyone in Sweden speaks English.'

They walked down the stairs to the ground floor, where Elena collected a sports bag from reception, before leading them to her car and inviting Marcus to sit in the front passenger seat. Once out on the main road, Elena briefly turned her head to him. 'The hotels are usually full at this time of year, but I have a sure-fire way of getting a room.'

He suggested, 'Claim it's for national security?'

She laughed and glanced again at him. 'No; I ask, "Do you have a room for the King of Sweden?" And they say, "Of course; it will be a great honour." And I say, "Well, sorry, but he isn't coming, so I'll have his room." Good, huh?' Marcus gave a hearty laugh. Lin pretended to be preoccupied with staring out of the window, as she wondered if Elena was making a play for him.

After Marcus had eventually quietened down, Elena explained, 'Actually, the hotels do get fully booked, but we have a couple of rooms that we reserve for urgent needs. We're supposed to let the hotel know by eight p.m. if they can use them for other guests, so that we get a rebate on our reservation fee. It works well, except when something happens very late at night; then, we just have to hope we can find some place, somewhere.'

Marcus responded with genuine gratitude. 'I don't know where we'd be without you.'

After a quarter of an hour, Elena drove them into a hotel car park and turned off the engine. 'I'll do the registering, so you won't need to provide identification. What name would you like?'

As he pondered, Lin answered for him. 'Dr John Watson.'

Elena looked around. 'You sound very certain.'

Marcus explained, 'He's a character in the Sherlock Holmes stories. Married to Mrs Mary Watson.'

Elena responded to him, 'Oh; right.' She turned to Lin. 'And you?'

She answered quickly. 'Mrs Mary Watson.'

Elena extracted her car keys. 'I'll be as quick as I can. Next, we should have a meal, I think.'

Marcus responded, 'Yes, I'm quite hungry. Does it have a good restaurant?'

She shook her head. 'We'll have to have Room Service, so we're not seen together by other people.'

He argued, 'But we've already been seen together, at the airport and in this car.'

She argued back, 'We shouldn't make it worse.'

Ten minutes later, Elena returned to the car and opened the boot. After Lin had declined his offer to help her into her parka, he put on his overcoat before removing the luggage.

As well as his travel bag, Marcus took the suitcase containing Lin's disguises. When Elena picked up a large holdall from reception and lugged it to the lift along with her sports bag, Lin felt underemployed with just a small travel bag and a box of chocolates to carry.

Elena led them into the lift and selected floor two. They emerged onto a dimly lit corridor. At room 205, Elena stopped, took out her key card, and spoke to Marcus. 'We're in this room.' He felt a momentary shock as he thought she meant him and her. 'You're two doors down at two-o-nine; here's your card.'

Lin involuntarily swung around to look at Marcus. He hid his disappointment and smiled at Elena. 'I'll leave Lin's things here, then. Will we be eating in the same room, or is that also best avoided?'

She smiled back. 'Yours is a large room; we'll all eat together there, if you wish, once we've unpacked.'

He nodded. 'Yes, that would be nice.' When he had put down the suitcase, Lin handed him the box of chocolates. He commented, 'And we can share these, as well, unless you're both on a diet.'

Lin tried to sound upbeat. 'There's no point in *me* dieting; I'm expecting to be getting much fatter, soon.'

Marcus left them at their door and went to his room. As he looked at the extra-wide bed, he wished Lin could have been sharing it with him, and concocted the flimsy moral defence that being in a different country to his wife meant it would not constitute being unfaithful.

Before unpacking, he carefully opened the gift from Virginia and found two layers of chocolates, concealed under which was a pile of Swedish currency. Counting out the twenty thousand kroner, he assumed it was all in high denomination notes to minimise their total depth. He took a sock from his bag, rolled the money into a tight bundle and stashed it inside. Realising he would be unable to make the box now appear unopened, he selected a dark chocolate and popped it into his mouth.

After unpacking, he sat and looked at the Room Service menu. There was a gentle knock at the door. He checked through the spyhole and saw it was Lin. As he let her in, he asked, 'Has she thrown you out, then?'

She sighed. 'No such luck. She'll be along soon, once she's made her calls.'

He nodded toward the bed. 'It's such a pity to waste it. So, is your room similar to this? Are you and your VBF going to be cuddling up all night, do you think?'

She punched his arm. 'Twin beds! And people use BFF, now.' She saw the opened box of chocolates and noticed one was missing. Pointing an accusing finger at the gap, she complained, 'Couldn't you wait?'

He looked hurt. 'I was being brave, taking the first one in case they were all poisoned.'

She gave a dismissive, 'Yeah; right.'

'And I needed to get the bread out.'

'The what?'

'The bread and honey.' He interpreted her frown as an indication of incomprehension. 'The money from Honey. I thought it might be better if Elena doesn't know we've another sponsor. There's twenty bag.' He waited for her questioning look. 'Twenty bag of sand; twenty grand. If we don't need it all, we can always return it, later.'

Her eyes lit up. 'Or go on a shopping spree!'

He handed her the Room Service menu. 'First things first; let's work out what we'd like to eat.'

Lin was reading through the options when there was another knock at the door. Marcus checked the spyhole and opened up for Elena. 'Come in; we're just looking at the menu. But are you sure it wouldn't be simpler to eat at a restaurant, somewhere?'

Elena shook her head. 'We have a lot to discuss that we wouldn't want to be overheard; we should eat here while we make plans. Decide what you'd like to have, and I'll fetch a chair from my room.' She immediately left them to pore over the menu.

Lin spoke hurriedly, 'Should we tell her?'

Marcus replied equally rapidly, 'No; but persuade her she isn't needed after tonight, though.'

'How do I do that?'

'Say you're no longer worried about being alone. No, say you'd feel braver if you were on your own.'

'Should I tell her tonight, or in the morning?'

'Maybe morning, after you've had…'

Any further discussion was interrupted by a knock. Though certain it would be Elena, Marcus nevertheless checked through the spyhole. She bustled in with the chair held forward, hurrying so as not to be caught by the door as it automatically swung closed behind her. After placing her seat at the table, she picked up the menu. 'Disappointing, isn't it. I'll have Fried chicken with coriander yoghurt sauce and a tomato salad.'

Marcus saw Lin looking to him to order next. 'Rib eye steak, red wine sauce and chips will do me.' He added seamlessly, 'And I suppose you'll be having a Béarnaise sauce with your trout.'

She smiled in appreciation. 'And a mixed salad.'

He salivated in anticipation as he contemplated the list of three sweets. 'Chocolate Cake and cream with berries; sorbet and ice cream with berries; or a selection of cheeses, presumably without berries. Which would you recommend, Elena?'

'I'd recommend you watch your weight!' She saw how hurt he looked. 'Only joking. I won't be having a sweet, myself, but you might like to try the cheese; if there's anything local, I'll explain what it is.'

He nodded. 'We could maybe share two between three; that will keep my calories down.'

Lin added quickly, 'Cheese would be good, for me.'

He looked at Elena. 'How does a bottle of house red sound?'

She shook her head. 'Tomorrow will be a long day for me; alcohol helps me go to sleep, but then it disturbs my dreams. I'll just have water.'

He grinned, 'Wrong answer!' With his right index

finger stiffly in his mouth, he flicked his left cheek to make a cork-popping sound, then quickly tapped the right cheek repeatedly as he progressively closed his mouth, making an imitation of wine being poured.

Taken by surprise, Elena laughed loudly. Lin seethed at him for repeating with someone else the joke he had first shared with her. When he saw her looking daggers at him, he knew he would need to make an apology.

Elena placed the meal order, and then proceeded to give them background information about Stockholm, which Marcus understood was largely for Lin's benefit.

The waiter who arrived with the food trolley was old and thin and unreasonably tall. As he pushed it into the room, he glanced at the two women, and then looked at the man for rather longer. Marcus imagined the waiter must be wondering how he had succeeded in enticing two attractive women into his room.

Elena spoke briefly with him in Swedish. As he headed out, he turned and glanced at Marcus one more time, before encouraging the door to close quicker.

During the meal, Elena continued her narrative, until Marcus suggested she eat her chicken before it goes cold. As she spoke very little after that, he thought she may have misinterpreted his well-intentioned words as a request for silence. After Lin had eaten just one cracker with cheese, Elena stood up. 'We'll go to our room, now; there's a lot I need to explain to you about the places we'll be going.' Lin glanced at Marcus, and then at the bed, before reluctantly allowing herself to be ushered out.

CHAPTER 22

Marcus looked at the remains of the day's only proper meal; there were still two almost full servings of cheese and crackers. He decided to eat every last morsel. When he had finished, he still felt hungry, so tentatively started on the chocolates; a growing feeling of guilt limited him to just three. Knowing from his army training days that his need for food was now only in his mind, he pushed the trolley outside, where he found Lin heading for his door. She looked at the empty plates. He grimaced. 'I was hungry; sorry if you've come back for your cheese.' Seeing a spec of rye flatbread, she picked it up, placed it on her tongue and closed her eyes in rapture. 'If you're trying to make me feel guilty, I can tell you, you're succeeding.'

She motioned him to go first. As the door began to close behind her, she stepped forward and pointed to her feet. 'What do you think of my boots?'

He looked down at the black patent leather mid-calf stilettoes. 'Very nice.'

'They fit me better than they fit Elena. Her feet are just a bit smaller, but she likes enough room for thick socks in the winter. The heels must be six inches long.'

'It sounds like you're enjoying some "girl time".'

'Yes. I've tried on boots, earrings, and a nice coat; she thought my parka wasn't right for going to a ball.'

'And has she now given you time off for good behaviour? Or is it bad behaviour she's wanting?' He was surprised not to receive a punch on the arm.

'Why can't we just tell her about us? It's hardly likely it'll get back to England.'

'Don't forget she's only here because she thought you wanted her to be; think about her feelings.'

'You're right, of course. I'm sure her "hard woman" attitude with us at the airport was all an act; she's really nice, once you get to know her. She told me all about where her various boots came from, and said I can keep the pair I'm using; but I couldn't accept them, so I said there's no room in my travel bag. It sounded lame, but I couldn't think of anything else to say.' She changed subjects with barely a pause. 'I'm a bit worried about tomorrow, because I think she's worried, and that's why she's uptight about making sure she's briefed me as well as she can. I wish I was staying in your bed; I'd feel safer, somehow, and less anxious about things.'

'But before, you said you weren't at all anxious.'

'I wasn't when I said it; but now, I've had more time to think about it.'

'Well, if you really believe it would help, I suppose we could let her in on our secret.'

'But then, what about her, being left on her own? Like you said, she's only here as a favour to me.'

'She could join us; the bed's big enough for a touch of troilism.' He was relieved to feel a punch on the arm.

'I'm not sharing you with anybody.' They both did a double take. 'Except Helen, of course. Anyway, why were you trying to be so charming with her? I can tell she's attracted to you, so why are you leading her on?'

He shrugged. 'I didn't think I had been. Oh, having a bit of fun with our popping bottle gag; I apologise, though I was only trying to lighten the mood. Maybe I was compensating for winding her up, earlier.'

Seeing his earnest, pleading face, she relented. 'I forgive you. But turn off the charm with her, will you?'

He smiled. 'If she is a bit attracted to me, at least it probably means she isn't quite as attracted to you as I thought she was.'

Her eyes widened. 'Now I'm really not going to get any sleep. I was only dropping in to let you know we'll be having breakfast in our room at seven thirty, and going out at a quarter to ten. She needs time in between to check on work, and I said you and I would meet up to get things straight.'

'I would like to get things straight with you, Lin; but I really believe we need Elena with us as well.'

'Erm, are you still talking troilism?'

He laughed. 'Let's turn our hormones off for now, shall we? Tomorrow, we're going to be walking into the lion's den, so we need to prepare thoroughly, only I don't yet know what that preparation should be. Let's all have a working breakfast in my room at seven thirty; I still have three chairs. Ask her to arrange it, will you? And will you make sure I get a full breakfast. I do some of my best planning overnight in my sleep, so by morning I should have a clearer idea of what needs to be on the agenda. But if you or Elena think you've spotted a major flaw in the plan, don't wait until half seven; just come and wake me.'

'Alright. I'll get back, then.'

He saw how she kept her eyes open as she kissed him on the lips, as though searching for something; he guessed it was reassurance. 'And don't worry; I *think* she'll leave you alone if you tell her you're not that type.' She scowled at him before stepping outside. He hoped the anxiety transference would be effective.

Two phones were charging. He picked up the third and called Helen. 'Hi, it's me. I'm in Stockholm.'

'What? And you didn't think to tell me?'

'I didn't want to worry you.'

'Well, sometimes I like to worry; it reminds me what you mean to me. Where exactly are you?'

'Exactly? Room 209... hold on.' He picked up the Welcome brochure and read out the address.

'Are you on your own?'

'Yes.'

'Didn't Lin go with you?'

'Yes, she did.'

'Where is she?'

'Room 205. She's sleeping with a woman from the secret service.'

'Marcus, stop messing about and tell me the truth.'

'I am telling you the truth; she's called Elena. Lin's been trying on her clothes and jewellery, and tomorrow they're going to be doing some sightseeing together.'

'How does that fit into the investigation?'

'Background, orientation, call it what you will.'

'What are your plans for tomorrow?'

'I'll try and see some of the sights myself.'

'Why can't you go with Lin?'

'She'll be incognito, looking like a Swedish tourist.'

'So, is everything alright.'

'Yes, fine. I'm registered here as a Dr John Watson, if you need to leave a message with reception. There isn't anything to report yet, so I'll save my phone bill.'

'It's nice to hear your voice, Marcus. Make sure you let me know if something's going to happen; let me worry, if I want to.'

'Alright, love. I'll call you tomorrow.'

Seeing the new smartphone's battery was showing one hundred per cent, he unplugged its charger and replaced it with the one for the phone he had just used. After a few moments spent thinking what he would say to Pamela, he called her and waited patiently, as the delay proved to be substantial. When she answered, he responded, 'Hi, Honey. Is this an inconvenient time?'

Her voice acquired a soft, seductive edge. 'It's never an inconvenient time to hear from you.' She laughed down the phone. 'Have you something to say to me, like how incredibly attractive you find me?'

He laughed back. 'Of course that's perfectly true, but it isn't why I called. There are some plans you might like to look over, only I'm not sure how best to present them to you. If someone could come here, I'd be able to explain them face-to-face.'

'Sounds a good idea to me. What room are you in?'

'Two o-nine. Don't you want to know the hotel?'

'Oh, yes, of course.'

He again read out the address from the Welcome brochure, then added, 'My colleague is just down the corridor; perhaps I should ask her to join us?'

'Hold that thought. First, you need to talk to my rep. When I get their sit-rep, I'll tell you who... I'll suggest who might best be brought into the discussion.'

'Alright, Honey. Oh, and thanks for the chocolates and the other stuff. By the way, if I don't need all of it, how do I return any leftovers?'

'No can do; the system only does issues. You'd have to dispose of the excess locally, however you like.'

'Well, you know I'm happy to handle anything you give me. Talk to you soon.'

She giggled. 'Bye, sweetie.'

He took the old phone out of the charger, as it was incapable of being operated in situ. When he called Ben, he found there were a few strange sounds on the line before it connected through. Ben answered, 'Yes?'

'I thought you might like to hear from me.'

'Of course, though I'm being kept in the loop by other friends and relations. I've arranged for Cinderella to go to the ball, and I understand you've already been paired for the dance, yourself.'

'In that case, you're the one that needs to keep me in the picture; you know more than I do.'

'I'm sure you would have been informed very soon, so don't take it to heart. Now, is there anything I can do for you?'

'Yes, you could tell me how unofficial everything is; the size of the bundle I received suggests your hands are still firmly tied.'

'Hmm; it was only meant to cover one night. I'll make sure you receive a bigger bundle, next time. What about coming to the big house tomorrow at, say, eleven o'clock? Ask for Michael Mouse.'

'That'll give me something to do; my colleague is having a day out with a friend.'

'Indeed? I'll have to arrange a friend for you, in that case. Anything else?'

'No, that's everything.'

'Well, have a good night's sleep; you have a long day ahead of you tomorrow.'

'Yes, it's New Year's eve, so I expect I'll still be up at midnight. Talk to you soon.'

As the battery tended to run down very quickly, he put the phone back into the charger. Having made all his calls, he reflected on who had already known what.

There was a gentle knock at the door. He checked through the spyhole and saw it was Virginia Long, holding a large bag. When he opened up and stepped aside, she breezed in. 'Hi, Marcus.'

'Hi, Virginia. Do you know, it sounds strange to hear someone call me by my name; my phone contacts don't use it, or call me something else.'

'What do your womenfolk call you?'

'Simply Marcus; it's never really been altered.'

'Marcus, like that Swedish model. Then I'll call you Marky-Marcus; no, just Marky. And you can call me Ginny.' She laid the bag on the bed. 'We're going to a party tomorrow, so I've brought you a tux. If we're to look convincing as a couple, we need to get familiar with each other.' She intercepted the thought that flashed across his mind. 'Just to be clear, when we're in public, we need to be *very* friendly; I have a bad reputation to uphold. But when we're alone, we keep it strictly professional; it's a rule I have. OK?'

'Sure, Ginny.'

'OK. But we'll have to try out the friendly bit in private, first, to make sure we're convincing in public.' He remained stock-still, unsure what was expected of him. She stepped forward, placed her hands behind his head, and pulled him toward her. When she kissed him, he felt like she really meant it, and yet he knew what she had just said. She pushed him away and looked him in the eye. 'I don't think you're trying. We'll have to work at this until you get it right.'

He sighed. 'Alright, Ginny, but I have to tell you, I'm a very slow learner. A very, very slow learner.'

By the time the training was over, she was satisfied he was consistently achieving top marks. 'Now you can tell me what you couldn't say to Pammie on the phone.'

He gave an outline of the plan, and explained how Lin would be made to look very pregnant.

She responded by spelling out their own schedule. 'I'll pick you up here at seven forty; that gives enough time to get to the Russian embassy for eight. The first call to the Russian's iPhone will be at eight twenty-six. If it's successful, we leave at nine fifteen. If it isn't, we stay for the next attempt at nine thirty-nine. If that's successful, we leave at ten twenty. If it isn't, we stay for the next attempt at ten fifty-two. Whatever happens, we leave at eleven o'clock.'

'Could you repeat the times.'

'Don't worry; I have it all committed to memory.'

'Yes, but I need to let Lin know, in case she's in a better position to see who answers the phone.'

'Oh, sure. She's obviously not the stay-at-home type she claimed to be. Calls come in at eight twenty-six, nine thirty-nine, ten fifty-two. We leave at nine fifteen, ten twenty, eleven o'clock.'

'Who came up with these timings?'

'Langley Logistics.'

'How do we explain leaving so early, if the eight twenty-six is successful?'

'I'll be all over you; can't wait to get you alone.'

'Well, you can rely on me to rise to the occasion.'

She smiled. 'I'd feel professionally insulted if you didn't, Marky. Now, I could do with a bite. Am I OK to have something here? I've been on the go all day.'

'Yes, sure; I'll join you.' He handed her the room service menu.

'Burger and chips with barbeque sauce should do nicely.'

'Great; I'll have the same. And a beer?'

'Sounds good.'

He phoned for Room Service and placed the order.

She unzipped the bag and extracted a dinner jacket. 'This should be your size.'

He tried it on. 'Well, someone has a good eye; it's a perfect fit.'

She shook her head. 'It's done by computer, working off images from CCTV.'

'What CCTV? Where was it? I thought Sweden had very little video surveillance.' Her laughter sounded to him like water babbling in a brook, sweet and clear.

'Love is all around, and so is CCTV.'

'I didn't realise it was ubiquitous in Sweden.'

'You swallowed a dictionary, Marky?'

'Sorry; anyway, your description was much nicer.' Her heard her laughter again, and understood how well-suited she was for her line of work.

He removed his jacket. She took it from him and hung it in the wardrobe. 'You need to try on the rest.'

As she showed no sign of turning away, he brazenly stripped down to his boxer shorts, and then put on the trousers. She extracted two pairs of black socks and three pairs of patent leather shoes from the bag. 'The computer sometimes gets the feet wrong.'

He put on the first pair of socks, which seemed fine to him. The first pair of shoes was too tight, whereas the other two pairs would have been acceptable; she chose the ones he had said were the more comfortable.

After comparing two shirts, she handed him the less frilly one. 'This is more you, Marky; an understated Brit.' As he put it on, she extracted a small jewellery box. 'Do you like these cufflinks?'

He held one up close, and found the plain gold rectangle was in fact finely tooled. 'It's very "me"; how did the computer know?'

She gave her sweet laugh again. 'It didn't; I chose them for you. They're a gift from me; I'd like you to keep them to remember me by.'

At she took the cufflink back and slipped it into position on the shirt, he understood how irresistible she must be to anyone unaware she was acting a part.

She fitted the second cufflink, before offering him a black bow tie. 'I'll be disappointed if you say you want the clip-on.' He extended his hand to take it. At the last moment, she whisked it away. 'I'll fasten it for you; sit down, so I can reach better.' He lifted a chair from under the table and positioned it where there was some floor space. She stood behind him. 'I find it easier with a mirror, but I can manage.' She leaned over him. As she imbued with a seductive air the simple process of fastening a tie, he wondered how much was taught and how much came naturally to her.

When the knot was complete, she leaned over him from behind for one last time, as though needing to give a final check. To breathe in her scent more deeply, he turned his head slightly. She slowly brushed her cheek against his nose before moving away, knowing she was leaving him wanting more of the moment.

She walked around him. 'Let me see you from the front.' He stood up. 'Good. Now I'll check the shirt. Turn around. Slowly!' He completed one revolution. She fetched the jacket. 'Put it on; let me see the whole effect.' He did as instructed. She turned him full circle, handling him easily and confidently. 'We'll look great together. You'd better take it all off again, now.'

When he was again down to his boxer shorts, there was a knock at the door. Ginny checked at the spyhole and opened up. The tall waiter trundled in with the trolley. Seeing Marcus standing away to one side in silence, he glanced at her for a moment. As he ambled out, he was unable to avoid raising an eyebrow.

Marcus waited until the door had closed fully, before turning to Ginny. 'Well, there goes my reputation.'

She smiled. 'And mine... I hope.'

He put on a pair of trousers and a shirt, while she laid out the food and drink. As they sat eating together, he understood how any unsuspecting red-blooded male would be utterly defenceless to her form of attack.

She knew he kept sneaking looks at her, and felt certain she had scored another success. When they were down to the last of the beer, she gave him a tiny smile. 'I'd better be going, now; we both have a long day ahead of us. And I'm sorry for disturbing your sleep.'

Puzzled, he responded, 'But you haven't disturbed my sleep.'

Her smile increased. 'Not yet I haven't; but I think I will have by morning.'

He laughed as he comprehended her meaning. 'Have you ever broken your rule about remaining professional in private?'

She replied confidently, 'No; never.' After a moment of reflection, she added hesitantly, 'At least, not yet.'

CHAPTER 23

At seven twenty-nine, Elena and Lin stepped out of their room and down the corridor to 209. Elena saw the old waiter approaching with a food trolley, so wished him, '*God morgon.*' He responded at length, Lin listening uncomprehendingly. When he headed away, Elena explained, 'It's breakfast for three, but he was concerned there had been a mistake and it should have been for four.'

Lin rapped at the door. Marcus opened it almost immediately. Lin motioned him away without a word, as she stepped inside. After looking in the bathroom, she opened up the wardrobe. 'Where is she?'

Assuming Lin knew about Ginny's visit, he quickly responded, 'She isn't here; she left last night.'

An awkward silence hung in the air, which Elena broke with the sound of unlubricated wheels as she dragged the trolley to the table. She looked from Lin to Marcus. 'Who are you talking about?'

He replied, 'Ginny Long. We had a meeting.'

Lin asked, 'Why weren't we invited? Or wasn't it that type of meeting?'

He frowned at Lin. 'How did you know, anyway?'

Lin shook her head. 'I didn't; I was just having a laugh with Elena, because the waiter thought he should have been bringing breakfast for four.'

He laughed unconvincingly. 'I need to up my game, don't I? Falling for that one.'

Lin smiled, 'You certainly do.' Then, she mouthed,

'You bastard!', as she looked daggers at him.

He gave a tiny shake of the head, to let Lin know he was reserving his defence.

Elena asked, provocatively, 'Is she as good as the rumours say she is?'

He pretended not to understand her true meaning. 'She certainly comes over as extremely professional.'

Lin asked, 'So, you feel safe in her hands?'

He decided to take control of the conversation. 'We'll have breakfast, and then I'll explain what the game plan is. Oh, and let me say from the outset, part of that plan involves my appearing to be intimate with Ginny, but it will all be an act.'

Lin spoke through clenched teeth. 'Yesterday, you were saying I had to really immerse myself in my rôle, not just act it. What depth do you hope to achieve with your performance?'

He ignored the innuendo, and sat at the table. 'Come on; let's get stuck in.'

Lin dropped heavily onto the seat next to him, and whispered, 'Or not!'

Elena settled next to Lin and removed the nearest lid, revealing a plate of sausage, bacon and scrambled eggs. 'This one is yours, Marcus.' He took it from her. For herself, she collected a large, dark flatbread, along with slices of cold meat and cheese. Unsure how to proceed, Lin copied her every move.

When he had finished his meal, and Elena and Lin had had enough of theirs, Lin cleared the table and prepared to remove the trolley. He stayed her hand. 'I'll take it out later. Let's get on with the meeting.'

They arranged their chairs into a tight triangle, and Marcus began with an explanation of the game plan.

Elena followed by detailing the arrangements put in place for Lin. 'The British Ambassador will collect her from the hotel at seven forty-five. The journey to the Russian embassy takes nearly twenty minutes; they will use that time to get to know each other a little, so that he can present her to the Russian Ambassador. He will also apologise for his wife's absence due to a migraine.' She sat back and waited for the next contributor.

Marcus informed them he had a meeting scheduled for eleven o'clock at the British embassy. He then asked Elena for her plans for their day.

She rapidly read out a handwritten itinerary. 'Depart hotel zero nine fifty hours. Drive for nine minutes to Hamngatan. Visit two shopping centres that open at ten hundred hours: Gallerian and NK. Depart ten twenty hours for Stadsholmen island in the old town and see the Palace apartments; the Museum and Treasury will be closed, unfortunately. Depart ten fifty-eight hours for the Nobel Museum. Arrive at eleven hundred hours, when it opens. Depart twelve hundred hours for the Vasa Museum on Djurgården island. Twelve minutes journey time and eighteen minutes for food. Enter at twelve thirty hours and stay for one hour. Thirteen thirty hours, seven minutes' journey to Skansen Living History Museum. Stay two hours. Fifteen thirty-seven hours, nine minutes' drive to the National Museum of Science and Technology. Stay one hour. Sixteen forty-six hours, sixteen minutes' drive to the Natural History museum. Stay fifty-eight minutes, until it closes at eighteen hundred hours. Drive for five minutes; obtain food. Eat for forty-five minutes. Drive remaining ten minutes back to hotel, arriving nineteen hundred hours.'

He picked up his mobile phone. 'I couldn't follow

some of that; let me just photograph your notes.' She handed over the sheet of paper. He took a picture, checked it for clarity, and passed it back.

Elena continued, 'I shall help Lin to dress, ready for collection by the Ambassador. And then, I'm officially off duty, but either of you can phone me at any time.'

Marcus responded, 'That's very much appreciated. And do you think I might like to see any of those places you're visiting, myself?'

She replied, 'The Vasa Museum may be first choice for you. It's dedicated to the *Vasa* warship. Way back in seventeen twenty-eight it sank on its first ever voyage, because it was top-heavy with cannon. After it was raised in nineteen sixty-one, it was put into a museum and became a very popular tourist attraction.'

Marcus shook his head and sighed. 'If only the designers had studied English history, the Battle of the Solent, fifteen forty-five. We hit a similar problem after the *Mary Rose* had been rebuilt to take extra guns. It toppled over when it was hit by a strong gust of wind. We salvaged it in nineteen eighty-two and then put it into a museum, but at least the *Mary Rose* wasn't on its maiden voyage when it went down; it had had years of active service before then. You know, it does seem a bit strange that you have a museum dedicated to a failure.'

Elena snapped at him. 'It wasn't a failure!' Realising how chauvinistic she had sounded, she gave a little embarrassed laugh. 'Well, it was at the time, but it isn't now. Since it was raised, we've learned lots of things from it, because it's so well-preserved.'

Marcus smiled. 'We can learn a lot from failures; just look at Napoleon Bonaparte. The English thrashed him and exiled him twice, but the French still regard him as some sort of hero.'

Lin twisted to look directly at Marcus. 'Have you ever considered yourself for international diplomacy? Because, if you have, I suggest you think again.'

Marcus gave a self-deprecating laugh. 'Alright, let's not talk of failures; we need to be focused on success.' He turned to Elena. 'Well done, by the way; you've put together a very comprehensive plan. And I suppose Lin could be tired out by the end of it, which might make her seem more the part when she's dressed to look pregnant. But I do think she'll really need her wits about her this evening, so it might be better if you schedule time for her to come back to the hotel for a rest, before the main event. Not that I don't think your plan sounds tremendous.'

Elena responded, 'We'll be flexible. If we think we need to change the plan, we will.'

He nodded. 'Great. I'll check on you both at seven o'clock, or you can come and see me earlier if you wish. I'll make sure I'm back by five p.m.'

Elena liked the idea of correcting him, after he had insulted Sweden's favourite ship. 'Seventeen hundred hours, you mean.' After a moment, she smiled.

He smiled back. 'Indeed.'

After they had forensically dissected the plans for the evening, Lin suggested she and Elena change into their tourist clothes and let Marcus check them out. He responded, 'That would be good, but first, there's one important question you haven't yet considered.'

Lin stared at him. 'What is it?'

He replied, 'What's the name of the father?'

She blinked hard. 'How could I be so stupid!'

Elena rushed to cover up their joint discomfort. 'I

could make up a Swedish name, if you like; what about Lucas Ljungberg?'

He shook his head at Elena and then addressed Lin. 'What would your airhead character think if someone introduced themselves as Henrik Ibsen?'

'Henry Gibson, obviously.'

'Then that's who he should be. Or at least, that's who you think he is. If anyone gets it, they'll assume you misheard, and being an airhead, you wouldn't have recognised the name of the famous Norwegian writer.'

Lin's eyes opened wide. 'He's a writer?'

Marcus felt embarrassed at having unexpectedly exposed her literary shortcomings. 'He was. He died over a century ago. He was really quite famous.'

'Well, I've never heard of him.' She turned to Elena. 'Let's get back to our room, shall we? When I'm all dressed up, it could be called A Doll's House.' She looked again at Marcus. 'Later, you and I can focus on tracking down An Enemy of the People.'

He looked anxiously at her. 'Do *not* be clever like that when you're being a dumb blonde.'

She smiled at him. 'I know. I know.'

He eventually smiled back. 'Before you go, have you thought about how to describe the mythical father?'

She responded immediately. 'I could just choose one of the three suspects.'

He stood and picked up his old phone. 'Let's see if we can narrow the field, shall we? Elena, have you had the chance to research the Swedish guy?'

'I set the hare running yesterday; I'll check, shall I?'

'Please. And I'll see if my contact has anything.'

Elena took out her mobile phone and walked to the window to make the call. Marcus rang Ben. 'Morning;

hope this isn't too early for you. ... Your man at the airport said he'd pass on our shortlist. ... So, what have you found? ... That's great. I'll be at the big house at eleven, if you'd like to talk on a secure line. ... Bye.'

Elena had concluded her call, and had delayed returning to her seat while Marcus finished his. As she walked back, she stated, 'The Swedish guy is clean. We didn't find anything negative about the other two.'

Marcus responded, 'The English chap's in the clear, as well, which makes the one with the Irish passport our prime suspect. My guys are still investigating him, but they aren't making much headway. So, if we spot him at the Russian embassy this evening, that alone is enough for us to build a *prima facie* case; and if he answers the iPhone there, that pretty well seals it.' He turned to Lin. 'You remember I asked you how to describe the father; have you thought any further?'

Having had time to reconsider her earlier response, she began tentatively. 'I could describe the Irish guy from the photo...'

He now felt sure she had spotted the flaw. 'But...?'

'If he's our man, the Russian Ambassador will keep him hidden. So, I should make up someone who doesn't look anything like him.'

'And how would you do that?'

'Think it all through from head to foot, and reinforce my mental image with details I'm unlikely to forget.'

He moved his head from side to side as an indication of ambivalence, before giving his personal preference. 'That could work in theory, but I believe there may be a better way. What about choosing someone you actually know? That way, if you're repeatedly asked to describe him in the future, you won't give inconsistent replies because you'll simply be recalling him from memory.'

Lin looked doubtful. 'Hmm, but that conjures up the idea of having had sex with him.'

As she paused for further thought, Elena suggested, 'You could simply choose one of your past lovers.'

Seeing Lin turn to him with a look of concern, Marcus covered for her by putting on an amused voice. 'Yes, Lin; surely one of them must fit the bill.'

Knowing he knew she had no former lovers, Lin felt a momentary swell of anger, which quickly subsided as she accepted he was merely trying to protect their secret. After a lengthy pause, she responded, 'I'm going to choose a boy I was at school with. All the girls wanted him to be their boyfriend, until it turned out he was looking for a boyfriend as well.'

Marcus glimpsed something in Elena's expression that suggested to him she may now be reinterpreting his latest interchange with Lin, so hurried to break her chain of thought. 'Right; that was an effective meeting. Now, you girls go and put on your smart clothes, and come back and let me have a look at you.'

Elena turned to Lin. 'Is it acceptable in England for male officers to refer to female officers as girls? They can't do that in Sweden.'

Lin lowered her voice conspiratorially. 'They can't in the UK, either; it isn't Politically Correct. Except, he doesn't know that, and no one wants to tell him.'

Deliberately ignoring him, they headed for the door, continuing their discussion of what was not PC.

As he waited for their return, he picked away at the remains of their breakfasts until there was nothing left.

There was a knock at the door; he checked it was them, before opening it. After quickly reviewing Lin's outfit and giving his approval, he turned to Elena. 'Put your shades on, as well.' She carefully slotted the arms of her matching large black sunglasses under the mass of raven hair she had just acquired. He pushed a few strands to one side that were out of place. 'Now everyone's going to think there are two supermodels let loose on an unsuspecting public. Where did you get the thigh length boots at such short notice, by the way?'

She shook her head as though trying to throw off the blush she felt glowing in her cheeks.

Lin answered for her. 'She already had them!'

There was a hint of embarrassment in Elena's smile to Marcus. 'I really like these boots.'

He smiled back. 'So do I. In my army days I took an officer aptitude test that involved undressing a woman who was wearing thigh length boots... on a computer!'

Lin tugged at Elena's arm. 'Another time, Marcus; the two of us still have a lot to go through, to prepare me for my whistle-stop tour.'

He followed them out with the trolley. Their waiter saw him from further up the corridor, and wondered how many more women would visit. Adding the red-headed and raven-haired beauties to the earlier tally of three, he inwardly revised his running total. '*Fem.*'

After his ablutions, Marcus considered what he might usefully do to fill the day. Ginny would no doubt ensure Pammie was *au courant*, and he was leaving it to Elena to update Max. Ben might appreciate another call, though he seemed to know what was going on well enough without his input; and besides, he could always make contact at the embassy.

He thought about telling Helen what was really happening, but decided that would only worry her. She had done so much to rebuild him in the past, devoting herself to helping him over his PTSD, that he felt it was the least he owed her. But then, he felt much more for her than love, gratitude and obligation; she was also his solid rock, his certain solace if things were to go wrong. Except, things never did go wrong, nowadays; it was as though the gods were watching over him, giving him a helping hand. As the Chief Constable had once said to him, "If you fell into a sewage plant, you'd still come up smelling of roses." Napoleon would have approved of him, but then Nappie was a loser, though he did always try to anticipate problems and have a strategy ready for dealing with them. Yet, what could go wrong this evening? Everyone would be together, and all they were doing was trying to identify someone. No, he need not spend time fretting about something that would never happen; he should simply be ready to react if anything failed to go according to plan.

Having satisfied himself there was nothing else he had to do, he decided to visit the shopping centres Elena had mentioned. Using a map he obtained from hotel reception, he worked out a simple route: along Olof Palmes gata, a right onto Drottninggatan, then a left onto Klarabersgatan, and over at the roundabout onto Hamngatan.

He set off at ten o'clock. After twenty minutes of walking, he found himself at the Gallerian, and recalled this was the time Lin and Elena should be leaving for the Palace. The H&M on the other side of the road reminded him there was one on Sheffield's Fargate. He recalled learning as a child on a school trip to York how "gate" was derived from "gata" meaning "street", so "Fargate" was really "Far Street".

Noting how impressive the NK building was, he decided to take a closer look. As he began to cross the road, a blue-fronted tram hove into view; he thought it was much longer than those back home in Sheffield.

Content with window-shopping, he continued past two familiar brands, Starbucks and Victoria's Secret. When he saw the ubiquitous McDonald's sign, he contemplated having a quick bite to eat, and put his increased appetite down to the cold. He found himself amused by a sudden afterthought: the craving for food must be a sympathetic symptom connected to Lin's planned pregnancy.

At twenty minutes to eleven, he found a taxi and headed for the British Embassy. When he presented himself at Security and asked for Michael Mouse, the guard enquired as to his name. Guessing which one to use, he offered 'Don Duck.' With the changing of the guard's expression from barely concealed mirth to determined seriousness, he imagined him as an old man telling his grandchildren about it and being disbelieved.

CHAPTER 24

Priestley was greeted by the same young man as had delivered the small package of kroner to him at the airport. 'Mr Duck, so nice to see you again. I'm Piers Fotherington, by the way. I have something for you, if you'd like to follow me.' He led him to a small office and placed a receipt in front of him, without inviting him to sit. 'My instructions are to provide you with up to five thousand kroner a day, on demand. If you'd just like to sign here.' Priestley again signed, "Don Duck". Piers unlocked a small cashbox and counted out ten notes, each of five hundred kroner.

Priestley asked, 'Do you mind changing a couple for something smaller?' Piers returned two to the cashbox and extracted a variety of lower denominations. When Priestley had put the money into his wallet, he asked, 'Do you know if anyone is wishing to speak with me? In person, or on the phone?'

Piers responded respectfully, 'Yes, Mr Duck; I have been requested to escort you to the Ambassador. If you will come this way.' Priestley followed him out of the office and along the corridor, until they eventually reached the Ambassador's door. Piers knocked lightly and was invited to enter. He walked ahead of Priestley into the brightly lit room, and gestured in his direction. 'This is Mr Don Duck, sir; you asked to see him.'

The Ambassador eased himself out of his red leather chair and walked around the mahogany inlaid desk, his hand extended. 'Good to meet you, Mr Duck.'

Priestley grasped the hand. 'And you, Mr Mouse.'

Hearing Piers' involuntary sharp intake of breath, the Ambassador turned to him. 'That will be all, Piers.' Once the door had closed, leaving only the two of them together, the Ambassador gave a hearty laugh. 'You people do like playing your games, don't you just. I'm Humphrey Blessingby-Smythe. Call me Humph.'

Priestley smiled. 'And I'm Marcus.'

Humph walked to a red leather Chesterfield. 'I'm not supposed to take part in any of your skulduggery.' He gave a prolonged wink. 'Let's have a chat, shall we? Now, tell me from the beginning, what's all this about a girl in the family way looking for the father?'

Unsure how much Humph already knew, he took him at his word and laid out the entire plan. 'So, if you introduce Lin to the Russian Ambassador, she'll take it from there.'

Humph steepled, his manicured hands displaying long slender fingers. 'His name's Nikita Arkadyevitch Romanov; friends calls him Niki. So, the plan is for Linda... What sort of a girl is she, by the way? Is she no better than she ought to be? Where is she coming from? Does she hail from the Shires, or is she more Home Counties?'

Marcus thought Humph's old-fashioned manner of speaking came more naturally to him than it perhaps should have. He responded in a matching style. 'She's from good, northern stock, and highly intelligent. Her real character is to be modest and well-behaved, but she'll be performing like a high-spirited filly with next to no sense.'

'And she'll be convincing, will she? What with the pregnancy, and all?'

'I've every confidence in her. She answers to "Lin", by the way.'

'Fine, though for the formal introduction, I shall use "Linda". And I'll need a surname, too.'

'Make it "Linda Jones"; I'll let her know.'

'A common name; how apposite. There's only one problem I see with your plan: it's this early departure malarkey. There are rules on who leaves when.'

'Are they like ours? Everyone has to stay until the guest of honour leaves the shindig?'

'Either you've been doing your homework, or you're one of us. Which is it, Marcus?'

'Perhaps a bit of both; but I was in the army, as well. I remember one occasion when the royal guest refused to leave when she should have, because she was having such a good time; you can imagine what the married officers with children thought about that, having to stay up 'til the early hours. Is there a guest of honour?'

'Yes, me! I can't leave early, but Lin could always play the pregnancy card. I'll make sure my chauffer is primed to whisk her away if she raises an inverted union flag, so to speak.'

'Thank you, Humph; I really appreciate your help.'

'And there won't be any ructions, will there? I wear two hats, don't forget: diplomacy and trade. We mustn't go upsetting the natives, what?'

'You can rely on us; and the natives have been very friendly, so far.'

'Then make sure you keep them that way. Now, is there anything else I can do for you?'

'I'd just like to make contact with London on a secure line, in case there's something they wish to let me know. And I spot of lunch wouldn't go amiss. But apart from that, I don't have any obligations 'til five o'clock, when I need to be back at my hotel. So, if you can suggest something to keep me occupied…?'

'We'll dine together, and then you can have Piers for the afternoon. He'll drive you wherever you wish.'

'That sounds like an excellent plan.'

Humph walked to his desk and picked up the telephone. 'Piers, would you mind?' A minute later, he recognised the familiar knock at the door, and invited him to enter. 'This is Marcus; the other name was just for cover. He needs to contact London, and then you're to keep him amused until luncheon. In the afternoon you can drive him somewhere.' He turned to Marcus. 'Anywhere particular you'd like to see?'

He nodded. 'Yes, the Vasa Museum. I've always been interested in history, so I'd quite like to take a look at the old warship and see what I can learn… beyond how not to build one.'

Humph sucked in air noisily. 'I could never say that; it's not diplomatic, you see.'

Marcus smiled. 'Yes, I've already found that out.'

Piers took Marcus to a small, secure room. 'I'll be in my office when you're finished.'

He contacted Ben. 'Hello, it's Marcus. We're all set for this evening. Is there anything I need to know?'

'I'm sure you're already fully aware you can't take any action inside the Russian embassy.'

He heard the pause as Ben waited for confirmation. 'Of course; it's identification only, at this stage. Did you make any further progress with the Irish passport?'

'A little. It was part of a batch stolen from one of their embassies, so we can assume "Michael Collins" isn't our man's real name. On the other hand, it does suggest he could pass muster as an Irishman, so he must surely be able to speak English, or Irish Gaelic, or both. Perhaps he is Irish; he could be an ex-IRA mercenary.'

'Choosing a name from the IRA's past does suggest someone who either knew Irish history or was prepared to do some research. But is the name too obvious? Is it a bluff or is it a double-bluff? And who's to say the person who came up with the name is the same as the one who was using it? I would say, the fact that he was assigned to make a hit in England makes it very likely he can speak English well enough not to stand out.'

'Actually, Marcus, there are areas of the UK where a significant proportion of the population don't speak English; we now have to recruit listeners to cover an ever broadening range of foreign languages.'

'Yes, but surely there aren't any areas where the common language is Irish Gaelic.'

'There are places you might get by with it; Clapham is the new Cricklewood for the Irish.'

'Alright Ben, I understand you wish me to keep an open mind, but realistically I'd say the guy travelled on an Irish passport under an Irish name and came to England to do a job, so he very probably speaks good English. Whether he's Irish or Russian or something else entirely is immaterial; it's only what he appears to be that will have a bearing on how we take things forward. In the final analysis, I wouldn't expect to encounter a language barrier if I can find a way of starting a conversation with him.'

'I can't fault your reasoning, Marcus. Of course, he may not even be the man you see behind the mask.'

'What on earth do you mean by that, Ben?'

'It's all about layers; and layers upon layers. He

could be a Kosovar who was pretending to be a Russian when he took on an Irish identity. To lose it, he drops back to being a Russian or a Kosovar, or even takes on an entirely new identity. All I'm saying is, in this line of business you never accept anyone is who they say they are; not unless you were present at their birth. Or better still, conception.'

'Understood. But if I make the connection between the man who committed the offence back in England, and the man who used the Irish passport, then it doesn't matter to me who he really is. Whatever his history, he's still my target.'

'True; true. But if he's a foreign national, or at least some foreign power claims him as one of theirs, then you may have a problem in bringing him back to face justice in the UK. Which is why I'd like to explore with you the extent to which our objectives are aligned, and where they may diverge. I previously emphasised the desire to expose any cover-up, which I know is also an objective of yours. But now, having spoken further with our cousins, I would say that understanding the reason for the assassination is paramount. Beyond that, is the question of whether the assassin may then be brought to justice. So, to clarify. Objective one is to find out why our man was killed. Objective two is to obtain the information that would enable the cover-up to be exposed, if appropriate. And objective three is to bring the assassin to justice, if practicable.'

'Are you saying objective two does not necessarily include actually *exposing* any cover-up?'

'Reasons may emerge that could indicate it would be undesirable to put the information in the public domain. I trust you can be prevailed upon to place the national interest above your personal objective as a policeman.'

'I can see little likelihood of bringing the assassin to book, without first making the underlying reasons for the killing available to the courts, which may well include exposing any cover-up.'

'Let me run through the objectives another way. If you achieve objective one only, your mission will be deemed a partial success. If you achieve objective two without achieving objective one, it will be regarded as a substantive failure. If you achieve objectives one and two, the mission will be treated by the intelligence services as a complete success. Objective three may be your personal goal, but for others it would be no more than a thin layer of icing on the cake.'

'I hear what you say, Ben; but why would you wish me to find out about any cover-up and then not use it? Hmm, you don't need to answer that question; I think I've just worked it out for myself.'

'Yes, there may be good reasons for covering up the cover-up. Do I have your word you will not go public without first obtaining the appropriate approval?'

'What would constitute appropriate approval?'

'That may become obvious in due course. Will you at least accept the need to discuss the matter before taking it forward?'

'Yes, of course. But will you accept that I should be allowed to continue with the investigation until I've completed it to my own personal satisfaction? I would take a very dim view of things if you tried pulling the rug from under me, before I've finished the job.'

'Yes, within reason, Marcus. Just how far would you wish to take your quest for justice?'

'The fact that I'm here in the first place should tell

you I intend to pursue my quarry to the bitter end.'

'Then let's simply agree that you won't act in haste or do anything precipitate, and that we'll discuss ways forward at every step. Do you agree to this?'

'I agree to discuss matters; but I don't agree to be bound by any restrictions I believe are unjustified.'

'Then we must aim for consensus at every turn.'

Having achieved a degree of concord, Marcus chose to close the conversation. 'Until there's some actual progress, I don't think there's really anything further to discuss.'

'I agree; we've covered all the key issues.'

'I'll be in touch again soon, then. Cheerio, Ben.'

'Cheerio, Marcus; and good luck.'

Marcus found Piers, who led him to an airy lounge containing magazines and a few books. He glanced at the reading matter before settling to look out of the window, his favourite way of thinking laterally about a mission. When Humph came to take him to lunch at one o'clock, he was disappointed in himself for having failed to add much detail to the plans for the evening. He took a quantum of solace from the implication there was no obvious way of improving on them.

Lunch proved a disappointment to Marcus. Having expected a choice of high calorie meals to ward off the cold, he found his acceptable options limited him to minced meat pie with potato and veg, followed by mincemeat tart with custard. As he looked down from high table, he wondered how so many employees could sustain themselves on salad in the depth of winter.

Marcus was also disappointed with the conversation. Humph seemed a different person, saying nothing of any importance, as though he suspected his every word was being monitored. There was no mention of their plans for the Russian embassy, or of Linda Jones, or Niki. He wondered to what extent Humph distrusted his staff, or whether he was simply being cautious. On reflection, he decided Humph was acting professionally to minimise the risk of leaks.

After lunch, Marcus asked Piers to drive him to the Vasa Museum. When Piers respectfully invited him to sit in the back seat, he declined and sat in the front. Once they were on the road, Marcus asked, 'Have you seen the *Vasa*, yourself?'

He kept his eyes focused on the road ahead. 'Yes; just the once. Am I allowed to know what you intend to do there? Are you meeting someone?'

Marcus felt amused, and showed it in a smile. 'I'm just doing something touristy, to pass the time.'

Piers nodded. 'Maintaining your cover.'

Marcus remained silent until they were parked up. 'If you've been here before, maybe you can fill me in on the background.'

'Yes; it would be a pleasure.'

As they traipsed around the multi-level walk-ways, he listened as Piers earnestly gave him exactly the same information he could easily read for himself on the English version descriptions. He checked his watch; it was showing twenty past three. 'I'll head back to the hotel, unless you think there's some other place I might like to see.'

Piers glanced at him. 'What sort of place?'

Marcus decided he would need different company to enjoy being a tourist. 'On second thoughts, let's just go to the hotel.'

As he was about to climb into the car, Marcus saw

two familiar figures heading for the entrance. He called up the photograph of Elena's schedule, to check what time they were due to enter the museum. Checking his watch again, he calculated they were almost three hours late. Not wishing to break their cover, he made no movement to attract their attention.

In the car, Piers asked, 'Were they your contacts, then? I didn't see what you did to let them know you were here.'

Marcus decided to be what Piers imagined him to be. 'They'll get my message, soon enough.'

Piers nodded. 'Ah! So you left something for them inside the museum.' Marcus remained silent for the drive back to the hotel, thereby confirming to Piers all his mistaken beliefs.

CHAPTER 25

At ten minutes to six, Lin and Elena returned to the hotel room with a new suitcase and a mountain of shopping. Elena opened the wardrobe door. 'There isn't much space in here to hang everything up.'

Lin ignored the wardrobe and looked directly at Elena as though only now contemplating something. 'I've really enjoyed our day out together, and I'm excited about this evening, but I'm feeling guilty about taking up so much of your time.'

Elena responded immediately, 'Don't give it another thought. I've enjoyed it, too.'

Lin slowed her delivery. 'Yes, but, when I go out this evening, you'll not be able to come with me. So it seems to me it would make more sense if you went home when I'm picked up at a quarter to eight.'

Elena nodded. 'That would be very convenient. I'll make sure I'm back by, say, ten o'clock.'

Lin looked down, aiming to appear ashamed. 'The thing is, I feel such a fraud. It would be nice to have you staying the night, but it makes me think I'm not as brave as I want to be.'

'Are you saying you don't want me here, tonight?'

Lin thought Elena appeared hurt by the suggestion, so tried a different tack. 'No, of course not; I'd really like you to be here. But I don't want Marcus thinking I'm a weak woman who can't take care of herself.'

Elena tried to hide her relief. 'In that case, I'll pack my things and leave when you do. If anything happens to make you change your mind, give me a call straight away. And tomorrow we'll need to review how things went; I could come over early?'

Lin shook her head. 'It's best if you wait until I call; I could be up very late. It is New Year's eve, after all.'

'OK. Are you certain you don't need me tonight?'

'Yes, definitely.'

'In that case, I'll phone Max. Now he's lost his date, he might be free to let the New Year in with me.' She immediately speed-dialled him and had a quick-fire conversation. 'That's me sorted, then.'

Lin made an excuse to give Marcus her good news. She was surprised to find herself kept waiting.

Marcus had just phoned Pamela. 'Hi Honey.'

'Hi Sweetie.'

'We're all set for this evening.'

'Have you been interfering with my rep?'

He heard a knock at the door. Without interrupting the conversation, he went to check through the spyhole and saw it was Lin, so decided not to open it until he had finished on the phone. 'What do you mean.'

'You Brits! You all think you're James Bond. She spent far too long in your room last night.'

'It must just be the hour difference with Sweden.'

'Ridiculous! And now she seems very keen on you.'

'You know you're the only girl for me, Honey.'

'Don't go sweet-talking me, Marcus. She needs to be totally focused on her job, so no distracting her.'

'I wouldn't dream of it.'

'Liar!' She laughed. 'Let me know how things go.'

'Sure, Honey. Bye.'

He put down the phone and opened the door.

Lin began, 'What were you doing, then? And don't

say you were on the loo, because it would still be flushing. Just like you are.'

'It's the air conditioning; I should turn it down.'

'That doesn't answer my question.'

'I was making my six-o-five call.'

'Oh, right. Anyway, good news: Elena won't be in my room tonight, so I can be in yours. Unless you're hoping to get off with Ginny?'

'Of course not! I told you, it's entirely professional.'

'If I find out you've been having it off with her, I'll be so mad with you, I'll... I don't know what I'd do.'

'Well, you won't.'

'Won't what? Won't find out?'

'That's right!'

She interpreted his willingness to joke about it as an indication of his innocence, so gave him a begrudging smile. 'I'd better go and get ready.'

'Shall we have something to eat?'

'We've already had something.'

'Was that on schedule, just after you left the Natural History Museum?'

'No, we changed the schedule.'

'Much, or just a bit?'

'Some.'

'Don't beat about the bush; tell me how much you changed it.'

'A reasonable amount.'

'That's still beating about the bush. Come on, give me a full breakdown.'

Lin took a few moments to decide how to play it. 'We discussed the plan and concluded your earlier analysis was not entirely reliable; we thought an airhead would not be spending so much time visiting museums.

So we began with the original plan, insofar as we went to the first two shopping centres, but we extended the duration in preference to certain other activities. We did visit the Vasa Museum as planned, though a little later than scheduled, before going to another shopping centre, because we were in the mood for it. That's its name, by the way, MOOD. After that, we had a meal together as per the original plan. And then we came back here, a creditable hour ahead of schedule.'

'So, just how long did you spend shopping?'

'Not so long.'

'How long in hours and minutes?'

'Less than six hours.'

'Five hours fifty-nine minutes?'

'About that.'

'Well done, Lin! You seem to have made a good job of putting yourself into airhead mode.'

'I'll take that as a compliment. Now, I'd better go and get myself pregnant. Without your input!'

After she had left, he called home. 'Hello, Helen.'

'Hello, love. How are things?''

'Fine. There's nothing much happening yet, so I had a trip out to see an old wooden warship they dredged up and put on display in a museum.'

'The *Vasa*.'

'Yes. How did you know?'

'I've been looking on the web and finding places for tourists to visit; I was wondering if I might come over and see you for a few days, if you're not too busy? It sounds like you're just killing time at the moment.'

He gulped. 'It would be great to see you over here, to stop the boredom from setting in, but I'm optimistic something will kick off anytime soon. Until the position becomes clearer, it's probably best if you stay put; but if I'm confident nothing will happen for a day or two, I'll let you know straight away.'

'Alright; I'll be packed and ready.'

'So, how are the children? How's my train set?'

'You told me I had to call it a model railway.'

'That's what I meant; I stand corrected.'

'They're all still in good order.' She added with emphasis, 'We're really missing you, love.'

'I'm missing all of you, too.'

'Will you be on your own by midnight? I could give you a call, when it's your New Year or mine. Or both.'

'Oh, of course; the hour difference. It isn't the same when we're not together, so let's skip it this year.'

'I might just try you, anyway; keep your phone on.'

'Alright, love. Talk to you tomorrow.'

After a while, he called up room service and ordered steak and chips followed by chocolate cake with cream and raspberries; to keep a clear head, he limited himself to water and coffee.

There was a knock at the door. He barely recognised Lin in her long blonde hair and gold dress. When he let her in, she walked as though on eggshells. 'I have to be careful in my condition; no rushing about.'

He took his time examining her from all angles, checking there were no telltale signs that the pregnancy bump was a fake. 'It really is completely believable.'

'What do you think of my breasts?'

'They're great; you know that.'

'No, what do you think of them now?'

He looked closer. 'They're bigger! How on earth did you manage that?'

'It's the bra I bought today; it pushes them up.'

'Make sure you keep it for when we're back home!'

She laughed. 'I really feel ever so confident, but that doesn't stop my heart from racing. Anyway, Elena should have made her phone calls by now, so I'll get back and apply the finishing touches.'

As she stepped outside, the old waiter arrived with the food trolley. He counted to himself, '*Sex.*'

Marcus was nearly dressed by seven thirty. Rather than threading the cufflinks for himself, he used them as a distraction for Lin when he went to give her his final briefing. She eased one of them from its retaining band. As she pressed it through a pair of buttonholes, Elena helpfully took out the other and worked it into place. He thought to himself, 'I rather like the idea of having two handmaidens.'

When he invited their opinion of his clothes, Lin asked, 'What about a tie?'

He felt at the open collar. 'I'll put it on last thing, to give my neck some breathing space. So, are you all set to waddle down? Don't go keeping Humph waiting.'

'Humph? That isn't really his name, is it?'

'Short for Humphrey. I suppose you'd better wait to be invited to call him that. He'll introduce you as Linda Jones, by the way; known as Lin. And don't forget the missing father is Henry Gibson. Any last requests?'

'You make it sound like I'm going to face a firing squad. I've no questions, if that's what you mean.'

He headed back to his room and found his consort standing outside, shimmering in a green dress. 'Sorry to keep you waiting, Ginny. I was doing a final check with my colleague.'

She flashed a smile. 'You're looking good, Marky.'

He waited until they were inside and the door was

closed. 'You're looking incredible, breathtaking!' He slowly checked her out from head to foot and back again, ending with her eyes. 'That certainly is low-cut, Ginny; I can see right down to your socks.'

She burst out giggling, less restrained and glistening than her babbling brook interpretation. 'I've always wanted a man who can make me laugh.'

He picked up his bow tie. 'I thought I'd leave this for you to do; you do it so nicely.'

'OK, but we don't have much time.' As she quickly fastened it from the front, he tried not to look down the dress's sizeable gap at her cleavage. When she had finished, she stood directly in front of him. 'I can see you're too distracted to think straight. You'd better have a good look now, before we go, so you can keep your mind on the job.' As he accepted the invitation to lower his eyes, she eased the dress open a little further, enough to allow him to glimpse the edges of her pink areolae. 'Can you see my nipples?'

He looked even more closely. 'Not quite.'

'Good. That's how it's supposed to be; always leave 'em wanting more. These are home-grown, you know.'

'That's the best type by a long way; you can't touch home-grown.'

She smiled at him. 'Well, maybe *you* can.'

As they stepped out and headed for the lift, Elena wheeled a case from her room. She glanced at Marcus for a moment, and then glared at Ginny. 'It's very cold outside, Virginia; shall I lend you a jumper?'

Ginny bared her teeth. 'You're too kind, Elena; but my chauffer is downstairs with my mink stole.'

'And did you skin all the little animals yourself?'

Marcus stepped forward as though breaking up a

fight. 'Now, now, girls; put your claws away.'

Lin closed the door behind her. 'Marcus, I'm so glad I caught you; I forgot to remind you to call your wife.'

He said nothing, as he recognised how the female of the species was so much deadlier than the male.

At Elena's insistence, Ginny and Marcus took the lift alone, to avoid Lin being seen with them. They exited at the ground floor and walked arm-in-arm through the lobby, guided by her to a man in a dark suit who presented him with a honey-coloured fur stole; he placed it gently around her shoulders. They followed their driver out, crossing the path of the Ambassador's chauffeur on his way in, peaked cap in hand.

Elena spoke to Lin as they stood together hiding behind a pillar, waiting for her to be officially collected. 'Here's your driver. He's a proper chauffeur, not just a goon. I can't believe even she would wear something like that; if she turns around too fast, her tits will drop out, and then people will see if they really don't need any support.'

Lin whispered conspiratorially. 'I'll keep a look out, and if it happens, I'll report back.'

Elena smiled. 'Anyway, you look better than her; pregnancy has made you bloom.'

Lin accepted the chauffeur's invitation to join the Ambassador. In the back of the black limousine, Humph introduced himself formally and informally, and checked she was indeed Linda Jones, familiarly known as Lin. He chatted with her as though she really were pregnant by one Henry Gibson. She wondered if it was all part of getting her into the correct frame of mind, or whether he suspected someone was listening.

CHAPTER 26

Ginny and Marcus stood in line, waiting to be formally presented to Nikita Arkadyevitch Romanov. When it was their turn, the Russian Ambassador ignored Marcus and leaned over to kiss Ginny several times on the cheeks, repeatedly lingering to look down her dress. She waited until he had finished examining her, before explaining, 'Marcus Holmes is standing in for Max Ahlberg, who was unavoidably detained.'

Having a little theoretical knowledge of the rules of Russian etiquette relating to greetings between men, Marcus steeled himself for three kisses; if one was on the lips, he hoped it would not be the French variety. When Niki thrust out a hand, he felt a wave of relief. The introductions were minimal as befitting his lack of status, but nevertheless he was officially on first name terms by the time he walked away with Ginny.

They accepted glasses of champagne from one of the circling waiters. He touched his to his lips without drinking any. She smiled. 'You've been reading your secret agent's manual on how not to get poisoned, haven't you, Marky. But what if the poison's on the glass itself?' She took a swig from her own and held it in her mouth to give the fizz time to subside, before gulping it down. 'This stuff won't kill you.'

He looked embarrassed. 'I was simply trying to make sure I stay sober; but thanks for the advice.' He took a sip. 'Are you sure it won't kill me? Whatever it is, it isn't French champagne.'

'It may be from Rostov-on-Don. They agreed to ban the *Sovetskoye Shampanskoye* trademark some years ago, but people still call this stuff champagne.'

He gazed upward wistfully. 'Ah, Rostov-on-Don; the Don quietly flows through my home town, too.'

She allowed the tiniest frown fleetingly to crease her forehead. 'But you're from England, aren't you?'

He smiled. 'It's a different River Don, though it also flows home to the sea. It used to be highly polluted, but now there are trout and...' He turned to where Ginny was indicating. The introduction line had been broken by the arrival of two special guests, one of them heavily pregnant. Marcus noted how Niki was indulging Lin with a considerably lengthier audience than he himself had been granted. He wondered what was happening when Niki called over a nearby waiter, so edged around Ginny to look over her shoulder for a better view. He guessed that the fluted glass which the waiter brought on a silver salver probably contained freshly squeezed orange juice, in consideration of Lin's condition.

Lin accepted the drink and walked into the room, leaning heavily on Humph's arm. Marcus and Ginny moved away to the furthest corner, as though the new arrivals were unknown to them. Counting down to the first planned call at eight twenty-six, they sallied forth from one group of Ginny's friends to another, looking out all the time for the man with the Irish passport.

Having had no success by eight thirty, they decided to indulge in caviar and vodka. Marcus looked along the serving table at the mother-of-pearl spoons that glimmered incandescent by the small crystal bowls sitting in crushed ice. Ginny scrutinised the black eggs and gave her assessment. 'It's good quality, but not the best; Niki reserves that for his special friends, I'm told.'

Marcus swallowed his pride. 'How do you assess caviar before you taste it?'

'The eggs could be a bit bigger and rounder, and maybe a shinier, clearer black. Put some on a piece of bread and try it, and tell me what you think.'

He transferred a small spoonful onto a tiny triangle of white bread cradled in the palm of his hand. 'It's been a while since I had any of this.' After sniffing it, he put it into his mouth and squeezed the eggs until they burst in little explosions of taste. When he had allowed himself enough time to enjoy the experience, he delivered his verdict. 'It didn't smell fishy; maybe there was just a hint of seaweed. And it tasted less salty than I was expecting. If I hadn't been with an expert, I'd have said it was very good indeed. Now your turn.'

She took hold of his hand and turned it upward, then picked up a piece of bread and placed it where his own had been. 'Do this one for me; I'll eat it off you.'

He transferred a larger spoonful of caviar onto the bread. She proceeded to lick up the eggs, pursuing some of them around his palm. When the escapees had all been captured, he offered her the bread with the remainder of the spheres. She opened her mouth, forming a tight circle; he edged the bread into it. The circle opened wider; he pushed it in, gently. Seeing three eggs had attached themselves to her cupid's-bow lips and were in danger of falling, he thought of using a finger to rescue them, but eschewed the idea in favour of his mouth. As he sucked off the stray eggs, he felt the tip of her tongue begin to chase them down, so opened his mouth wider and took grateful delivery of two more exploding globes.

She whispered, 'Nicely done.' As she looked into his eyes, he had to remind himself she was only acting a part in a play. Except, the play was still being written.

When they moved toward the vodka, a young man stepped up to her. 'Virginia, your eyes match dress.'

She held his gaze. 'Misha, your eyes match borscht; stop drinking. And pour two shots for me and my boyfriend.'

He poured three. 'A toast: to most beautiful woman on planet.' In case she had failed to understand the compliment, he added, 'I mean you, of course.'

When the young man raised his glass, Marcus thought he appeared to be in danger of falling, so grabbed his shoulder to hold him up. 'Yes, to the most beautiful woman on the planet.' The two downed their shots together in a show of camaraderie, quickly followed by Ginny.

Misha picked up the bottle and refilled their glasses before they could object. 'And now, toast to handsome man with most beautiful woman on planet.'

Misha and Ginny downed theirs at once. Seeing Marcus still holding his glass, Misha explained, 'You also must drink; it is Russian way.'

Marcus looked to Ginny for advice. 'He's right; you have to drink, even if you're the one being toasted.' He immediately emptied his glass and poured another drink each. 'And now a toast to Misha, who is a friend of the most beautiful woman on the planet.' The three drained their glasses.

Ginny took the bottle off Marcus. 'And that's all, Misha. You should go and sit down, somewhere.'

Misha looked at her with pleading, bloodshot eyes. 'You must walk with me or I will fall. And bring bottle, to toast some more.' Marcus took his arm.

Misha held his pass card next to an electronic reader until a green light came on, and then opened a nearby unmarked door. 'My office is this way.'

Marcus supported him as they walked along a dingy corridor. When Misha stopped, Marcus asked, 'Is this where you want to be?'

Misha swayed. 'Yes, in here.' He held himself up by the handle. The other two saw the door was unlocked.

Ginny turned on the light and instructed Marcus, 'Sit him down in that chair.' She placed the bottle on a desk nearby. 'Are you alright, Misha?'

'Yes, I am fine, thank you very much. Now we have toast to friendship.' He grabbed the bottle.

Ginny shook her head. 'We don't have any glasses.'

Misha smiled like an idiot. 'Then we shall take turns with bottle.' He took a swig. Marcus accepted the bottle and took a small taste. Ginny touched the bottle to her lips, drinking none at all, before handing it back to Misha. As the two guests were still standing, she was able to make a sideways chopping motion with her hand for only Marcus to see; he interpreted it as an instruction to consume no more alcohol.

Marcus gave the next toast. 'To the Ambassador, for inviting us to his party.'

Misha mumbled, 'To Nikita Arkadyevitch.' He took a swig and then held the bottle in the air. Marcus grabbed it before it fell, and pretended to take another drink.

Ginny saw Misha's eyes had closed, so took the bottle off Marcus and placed it back on the desk, before using a single finger to motion him to leave. She turned off the light and led the way out of the room, with a little accompaniment from the unoiled door hinges. He whispered, 'Now let's go looking for our Irishman.'

As they walked in silence along the corridor, away from the party, they discovered all the rooms were in darkness, so assumed they would not find their quarry there. She suggested, 'Shall we take a look around?'

Marcus shook his head. 'We need to stay focused on the mission.'

She nodded. 'At least I have an idea of the layout of this section, if I ever come back.'

With nowhere else to go, they returned to the original entrance door, but found it had no manual release mechanism. Marcus was about to speak, when Ginny silenced him with a finger to his lips. She led the way back to Misha, who was now snoring heavily. In the dim light from the corridor, she extracted the pass card from Misha's pocket without him noticing.

Marcus quietly suggested they go and open the door, and then he would return the card to Misha before they both left together. She shook her head, and removed a slender electronic card reader from her purse. After one swipe to copy it and another to check that the process had worked correctly, she slipped the card back into Misha's pocket.

Back at the entrance, she touched the little gizmo's screen. They saw a green diode light up on the wall, and heard the lock release activate. She carefully eased the door open and slipped through. Marcus followed her out and quietly closed it. A few steps away, she pushed him against the wall. 'Look over my shoulder.' She tilted her head as she began to kiss him, enabling him to have a better view of the room.

At the first break, he whispered, 'No one's looking.'

She kissed him a little more, then took his hand and walked with him further into the room. 'Next call is at nine thirty-nine, but we haven't found the target yet.'

He looked around for Lin. Though he heard Humph holding forth, he could see no sign of his colleague. Without a subtle way of isolating Humph from his group, he had to accept he would be unable to ask him for the explanation behind their separation.

As the time to the next phone contact grew closer, Ginny guided Marcus away from some Swedish friends and toward her own people, other US embassy staff. With still no sign of the target, the moment came and went without incident. Shortly after, Lin appeared, leaning heavily on Niki. Marcus and Ginny glanced in their direction only briefly, determinedly displaying disinterest. Humph broke away from his audience and went to see Lin. Marcus and Ginny wandered closer, to overhear the conversation.

Niki explained to Humph, 'It's all been a bit too much for the child; she's become quite faint. I would have taken her to lie down, but she wants a proper bed.'

Humph responded, 'Did you have any luck with identifying the father?'

Niki shook his head. 'No, though we did our best.' He gave Lin an avuncular kiss on the forehead. 'Didn't we, my sweet?'

She kissed him on the cheek. 'Yes, uncle Niki. Now, I think I'll never find him. I don't even think Henry is his real name, after what you told me about that writer. I'll do what you say, and try to forget all about him, and look for someone else to take care of me and my child.'

'And don't forget you need to find yourself a Wise Woman in Sweden before it's too late. You can't go back to England in your condition.'

'I'll make sure I find a midwife, uncle Niki.'

Humph addressed Niki. 'I could send her back in my car on her own, unless you don't mind my running out on you while the party's in full swing.'

Niki looked pathetically sad. 'My dear friend, at times like this, the most important thing is to take care of the poor girl. You should go at once.'

'Dashed decent of you, old man. Well, I'll wish you a Happy New Year.'

'And the same to you, Humph.' He released his hold of Lin, allowing her to grab onto Humph's arm. 'And you must let me know how things are progressing, my dear. I insist on coming to see you and the child as soon as you are well enough to receive visitors.'

Humph and Lin staggered off, as she had now reached a point of apparent total exhaustion. Marcus thought to himself, 'Don't bury yourself in the part.'

After a sufficient interval to avoid her next action being readily connected to the previous event, Ginny led Marcus to an alcove and pinned him against the wall. 'Put your arms around me and stroke my back.'

He whispered, 'I don't need any more coaching; I know exactly what to do.' He ran his hands down to her waist and then plunged them lower, his fingers edging inside her backless dress.

She kissed him the way she had demonstrated the previous evening, though this time he felt there was an added frisson. After unfastening his jacket, she made him hold it open to either side of her as though shielding her from the wind. Hidden from everyone else, she pulled her bodice apart to reveal her breasts, and whispered, 'For your eyes only.'

He quickly brought one hand into their intimate space and ran the back of his fingers up to the more distant breast, then located the right point to take hold of the material. After a moment's exquisite delay, he drew it over her bust. Perceiving no hint of disapproval for the act or the manner of its execution, he repeated the process at the other side, delaying to linger longer at the point where he brushed her left nipple.

Knowing he had had to release the windbreak to perform the redressing, he glanced around to see if anyone had noticed their act of intimacy, and was unsure whether to feel relieved or disappointed that no one appeared to be looking in their direction. He wondered if her indecorous behaviour was down to her stated intention of enhancing her reputation as a wicked woman, or whether it was entirely for his benefit. She distracted his thoughts with yet more kisses, before whispering, 'It's time we were off.'

They clung to each other as they exited. Her driver appeared out of nowhere to deliver her wrap. She told him to take them to the hotel. At the car, he opened the rear door for her. Marcus climbed in at the other side.

She kept her arms around Marcus only until they had cleared the area, at which point she sat up, fastened her seat belt, and spoke calmly. 'We're assuming Lin's early departure means she was successful, but we need to check. I'll cancel the last call, anyway, as there's no one there to see who takes it.' She took out her cell phone and contacted someone on speed dial. 'Hi. Kill the final shot. I'll update you in half an hour.'

Marcus carried Ginny's small case for her to room 205. Lin had removed her pregnancy bump but not her gold dress. While Marcus occupied the only chair, Lin sat on her bed with Ginny, and explained, 'I asked Niki to take me somewhere quieter, and he said he had a place I could go and lie down, but I said I didn't want to, so he took me to his private office instead. Then, when it was nearly time, I said I needed a cup of tea. He was going to have one brought in, but I'd passed a little dining room on the way through, where half a dozen people were sitting around, so I asked just to go there. Right on time, some guy with his back to me took a phone call. When it rang, he turned away from the people he was sitting with, and I saw it was him.'

Marcus asked, 'Did you hear him say anything?'

Lin replied, 'No, he cut the call off straight away.'

Marcus wanted to touch her, to tell her how brave she had been, but knew it would betray their secret to Ginny. He therefore merely responded, 'That's brilliant, Lin. You'd better try and settle down now and get some sleep; you must be exhausted.'

Ginny added, 'Yes, it's the best thing after all that excitement. And well done.' She turned to Marcus. 'I need to make a full report; it could take quite a while. I'll phone from your room, so I don't disturb Lin.'

In his room, Ginny took out her phone and made a quick call. 'Hi, mission accomplished; it's the guy on the Irish passport. Keep a lookout for him and let me know if you spot him. ... He's with me right now. ... Well, the easiest solution is if I stay here tonight so we can be ready at a moment's notice. ... I'm sure he won't mind; just a minute, I'll put him on.'

Pammie spoke to Marcus. 'Hi, sweetie. She seems to think it's a good idea to spend the night in your room on the grounds of expediency, in case we spot the target. But I'm concerned that you're a married man and may object. After all, you implied you didn't sleep with her last night. Or were you lying before?'

He deflected her question. 'There's a spare bed in Lin's room; she can have that.'

'Still refusing to answer; OK, put her back on.'

'Hi. … Good idea; that's what I'll do. Bye.'

She opened the bag she had brought the tuxedo in. 'Sorry, Cinderella, but all the clothes have to go back tomorrow. All except the cufflinks; they were from me.' She began to strip off.

He followed suit, down to his boxer shorts. She took her spare clothes out of her case and piled them into the wardrobe, before collecting together their evening attire and packing away everything except his socks. He placed the case on the stand by the door, then turned and looked at her as she stood unashamed in just her bikini knickers. 'It looks like you're planning to stay.'

'I can go to Lin's room later if you like, for the sake of appearances, but first we have some unfinished business. You know we do.'

While Lin was waiting for Marcus to let her know the coast was clear, she packed everything away into her bag and suitcases, before sitting to stare out of the window. As time dragged by, she started to wonder how much longer Ginny would need to make her report, and then began to doubt whether Marcus would ever come for her. Eventually, there was a knock at the door, and she rushed to open it. Seeing Ginny standing there with her bag and case, she was lost for words.

Ginny explained, 'I need to stay here so we can respond at a moment's notice if there's a sighting.' When Lin stepped back, she carried her luggage into the room. Seeing Lin's bag and cases already packed, she asked, 'Are you planning to move out? Did he sling me out to make room for you?'

Lin made a desperate attempt to save their lie. 'Elena stayed with me last night, because I get nervous; but she had to go home. So I was moving in with Marcus.'

Ginny totally disbelieved her. Mischievously, she responded, 'It's a good thing I came along, then; I can keep you company.' She read the dismay on Lin's face. 'Go on, Lin; you've earned it. Don't worry; I'll keep your secret.' As Lin struggled out with her luggage, Ginny called after her, 'Ask him if I can come as well, won't you? Just so I don't get nervous in the night, like you do.' There was no reply.

Marcus heard the knock at the door and was unsure whom to expect. Seeing Lin standing there, he opened it and let her in. 'What are you doing here?'

She trundled her suitcases into the room and threw down her bag. 'She'd guessed, anyway, so there was no point in covering up.' Her voice became sharp. 'Why are you wearing your pyjamas? She's only just left.'

'I had a shower while she was making all her phone calls, and as soon as she'd gone I put my pyjamas on and went straight to bed. I thought I was going to be on my own, so there wasn't much point in staying up to see in the New Year.'

Lin suspected he was lying, but knew she had no wish to learn the truth at that precise moment; the last two days had been so exciting for her, she refused to lose their magic by giving credence to her doubts. 'I have an idea, why don't you put your evening suit back on and I'll change into the blue dress.'

'I don't have it anymore; she has to take everything back in the morning, so she's been carefully packing it all away.' He saw an opportunity to support his falsity with true lies. 'That's why I had to get changed while she was still here. And then I thought, I may as well have a shower. But I like the idea about the blue dress. I'll put some trousers and a shirt on.'

Lin waited until Marcus was decent again, before slipping out of the gold dress. He noticed she was wearing just a simple bra and knickers, and wondered what underwear she had had on earlier, but decided this was not the time to ask.

Knowing she normally stepped into and out of her dresses, he saw how she was making an exception with the blue one. Once it was in place, she twisted her arms up her back and unfastened her bra, then extracted it without revealing herself. He wondered why she had adopted that technique, as she generally stripped off without keeping him in suspense. When she began to ruckle up the hem, he guessed she intended to remove her last item of underwear. Feeling a physical need to delay what would undoubtedly follow, he stayed her hand. 'Let's wait until midnight, shall we? Let the New Year in with a bang, so to speak.'

'I'm not sure I can wait that long; I want some fireworks now. I'm so excited after all that's happened. It's as though it isn't even me who's been doing those things, what with the aeroplane, the chauffeur-driven car, two ambassadors, and clothes I could die for.'

'Let's take it slowly, shall we? I want time to savour every moment. You're almost falling out of that dress; why don't you pop them out.' She complied too quickly by professional standards. He felt how hard her nipples were, and knew she was wanting to hurry things along. 'I'll take my shirt off and we'll have a dance.'

He softly sang snatches of classics from the sixties, while they moved rhythmically together. With midnight approaching, he turned off the lights and opened the curtains, before wantonly wrecking Nessun Dorma by crooning in Italian in the wrong key and with dreadful pronunciation. After he inappropriately delivered the final *vincerò sotto voce*, she slipped off her knickers, and then stripped him. He eased her dress over her head, then pulled down the sheets and laid her on her back, relieved he was now able to rise to the occasion.

She grew excited at the first touch of his fingers, and insisted he continue in that manner. In seconds, her delight had escalated to new heights. When she began to scream, he put his hand over her mouth for fear of being interrupted by irate guests or the night manager. She managed to tone it down, even though her ecstasy was now in spate. Believing she had begun to drift into unconsciousness, he eased off. She found a new lease of life and climbed on top of him, vigorously insisting he should achieve his own burst of pleasure. When certain he was satisfied, she peeled her sweaty body off him and lay on her side. After a moment, she spoke in a hoarse voice. 'It's wet all over; get some hankies.' He grabbed a handful and tried to mop up. Suddenly, there was a loud bang followed by a burst of bright red points of light in the sky.

He kissed her on the lips. 'Happy New Year.'

She smiled sweetly. 'Will it always be like this?'

Before he could respond to her humour, his phone began to ring. He ignored it for fear of destroying Lin's special moment. When it stopped, he turned it off to avoid the same problem an hour later.

CHAPTER 27

At eight o'clock, Marcus reluctantly left Lin's sleeping, radiant body and went for a shower. By the time he was out, she had roused herself and was standing patiently awaiting her turn. He made room for her to pass. She stopped for a moment to kiss him on the lips, while avoiding contaminating his clean body with her sweaty one. He recognised their relationship had escalated to a higher level of intimacy, and wondered where it might lead. A flash of insight struck him as he saw a parallel with the one in five US soldiers who had become addicted to heroin in Vietnam; nineteen out of twenty of them had instantly kicked the habit when they had returned from a foreign land to a radically different environment where they were no longer constantly subjected to unfamiliar stimuli. He asked himself if Lin was his heroin, before being diverted by the thought that she was indeed a heroine.

He heard a rap at the door. Seeing Ginny through the spyhole, he let her in. As she bumped past with her luggage, she indicated she could hear someone in the bathroom. He explained unnecessarily, 'Lin's having a shower.' The sound of water ceased.

She pointed to her case. 'I've moved out. Did she tell you I offered to join you both last night?'

His eyes sprang wide open. 'No, she didn't. Did you mean it? Were you still playing the bad girl?'

'Bad girl is as bad girl does; it's my job.'

He stretched out a hand and touched her gently on

the cheek. 'You have the kind of beauty that makes men want to do anything for you. I don't think you have to be a bad girl to twist men around your little finger; you could do it with simple charm and personality.'

She looked puzzled. 'Why are you telling me this? Are you wanting to reform me?'

He smiled. 'Well, now that you mention it.'

'But you were happy enough for me to be a bad girl last night, weren't you?'

Lin flung open the bathroom door, being unable to hear well enough from behind it. She stepped out, still dripping wet, wearing only a towel. 'How exactly *were* you a bad girl, Ginny? Do tell me; I'd like to know.'

Ginny gave her a huge smile. 'Lin, the star of the show; you were brilliant. Did you have to do anything bad, yourself?'

Lin directed her reply more at Marcus than at Ginny. 'Not in the slightest; Niki was a perfect gentlemen.'

Ginny responded, 'Classic first date behaviour to create the right impression. But if you meet him again, you can expect his hands to be all over you.'

Lin allowed a hard edge to creep into her voice. 'That may be your experience, but it's probably down to you encouraging it. Maybe you should simply try being nice... like me!' Marcus wondered just how nice she was being at that precise moment.

Ginny responded to Lin. 'That's both of you picking on me, trying to reform me, but I don't need it; I'm Catholic. We can sin all we like so long as we obtain absolution before the end; it's a system that positively encourages sinning.'

Marcus gently tugged Ginny further into the room. 'Aren't you supposed to be keeping an eye on me? My guardian angel? It might have to be the other way around. If I find you misbehaving, I may have to pull your pants down and smack your bottom.'

Seeing Ginny looking perplexed, he explained, 'It's what they used to say in England to naughty children, before someone decided it should be seen as assault.'

Interpreting his inflections, she asked, 'So, do you approve of smacking?'

He thought for a moment. 'It's like nuclear weapons: to be a credible deterrent, others have to believe they would be used under certain circumstances.'

She laughed lightly. 'When it comes to the arms race and escalation, I think you now hold the world record: from smack to nuclear bomb in one small step.'

He smiled. 'Yes, it turned into a giant leap; though, now I think about it, I can see it isn't really such a good analogy. There are children who probably could do with a little smack if they try something that's life-threateningly dangerous; it may be the only way to persuade them not to do it again, to keep them safe. But other children would simply need to be told, so they wouldn't need physical chastisement. Really, it's horses for courses. The trouble with a blanket ban is that the ones who need correction when they're young never get it, so they grow up to be the lawless juveniles and adults that the police have to deal with every day.'

Ginny held his gaze. 'You're not really going back to being a policeman, are you? Don't you feel more at home in my world? You could even come and work for us, if you didn't want to stick with the Brits. I reckon if you asked Pammie, she'd recruit you, no problem. You and I could be partners.'

Lin gritted her teeth, but said nothing.

Marcus shook his head. 'This is all a bit heavy; we haven't even had breakfast, yet.'

Ginny looked at her watch. 'Speaking of which, it will be arriving any time soon. I checked what you'd had before, so yours is sausage, egg and bacon.'

Lin complained, 'But I'm not dressed.'

Ginny responded, 'Go right ahead; I'd quite like a good look at your body…' She turned to Marcus. '…to see what I'm up against.' Lin collected her clothes and scuttled back to the bathroom, locking it behind her.

Marcus invited Ginny to sit at the table. Shortly after, hearing the rattle of an approaching trolley, he stepped outside. The old waiter was about to park it, so offered to push it into the room. Seeing just the one young woman seated, he checked that the order was for three breakfasts, and was relieved but unsurprised when another stepped out of the bathroom.

After breakfast, Ginny spoke to Marcus. 'If there's a sighting, I'll call you.' She took out her mobile. 'Put me on the same cell phone you use with Pammie.' She Bluetoothed the number.

Lin asked, 'Don't I need your number, as well? I've already been given Pamela's.' Ginny agreed she did, and repeated the process with Lin's mobile.

Seeing Ginny preparing to leave, Marcus offered to help her with her luggage. She accepted, before asking, 'What do you two intend to do with yourselves today? You could be here for ages before anything happens.'

He glanced at Lin for a moment. 'We might do some touristy things.'

'Well, don't stray too far; we know where our man is, and we'll have a tail on him if he steps outside.'

'Alright. Here, let me take that.' He led the way.

Ginny called out over her shoulder, 'Bye, Lin.'

She called back, pleasantly enough, 'Bye, Ginny.'

Having the lift to themselves, Ginny asked, 'Do I get a goodbye kiss?' She interpreted Marcus's lack of an immediate refusal as equivalent to the granting of permission, so demonstrated her expertise once again.

As they were passing through the lobby, she stopped off at reception. 'Room two-o-five is vacant now. Just charge it to two-o-nine.'

The receptionist asked Marcus, 'Is that satisfactory, Dr Watson?' He nodded in affirmation, believing it to be too late to maintain the deception regarding Lin. 'Do you wish to clear the bill now, sir?'

With so much currency stuffed into his wallet, he decided to reduce his load. 'Yes, and two-o-nine up to and including tonight, but I'll be needing the room for some time yet. And I'd like a second key card.'

'Do you know how long you might be staying, sir?'

'I really couldn't say. Is that a problem?'

'No, sir, not a problem; it just helps us with room allocations to know when it might become available. We're always full at this time of year, so when we know a large room is due to become vacant, we note it down on our manual system; if we were to put it online, it would probably be booked by someone straight away. It's so that we can accommodate any special guests.'

'So, if the King of Sweden were to call you without booking in advance, you could find him a room.'

The man allowed his professional mask to slip. 'I really don't expect that to happen.'

'Well, if he does, don't give him my room, will you? It sounds like I'd struggle to find another one.'

'Don't worry; your room is specially reserved.'

He almost drained his wallet of kroner, and was relieved he was spending someone else's money.

After escorting Ginny to her car, he returned to his room and found Lin looking through brochures. She gratefully accepted the new key card, and then asked, 'Does she really think she can steal you away? If only she understood how special our relationship is, she'd know she doesn't stand a chance.' She watched his reaction, her words having been aimed at influencing him, rather than genuinely expressing her confidence.

'Yes, what we have is very special.' After delaying a while, out of respect for Lin's feelings, he picked up his phone. 'I need to ring Helen.' He was surprised to find she failed to answer, as they had made no plans for the children to be away from home that Sunday morning. Aware the system would alert Helen to the missed call, he broke the connection without leaving a message.

Lin asked, 'No one in? And they're an hour behind us. I'd have thought only churchgoers would be out this early on New Year's Day.'

He frowned. 'I hope nothing's happened.'

'Does this mean we have to stay here in case she calls the hotel? I don't mind spending all day in bed with you if you want me to, but I do feel a bit drained from last night. It's never been quite like that before.'

He grinned. 'It was pretty good, wasn't it.'

She gazed at him. 'You know it was more than just good. But is it normal, what I did?'

'Yes, if you're lucky enough to be the kind of girl who can let it all go. Only, don't expect fireworks in the sky every time; it won't always be like that.'

She smiled for a moment, before looking pensive. 'I doubt if things could ever be quite so perfect again.'

He frowned. 'Which means it's downhill all the way from here. Are you thinking we should quit while we're at the top?'

She looked shocked. 'No, never! You and me are as permanent as you and Helen. I don't worry about you and her; I know it's just the way it has to be.'

Realising she had never spelled it out quite so clearly before, he wondered if it really could be that simple.

She waved a brochure at him. 'If we don't have to stay in, could we go to the Living History Museum? It looks like there are plenty of things to see there.'

After replenishing his wallet from the sock, they decided to go to the museum on Djurgården Island, using public transport. Lin remarked, as she picked up her parka, 'I was getting used to going out as other people; being myself again feels quite strange.'

They made their way to Drottninggatan and then continued along to Klarabergsgatan, where they found steps leading down to a square, the Sergels Torg sunken shopping plaza. After looking around, he suggested they walk to Kungsträdgården, rather than catching the tram at the nearest stop. As they reached the NK shopping centre on Hamngatan, she began to describe all the items she had bought there the previous day; he was relieved it was currently unable to tempt her again, as it had not yet opened.

When they were approaching the Kungsträdgården tram stop, he diverted them into the nearby park. They strolled around together, for once risking linking arms, and came upon a winter scene they found aesthetically pleasing: skaters were circling a statue of Charles XIII, within a sunken octagonal enclosure that had been turned into an ice rink.

Eventually, they meandered back to Hamngarten and the Kungsträdgården tram stop. A blue caterpillar hove into view within minutes. They sat together looking out of the window and drawing each other's attention to the sights along the way. On Djurgårdsvägen, they saw a sign for the Skansen museum on Hazeliusporten, then passed several more museums before reaching the next stop. After they had disembarked, he looked around and saw the Abba museum. She crushed his enthusiasm for a detour by suggesting it would appeal to an earlier generation than hers. He made no mention of his liking for their music, as they walked back up the road to their planned destination.

Inside the Skansen museum, they speculated that the dearth of animals was probably due to hibernation, or to the presence of a thick crust of ice covering their pools. Many of the traditional buildings were also closed, though various shops were open. He checked at the quaint Tavern restaurant and received confirmation they could have Christmas Platters at noon.

To kill time, they looked around the Pottery and Glasswork shops, and then the Barn Store. He saw a phalanx of highly stylised wooden, squat, red-painted horses with unarticulated legs; green-and-yellow flower designs represented their saddles, and red-and-green swirls the girth straps. Thinking it would be a nice little present for Alice, he bought one. For Edwin, he chose a wooden three-masted ship of a similar size, white with a red keel, the sails cream with brown pinstripes. Lin bought a small figure of a round-nosed man wearing a red felt cone as a hat, his face almost entirely obscured by curly white whiskers, and with shiny black shoes peeping out from under his frustum-shaped grey body.

When they went to eat, he complained about the cold keeping him perpetually hungry. After the platters, he scoured the menu for a sweet that would be highly calorific. Torn between two contenders, he suggested they have one each and share them to discover more about Swedish cuisine. She understood what was expected of her, so had a third of the first and even less of the second, and left the rest to him.

In the afternoon, they caught the tram and headed back to the hotel. Only a few minutes into the journey, he took a call from Ginny. 'Hi, Marky. Our Rabbit has come out of his hole.'

'Burrow,' he suggested.

'Focus,' she demanded, then declared defensively, 'It was my surveillance team, but I wasn't the Eye who lost him. He obviously expected to be surveilled; he tried a couple of choke points with me, but he didn't spot me on his tail. I set my first Eye on him at Molly Malone's; it's an Irish pub on Odengatan, about ten or fifteen minutes' walk from your hotel. We didn't lose him straight away; we rotated a few times before he disappeared. I can show you where he went, but I don't know if he'll come back this way.'

'I would like to see where he started out, and where your Eye lost him, but I'll be half an hour.'

'Half an hour? Why? Where are you?'

'Coming back from Djurgården Island; we were at the Skansen Living History Museum. We're on a tram.'

'On a tram?' Her tone suggested surprise. 'Shall I pick you up in the car?'

'You stay on tracking him down. If you find him, give me another call, but otherwise there's no point in rushing. I'll phone you once I'm back at the hotel, if I don't hear from you first.'

He returned to the hotel room with Lin, and then phoned Ginny. 'I'm back. Still no sign of him?'

'Not yet.'

'Shall I walk to the pub, then?'

'Yes, but scan it from a distance first, in case he's in the vicinity. Don't go up Västmannagatan, as it would be just around the corner on your right as soon as you reached Odengatan. Go along Dalagatan instead, and then turn right when you reach the end of Vasaparken on your left. That's a park, by the way, if you hadn't guessed.'

'Thanks for that, though I think I might have been able to work it out for myself. Where will I meet you?'

'Just keep going until I meet you; you won't see me first, if I'm as good as I think I am.'

'That sounds like a challenge. What do I win if I see you before you see me?'

'Be serious! This isn't a game.' He heard her laugh. 'You can have any prize you like, so long as I'm the one presenting it. And what do I win?'

'The same, I suppose.'

'Sounds a fair trade.'

When he had terminated the call, Lin asked, 'Am I invited?'

He grinned. 'Not officially. I'm going to an Irish pub called Molly Malone's. You know that cagoule you bought yourself, with the money Max authorised for Elena to give to me for essential expenses…?'

'I feel you're trying to make a point, Marcus.'

'… Put it on over your two new jumpers; you don't want to get cold. Put your red wig on, as well. And then follow me along Dalagatan; take this map. But keep twice the normal tracking distance. At some point, Ginny's going to be meeting me, only she wants to prove herself by not letting me see her first. If you see her before she makes contact, give me a call, and I'll do a disappearing act. After that, come back here, so she doesn't know how I knew where she was.'

A few hurried minutes later, Marcus threw on his thick overcoat without his jacket, and took the stairs while Lin waited for the lift. Outside, he set off at a steady pace, and was at the end of Eastmansvägen when his phone vibrated; he answered quietly, 'Yes?'

Lin spoke in hushed tones, in keeping with the spirit of subterfuge rather than out of necessity. 'I'm sure it's her, wearing a brown duffel coat with the hood up. She came out of Observatoriegatan, which was on your right. Then she followed you at an even distance, except when she stopped and turned away from you at Hostel Dalagatan, and then again at the Pizzeria. When you reached the restaurants opposite the park, she rushed back to Observatoriegatan, where she was picked up in a white van with a water tap painted on the side; it was probably meant to indicate a plumber. My guess is she's being driven around, to meet you at the end of Vasaparken.'

He stepped into the park and headed for an ancient linden tree in the shape of a candelabra, before turning to look along Odengatan. The plumber's van drew up near the corner with Dalagatan and jettisoned a duffel-coated passenger, who glanced in all directions. Not seeing her target, she also headed into the park. He edged around a tree to avoid being seen by her, occasionally taking a sly glance to check on her progress. When she was passing close by, he stepped out and walked behind her a few paces. Sensing someone was there, she stopped. He made his voice sound gravelly. 'Don't turn around.'

She still recognised it was Marcus, so ignored his instruction. 'How the hell did you do that?' Her words were dripping with irritation.

He smiled innocently. 'I'll tell you later... what I want to claim as my prize.'

She dropped her annoyed tone. 'You didn't need to do this; you know you only have to ask, if you want me. Now, I'd better show you where our target went.'

They walked along Odengatan, turned right onto Upplansgatan, and then left onto Observatoriegatan. 'This is about where we lost him.'

'Maybe he called in there for a burger.'

'If he did, he came out looking totally different. We watched the place for a while, and then one of my team went in and checked who was inside; there was nobody even remotely similar.'

'Back entrance? Car park?'

'We couldn't tell, but he was long gone. So, do you have any brilliant ideas?'

'I could take you to the pub for a drink.'

She smiled. 'I'd like that, but it wouldn't be smart for us to be seen in there together; I'm the kind of girl who gets noticed, and you need to be a ghost.'

'In that case, I'll go in on my own. If we're lucky, he might just walk in; we know he used an Irish passport, so maybe he likes Irish bars.'

CHAPTER 28

Marcus wandered into Molly Malone's pub and glanced around. He thought the place was being overseen by a model of a jolly Irishman sitting astride a clock and drinking a flagon of ale, until he saw the painted eyes were raised heavenward. He found the old-fashioned décor pleasantly subdued, with yellows and earthy reds. As he scanned down the long list of Scotch whiskies, he decided he really should have Irish whiskey. With two to choose from, he opted for Bushmills over Paddy.

Sitting in a corner, he watched the door. Within ten minutes, his target appeared, unaccompanied. He thanked the gods for their continued dispensing of thick wodges of luck, and wondered if Freya was standing in for Pallas Athena. The man did not even glance at him, as he obtained a glass of whiskey and then ruined it with a glacier of ice, before sitting at a distant table.

Marcus recalled his plan for a casual meeting in a pub: get the man drunk to loosen his tongue, and pump him for information without him realising. The first hurdle was making contact without being too obvious. He drained his glass, obtained another Bushmills, and headed for a table near the target; if someone would start a conversation with the man, he might be able to join in. As he was walking by, he accidentally tripped over the man's foot when he moved it at just the wrong moment. A few drops spilled from his glass.

The man stood up immediately and addressed him in English, the assumed *lingua franca* in places where tourists may outnumber natives. 'I'm so sorry; it's my big feet. Let me get you another.'

Marcus could hardly believe his luck. 'No need; there were only a few drops spilled.' He waited, hoping his attempt to be subtle would not have lost him his golden opportunity.

'But I insist; what is it you're drinking?'

'Well, Bushmills, as a matter of fact.'

'I'm drinking Paddy, myself; but I'll join you in a Bushmills. Do sit down.'

Marcus poured his old drink in with his new. 'Slainte! as they say in Ireland.'

'Na zdorovie! as we say in Russia.'

'Nostrovia!' Marcus mis-repeated.

'Nah zda-ROVH-yeh!' the man corrected.

Marcus had a sip. The man emptied his glass. 'When we make a toast, you must drink it all.' Marcus drained his in one, regretting being unable to savour it.

The man banged down his glass. 'I'm Sergei.'

Marcus banged down his own glass. 'I'm James.'

'Pleased to meet you, James.'

'And you too, Sergei. I'll get the next round. Same again?'

'Yes, fine.'

When Marcus returned with two double Bushmills, Sergei asked him, 'Is this your favourite drink?'

He replied, 'I think Moonshine is my favourite.'

'Ah, moonshine; illegally distilled spirit.'

'No, it's the name of a beer made by a small brewery in England.' He immediately realised he had divulged more information than he had intended.

Sergei smiled. 'Mine is Gold Symphony vodka; it contains real twenty-three carat gold leaf. They sell it at a bar I often visit, not too far away. I'll be going there, later; you should come and try some.'

'That sounds good. But tell me, Sergei, where did you learn to speak such excellent English?'

'I studied at the London School of Economics for three years, where I took a double first in Capitalist Corruption and Western Political Hypocrisy.'

'You sound like you're not exactly enamoured of the way we do things in the West.'

'That's because you all live with so many Big Lies that the media won't mention and no one will talk about. Unless you move to a more open society, like we have in Russia, you'll never even start to address them.'

Marcus suppressed a smile at what he perceived to be a Giant Lie. 'I can think of some Big Lies, myself; but which ones did you have in mind?'

'I'll start with something that affects everyone: all people are equal, no matter who they are or where they come from. It's such a convincing lie, people in the Western media don't even realise it's an underlying assumption behind much of their reporting.'

'Perhaps it's more of an ideal they wish to support on principle, regardless of reality? I know of a good Big Lie, aimed at reducing assaults on homosexuals, that's been propagated in the media, and has proponents in the academic world; it's the claim that anyone who displays antipathy toward homosexuals must themselves have homosexual tendencies. The idea behind it was that hostile heterosexual men would fear being labelled the very thing they hated. The reality for many of them is that their naked aggression stems from some primitive, socially unacceptable heterosexual instinct.'

'That lie affects only a minority, though. My earlier

example, of the idea that all people are equal, relates to everyone. Here's an obvious scenario you can relate to: if anyone tries to shoot the US president, someone in the security service is expected to jump in front of them and take the bullet. Imagine that was your job; could you believe all people are equal, and at the same time sacrifice yourself for someone else? What greater right to life do they have if the two of you are equal? And if you were prepared to sacrifice yourself for anyone, then you're hardly going to be any good at defending the president in the first place. What would you say to a terrorist with a gun? "Please don't kill anyone, but be aware I won't shoot you as you have the same right to life as I have." So equality clearly doesn't apply there.'

'I accept your argument, but it is something of an extreme example.'

'There are many other examples that affect all levels of society. Imagine a man on a crowded train. Another man says to him, politely and in a non-threatening way, that he'd like their seat. Does the seated man stand up?'

'Actually, in an experiment in New York designed to breach social norms, they found that more than half did exactly that.'

'But there, the request would not have been normal, so he probably thinks the man is a mentally defective. We lock up our mentally defectives, so in Russia the interpretation would be different; the man would be saying he is more important.'

'Or ill. What if he really needed to sit down?'

'The seated man should ask him why he wanted the seat; then he could decide whether or not to stand.'

'So how is that about equality?'

'If he had a good reason, he could stand; but if he

had no good reason, he may stay seated, showing the two of them are unequal.'

'Or that, for people who are equal, the rule is simply, the first on the train gets the seat.'

'Hmm, you argue very well; I can see you would make a formidable opponent. In a debate, I mean.'

'Maybe it's because I'm employing the superior forces of Western arguments, and there isn't quite so much wrong with our society as you first thought.'

'On the contrary, there are many fundamental flaws with the way the West operates.'

'Which wicked ways of the West are the worst?'

'Corporate greed comes first. So many people who are at the top of an organisation take advantage of the lack of any higher authority to restrict how much they can milk from it. Should anyone be paid a fortune to do a job they enjoy? The top executives of a company are often the happiest, and yet they receive what are stupidly called "compensation packages" that are worth far more than is given to any worker. The unhappiest employees would be those at the bottom, so they are the ones who should receive compensation to make up for their suffering. The reality is, there are no limits to greed. Do you not see it yourself, all over the Western world? Not just in companies, but everywhere.'

'Well, now that you mention it, we do seem to have let things get out of hand. In Britain, there are Hospital Trust managers who pay themselves far more than the doctors, even though it's the medics who are essential. School principals arrange to have themselves paid more than our prime minister, because there's no effective governance to keep them in check; and they're forever bleating on about how many millions their budgets are, when the country's accounts are measured in billions.'

'Speaking as an economist, heads of schools should really be recognised as simple administrators of cost centres. They take in government funds and then spend them on the things that are essential, such as books and teachers. Anything left over goes into the trough where they thrust their snouts. Tell me if I'm wrong.'

'I can't fault your argument; it's why we have heads of schools who behave like tinpot dictators, and who syphon off funds given to them by taxpayers.'

'The concept of public service in Britain has been replaced by a culture of greed. They should have our system; the President is the only one who is allowed to be greedy. Anyone else can only grow fat off the state with his permission. Even the wealthiest can become paupers overnight if he decrees it, which is why so many move to London to protect their assets. The breadth of his personal control is what makes him the most powerful political leader in the world.'

'But isn't the US president the most powerful?'

'No; that's just another lie. In Russia, the president can make any laws he wishes, and then choose to apply them or ignore them entirely. Putin's view was always: for my friends, everything; for my enemies, the law. A US president has to gain approval from Congress to implement legislation, or appoint judges who might reinterpret the statutes. When an outgoing US president has to admit his biggest failing was being unable to revise the Second Amendment to the Constitution, the right to bear arms, you can see how weak US Presidents really are. If you look at the history of gun crime in the US, you realise it's because the president doesn't have the power of a Russian Federation president.'

'But there's a history of gun crime in Russia, too.'

'It's relatively small, compared to the authorised use of weapons by the state; just ask the people living in the Ukraine.'

'I think many people living in Ukraine would say the Russian invasion should never have been authorised; they would argue it was an act of naked aggression in support of Putin's stated objective of a greater Russia.'

'Invasion? Who said anything about an invasion? It was an intervention designed to relieve the suffering of Russian people living there.'

'So, if a Russian is living in another country, do you see an intervention as justified to support them?'

'Anyone who is Russian, or is working in another country for the Russian state, should be subjected to the laws of Russia... as well as to the laws of the country they are living in.'

'What if there's a conflict between the two?'

'Russian laws must prevail.'

'Well, Sergei, that was interesting. What else is on your list of things wrong with the West?'

'I have to say, it's a very long list. Look at American television, for example; there are now so many action programmes featuring women beating men in physical combat. The idea that a small woman can overpower a large man is a stupid lie; I can tell you, if any of those little women attacked me, I would just snap their neck.'

Marcus realised his eyes had opened a little wider, so tried to mask his unintended sign of cognition by quickly supporting the polemic. 'I completely agree with you; scenes like that are totally ridiculous.'

'Yes, almost as ridiculous as those where people are pointing guns at each other and talking at the same time. It would never be like that; the first to take aim would fire before the second was ready. If I were in that situation, I would already have shot him through the head before he could start to discuss why we were standing there. It's just so unbelievable.'

'You'd shoot him or her straight away?'

'Him or her! Have you heard the British are now allowing women to be recruited as frontline soldiers? You're probably too young to know this, but when a female rear-line soldier was captured by the Iraqis in the first Iraq war, all the media focused on was whether she would be raped. It was as though the rest of the war didn't matter to them. What do you think would happen to a female soldier captured by an enemy who regarded women as having little or no value? When you look at how their own women are treated in some of these supposedly civilised Islamic countries, you can hardly expect them to treat captured women any better. The Western powers need to understand the minds of those people, and not expect them to behave decently, the way we Russians behave.'

He recalled the level of rape by Russian soldiers against German women toward the end of the Second World War, but thought it would be counterproductive to a free-flowing conversation if he were to mention it. 'There's a lot of truth in what you say, Sergei. But isn't the way forward to civilise the rest of the world?'

'What is it to be civilised? You must know people in the US who seem to think Political Correctness makes them more civilised than anyone else, yet in reality it merely curbs the freedom of speech enjoyed by others. In Russia, we're free to say what we like on anything, so long as it doesn't include direct or indirect criticism of our president, which is only a small price to pay.'

He decided now was the right time to poke the Russian bear. 'Yes, it is a *small* price to pay; he's only slightly taller than Napoleon was. And is there any truth in the rumour he likes little boys a bit too much?'

'There's no truth in it whatsoever. He works hard to control and restrict all types of degeneracy, including suppressing homosexuality of any age or gender.'

'So, if he defected to the West, we shouldn't expect to see him on Brighton Beach.'

'Why not Brighton Beach? Half the male population of Brighton Beach is Russian. He often wears a leather jacket; if he grew a beard, he would fit in very easily.'

'Ah, I was meaning Brighton on the south coast of England, a favourite town for Gays.'

'My mistake; I was thinking of New York City.'

'You must be quite well-travelled, Sergei. Is it work that takes you to other countries?'

'I go where I'm told. But what about you, James? What brings you to Sweden?'

He knew he had learned a considerable amount from letting Sergei vent his views, but believed the flow would dry up if he failed to reciprocate. 'I'm here to do the touristy things. Yesterday I went to see the *Vasa*, and earlier today, an open air Living History museum, except it was mostly closed.'

'You were not alone, I assume.' Marcus hesitated. 'Ah, let me guess: you're married, but came with your mistress. It's the typical Russian way, too.' Marcus grinned to indicate he had been caught out. 'While you still have your freedom, let me take you to the bar where they serve my favourite vodka; yes?'

'Sure. I'll just make a quick call, so my little friend

isn't waiting for me.'

'And I'll make a call, too.'

Marcus phoned Lin. 'I'm having a drink at a pub with a foreign pal, and now we're going to another one. I'll make sure I'm back in time to have a chat with our friends.' He cut the conversation short, having seen that Sergei's call had been even briefer.

Sergei stood up. 'I arranged a lift; it's right outside.' When Marcus hesitated, he added, 'It's too far to walk.'

The large white van had two rows of seats and plenty of space behind them. Sergei pulled back the sliding door and waited for him to climb inside. Feeling no hint of coercion, he stepped in and sat behind the driver. Sergei followed him and pulled the door shut. 'This is Vladimir; you can call him Vlad.'

The weasel-faced man turned his head for a moment. Marcus thought he looked quite like Putin. When he growled 'Hi,' Marcus responded similarly.

Vlad drove them at a leisurely pace across to the island of Stadsholmen, where he suddenly speeded up and headed down a narrow street. Marcus began to feel distinctly uneasy, his misapprehension increasing as Vlad executed several quick turns before braking sharply outside a small, dimly-lit bar. Sergei jumped out smartly. 'Come on, we're here.' Marcus's level of concern ratcheted up when Vlad sped away, but dipped again when Sergei entered the bar ahead of him, as he was now free to walk away if he so wished.

He pushed open one of a pair of narrow wooden doors, and stepped inside. Finding they were the only two customers, he looked over at the barman: wiry, not very muscular, probably not much good in a fight. He decided that may be a good thing if he ended up scrapping with Sergei, as the barman would probably be on the side of his regular customer.

Sergei called over from the counter, 'It's small, but it has character. Come, my friend.' He walked toward Marcus with his arms outstretched, clearly intent on a man-hug. When they accidentally crashed their heads together, he pulled himself away. 'Ah, yes; in Russia, we move our heads to the right, but in North America the move is to the left. You have clearly adopted the American way.'

In a spirit of entente, Marcus leaned his head far over to the right for a Russian-style man-hug, before walking around and looking at the décor as though he were interested. Finally, he sat at the table nearest the door. The barman brought them two shots of vodka. Sergei held the glasses up to the dim light, to display the gold flakes. 'A toast: to our noble profession.'

Marcus stopped dead. 'Exactly what profession is that, Sergei?'

'You do for the US what I do for mother Russia: we support the national interest. If you don't want your drink, James, I'll have it for you; it isn't poisonous.'

Marcus touched it with the tip of his tongue, before knocking it back. Finding no evidence of the gold in the taste, he decided it was more for show than for flavour. As it coursed its way down his gullet, he reflected on the significance of having been addressed as James, and concluded a connection must only have been made with Ginny, leaving his true identity still hidden.

Sergei asked, 'Are you actually English, James; or are you that incredibly rare creature, an American who can put on a convincing English accent?'

Marcus obfuscated. 'Do I really wish to answer that

question, I ask myself. I can see little point in disclosing more of my identity than is essential at this juncture.'

Sergei nodded. 'Never heard a Yank say "juncture", so I guess you're originally English.'

Marcus countered with a ruse of his own. 'Are you really Russian? We know you have an Irish passport, which suggests you have at least one Irish grandparent.'

He swept away any doubt with a wave of his hand. 'If I had been from St Petersburg, I could have risen up the ranks. But being from Moscow, I could never really get in with Putin's cronies.' He called for two more shots of vodka, this time offering both to Marcus for him to choose. 'Now it's your turn to raise a toast.'

Marcus thought long and hard. 'To professional courtesy.' They downed their drinks simultaneously.

Sergei asked, 'So, why have all you US operatives been watching me, today?'

Marcus replied immediately to support the erroneous assumption. 'Because you killed a guy called Stanley Hicks, and the Brits are refusing to investigate; they think it might show them in a bad light. Professionally, it didn't make any sense to us for you to delete an asset who was out of the game, especially as you performed the termination too quickly to have had the time to extract any intel from him.'

Sergei sat and pondered, and then called for more drinks. The barman placed them on the table. Marcus chose the one nearer his right hand. Sergei proposed, 'Here's to Stanley Hicks, and to anyone else who wants to get out of the game.' As Marcus downed his shot, he caught Sergei's eye, and knew something was wrong.

CHAPTER 29

Lin tried again to contact Marcus by phone. He had said he would be back in time for the six-o-five phone call, but it now looked like he would be late. When she heard a rap at the door, she felt a huge swell of relief, and rushed to open it. The shock of seeing Helen there left her speechless.

Helen hurried in, wheeling her bag. 'Hello, Lin; where's Marcus?'

Her words tumbled out. 'I don't know. I haven't been able to contact him, and he's due to make a phone call in a few minutes. I really can't imagine what's keeping him.'

Helen put her bag on the stand, then opened the wardrobe. 'What are your things doing in here? Marcus told me you were sleeping in two-o-five with a Swedish woman called Elena.'

'That was the night before last.'

'So, what about last night?'

'There was an American woman.' Helen silently waited for more information. 'She's called Ginny.'

'And tonight?' Lin failed to respond. 'Were you intending to sleep here tonight?'

'The other room isn't available anymore and all the hotels are full. I thought it would be alright; it's a wide enough bed, and he knows I'm not attracted to his type.' Helen stared at her. She flinched, and then checked the time. 'I have to make a phone call in a minute if Marcus doesn't show up.'

'Well, if he's gone missing, shouldn't you have told someone? Anything could have happened to him.'

'I was going to, if he wasn't back by five past six; that's when he makes contact with our support team. I'm going to tell them right now.'

'Put your phone on speaker; I want to know what's happening.'

She called Pamela, who quickly answered, 'Yes?'

Lin remembered to use the code word. 'Hello, gorgeous.'

The response was immediate. 'Hello, lover. I know he's gone missing, but I can't talk to you right now; wait for my local rep to contact you.'

'Will do.' The phone went dead.

Helen asked, 'So, was that your Swedish girlfriend, or your American one.'

'Neither; I mean, it was a different American one.' Receiving the silent stare again, she added, 'She's called Pamela.'

Helen guessed this Pamela was Marcus's Honey. 'I'll unpack my things. You'll have to sort out somewhere to sleep when Marcus is back. I need to get something to eat; how's room service?'

'Very limited. You go down to the restaurant and I'll hold the fort.'

Helen unpacked, grabbed her handbag and headed down to reception, where she demanded a key card for her husband's room. The man frowned at her. 'So, you're another Mrs Watson.'

'No.' Helen recovered quickly from having forgotten about the alias. 'I mean yes; Mrs Helen Watson. Just how many Mrs Watsons are there?'

'You're the seventh.' Realising she may be unaware

of the other women, he covered for Dr Watson. 'It must be a very popular name; we've never had so many Mrs Watsons staying in different rooms at the same time.'

When Helen returned after her meal, Lin let her in and told her about a brief call from Ginny. 'She says they're doing everything they can to find him, and I should stay around and wait in case he comes back.'

Being more than a little uncomfortable with the situation, Lin decided to leave Helen alone, relying on her phone for updates on the search for Marcus. 'I think I'll go and get a bite to eat.' She found Marcus's money sock and extracted a small amount of currency, having previously stowed the funds that came from the British embassy, and what remained from Elena following their shopping expedition. Seeing Helen watching closely, she explained, 'It's been provided for expenses; we're supposed to use cash, to stay under the radar.'

Helen frowned. 'Does that apply to me, as well?'

'I suppose it does; you should take some yourself.'

'I've just charged my meal to this room.'

'They let you do that?'

'I had my room key, so no one objected.'

'How did you get a room key?'

'I just asked at reception. The guy accepted my word that I was who I said I was. He gave me a funny look, at first, but then he must have realised I was genuine. Except I wasn't, was I? I'm Mrs Helen Watson, now. So, who are you?'

'Mrs Mary Watson. It was meant to be a joke.'

'That could go some way toward explaining the surfeit of Mrs Watsons the receptionist was on about.' She emptied the sock and counted the money, then took a few thousand kroner. 'Is anyone keeping a record?'

'It's an off-the-books operation, so we simply have to ask for more when we're running out.'

'How long are you expecting to stay here?'

'I'm due at work on Tuesday, so I don't know what will happen if Marcus doesn't come back to clear it with them for me to stay longer. But I can't just leave him here, so I suppose the answer is, I'm staying as long as he needs me. To help him. With the case.'

'I've made arrangements for the children 'til Friday evening, so I could take over as his support. Have you any idea where he might have gone?' She saw Lin's hesitation. 'Tell me what you know. Now!'

She took a deep breath. 'He phoned me to say he was at a pub with a foreign pal, which must mean the Russian assassin.' She saw the look of horror on Helen's face, and wished she had simply lied.

'Oh God; what's he got himself into.' She looked at Lin and saw her eyes were watering. As much to bolster her own troubled emotions as Lin's, she put on a confident visage. 'We don't need to worry. He's bound to be back soon, probably after drinking far too much. You go and get something to eat. If I hear anything, I'll go and find you in the restaurant. Alright, Lin?'

'Alright, Helen.' Lin hurried out before Helen could see how deeply upset she was feeling from the thoughts now flooding her mind.

When Lin returned, the two sat together and watched Swedish television without taking any of it in. It was almost ten o'clock when a couple of questions occurred to Lin. 'I forgot to ask, how did you get here? And what made you decide to come over?'

Helen turned off the television. 'I tried to phone Marcus at midnight your time but there was no answer.

Then I tried again an hour later, but he must have switched the phone off. So I tried again at seven this morning, and still no reply. And that's when I decided to come and see what was happening for myself. It was a bit of a trek: seven fifty-one train to Manchester; KLM flight to Amsterdam; KLM from Schiphol to Stockholm; train from Arlanda to the central station; and taxi here. I'm so weary, I could do with going to bed. But he isn't back, and you need somewhere to go.'

Lin smiled sympathetically. 'It's alright, Helen; I'm sure he wouldn't expect you to stay up after all that travelling. Why don't you go to bed; I'll join you soon.'

Helen gulped hard. 'I can stay up a few more hours.'

Lin assumed it was for her benefit. 'There's no point in staying up if you're feeling shattered; you need to go to bed now, don't you. Don't worry about me having to get up later; at least I'll have had some sleep.'

Helen, accepting how exhausted she felt, changed into her night clothes in the bathroom and went to bed. Ten minutes later, when Lin heard the sounds of her sleeping deeply, she quietly joined her, unnoticed.

A little before her morning alarm call, Helen became aware of Lin lying pressed against her back, her arm around her; she froze, hoping Lin was still asleep. At seven o'clock, Helen was relieved to hear her phone beeping. Lin woke, and discovered she had unwittingly placed her arm around Helen, so quickly withdrew it.

As soon as Helen was released, she scrambled out of bed, snatched up the phone, turned off the alarm, grabbed some clothes and hurried into the bathroom, remaining closeted until she was showered and dressed.

Wishing to stay in the room in case Marcus returned, Helen ordered room service breakfast for two. At seven thirty, she opened the door to collect the trolley that the old waiter had just delivered, thereby confirming to him the tally now stood at seven.

At seven fifty, Lin phoned Ginny. 'Any news?'

Ginny tried to sound optimistic. 'We're bound to locate him sometime soon. I suggest you just pretend it's a normal day and do something you like doing. Maybe go shopping; there's a centre not far away. I'll phone you as soon as we have anything. Honestly, Lin, you'll only feel worse if you just wait around.'

Despite the enmity she felt she should have toward Ginny, she nevertheless appreciated the sympathy. 'If you think there's anything I can do to help, just let me know. I'm sure you're doing your best, Ginny, so you keep your pecker up as well.'

'That's so nice of you to think about me, Lin; you really are a lovely person. I'll talk to you soon.'

Lin relayed Ginny's advice and then supported the proposal, persuading Helen to recognise the wisdom of therapeutic shopping. Numerous phone calls during the day only confirmed lack of progress, so in the evening they stared at the television, before finally going to bed.

In the night, Lin woke to find Helen with her arms around her, still sleeping soundly. She wondered if Marcus's desire to continue his affair with her may have been in part due to his having discovered Helen's hidden inclinations. But then she realised Helen must simply be missing her husband, and decided she owed it to her to act as a surrogate by reciprocating. As the two lay in each other's arms, Lin drifted back to sleep, appreciating the sisterly companionship.

CHAPTER 30

Marcus fought to regain consciousness, only to find the drug repeatedly overcame him. When he finally won the battle, he took stock. The cold was intense. There was an absence of sound or light. Something was covering his face down to his neck. A pressure line was tracing an arc around the back of his head, with another on his lower forehead, and a third a few inches below that, across his cheeks. He heard the sea in his warm ears. Interpretation: he had no coat, and he was wearing a hood, plus visor and ear covers.

He began another assessment at the lower extremity. His feet were still shod. Something cold encircled his ankles outside his socks; he guessed they were iron fetters. Finding his range of leg movement severely limited, he recognised he had been shackled.

Transferring his focus to his wrists, he knew there were manacles that were broad and heavy; he guessed they might be of a type familiar from ancient times. The short distance he could move one arm without the other being dragged along with it, enabled him to visualise the length of chain that joined them together.

His fundamental numbness suggested he was sitting on a stone or concrete floor. The intense cold that was biting into his back indicated a wall of similar material; he leaned away from it, to reduce his heat loss.

Knowing he could neither see nor hear nor touch nor taste, he tried sniffing the air. All that came back from within the hood was his own damp breath.

He attempted to uncover his head. There was an immediate sharp impact on his thigh, which he took to be a kick. He reverted to being motionless.

The sensory deprivation left him unable to tell the passing of the hours, except by considering what he found the time to contemplate. He began to think of all the torture techniques he had ever come across, so he would know what he might expect, and how he could try to endure any that were employed against him.

Number one: string you up and beat you with cables or sticks. That makes two different ones, cables and sticks. But stringing up is torture as well, so that makes three. I'll just keep them together as one, and include kicking or hitting with other things, such as fists or leather straps. What's the name of the thing the South African police use? What about lashes in Saudi Arabia? Does anyone still use the Cat o' Nine Tails?

Number two: walling. Grab your head and smack it backward against the wall, until you can't see straight and everything's swimming around you.

Number three: keep you standing up for hour after hour. Maybe with your hands out. That's two variations on a theme. By Paganini. Or Tchaikovsky. Or Haydn. Or Corelli. I love classical music and I despise rap.

Number four: force you to listen to some rap. That's not short for rhapsody. Rap in C. C-rap.

Number five: variations on a theme of crap. Smear it all over you. Force you to eat it. Disgusting.

Number six: insert objects into your orifices. Edward the Second had a red hot poker shoved up his back passage, but that was fatal, so it wasn't for extracting information. It's been done to tigers as well, so some stupid person can buy a rug that has no damage marks.

Number six, again: forget the red hot pokers, but stick with the back passage. A stick. Didn't that happen to Gaddafi? Or use an M-16. Or anything else, for that matter. Water hose shoved up and turned on full blast; that was used under a Greek military junta in the sixties or the seventies. At least I don't have to consider what the Argentinians used water for, with women: shoving up a full glass bottle that sealed itself in place and had to be smashed to release it. They also trained a dog to rape women political prisoners, but that wasn't original; the ancient Romans used bulls, only it was always fatal, and they weren't political, so it wasn't really the same.

Number seven: normal rape. Except it isn't normal. Unless you're a Russian and it's the end of the Second World War. I don't know whether it's worse for men or for women. Some people have been able to get over it entirely, and others have let it ruin their lives. But I'm buggered if I'll let someone do that to me. Very good, Marcus; keeping your sense of humour. I mean, James. But James who? I haven't even thought about a surname. Maybe Blond. Hi, I'm James Blond. It'll never wash. The hair, it'll never wash. I'm going to wash that man right out of my hair.

Number eight: water boarding. Or water spray to keep you soaking wet. Pepper spray on a blindfold. No, that's different; it uses an organic chemical.

Number nine: pepper spray. No thank you, sir; I only use organic foods, now. Oh, you have organic pepper spray? I'll take a face full of that, then.

Number ten: noise. I should have included this with rap, which was number… One was physical assault. Two was walling, only that's another form of physical assault. Too late to change it now. Three was standing with the hands out. Four was rap. I'll include all noise in four. White noise, techno-noise, rock music bass noise. And barking dogs, like the one that just suddenly starts wailing, and ruins it for me and my neighbours, who are lazing on a sunny afternoon in their gardens. Or not sunny; it's still as annoying whatever the weather. God, I hope I see my garden again, and the things that are growing up in it. No, I refuse to think about my children.

Number eleven: pull out your fingernails or toenails. As favoured by the Nazis.

Number twelve: remove other parts of your body. Hang, draw and quarter, and have your entrails burned on the fire in front of you. Lose your limbs, like in *Le Silence de la Mer*, where the girl tears the legs off a mosquito that bit her. Or that film where the injuns tie a white man to two hosses and set them off in opposite directions. Torn between two horses. Make that lovers; it was in a song, but not by Iron Maiden, who're named after a box with spikes in it. Anyway, that was more suited to execution than torture.

Number thirteen: put you in a box, one without spikes. It could be a coffin, to mess with your mind; or just a very small box, to make you totally cramped up.

Number fourteen: go for your pressure points. Or the natural varieties: toothache; earache; whatever-ache.

Number fifteen: being eaten alive by animals. Rats. Cats. Jam on the face, and bring on the ants. They're only getting their own back, for the Japanese and their ikizukuri, preparing sashimi from living fish.

Number sixteen: make you sweat and overheat. Could use powerful lights.

Number seventeen: force you to stay awake. To die,

to sleep, to sleep perchance to dream. If I get out of this alive, I don't think I'll want to dream; it'll be just like it was when I left the army.

Number eighteen: starve you of food and drink. That can only be taken so far, if they want you alive. Anyway, I needed to diet; my weight's gone up a bit, and I haven't been spending enough time in the gym to burn it off and pump up my muscles. I'm still in good shape, though. And I'm quite a bit younger than Sergei, so I think I could take him in a fair fight. But I'm chained up, so I don't expect it would be a fair fight.

Number nineteen: force you to strip in front of women, as a form of humiliation. I don't think I'd mind that too much. Or in front of men? Depends.

Number twenty: threats to your family. No, you have to stop right there. Don't even think about it. Think about something else.

I've lost sight of the real objective: it isn't all about withstanding torture; it's to do with not disclosing confidential information. Except I don't have any, other than the names of a few operatives, so it's about giving them time to get away. Only that doesn't apply, either; they don't need to go anywhere. Not only that, but I'd expect they're probably already known to the Russians; certainly Ginny is. So it's me who's the only one at risk. And Lin. That means I simply need to make sure I don't mention her. Right; that's that sorted.

Now to think about information extraction methods. Some of the torture techniques may apply that I thought of earlier, but there are others that are harder to resist.

Number one: drugs. I hope they don't scramble my brain with their truth serum.

Number two: intimidation. Just because I'm tied up

with a black hood over my head doesn't mean I have to feel intimidated. Much! I assume it's a black hood. They're always black, never brown. Who said brown is the new black? Someone from the world of fashion, probably. I don't think it extends to prisoner-wear.

Number three: number three? You're doing this all wrong. Think back to your army training. What was the routine? Some Harshing; a short sharp interrogation; stick me in a stress position; no food, no sleep; keep me guessing what's going to happen next; do things all of a sudden when I'm not expecting them.

What about defence techniques?

Number one: humanise myself. Come on, James... Well done for remembering that's who you are. James Blond, you've already been drinking shots with Sergei, so how much more human can you be with him? It will be his weakness, his Achilles' heel. He won't be able to treat you as a non-person. Work on him, but don't overdo it, as that would give him an excuse to drop his friendship with you. Of course, it wasn't the friendliest thing he could ever have done, kidnapping you and putting you in chains, but don't underestimate how much residual feeling he may have. He did hug you, after all. So, try making yourself a bit vulnerable, someone he might empathise with and feel sympathy for. Imagine he's releasing you; maybe a hug or a slap on the back, and a "Don't forget to write."

Having reached a point where he felt satisfied with his outlook, he fell back on thinking about the usual mainstay for men with nothing else on their minds.

Without a way of measuring time, he had no idea how long his thoughts had been wandering before his captors made their first harsh contact. His goggles and ear covers were pulled off, and then his hood. With a bank of dazzlingly bright lights blinding him, two men in balaclavas bombarded him simultaneously with shouted questions that came so fast there was no time to answer any of them.

'What's your name?'

'When did you join the CIA?'

'Who's your handler.'

'What are the names of the rest of your team?'

'Are the British involved?'

'What do you know about Stanley Hicks?'

'Are the Swedes in on this operation?'

'How did you track us down?'

'Was your plan to kidnap us or to kill us?'

'Who's your boss at the CIA?'

Amid the swirl of questions that he registered, there were many others that he failed to comprehend. He anticipated they would stop and he would be returned to the darkness, but they kept on coming, many of them repeated numerous times. Finally, the man he assumed was Vlad, punched him on the jaw. The other man, no doubt Sergei, immediately terminated his flood of questions and pulled Vlad away, then put the hood back over the prisoner's head. James heard what he thought was perhaps a heated debate in Russian, and then the goggles and ear covers were forced back onto him.

After what seemed like ages, James felt his head-coverings being removed, and this time there was no bright light. Sergei, no longer wearing a balaclava, placed a solid wooden chair next to him and invited him to sit on it. Then he brought another chair for himself, and sat directly facing. 'James, my friend, you know I hate to have to do this, but you'll suffer horribly unless you tell me everything you know about this operation. In the end, you will tell me; so it makes no sense to put yourself through this pain and suffering, simply to delay giving me what I need to know.'

James attempted a smile, though his jaw still ached from the punch. 'Sergei, my friend, I know how much you must hate putting me through this, and I have no wish to suffer for no good reason, but I really don't know anything that might be of any use to you.'

'I knew you'd be reasonable, James; but I do need you to tell me everything you do know. First of all, who's your handler?'

He made a snap decision to reveal Ginny's name, on the basis that she must already be known to him, and was almost certainly the contact by which he had been identified as part of the surveillance operation. 'Have you ever come across Virginia Long?' By responding in the form of a question, he hoped to alter the nature of their interaction to a less one-sided dialogue.

'Is she your handler?'

'It's more of a mutual benefit type of relationship: she handles me and I handle her.' He gave an extended wink.

'James, you don't seem to appreciate the seriousness of your predicament.'

'I do, Sergei; but you need to understand I'm simply someone who was brought in at the last moment because I'm an unknown face. I was told to trail you, but I wasn't told why. I'm sorry to say I'm just a small cog in the machine; if I knew more, I'd tell you.'

When Sergei heard Vlad speak from the shadows, he responded with what James interpreted as a degree of irritation. Sergei quietly informed James, 'Vlad will hit you and then ask you some questions.' He stood and removed his chair, before shouting, 'Get up!'

James jumped to his feet as Vlad walked over. Vlad positioned himself in front of James and punched him in the solar plexus. James tried hard not to show he had felt the powerful blow. Sergei took Vlad to one side, before conversing with him at length in Russian.

As Vlad moved further away, Sergei again spoke quietly to James. 'We've agreed I shall use you as a punch-bag, because I'm much more powerful; and he will ask you questions, because he thinks he's the one with the brains. When I hit you, it will hurt you so much you must double up in pain.'

Sergei took his stance in the textbook manner, as though focused to strike thirty centimetres beyond the target. James felt the blow but knew he had pulled his punch. Acting on instinct coupled with reinterpretation of Sergei's words, he doubled up and crashed to the ground, then proceeded to groan pitifully.

Vlad walked over to them. 'Who ordered the search for Sergei?'

James stayed on the floor and groaned some more. 'Virginia told me what I had to do; that's all I know.'

'Where did she get her orders?'

'From someone higher up, I suppose.'

'Who in Britain is involved?'

'No one, as far as I know.'

There was another exchange in Russian. Sergei yanked James to his feet, then set himself to rain body punches on him, delaying long enough for James to prepare himself for the onslaught. Though each blow made contact firmly enough to give a little pain, he knew Sergei was performing for Vlad's benefit. As he reeled under the pressure, he tried to imagine what was behind the show, but had no time to reach any sort of conclusion. When Sergei delivered a particularly well-telegraphed imitation blockbuster to the stomach, he managed to let out a yelp that extended to a scream, as he crashed onto his chair and then to the ground.

Vlad stood over him and kicked him hard on the thigh. James ignored it, as though it were nothing in comparison to what he had just suffered. Vlad asked, 'What is the name of the British operative who makes contact with Virginia Long?'

James responded one word at a time, punctuated by an audible wince that accompanied each shallow breath. 'I... don't... know... who... she... talks... to...'

Vlad and Sergei held another exchange in Russian, and then left him alone. He stood the chair back up and sat on it. With his hood removed, he scanned the entire room and concluded it was a cellar.

James guessed about half an hour had passed before Sergei returned with a young woman holding a camera. He thought her heavy brow and prominent jawline would have better suited a boxer than a photographer. Sergei quickly placed the hood over James's head.

The woman stepped closer to James and spoke to him in halting English. 'I will photograph you naked.'

James responded from underneath the hood. 'That would be very nice.'

There followed an exchange in Russian, before Sergei asked James, 'Why do you think that would be very nice?'

He replied into his darkness, 'Because she looks rather attractive, so I would quite like to see her naked body when she takes a photograph of me. Does she double as bait in a honeytrap? Is she a Sparrow?'

During the exchange in Russian that followed, he heard her laugh for a moment, and hoped that was due to his attempted charm. Suddenly, he felt a hard slap across his face, cushioned only by the hood. Sergei explained, 'She says she's insulted by you, to think she's that kind of a girl. She also says you must be stupid to make that interpretation. She says she will make a photograph with you naked with a frightened child, so people will think you're a paedophile.'

Unsure who was listening, James remained silent. When he heard two pairs of footsteps diminish into the distance, he assumed he was alone again.

Though he knew his body was demanding food, his brain was overriding the messages of hunger, as it focused on processing the scant information he had obtained so far. His first tentative conclusion was that Sergei was in some sense a good man despite being an assassin, and was protecting James from serious harm out of a spirit of friendship. After further reflection, he considered whether Sergei and Vlad were playing a variant of the "Good guard, bad guard" game. His final interpretation seemed to him the most probable, that the two guards were competing for power in their working relationship, and that he was merely a pawn.

He reminded himself of what he had said and what he had kept obscured: he knew nothing about anything, beyond Virginia Long having invited him to take part in a surveillance operation, relating to someone accused of assassinating a man in England.

After another period of cold, quiet contemplation, he heard steps approaching. Sergei removed James's hood and held up his new smartphone. 'I wish to contact

Virginia Long; I assume you have her number on here.'

Knowing the other number it held was Pamela's, he tried to think of a way of avoiding giving Sergei access. 'It's a new phone and I've forgotten the code number, what with everything else that's been happening.'

Sergei shook his head. 'James, you know and I know that that is not true. I wish to have her number straight away. If you will do this little thing for me, I will do something for you in return. What would you like me to do for you?'

'Let me go?'

'Seriously, James.'

'A lavatory would be good. And something to eat.'

'Of course. So, first you give me the number.'

'Would you mind doing it the other way around, Sergei? I'm really quite desperate. Remember when we toasted to professional courtesy?'

'A compromise. You go to the toilet. I receive her phone number. You get some food. In that order.'

'That would be great; thanks, Sergei.' He wondered if the chains would be removed and this might be the moment he could take on his captor in a fight. Sergei unfastened only the chain that attached James to the wall. With his wrists and ankles remaining linked together, he decided this loaded the odds too heavily against him. Following directions issued from behind by Sergei, James trudged to a small room on the same floor and found a chemical toilet.

Sergei waited patiently, before following James back to his original place. After reattaching him, he held up the new smartphone. 'If you attempt to use this for any purpose other than obtaining the number, I shall have to punish you.'

James replied, 'No problem, Sergei. Shall I simply read out the number, or should I Bluetooth it to you?'

Sergei opened up his own phone. 'I don't have that facility; just call it out, slowly.'

When the number had been logged, Sergei watched and waited while James turned off his phone. 'I'll take that back, now.' He handed it over.

Cheeseburger and chips with a can of fizzy orange was not exactly the meal he had been hoping for, but it served the essential purpose. Sergei removed the manacles to allow him to eat more easily, and then left them unattached on the floor as he departed again.

James estimated it was perhaps ten minutes before Sergei returned. 'You would like the toilet again?'

'I'm alright at the moment, thanks.'

Sergei repeated, more insistently, 'You would like the toilet again!'

Unsure where this was leading, he watched as Sergei detached him from the wall. As his ankles remained chained together, James felt the odds were still not in his favour, so made the same journey as before. When he returned to the chaining point, Sergei made no move to reattach him. 'You can't run far like that, can you? If you promise to behave, I'll not fasten you up again.'

Before he could respond, James heard footsteps approaching. Vlad appeared, along with the prospective photographer. Sergei yawned and stretched himself lazily, which opened his coat and revealed a gun in a holster high up on his chest. James wondered if this was simply carelessness, or whether he was employing the technique allegedly used for disposing of problem detainees at Guantanamo Bay: the inmate snatches the gun, thereby justifying a guard's action in shooting him.

He decided to take his chance. With his right hand, James grabbed the gun and quickly released the safety catch. While keeping his back to Vlad, Sergei used his left hand to grasp James's right hand together with the gun, before shouting something in Russian. Vlad pulled out his own gun and moved to Sergei's left, looking for a line of sight.

James jerked his hand away and held the gun over to his right, keeping it out of reach. Sergei grabbed the lower side of his right arm with his left hand, and pulled it close enough to grasp the gun with his right hand over the top of James's hand, positioning his finger on the trigger. James tensed his muscles to resist Sergei forcing his arm upward to point the gun at his head. Instead, Sergei turned through ninety degrees so that his right shoulder was up against James's chest.

A single shot rang out. The woman screamed. Sergei released his hold over James's gun hand and jumped well away from him, before backing away even further. Vlad had crumpled to the ground, a bullet through his forehead. Very slowly, Sergei began to approach James, his hands outstretched like a big Russian bear. James aimed a warning shot over his head just as Sergei lunged forward. When Sergei fell to the floor, face down, the woman sprinted for the door.

James looked accusingly at the gun as he put the safety on, having been determined to take Sergei alive. He put it on the chair behind him, and then hobbled to Sergei's body to extract the keys to his fetters. As he bent low, Sergei whispered, 'The left pocket.' James quickly dragged his chain back to the chair and grabbed the gun again. Sergei remained on the floor as he pulled out the keys and threw them along the ground.

James picked them up and freed himself, then sat down on his chair and looked at Sergei. 'Would you mind explaining what's going on?'

Sergei replied, 'Not so loud; she might come back.'

The sound of approaching footsteps made them look to the doorway, Sergei twisting around while remaining on the floor. Three people entered, one large and two small, wearing white scene suits that hid their contours; James saw the large one had a beard. When the man detached his mask, James recognised Max Ahlberg from Säpo. Max unzipped his suit, stepped out, and handed it over. 'Put this on, and don't say anything.'

Once James was dressed in the suit and face-mask, one of the other white-suited people took him by the arm and led him away, upstairs and out to a waiting Crime Scene van. They climbed into the back, and the driver set off immediately. As they lay on the floor, she lifted her face mask, confirming to James it was indeed Ginny. He removed his own mask, and then began to unzip his scene suit as she slipped out of hers. After kicking the thin clothing away, he realised how cold he felt. She understood instinctively, and nestled up to him, as they sat with their backs against the cold side-panel. He was pleased to feel the warmth of her body coming through his shirt. She hugged him a little tighter. 'I have your things, but your overcoat is still needed for a little deception about you fleeing the country. I'll bring it in the morning. Until then, you'll have to make do with me around you.'

He responded, 'No man could wish for more. Now, can you tell me what just happened?'

She countered, 'What do you think happened?'

He tugged his ear. 'You and Sergei arranged it.'

She laughed sweetly. 'And it worked like a charm.'

'But how did you know I wouldn't just shoot him?'

She smiled up at him. 'He had confidence in you, and he was the one in the firing line, so I was happy to go along with it.'

'But why the charade?'

'I'm sure you can work it out. See tomorrow's front page: two men, one Irish, one of unknown nationality, were shot and killed by an allegedly British man named James, surname unknown. See photograph.'

'Which makes me a target for the Russians!'

'Except the photograph won't actually be of you, but of someone who looks just similar enough to convince the Russian woman that it's the man she saw shoot and kill two of her brave compatriots, who will no doubt be awarded Hero of the Russian Federation or some such medal. And the detailed description will be nothing like you. Plus, you're believed to have left the country by road immediately after, with the trail being picked up in Denmark and then going cold again. You'll need to stay in Sweden for a few days, just so that there's no one still looking out for the killer at the airport and thinking it could be you.'

'It really wasn't me, Ginny; Sergei was the one who pulled the trigger. It matters to me that you know that.'

'I don't doubt it for an instant. So, we're going back to your hotel; you must be shattered.'

'What time is it? I completely lost track after I'd been kidnapped.'

She looked at her watch. 'It's just after midnight.'

'How many days?'

'Three.'

'That's a lot more than I thought it was. Three whole

days, so it's now Thursday.'

She laughed. 'It's only just Tuesday, and you were zonked for most of Monday. You drama queen!' She hoped her casual attitude to his abduction and rescue would minimise the trauma he might otherwise suffer.

'You're not taking this seriously. I should be given therapy, or something.'

'Whatever.'

'So, where's Sergei? He should be sent back to England to face justice.'

'Not gonna happen; he's heading for the States.'

'Am I going to have to pursue him there, as well?'

'Are you a Mountie, or something? Always gets your man? You need to see the bigger picture.'

'Well, obviously I don't at the moment. What is the bigger picture?'

'Hmm. I don't really know myself, yet. We'll have a debriefing in the morning, once I'm read in and cleared to give you the low-down.'

They arrived at the hotel and were let out of the van. As they walked through the lobby, Ginny clung onto him. 'I'm going to see you safely back to your room.' In the lift, she suggested, 'Maybe I should stay all night to make sure you're OK?'

As tempting as the offer sounded, he responded, 'No need; Lin will be there.'

She smiled. 'Old American Indians used to take a couple of teenage girls to sleep either side of them, to keep them warm at night. You're still frozen through, so maybe Lin and I can be your squaws.' Though he thought that seemed an excellent suggestion, he was fairly sure Lin would baulk at the idea.

At the door, she handed him his wallet, and he took

out the key card. Inside, he turned on the small light at the entrance, in case Lin was asleep. They edged into the room and saw two women in each other's arms. Ginny whispered, 'Looks like Lin's found what she really wanted. You should come back with me.'

The light woke Helen, who flinched, which in turn woke Lin. Ginny called over to them as they unwrapped from each other. 'I'll take him back to my place tonight, if you like.'

Helen screeched, 'You're not taking him anywhere! Who the hell are you?'

Marcus thought he had just suffered more shock than in the whole of the time since his abduction. 'Helen, what are *you* doing here?'

'I came to see what was happening, and I think I'm just starting to understand.'

'You're getting it all wrong; Ginny only wants to keep me safe. And would you like to explain exactly what you and Lin were up to, please?'

'You're getting it all wrong as well, Marcus. Lin and I were just asleep together. Alright, I know she's a promiscuous lesbian, but that doesn't mean we were doing anything.'

Lin opened her mouth to speak, but closed it again.

Ginny turned to Marcus. 'You decide: which women do you want in your bed, tonight?'

Lin answered for him. 'Just the two of *us* will be enough, thank you very much.'

As Marcus said nothing to correct her, Ginny assumed he was in agreement. 'OK; I'll leave you to it.' When she reached the door, she motioned Marcus to come closer, and whispered, 'Who's this one?'

He whispered back, 'Helen, my wife.'

'Whoops!' she breathed, before speaking normally. 'I'll come and debrief you in the morning; say, ten?'

'Alright. Oh, and, by the way, thanks for saving my life. I'll see if I can do something for you in return.'

Despite the gawping audience in the bed, she kissed him on the lips. 'It was a pleasure. See you tomorrow.'

As the door closed, Helen demanded, 'WHAT?'

'I was kidnapped on Sunday evening, and she's just rescued me. I was drugged and unconscious for most of the time, so it didn't really feel that long. But what are you doing here? Did you come over when you found out I'd gone missing?'

'No, I set off on Sunday morning, when you weren't answering your phone; it's so unlike you.'

'I hadn't really told you what was happening before; I didn't want to worry you. But doing undercover work, sometimes you have to turn off all communication devices; with GPS, mobile phones act like beacons for anyone wanting to track someone remotely.'

'So, that explains it.'

'Yes. I'll give you a full account in the morning, but now I really need some sleep.' And time to sanitise my story, he thought. 'I'll just brush my teeth.'

When he emerged from the bathroom, he went to Helen's side of the bed. 'Move up, then.'

She quickly climbed out. 'No; you go in the middle.'

Lin squeezed herself to the edge of the bed, until Helen had turned out the light.

As he lay on his back between the two women, he feared he would find their delicious juxtaposition would keep him awake all night, but within minutes he had succumbed to post-stress exhaustion.

CHAPTER 31

For an hour before Helen's phone woke the others, she lay formulating a plan. As soon as the two quieter beeps had sounded and the volume had increased, she reached over to put on the side light, and then turned off the alarm, before climbing out of bed. At the bathroom door, she called out, 'It's a nice big shower, isn't it, Marcus? Shall we have one together?'

He felt shocked that she would suggest it with Lin present. 'I don't think so, Helen.'

'What about you, Lin? It might be fun, soaping each other down.' She watched closely for her reaction.

'Erm, no, thank you, Helen.'

'We'll take it in turns, then.'

Once the bathroom door was closed, Lin asked, 'Why didn't you tell me she's into women? Does that mean we can let her know about our affair, because she won't be too bothered?'

Marcus pondered. 'I'm quite certain that she isn't into women. Maybe it's a trap; she could be trying to find out if there's something going on between us. We need to stick to our story that we're simply colleagues.'

'Except the story's changed a bit, hasn't it. When did you tell her I'm a promiscuous lesbian?'

'I didn't. Is it something you said? Or did? I know the two of you were holding onto each other last night.'

'That was just a bit of mutual support. My guess is she misinterpreted something I said about sleeping with Elena. Then I mentioned Ginny slept in my room, and I couldn't explain I wasn't there myself because I was here with you. Plus I had to call Pamela "gorgeous", and then she called me "lover". So she probably thinks that's three women I've had in double-quick time. Perhaps I should stick with that line; then she'll think I'm not a threat, and we can spend more time together.'

'I don't know; she's very insightful, generally. In fact, always, I'd say, except when it comes to us.'

'Do you think she'll be in the bathroom for long?'

'Why? Are you desperate to go?'

'No; I'm desperate to come!'

'You can't be serious! She could be out any time.'

'Don't panic; I was only joking.'

They lay motionless, neither touching nor speaking.

Helen stepped out of the bathroom, wrapped in two towels, one large and one small. 'You go next, Lin; he can make do with our towels when we're finished with them.' She dressed while Lin was in the shower.

He requested room service. His order of breakfast for three was taken without the least hint of surprise. When Lin emerged, fully clothed, he took her place. Helen maintained an inconsequential conversation with Lin, until Marcus returned, his shirt sticking to his torso due to insufficient dry towelling for his hirsute body. The sound of a trolley outside told him his timing was perfect. He opened the door and accepted the waiter's offer to wheel in the food. The old man registered with a touch of disappointment that the two women were already included in his count.

Though Lin was wanting to know exactly what had happened to Marcus from when he had gone missing, she felt it was Helen's prerogative to ask. Helen, on the other hand, was taking a similar line to Ginny's: play it down, so as not to encourage anxiety. Consequently, during their meal, no one asked him about his ordeal.

After breakfast, Marcus held out for ten minutes, before saying to them, 'Don't either of you want to know about my kidnapping?'

Helen responded, 'Yes, but all in due course. Before then, there's something important I wish to talk about.' Marcus and Lin looked at each other, trying to hide their concern at what might follow. She began, 'Lin, let me say, first of all, that I've nothing against lesbianism. However, you need to understand fully the various sociological and psychological factors that have resulted in the generation of an environment in which the small proportion of lesbians who are genetically predisposed to same-sex attraction has been dwarfed due to the growth of acceptability of lesbianism from mere toleration to misguided pride. I say misguided, because the concept of pride would appear to be inconsistent with the argument that their behaviour is in some sense normal. If the pride relates to someone who has inherited the requisite traits, then their pride is in being born, but that must surely be something only their mother can take pride in, unless we trace back the nine months or so to when a man made a miniscule but essential contribution to the process. On the other hand, if there is no genetic component, then their behaviour amounts to no more than a lifestyle choice, which hardly justifies the suggestion that they have in any real sense achieved something to be proud of.'

Lin looked at Marcus, hoping for a sign of how to react. He asked Helen, 'That's all very interesting, but why are we getting this lecture?'

She steepled. 'Judging by Lin's discomfort at the

idea of joining me in the shower, I would say her lesbianism has arisen from environmental rather than genetic factors. Working in the police force may have resulted in her developing a strong sense of competition that has become an obsession with male emulation.'

She turned to Lin. 'You suggested to me you're not attracted to people like Marcus, i.e. red-blooded males. But is this because you see them as rivals? One only has to look at the world of politics, or high finance, or big business, to find women who deny their true nature in order to get to the top of their chosen sphere.'

Marcus suggested helpfully, 'Like arctic explorers and the North Pole?'

Helen looked at him witheringly to silence him. 'The top of their profession, then. And yet, how can they be at the top, they may think, if they regularly return home to an environment in which there is a man on top.'

Marcus interjected, 'You do know there are other possible positions, don't you?'

Helen wagged her finger. 'This is not a subject for levity, Marcus. I'm trying to explain to Lin that there are signs which indicate her predilection for women is not, for her, the natural state of being. More likely, it may have resulted from a misguided belief that, for a woman to be successful at work, she cannot allow herself to be subsumed at home into a mixed gender relationship.'

She turned back to Lin. 'There are professions where lesbians make up a disproportionately large fraction, such as in television, or novel writing.'

Marcus asked, 'What about tennis? Is it connected to the relatively high levels of testosterone that can enable more masculine women to outperform the others?'

'There may well be a correlation.' He was relieved not to receive another finger-wagging. 'Horizontal slicing through organisational structures has provided evidence to suggest there is a higher concentration of women who display masculine traits in the upper echelons than the lower. You may wish to explore related topics; I can give you some references if you'd like to review research on Feminism, Queer theory, the subversion of identity, and so on and so forth.'

Marcus interjected, 'I really don't think Lin is interested in researching the subject.'

'Perhaps it would be of limited benefit, anyway, as there are other factors for which there's a dearth of academic material. For example, there has been little research into the extent to which women, brought up on a diet of soap-operas where the *de facto* rôle models are forever trying to win out over their male counterparts, have, at the next generation, led their own daughters into believing men are the enemy.'

He asked, 'Should you put that on your to-do list?'

Helen made it clear she was ignoring his question. 'Another area crying out for more research is the extent to which women who see themselves as conventionally ugly, and so believe they are unlikely ever to attract a man, consequently prefer to convince themselves they have no interest in men in the first place. I suspect the reason is that the concept of ugliness is far too subjective for most researchers to consider risking their professional reputations by basing their work on qualitative judgements. Now, for the sake of argument, let's say that the vast majority of men would generally find a woman unattractive if she might quantitatively be categorised as obese. To keep it simple, there's no need to consider Triceps Skinfold Thickness or Body Mass Index, and I'll ignore adiposity factors such as those relating to race, derived from anthropometric data. I'll simply say they're subjectively deemed to be fat.'

Marcus endeavoured to prove he was still paying attention. 'So you're saying that being fat can be used as an indicator of ugliness, based simply on perception by other people, irrespective of one's own attitude.'

'Indeed. Now, a fat woman may protect her ego by entering into a lesbian relationship, thereby avoiding rejection by otherwise available men.'

He interrupted. 'But Lin obviously isn't fat, or ugly.'

'Of course not, but by first discounting those factors that clearly don't apply, any which remain may be deemed worthy of further consideration.'

'But there must be masses of potential factors. Can't you just get straight to the bottom line?'

Helen stopped and reflected for a moment. 'Lin, the bottom line is simply this: have you ever considered having a relationship with a man? Because, until you try it, you won't be able to make a genuine comparison. When you have, I suspect you may decide that your unbridled lesbianism was not in accord with your biological make-up.'

Lin looked at Helen, and then at Marcus, and then back at Helen. 'You make it sound so simple, as though I can just go out and get myself one.'

Helen replied, 'With your looks, you could get any man you like. Well, almost any man.' She turned and gave Marcus a quick smile. 'But it's harder to get the right man. Perhaps what you need is a suitable boy, just emerging into manhood; not one that is old and full of bitter disappointment. Choose wisely and they can last you a lifetime; chose unwisely and you waste the best years of your life on them. So, what do you think?'

Lin looked down, and then around, and finally at Helen. 'Maybe I should test the water, first; perhaps try someone I know won't break my heart. I'm thinking... a slightly older man than you suggest, so they have some maturity and, erm, physical knowledge.'

Helen responded, 'Not that the two necessarily go hand-in-hand.' She turned to Marcus. 'And why have you not done anything to help Lin understand whether she's taking the right path in life? I know she looks up to you, so why haven't you given her some guidance?'

He put on a hang-dog expression. 'I wasn't sure it was my place to do that; but now, I realise it was.' He turned to Lin. 'Don't feel under any pressure to change, just because Helen has suggested it; but if you do decide you ought at least to try having a heterosexual relationship, then I'll give you any help I can in that direction.'

Helen wagged her finger at Marcus. 'Well, just see that you do. Fine words are one thing, but it's deeds that count.'

Secretly pleased with the outcome, Lin asked Helen, 'How did you come by your man?'

She smiled. 'I was fresh out of medical school, and he was fresh out of ideas for getting himself together.'

Lin smiled back. 'Marcus does that all the time; saying clever things, I mean. Did he get it from you?'

She shook her head. 'I was never noted for it. I think I must have picked it up from him.'

'Did you meet him when he was a patient? Aren't there rules about relationships with patients?'

'When I was in my first year as a psychiatry trainee

on a foundation programme, he was a patient suffering from PTSD. The more I thought about him, the more I thought what he really needed was the kind of woman who would understand him and take care of him when he needed support, and it seemed like a twenty-four hours-a-day type of job. Then it struck me that I fitted the bill precisely, so I made him an offer he couldn't refuse. He wasn't my patient when we started going out, so there were no breaches of medical ethics.'

Lin thought for a moment. 'Does that mean you married him as a form of therapy?'

She laughed. 'In a way, I suppose you could say that; but it was very much more.' She turned to him and smiled. 'It was love, wasn't it.'

He frowned at her. 'Am I just a dumb animal in one of your experiments? How will you know if it was successful? Only after I'm dead and gone?'

'Oh, don't be so melodramatic, Marcus. Actually, if the measure is whether you are dependent on me for support, then the test can come much earlier than death. If you were to prove your independence of me at any time, the experiment could then be deemed to have concluded with a successful outcome.'

'I may be misinterpreting you here, Helen, but are you saying that I would need to leave you in order for you to believe your treatment of me was a success?'

She pondered on this at some length. 'Technically, I suppose if you had an affair, and felt you didn't have to come back to me, even though you chose to, then that could also be deemed a successful outcome, so far as the original experiment was concerned. But that's not an invitation to misbehave, because I might then be the one in need of therapy, so true success would only be achieved if I also subsequently reached a point of independence. Yes, that's the definition, isn't it: the achievement of mutual independence.'

Marcus smiled at Helen. 'But if I were to have an affair, thereby asserting my independence of you, and you were not to feel threatened by it, thereby not causing you to need therapy, wouldn't that mean that we had achieved the mutual independence within our relationship essential for you to claim the attainment of a successful outcome to your experiment?'

She looked long and hard at him. 'I think you may be trying to put words into my mouth, Marcus. Don't forget that, at an emotional level, I am a woman, after all. So, if I discovered you hadn't been keeping it in your pants, you might wake up one morning to find I'd resorted to superglue, like that woman on the news.'

Marcus laughed. 'Well, that's rather grounded that particular line of thought. So, when do I get to tell my tale about abduction and torture and derring-do?'

Helen laughed back at him. 'Oh, go on, then; we've kept you waiting long enough.'

The story was into its second re-run when there was a knock at the door. Marcus invited Elena into the room and introduced her to Helen. Elena explained, 'Ginny says she's coming at ten. The two of us can't really be seen together; it isn't politic. Anyway, I'm glad we were able to extract you safely, Marcus. Now all you need to do is enjoy your visit to Stockholm. I'm sorry to say, this marks the end of our working relationship. It's still important for you to stay invisible, though; and not leave the country for a few days.' She turned her head. 'And the same applies to you, of course, Lin.' She looked at Helen for a moment. 'You're all booked on the same flight on Friday morning, if that's alright?'

After receiving acknowledgements, she continued, 'I've a few instructions for you. Don't use your credit or debit cards in Sweden; only use cash. I've settled your hotel bill up to Friday morning; you'll need to pay for any extras before you leave. Don't hire a car; public transport only. Don't get yourself arrested for anything. Don't get your picture in the newspapers for doing something heroic or stupid. Don't have an accident and end up in hospital. Do I need to go on?'

Marcus responded, 'We get the idea, thanks.'

She addressed Lin. 'And I need to take your bag of tricks with me.' Lin saw Helen looking questioningly at her, but decided to save the story for later.

Marcus was disappointed the formalities were being completed so quickly, having anticipated a long session of explanations and mutual congratulations. As he presented her with the suitcase containing the items Lin had borrowed for her disguises, he asked, 'What about the reason for my coming here in the first place?'

She shook her head. 'Säpo doesn't know anything about that, if you remember. You'll have to ask Ginny; she'll be here soon. Which means, I'd better be going.' After exchanging formal goodbyes, Elena decided that that was insufficient, so hugged Lin warmly and kissed Marcus on both cheeks, before grabbing the borrowed suitcase. At the door, she called out, 'Do stay in touch,' and then was gone in an instant.

As soon as she had departed, Helen asked Lin, 'What was in your bag of tricks?'

Lin smiled broadly. 'If you think Marcus had a good tale to tell, just wait until you hear mine.'

Helen listened with increasing amazement as Lin

moved on from the shopping redheaded model to the fake pregnancy and the trip to the Russian Embassy with the British Ambassador. At the end, Helen asked, 'How can you face going back to ordinary police work after all this? It'll seem so dull, won't it?'

Lin's face froze as she remembered work. 'I won't be allowed to go back if Marcus doesn't get in touch with them straight away; I'm due in, this morning.'

He took the hint and made a call, and then gave her the gist of it. 'You're currently on special assignment and aren't due back 'til Monday.'

'Good. Now my only problem is, I don't have a place to stay.'

Marcus avoided looking at Helen as he responded, 'You'll be staying here with us, of course.' He was relieved his wife made no objection.

The next visitor was Ginny, arriving with Marcus's overcoat around her shoulders. As Helen had been in bed with Lin when Ginny had brought Marcus home, he introduced her to Helen as though they had never met.

Ginny explained to Marcus, 'I'm sorry to have to tell you this, but I'm not cleared to have the full story myself, so I can't fill you in. It's compartmented; that means the left hand isn't allowed to know what the right hand is doing.'

He scowled to one side, so she would know it was not intended for her. 'I really believe I have a right to know what it was all about.'

She gave him the radiant smile that could make his heart skip a beat. 'So do I, Marcus; and I said so. That's why you've been invited to London on Saturday, for a meeting with Pammie and the Brits. She's organised overnight accommodation for you for Saturday night;

she's wanting to take you to a swanky 'do'. And then you're back to being a policeman on Monday, aren't you. Do you remember what I said about that?'

'Yes, Ginny, and I *would* like to discuss it with you at length; but now that the case is over, am I required to avoid any further contact with you?'

She did her best to put on a blank face. 'It's a serious question that needs thrashing out. There's no reason why the two of us can't meet up and go into the subject in some depth. But it's a sensitive matter, so not one for raising in front of anyone else.'

With a disappointed expression, he turned to Helen and then to Lin. 'I have to have a meeting with Ginny; sorry, but the two of you aren't invited.'

He turned back to Ginny. 'You tell me the where and the when, and I'll make myself available.'

'This evening at seven thirty, outside reception.'

'I'll be there. Anything else we need to discuss?'

'If there is, we'll go through it this evening.' She gave a formal goodbye to Helen, a warm one to Lin, and finally a quick, casual one to Marcus.

When she had gone, Helen asked, jokingly, 'Did you just arrange a date with that girl?'

Marcus gave a rumbling laugh. 'The very idea! No, she's wanting to give me a job, and the least I can do is to hear her out.'

'A job, as in, her line of business?'

'Yes; why not?'

'Because you could get yourself killed, playing their games; that's why not.'

'There's no chance of that. I'm convinced the gods are looking down on me to give me whatever protection I need. I suppose here it would be Odin or Thor.'

'Or Freya, more like. Does this mean you've come through your experience unscathed? Are you not going to relapse? No night terrors?'

'Do the text books say they might start again?'

'It's a not uncommon reaction, but you've gone the other way. Now you've a potentially bigger problem: you think you're invincible.'

'I'll try and get back to normal by the weekend.'

'Maybe we should explore how to define normalcy.'

'Maybe we should explore the city. Any thoughts on what we might do? Lin? Any preferences?'

Lin responded, 'I haven't exhausted the shops, yet.'

Marcus nodded. 'To cover our tracks, we shouldn't convert kroner back to Sterling, in case someone makes the connection with what happened here. So, we have an objective of spending all our currency before we go. You're the expert on shopping, aren't you, Lin? You can come up with a plan for us all. I'd quite like to have a look at some more museums, if you can include that.'

Helen added, 'And I may need some time out. I once collaborated with a woman at Stockholm university, and I'd like to meet up with her if she's available.'

Marcus went to his money sock. 'I need to return most of this, but we'll share out the rest.'

They passed the day being tourists, looking at the architecture and spending money in the shops. As seven thirty approached, Marcus shaved and changed into his suit and tie. Helen checked that he looked presentable. 'I'm sure I should be jealous, you know.'

He bent and kissed her on the lips. 'You can take solace in the traditional way; there are some chocolates to share with Lin. I'll try and be back by midnight.'

'Before your carriage turns into a pumpkin.'

'I think that implies a degree of gender reversal.' He reflected for a moment. 'Trying to match a foot to a boot mark was how this investigation started; not quite the same as fitting a glass slipper, but near enough.' He called a brief goodbye to Lin, and left the room.

Lin suddenly looked at Helen. 'I forgot to ask him about something; I'll catch him up.' She dashed out of the room and saw him standing by the lift. When the doors opened, she burst into a sprint and leapt inside.

Surprised, he asked, 'Have I forgotten something?'

She smacked the button for the first floor, and then punched him in the arm. 'Yes; me. Why can't I come with you? Are you and her going to be having it off? Again! Helen might not be jealous, but I am.'

He gave a delayed wince and felt his injured arm. 'I don't remember ever admitting anything of the sort. I'm just going to talk to her about her work.'

The lift reached the first floor. As there was no one about, she put her foot on the gap to keep the doors open. 'If you're trying to get a job with them, what about me as well? We make a great team.'

'I'll bear it in mind. Now, let me go; I don't wish to keep the lady waiting.'

'She's hardly a lady, is she!'

'Not yet, but she may become one. Now, off you go.' He gave her a gentle push in the back. She walked away, and then turned to throw a few more words at him, but the doors were already closing.

CHAPTER 32

Ginny was sitting in the foyer, receiving admiring or envious glances from the men and women passing through reception. When she saw Marcus, she stood and walked over to greet him. The kiss on the lips was perhaps a little too generous for the public place, but he willingly forgave her. 'I've booked us a table at a nice restaurant; is that alright with you?'

'That sounds marvellous.'

She took his arm and steered him away from the main entrance. 'I'm parked in the underground; it saves clearing the windscreen.' In the car park lift, she began kissing him lusciously.

He broke away. 'Where can we have a proper talk, in private?'

'I was intending to take you to my flat and park up, and then we'd go and eat nearby. I'm too dependent on my car to risk breaking the drink-drive limits, but I'll be sober by morning when I bring you home.'

'Actually, my wife expects me back by midnight.'

'That's the trouble with you married men: if it isn't your mistress you have to get back for, it's your wife! Which one's the more jealous?'

'That would be Lin. Helen trusts me implicitly.'

'Really? I must be slipping. I expect any woman to be jealous of me if I'm out with their husband.'

Ginny drove to her flat and garaged the car. They walked the short distance to the bijou restaurant where she had made a reservation. As they sat opposite each other at a small table, he found the tall red candle in a bottle was interfering with his line of sight, so moved it to one side. They kept their conversation away from anything work-related. She spoke of holidays and places visited. He talked about sport and politics. When he asked, 'Do you know who assassinated the...', she looked askance, but recovered quickly as he continued, '...Swedish Prime Minister, Olof Palme, in Stockholm back in nineteen eighty-six?'

She smiled. 'I thought it was unsolved.'

'I've been told the clue is on his gravestone. "Taken care of by the Church Council." What do you think?'

She laughed sweetly, causing several male diners to turn their heads and smile in her direction. 'I think you don't take life seriously, and I'm supposed to be the one who lives every day like there's no tomorrow.'

He gave her a tender smile. 'Actually, that's more or less what I wanted to talk to you about. But later.'

As they walked back to her flat, the snow began to fall in flakes as blinding as goose down suddenly spilled in a pillow fight. At her door, she turned the key until the first click, and then further until there was a second. She instructed him to wait while she disabled the alarm system, and then invited him in. 'You should feel really honoured; no one gets to come here.'

He looked around; the furniture and furnishings were surprisingly simple. 'I like it; sort of minimalist.' Now they were alone, it seemed to him she smiled less often.

'No point in making it homey; I may have to move in a heartbeat. I know you've been itching to talk to me about something all evening; do you want to get it out there right now, or shall I make a hot chocolate first?'

After all the unexpected turns of events, the idea that

she would have hot chocolate before bedtime seemed to him the most surprising. 'Hot choc would be nice.'

When she brought in the steaming mugs, he was surprised again when she sat in a chair away from him. She took a tiny sip, but found it too hot, so placed it back on the coaster. 'We'll keep our distance until we've dealt with the work issue that's on your mind, before you claim your prize and take me to bed.'

'You're making some assumptions there, Ginny. What I really wanted to talk to you about, isn't exactly work; it's about you. Have you thought of what you'll be doing in ten years' time? I know that doesn't fit with the idea of living always in the present, but for how long do you expect to be playing your "bad girl" rôle?'

'You seem to have an issue with what I do; or rather, how I do it.'

'I've seen enough of how you handle situations to know you're a highly professional operative, and I just wonder if you've ever considered how your "bad girl" style may limit your career prospects.'

'So, this is career guidance.'

'I suppose you could call it that. You see, I've seen beautiful women such as yourself gain promotion through the ranks because of their appearance. But in the upper echelons, I've also seen women who haven't been taken seriously because they're so attractive. And then there are those who've slept their way to the top. It's an unfair world, Ginny; appearance counts for so much. In the end, if you're ambitious, you need to map out a career path for yourself, and then decide whether the "bad girl" style is a help or a hindrance. Maybe it was a help to get you to where you are now, but could it be a hindrance to taking you as far as you wish to go?

People talk about a glass ceiling that limits women's promotion prospects, but there may be ways around barriers that are easier than smashing through them. Consider transmogrification as a valid career strategy.'

'I certainly would, Marcus, if I knew what it meant.'

'I'm just saying you might have reached a point in your career where you wish to be seen as a different type of person; and you may be more comfortable in your skin if it's closer to the real you.'

'So, you think there's a different me under the one that everybody else sees?'

'I'm sure of it.'

She remained silent for quite some time. Eventually, she noticed the mug of chocolate and took a drink. 'I'll certainly give your observations careful consideration; maybe we should talk some more in the morning.'

'Not really possible; I need to get back to the hotel.'

'Didn't you come to claim me as your prize? I'd be bitterly disappointed if you no longer fancied me.'

'I'd be having you under false pretences; I cheated. Lin was watching and relaying information to me on the phone.'

'So, that's how you did it, then! You really should consider coming to work for us; you and Lin both.'

'It's certainly something to think about. But I'd better be going.'

'You're not leaving.'

'I have to; I wouldn't want to upset Helen.'

'No, I just mean you can't go anywhere right now. Look out of the window; I don't have a snowmobile.'

When he saw the extent of the continuing snowfall, he called Helen. 'Hi, have you seen the snow?'

'Yes, it's quite impressive.'

'It's also blocking the roads. I'm going to have to stay where I am tonight.'

'And where's that?'

He knew it was pointless attempting to lie to her at that moment. 'I'm at Ginny's flat. She says she can put me up for the night.'

'That's fortunate, isn't it. I'll see you sometime tomorrow, then?'

'Yes, even if I have to make some snowshoes.'

'Don't do anything stupid; I know you'll get over here as soon as you can. Well, we're going to bed now. Phone me in the morning. Goodnight.'

Hearing the call terminate, he wondered how to interpret the conversation. Ginny asked, 'Is everything alright? Was she a bit sharp with you?'

'No, she was fine; she just said she's going to bed.'

'We'll do the same, then.'

'So, you're sticking with the "bad girl" routine?'

'I am tonight. Maybe I'll change once you've left.'

He went to his coat and extracted a small box from a pocket. 'I brought you these, by the way. I hope you like them, and if you don't, then at least they might be something to remember me by.' He opened the box.

She looked at the three-stone pendant gold earrings. 'They're lovely. They're not real diamonds, are they?'

'They're as real as you are.'

'But I'm not real, am I? Is that what you mean?'

'They're as real as the real you.' Seeing she still appeared uncertain, he added, 'I've put the receipt in an envelope, in case you want to insure them.'

She took the studs from her ears and put on the diamond earrings. 'They're brilliant. But why are you being so generous to me?'

He put his finger to his temple, as though in thought. 'Let me see. You saved my life…'

'No, I didn't; I think you did that yourself. Or at least, you lucked out.'

He waved away her objection. 'You saved my life. You gave me a glimpse into your world. You drove me mad with desire. Need I go on?'

'I really like that last one; you can give me some more of it in bed.'

'There's one more reason I have to give, only I'm afraid it'll spoil it for you. It was you who gave me the money in the first place.'

She smiled sweetly. 'But I know the routine; it was yours to do with as you please. And what you did was buy me a lovely present. Come on, now it's my turn to give you a lovely present.'

In the morning, though the snow lay in heaps by the side of the road, the public transport system was still functioning. He compared Stockholm with Sheffield, where the snow fell only rarely, but when it did, everything ground to a halt. As a sign of his keenness to return to Helen, he had set off as early as practicable, leaving Ginny still in bed. She had pressed him to stay longer, but accepted his unspoken reason.

As he knocked on his hotel room door before using his key card, he wondered what sort of reception he might receive from Helen and Lin. When they appeared to be entirely unfazed by his disappearance for the night, he wondered if they were both acting a part.

He asked what plans they had for the day. Helen stated, 'I'm having lunch at the University; I should be back by late afternoon.'

The three ventured out to look at the scenery and to

deliver Helen to the relevant part of the University. At Lin's insistence, Marcus returned with her to the hotel, to take advantage of Helen's absence. Once they were in bed, Lin desperately wished to ask about him and Ginny, but something told her it was better to feign disinterest. Nevertheless, Lin hoped the pleasure he felt with her was greater than any that she suspected he had found with Ginny.

No longer feeling obliged to hide away in their room at mealtimes, in the evening the three dined together in the hotel restaurant. The conversation focused on what they would do on their final full day in Stockholm. Marcus suggested a few museums, and the other two were happy to give their assent.

At bedtime, the routine continued to apply whereby each changed into their nightclothes in the bathroom. Marcus still slept between them. He felt relieved he had had enough sex recently for the arrangement not to disturb him too much.

On Thursday morning, Marcus took a phone call from Elena. After standard pleasantries, she continued, 'I know what I said about no contact, but I've been thinking, it wouldn't really matter if I spent some time with Lin. Do you think she'd like that?'

'I'm sure she would; let me put her on.'

Lin agreed to join Elena for an early lunch, and to spend the afternoon looking around the shops with her. After a walk together in the morning, Lin left Marcus and Helen to find her agreed meeting location.

When Marcus suggested to Helen they head for the first museum on their itinerary, she responded, 'How does it feel, sleeping between two women?'

Hoping it would be the best strategic response, he

replied, 'It's very frustrating, having Lin there. It would be so nice to make love to you; a new experience for us, our first time in Sweden.'

She took his arm and directed him back toward the hotel. 'You're not the only one who's frustrated; let's forget the museums.'

Much later, when Lin joined them in the hotel room, she saw the sheets lacked the crispness they had had when the maid had made the bed. She looked at Marcus, who indicated with a tiny nod and a lopsided smile that he had indeed been ruffling them with Helen.

After a pleasant meal with two bottles of wine between the three, they sat together in the hotel lounge and watched a news programme on an English channel. When a film came on, Helen asked, 'Have you seen this one before?' Lin and Marcus confirmed they had. 'I haven't. Why don't you two go up, and I'll see you in an hour and a half.'

Marcus and Lin instinctively knew Helen had some intent behind the offer, but neither could fathom it. Marcus responded first. 'No, I'll stay and watch it with you; I've only seen it the once.'

Lin understood his defensive manoeuvre. 'I'll go up on my own; I'm sure you two would like to have some time together without me playing gooseberry.'

Helen responded, 'No, don't feel pushed out, Lin. Now that you sleep with us, it would feel like there's someone missing if you're not here. Come and sit next to me.' Lin felt obliged to accept the offer.

When the film was over, they returned to their room and again employed the procedure for keeping their bodies hidden from each other. Back in the middle of the bed, Marcus wondered what would happen if the two women concurrently made advances toward him. He laughed inwardly as he thought, 'I wouldn't know which way to turn.'

In the morning, Helen woke before the alarm. There were a few white rays bouncing around the room; she thought it must be external lighting that was reflecting off the snow and finding its way under the blinds. She realised Marcus was lying on his side with his arm around Lin, so nudged him gently a few times and whispered, 'I'm this side.' He pretended he was still asleep, as he turned over and put his arm around her. Lin, still sleeping, turned and put her arm around Marcus; she woke immediately as she realised there was another body at the other side of him. Trying to appear still asleep, she turned back again and edged away from them, to the area where the sheets were cool.

When they went to check out, Marcus felt slightly embarrassed when the two Mrs Watsons came to stand either side of him, and even more so when he needed a supplement from the second Mrs Watson to pay the residual bill.

Before stepping out of the hotel, Helen collected together all their remaining funds, and calculated there was more than enough for a taxi and any excess luggage charge for Lin's new suitcase. At the airport, she organised spending the remainder, before finally draining the coffers into a charity collection.

When the plane was in the air, Marcus closed his eyes and wondered how difficult it would be to settle back into the life he had had before the Swedish experience.

CHAPTER 33

The radio station that burst into life just before seven o'clock confirmed to Marcus he was back in England. Immediately after the first of the louder beeps from Helen's phone alarm, the pips began sounding in close syncopation. She picked up her mobile and turned off the alert during the extended final pip. He asked, 'Shall we wait until it's light before we get up?'

She leisurely climbed out of bed. 'In Sweden, with that attitude you'd hardly get up at all in winter.'

'But we're not in Sweden. When's sunrise?'

She turned her head. 'In theory, somewhere between seven thirty and a quarter to eight. That's why we have these things called electric lights.'

The children had been excited to see their parents the previous evening, but now that everything was back to normal they were happy enough simply to play together in Edwin's room. When Helen insisted they come with her in the car to say goodbye to their father at Sheffield railway station, Edwin argued they should be allowed to stay home to finish their game of ludo. She claimed there was no babysitter available. He counterclaimed he was now old enough to take care of Alice. After he had lost to her spurious argument that credited the law with far more certainty than the legislators had provided, he asked, 'Why doesn't dad take a taxi?'

She used her pointing finger to bring him to his feet. 'Daddy is going away and won't be back 'til tomorrow, so we need to go and wave him goodbye, because he'll miss us such a lot.' Alice obediently stood and left the room, prompting Edwin to accept defeat and follow her.

As they approached the station, Marcus offered to be dropped off before the concourse and walk the last leg of the journey, so that they were not kept waiting. Helen declined, not only parking up, but also bringing the children to the platform. Edwin felt secretly pleased to be able to watch the trains, but stubbornly refused to admit as much. When Marcus waved to them from his window seat, he reflected how their positions had been reversed compared with Christmas eve.

Marcus took the underground from St. Pancras to Bond Street station, and followed Pamela's directions to the business lounge she had arranged for the meeting.

Ben Blue met him outside, ushered him in and made introductions. 'This is Marcus. Marcus, you know the lovely Pamela, of course.' She gave a cursory wave. 'And this is Mr Green.'

Smiling, Green stepped forward and stretched out a hand. 'Peregrine. I understand you're like a ferret with a rabbit, won't let go 'til it's been despatched.'

'I'm certainly determined to see this through to the right true end, but death isn't exactly the conclusion I had in mind.'

'Then let's sit and talk about what the right ending should look like.' Peregrine sat with Pamela, Ben with Marcus. 'Things have moved on since you last met with Pamela and Ben.'

Marcus looked around as though he might see other people. 'Brett and David aren't with us, this time.'

Pamela stated, 'Brett's minding the shop.'

No explanation was offered concerning the other absentee, so Marcus asked Peregrine, 'And David?'

Peregrine hesitated. 'He's been retired.'

Marcus smiled, thinking he might make a joke. 'As in, retired permanently? Sleeping with the fishes?' The lack of any reciprocation for his levity made him think he may have just spoken the truth in jest.

Peregrine continued. 'Mr Brown was found to have been a mole, supplying information to the Russians. It was he who tipped them off about where they might find Stanley Hicks. They sent an assassin, known to you as Sergei. And the rest, as they say, is history. Now, I know Pamela has arranged accommodation for you tonight, so I'll leave you in her care.' He stood up and proffered his hand as a parting gesture.

Marcus remained seated. 'Not so fast, Peregrine. I have a couple of unanswered questions. Number one: why did Sergei kill Hicks? Why did the Russians want him dead if he was genuinely retired and out of the game? And number two: why was Sergei allowed to leave Sweden for the States? So far as I'm aware, he didn't have diplomatic immunity, so why wasn't he arrested and extradited to Britain?'

Pamela turned to Peregrine. 'I told you he wouldn't let it go. We're going to have to come clean.'

Peregrine nodded, and then addressed Marcus. 'Hicks had himself been working for the Russians.'

Marcus stared at him. 'If what you say is true, why would the Russians have wanted him dead? Or was Sergei a rogue agent?'

Peregrine replied, 'Sergei was working under orders from the Russians. My interpretation is, they wanted him dead so he would never be able to admit to us what information he had supplied to them over the years.'

Marcus nodded. 'If we knew what secret information

the Russians had obtained, we could potentially take counter-measures. It's the importance of knowing what the enemy knows. And no doubt Sergei is now telling our cousins exactly what he knows about what Hicks knew, as well as anything else he may have to offer.'

Pamela again turned to Peregrine. 'Now do you see what I mean? He's a natural. But we have first refusal.'

Marcus stared at Pamela. 'Why do I feel like a horse at a country auction?'

She smiled at him. 'Because that's what you are, Marcus: a thoroughbred stallion. Once we've finished here, I'm taking you to my stud farm.'

Marcus momentarily contemplated laughing at her joke, but decided he was no longer confident he could distinguish truth from fiction.

She stood up suddenly. 'If any more loose ends occur to you, I'll do my best to answer them. Now, we'd better be going; we have things to do.'

Outside the building, Pamela hailed a taxi and gave directions to a property in Knightsbridge. She led him into a courtyard and through a private door to a two-storey apartment. Once inside, she explained, 'I'm staying here at the moment. It belongs to the firm.'

She took him into a room with a view over private landscaped gardens. He looked out, and then asked, 'Where am I staying, tonight? Do I need to book in?'

She took hold of his case. 'There's a room for you upstairs. This way.' She lugged his bag for him, despite his protestations. When she took it into a bedroom, he looked around. She answered his unspoken question. 'Yes, it's my bedroom. I knew there was chemistry between us the moment we first met.'

Up to now, he had assumed they were just flirting

with each other in jest. He quickly decided he had to set the record straight. 'Pammie, I'm a happily married man. I can't go sleeping with you; my wife might not approve.' He saw how crestfallen she appeared. 'I'm sorry if I've misled you.' He thought she might burst into tears.

'It's because I'm not good looking enough for you, isn't it. Or too old.'

'God, no! You're gorgeous, and I'm not saying that because I'm in danger! Remember? The code word? And you're a lot younger than me.' He estimated her age as mid-thirties, about the same as himself. 'What are you, twenty-four? Twenty-five?' He thought she still looked unconvinced.

'You're just saying that to make me feel better.'

'No, I'm not. How can I prove I really mean it?'

'There's only one way: make love to me right now.'

Feeling guilty at having led her on, he obliged with considerable enthusiasm, to erase any lingering doubts about her perceived attractiveness or youthfulness.

When they were both entirely satisfied, she kissed him on the cheek. 'I'll take a shower. You can have a rest; you've earned it.'

She returned, wrapped in a white towelling dressing-gown, and insisted he go for his own shower before she disrobe. He thought that perhaps she was not entirely confident her body would withstand the inevitably more critical post-coital scrutiny.

When he had showered and dressed, he returned to the living room. As he entered, she stood and gave him a peck on the cheek. After inviting him to sit, she chose a chair facing him. 'I have a complaint about you.'

He stared. 'I thought we were fantastic together.'

'Not about that; that was great! But about something that happened in Stockholm. Not to put too fine a point on it, you've buggered one of my best operatives!'

He looked shocked. 'I categorically deny having buggered any of your operatives. Which one of them has made that scurrilous allegation?'

'*She* didn't make the allegation; *I'm* making the allegation. I've been grooming her for quite a while, preparing her to go whoring for her country.'

'Well, grooming's a criminal offence, unless you're talking horses and so forth.'

'Horses and hunting; you British are still full of it. Well, if I understand your terminology correctly, she was ripe for blooding. Only now, she doesn't believe it's the right thing for her to do, and it's all your fault. She's gone down with a bad case of *lurve*. I don't know what you did to the girl, but she's fallen for your charms. Now, she wants me to recruit you, and to team you up with her.' Feeling entirely unsure how to react, he remained motionless. 'I have to say, I think she was genuinely impressed with the way you operated, which is why she's vouching for you.'

As she was clearly waiting for a response, he began, tentatively, 'So you'd like me to become one of your operatives, bravely risking life and limb as I perform heroic acts in far-flung corners of the world.'

She turned her palms upward and tilted her head in equivocation. 'Not exactly. The way you broke through the defences of my well-trained operative made me realise you could be a great asset to us, as a professional seducer. What do you think of that idea?'

He broke his silence only when he knew he had to accept she was determined to hold out the longer.

'What we just did, was that an entrance exam?'

'In a manner of speaking.' She saw the shockwave cross his features, so tried to soften the blow. 'But then, even if I knew for certain you wouldn't be interested in the work, I'd still have wanted you in my bed. I thought that from the very first moment I set eyes on you. You could call it love at first sight.'

'I think you mean lust at first sight, which I suppose, if I'm honest, is what I thought when I first saw you. But I would never have tried to do anything about it, because I'm happily married.'

She smiled at him and held it for a few seconds. 'Interesting definition of happily married, Marcus. As well as your wife, you've had your mistress, and me and my girl. And, I'd guess, that babe, Ruth.'

'But you seduced *me*! And with Ginny, even the weather conspired to make things happen. Anyway, you're trying to make her into something she isn't. She's such a nice girl, and I have the impression she's highly competent; surely you can use her in a way that's more suited to her true character.'

'Well, possibly; but her looks are her greatest asset. I said to her, if she doesn't want to lay down her body for her country, what about going deep undercover with another operative, and she said she'd only be happy as one half of a husband-and-wife team if you were the other half. So, if you want to be sure of saving her soul, you'll have to be a martyr yourself.'

'You certainly know how to find the pressure points, don't you, Pammie. Is there anything else I should be aware of, if I were to agree to be recruited?'

She gave a disarmingly cheeky grin. 'Yes. Everyone else has appraisals annually, but you'll be getting yours every month at the very least, and I'll personally be the one checking your performance comes up to scratch.'

He laughed. 'Now I know you're having me on, aren't you, Pammie. Aren't you? Honey? Tell me. I really don't know what to believe, anymore.'

'There'd be lots of details to work out, but for now, just consider the overall idea. While you're reassessing your view of the world, I suggest you get changed. You did bring a tux, didn't you? I mean "Dinner Jacket".'

'Yes, as requested.'

'Then you shall go to the ball!'

She waited until he was changed and back down, before going upstairs and putting on a midnight blue dress that relied heavily on two narrow shoulder straps. When she returned, he politely stood up for her. He thought she exuded such sophistication, any residual resentment he might have had for tricking him into her bed was replaced by a glow of remembered pleasure.

Another taxi ride took them to the party. As they entered the grand ballroom, she led him to one side. 'Sorry, Marcus, but I can't partner you this evening; I have other duties to attend to.' She waited until his intense disappointment had fully registered. 'But I've organised someone else for you.'

Seeing how she was looking past him, he assumed the stand-in was standing behind him. He turned, to see a young woman in a lace-trimmed black dress with a halter neckline, and wearing a familiar pair of earrings. She twirled around, revealing her bare back. 'What do you think of this, Marky?'

'You look fantastic. But what are you doing here?'

'I asked for rapid reassignment to London. Now we can see each other again. Isn't it great?'

Pamela moved to one side. 'I thought you both deserved it, after your successful joint mission; the first of many, I trust. Try to stay here long enough not to be too conspicuous by your absence, won't you.' She turned and walked away without a backward glance.

Ginny flicked the lace by her neck. 'Is this modest enough for your taste, Marky?'

He looked her up and down. 'It's a question of what you personally want, Ginny; not what you think other people want for you. I explained all that, didn't I?'

'Perhaps I wasn't listening closely enough. Tell me again in the morning.'

When dawn broke, in her borrowed flat, she woke him with delicate kisses, as though she had replaced her former professionalism with a tenderness that spoke of love. He reciprocated only briefly, before holding her far enough away to be able to look her in the eye. 'This wasn't supposed to happen, you know, Ginny. I don't want to break your heart, but I have a wife and family, and I'm not going to lose them.' He felt her shiver repeatedly, as though her intense emotion had translated itself into electrical form and was now being conducted up and down her spine.

'She needn't ever know about us; I'm trained to stay in the shadows.'

'So long as you understand there's no point in waiting for me to leave... her.' He had intended to say "Helen", but then wished to keep her more distant.

She interpreted the hesitation. 'That's a given. Now, tell me what you think about joining us.'

'It wouldn't work; my life's already sorted.'

'What if you kept your day job and we made an occasional request for you to join me on a mission?

Could you then live a different life for a while? I can imagine us spending time together, somewhere hot.'

'On some Greek island? It sounds idyllic.'

'You know I mean somewhere a lot hotter than that.'

'I'm very doubtful, but who knows?'

'But you must; and until then, make sure you come and see me as often as you can.'

'I'm really not going to commit to anything, Ginny. Besides, a week from now you might have changed your mind about me, and then I'll start to fade away and become nothing more than a distant memory.'

'That'll never happen, Marky. You see, when I met you, in theory I already knew everything there was to know about falling of love, because I was very well-trained in getting others to fall in love with me. But it was that same training that told me this is the real thing for me, even if it isn't for you.' Remembering his tender touch to her soft skin in Stockholm, she gave a distorted echo with her fingers to his stubbled cheek. 'Do you recall how I talked about information being compartmented? You can use that method yourself to lead a double life. All you have to do is not let one life know what the other life's doing. And in this life, we can be lovers.'

As he shared her silken cocoon, he found her arguments highly persuasive, though he wondered if they would lose their apparent cogency once he had returned to the bosom of his family.

ACKNOWLEDGEMENTS

I would like to thank the volunteers of Derbyshire's Peak Rail, who welcomed me behind the scenes of their Santa Special and gave generously of their time.

Thanks also to Elena Hildan, a Swedish resident of Stockholm, who helped with background information and checked my descriptions of her beautiful city.

I am grateful to Eileen Basford for her patient and thorough research of the many and varied subjects that would spontaneously pop into my head.

Finally, I am indebted to Dr John Basford of Colley Books Ltd, who offered sage advice on publishing.

SEND OFF SIR

The seminal Detective Marcus Priestley novel

A games master is red-carded at the annual school v. staff football match. His body is discovered shortly afterwards in the changing room, blood seeping from a wound to the back of the head.

The police set out to establish the underlying cause. A senior investigating officer has an ulterior motive when he assigns a particular policewoman to lead the investigation, which flounders due to her inexperience.

When a second teacher is found dead, the series' principal detective returns from secondment and takes over the two cases. In resolving the investigation he is forced to choose between a successful prosecution and a morally satisfactory outcome.

Send Off Sir was originally published in 2014 under the pen-name *Marc de Caen*. Copies are available in the UK from Colley Books Ltd while stocks last. Future reprints will be under the author name Mark Basford.

BIRDS IN THE GRAVES

Sequel to Send Off Sir

DCI Marcus Priestley is feeling bored with mundane police work. The presumed suicide of an artist is re-evaluated when a toxicology report suggests foul play. Priestley takes the case and sets about understanding art and artists, in order to apply his psychological approach to finding the perpetrator.

He has dinner with beautiful art expert Anna, where she explains her unconventional views on modern art. She shows a personal interest in him, but Priestley is happily married and fully intends to remain so; nevertheless, he cannot avoid being attracted to her. Being an essentially moral man, he strives to remain faithful to his wife in the face of mounting pressure.

CHRISTMAS EVE

A Short Story

'Listen up, everyone; this is the last leg of the journey. If you were worried about my team being mercenary people-traffickers, by now you must know that isn't the case.' He smiled reassuringly. 'I'm certain that you all appreciate the level of protection we've provided so far, but those of you who believe we're now safe had better think again; this final stage is notorious for attacks by bandits. Just because we have the "no camels" rule so we don't attract robbers who might think we're a group of merchants, that doesn't mean they'll leave us alone. My team are tough, all ex-legionnaires, but it's numbers that make the difference in hand-to-hand combat. So, every one of you needs to have your knives at the ready, and to get stuck in if necessary.' He scanned the group of fifty assorted travellers, young and old, men and women. Spotting one heavily pregnant young woman, he gestured with his hand toward her. 'I can see you won't be in a position to do much fighting, but keep your blade handy all the same.' He glanced at the old man who was standing with her. 'Your father will have to protect you as well as himself.' The old man chose not to correct the error, that the woman was in fact his wife.

The leader turned and addressed the people at the back. 'There's safety in numbers, so keep together at all times. Bandits are more likely to attack us under cover of darkness, so it's essential we reach the caravanserai before nightfall. If anyone is too slow and falls behind, I'll do my best to bring you back to the group; but in the end, it makes no sense to jeopardise the lives of the many for the sake of the few, or the one. Does anybody have any questions?'

A regular traveller standing to one side called out a question to which he already knew the answer. 'What about keeping quiet so no one hears us coming?'

The leader acknowledged him with a nod of the head. 'I'm glad you asked me that.' He raised his voice a notch as he addressed the central group. 'Any attacks are likely to come from our left side. Sound travels a long way in the desert, so unless we're in the lee of a barchan to our left, bandits could hear us from miles away. So, travel quietly. Even better, stay silent. And definitely no playing your instruments! I know some of you have brought lyres and harps, reed-pipes, frame-drums, shakers, finger cymbals and crotales; well, keep them packed away until we've arrived safely. Playing any music in the desert is just asking for trouble; you might as well blow on your shofars and trumpets.'

Accepting the leader's invitation, his lieutenant strode up beside him. 'Right, everyone, we're moving out; single men at the front, single ladies at the back, families in the middle.' A few knowing smiles rippled around the group at the euphemistic reference to single ladies.

The lieutenant and another bodyguard walked at the front, setting a fair pace that aimed to ensure arrival at least an hour before nightfall; two more walked on the left and one on the right. The leader stayed at the back, where he had the responsibility of keeping the caravan together, and had the fringe benefit of getting to know the single women better.

The road was no more than a dirt track; though

Roman authority had extended this far, Roman engineering had not. In a hollow, the leader saw a cloud of dust kicked up by the hooves of the donkeys; he watched as it dispersed in the dry breeze, hoping it had not signalled their approach to any scum of the desert.

At the first oasis, the group stopped to take food and water. Seeing the three single women sitting together, he sat down next to them without invitation. 'Hello, girls; I'm Bonifatius.' Two of the girls giggled. One of them spoke up boldly. 'We know who you are, Bonny. You were famous around these parts, once, when you were a centurion. What happened to your troops, then?'

He knew she knew exactly what had happened, but humoured her anyway as she was the most forward and therefore the likeliest to offer him her favours. 'There was a storm the likes of which you've never seen, I promise you. There were twenty-three of us caught out in it; we just had to stop and huddle together. The sand kept covering us up and we kept digging ourselves out; it carried on right throughout the night. At first light, the wind had dropped enough for us to get on our way again, except five of my men had disappeared. We did everything we could to find them, digging holes all around, but they were gone without a trace. I was court-martialled and had to leave the army, so I set up a travel agency, which of course is the one you chose for this journey.' He gave a cheesy smile to all three in turn. 'I thank you for your custom and hope you will travel with us again in the future.'

The bold girl responded, 'My name's Leila, and perhaps I'll have *your* custom.' She laughed dirtily.

The second girl spoke over Leila's laughter. 'I'm Ofra.' Her unflinching stare suggested she also would be open for business.

As the third girl was remaining silent, Bonny asked her, 'May I be permitted to ask your name, miss?'

Her eyes looked to the ground as she half-whispered, 'I'm Zakiya.'

Before he could respond, the lieutenant walked over to him. 'Time to go now, boss.' He held out a hand for him to grasp; Bonny pulled himself up.

Leila and Ofra had quickly scrambled to their feet, leaving only Zakiya to whom Bonny could offer his helping hand; she declined it with a modesty that cast doubt in his mind as to her assumed profession.

Back on the road, Bonny was passing the time of day with the girls, when he saw the pregnant woman on the donkey come to a halt ahead of him. He strode over to her. 'Is there a problem? We don't have time for extra breaks.'

The old man looked at Bonny and answered for her. 'The baby's kicking.'

Bonny tried to sound calm as he responded, 'I made it quite clear we can't stop for slow travellers. Is she about to have it?'

She whispered to the old man. 'I'm alright to carry on, now.'

He relayed the message to Bonny. 'She's alright to carry on.'

The other travellers having kept moving, the three were now at the back, just behind the girls. 'I'll walk with you and make sure you don't get left behind.'

Bonny chatted with the old man, but then decided it was making them slower, so he remained silent as they drifted further away from the back of the caravan.

When they arrived at the final oasis, the lieutenant

was already pacing anxiously. 'It's time we were off, boss. We'll have to leave them behind.'

Bonny shook his head. 'We had some time in hand; the woman has to have a break.'

As the woman was taking a drink, a large, heavy man came and stood over her. 'You shouldn't have come on this trip; you're slowing us down too much.'

Before the old man could respond for her, Bonny quickly stepped over to them. 'We have plenty of time; don't worry about it.'

The heavy man snapped back at him, 'I've done this journey before; we need to be going.'

Bonny tried to remain calm. 'I'm in charge of this trip, and I'll decide when we go. If you don't like it, you're free to drop out and make your own way there.'

The man flushed. 'You know we can't do that.'

Bonny tried to appease him. 'We'll all be setting off soon, anyway.'

After a fairly brief stop, Bonny gave his lieutenant instructions. 'Get them started, but don't go so fast that you leave us behind. And most important, don't let anyone break away; I've never lost a traveller, yet, and I don't want to start now.'

Bonny estimated the pace being set by his lieutenant was just about right to reach their destination before nightfall, but felt sure that the pregnant woman would be unable to maintain it. As she and the old man slowed to the back and then fell behind, Bonny gave them a final warning. 'I can't jeopardise the lives of everyone else by waiting for you to catch up.'

The old man responded. 'I know, but what can we do about it? She's hurting so much.'

Bonny walked with them a little longer, reluctant to

leave them.

When they were substantially adrift of the caravan, the woman spoke directly to Bonny. 'We can't ask you to stay with us; you go with the others.'

Bonny felt deeply troubled about leaving them, yet relieved the woman had given him permission. His parting words were, 'I'll keep a look out for you.'

He caught up with the three girls and walked close behind them in silence.

Seeing him glance around for the third time, Zakiya asked, 'Should I go back and walk with them? If she has the baby out here, she'll need a woman to help.'

Bonny felt deeply ashamed that this slight girl had displayed more bravery than he had. He looked directly into her eyes. 'If you're willing to stay with them, then so am I.' Her immediate response was to head back the way they had come. They returned to the two stragglers without speaking to each other.

Knowing that the most dangerous stretch of road was after the point where several paths merged, Bonny asked them all to travel in silence as they approached that position. Darkness had now fallen heavily, which the stars and crescent moon did little to attenuate. He peered to the left and to the right but saw no sign of robbers. Then, up ahead and just off to the left, he saw a pack of jackals biting and chewing at something on the ground; as they came parallel to it, he was certain they were tearing apart the body of a large man. 'Don't look,' he whispered, though certain they would all continue to watch the jackals.

A little further on, Bonny had the impression of movement over to their left. He turned to the old man. 'I think we have company. Do you have a knife to defend yourself? I'll look after your daughter.'

If they were to die, the old man wanted the truth to be known. 'She's my wife, but I'm not the father.'

Bonny acknowledged this revelation with a simple nod. He turned to Zakiya. 'How good are you with your blade?'

She shook her head. 'I don't have one.'

He handed her the shortest of his three. 'Take this.'

In the next moment, they saw several men coming toward them from the left. A gentle wind sprang up and brushed their cheeks, and then a vortex appeared in the desert; it grew heavy with sand, before moving away in the direction of the band of men. Taking advantage of this sudden screening, they did their best to hurry the final stage of the journey.

As they reached the gates of the caravanserai, they heard the sounds of musical instruments being played within the compound. Bonny's lieutenant hurried over to him and called out, 'It wasn't my fault, boss.' He stopped in front of him. 'He insisted on leaving us all behind, because he reckoned it would be safer than travelling in the dark. I tried to talk him out of it.' He stared at him. 'I saw it all. They took his clothes, and his two women, and the donkey he was on, and the other donkey that was carrying his baggage, and then they just left him lying on the ground. I didn't think I should leave the caravan to see if he was still alive.'

Bonny put an arm around his lieutenant's shoulder. 'Don't worry about it; he was the one who made the wrong decision. And you can be sure he was dead when they left him.'

The lieutenant felt relieved he would not be held personally responsible. He glanced at the woman on the donkey and saw she had not yet had the baby. 'I told the landlady here about her; she's kept a place in a stable because she knew she wouldn't want to be sharing with everyone else in her condition.' He leaned in closer and half-whispered. 'And what about you? There's a couple of girls waiting; I'll have whichever one you don't want.'

Bonny turned to Zakiya, who had heard enough to understand what was being discussed. She looked steadfastly at him. 'I'm not that sort; I'll be sleeping with the other women.'

He smiled at her. 'And I'll be sleeping with the other men. May I see you tomorrow? I could maybe show you around the place.'

She mirrored his smile. 'That would be nice; I was just a child the last time I was in Bethlehem.'

Christmas Eve (A Short Story)
Copyright © 2015 Mark Basford